Praise for Kimberly Frost's Southern Witch series

"Delivers a delicious buffet of supernatural creatures, served up Texas-style—hot, spicy, and with a bite!"

—Kerrelyn Sparks, *New York Times* bestselling author

"An utter delight. Wickedly entertaining with a surprise on every page. Keeps you guessing until the end. Kimberly Frost is a talent to watch."

—Annette Blair, national bestselling author

"One heck of a debut from Kimberly Frost . . . This is definitely an excellent read, and, for a debut, it's nothing less than fantastic."

—*ParaNormal Romance*

"Kimberly Frost's Southern Witch series is destined for great things. Full of action, suspense, romance, and humor, [*Barely Bewitched*] had me hooked from the first page until the last."

—*Huntress Book Reviews*

"Frost's latest Southern Witch novel has all the fun, fast, entertaining action readers have come to expect from her . . . Populated with fairies, goblins, vampires, wizards, rampant plants, and a few nasty-tempered humans thrown in for measure, there's no end to the things that can hilariously wrong."

"What an amazing author! Kimb series is fated for great things. of romance [and] magical havoc, scenario to another. I was definitely put it down."

—*Romance Junkies*

continued . . .

All That
Falls

Kimberly Frost

BERKLEY SENSATION, NEW YORK

THE BERKLEY PUBLISHING GROUP
Published by the Penguin Group
Penguin Group (USA) Inc.
375 Hudson Street, New York, New York 10014, USA

Penguin Group (Canada), 90 Eglinton Avenue East, Suite 700, Toronto, Ontario M4P 2Y3, Canada
(a division of Pearson Penguin Canada Inc.) • Penguin Books Ltd., 80 Strand, London WC2R 0RL,
England • Penguin Group Ireland, 25 St. Stephen's Green, Dublin 2, Ireland (a division of Penguin
Books Ltd.) • Penguin Group (Australia), 250 Camberwell Road, Camberwell, Victoria 3124, Australia
(a division of Pearson Australia Group Pty. Ltd.) • Penguin Books India Pvt. Ltd., 11 Community
Centre, Panchsheel Park, New Delhi—110 017, India • Penguin Group (NZ), 67 Apollo Drive,
Rosedale, Auckland 0632, New Zealand (a division of Pearson New Zealand Ltd.) • Penguin Books
(South Africa) (Pty.) Ltd., 24 Sturdee Avenue, Rosebank, Johannesburg 2196, South Africa

Penguin Books Ltd., Registered Offices: 80 Strand, London WC2R 0RL, England

This is a work of fiction. Names, characters, places, and incidents either are the product of the author's
imagination or are used fictitiously, and any resemblance to actual persons, living or dead, business
establishments, events, or locales is entirely coincidental. The publisher does not have any control over
and does not assume any responsibility for author or third-party websites or their content.

ALL THAT FALLS

A Berkley Sensation Book / published by arrangement with the author

PRINTING HISTORY
Berkley Sensation mass-market edition / June 2012

Copyright © 2012 by Kimberly Chambers.
Excerpt from *Revelation* by Erica Hayes copyright © 2012 by Erica Hayes.
Cover illustration by Melanie Delon.
Cover design by Rita Frangie.

ISBN: 978-0-425-25090-7

BERKLEY SENSATION®
Berkley Sensation Books are published by The Berkley Publishing Group,
a division of Penguin Group (USA) Inc.,
375 Hudson Street, New York, New York 10014.
BERKLEY SENSATION® is a regsitered trademark of PenguinGroup (USA) Inc.
The "B" design is a trademark of Penguin Group (USA) Inc.

PRINTED IN THE UNITED STATES OF AMERICA

10 9 8 7 6 5 4 3 2 1

For Kay T—
avid reader of paranormal fiction and
expert white-knuckled driver on English roundabouts.
This one's for you, amiga.

ACKNOWLEDGMENTS

I would like to thank my critique partner, David, for his thoughtful comments. For their hard work on behalf of my writing efforts, many thanks to my agent, Liz, my editor, Leis, and the team at Berkley. For their unflagging support, many thanks to my friends and family, the writing organizations of which I am a part, and the wonderful booksellers I've come to think of as friends.

This year I spent some time doing research for future books I plan to write. For showing me Seattle and for joining me on a trip to Ireland and England, thanks to Robert, Kay, and Sara.

Rick, Lorin, and David, who kept me company in coffee shops, by phone, and at large throughout 2011, I'm lucky to have you in my life. Thank you.

As always, many thanks to my paranormal readers everywhere, especially to those who have reached out electronically to connect with me or who have visited my book signings. I think of you often when I'm writing. It's been terrific to know that you think of me, too.

Prologue

The road to hell is paved with good intentions, Cerise thought, running a hand through her black cherry waves to smooth them into place. The famous "good intentions" quote seemed especially true in the Etherlin, the claustrophobic utopia where the most powerful descendants of the ancient muses had lived for three generations.

Tonight the muses were in a newly opened retreat center that was supposed to be a place of refuge and reflection, a place for the muses to come together. Instead the retreat had been tainted by crime, and the muses stood divided.

"Why the hell are all the lights on?" Cerise mumbled, looking around the lounge where the four Etherlin muses had been gathered along with a pair of ES—Etherlin Security—officers and Ileana Rella's brother, Troy. Only Cerise and Ileana were left in the room.

Ileana's coarse black hair stood on end, having overcome the restraint of the gel and hair spray that had been used to tame it for the day's photo shoots. Her rose-print pajamas strained as she propped herself up. Ileana was in her late thirties, but looked younger without makeup.

"And where is everyone?" she asked, her thick sculpted brows bobbing. Ileana scowled when she looked at the empty recliner where her brother had been sleeping. "Troy left without saying anything?"

"He probably didn't want to wake us," Cerise said, pulling

her black tank top down over her velour track pants. She slid her feet into velvet ballet flats that doubled as slippers. "Hopefully he's with Dorie," she said, her gaze stopping momentarily at the covers heaped on the temporary mattress where her younger sister had been lying when Cerise had fallen asleep. She wondered if Dorie had gone looking for trouble . . . or to cause it.

"I'll be back," Cerise said, crossing the room and walking out of the lounge.

Striding down the retreat center's deserted hallway, she caught glimpses of the shimmering snow outside. The retreat was on a mountaintop with stunning panoramic views. It was remote and even more isolated than the rest of the Etherlin, which was famous for its impassable walls. Unfortunately, tonight the walls had apparently been breached.

Alissa, arguably the most celebrated of the modern muses, had brought a private bodyguard into the retreat center, and Etherlin Security suspected the man of being a ventala—a human-vampire half-breed—in disguise. The bodyguard, who was thought to be concealing his identity using a magical glamour, wasn't just any ventala; he was presumed to be the most infamous ventala in the world, Merrick, a deadly syndicate enforcer.

Part of the reason the bodyguard had come under suspicion was that Cerise's sixteen-year-old sister Dorie had accused the man of attacking her. Alissa swore that Dorie was lying. As much as Cerise wanted to believe that her sister would never lie about something so serious, Dorie's story didn't quite ring true. Cerise hoped for Alissa's sake that the bodyguard didn't turn out to be a ventala, because if he was, ES would surely kill him.

A thumping sound drew Cerise to the door of an interrogation room. Was Alissa's father, Richard North, trapped inside? An ES officer wouldn't have let him bang on the door, which made Cerise wonder if he'd been left alone. She scowled. The man wasn't well. He shouldn't have been locked in a room on his own.

She felt a pang of sympathy for Alissa, who'd had to carry the burden of her dad's mental illness alone. As Cerise tried to pry the door open, she made a silent vow to be a closer friend to Alissa in the future, especially if the bodyguard, whom Alissa seemed attached to, turned out to be Merrick.

How could Alissa have gotten involved with a ventala? She was usually so smart and careful in her decisions. It just didn't make sense for her to get entangled with a member of the fallen, who were known to be violent and unpredictable. All the muses had been taught from childhood to be wary of the ventala.

Of course, five years earlier, Merrick had slain a demon in the Etherlin. When Alissa had met him that night, Cerise supposed Merrick must have looked like a conquering hero. He'd undoubtedly been gorgeous and charming. Trouble often came in attractive packages.

That's the way life was. Some things started off too wonderful to resist then morphed into something else. Like the Etherlin. Like Cerise's muse–aspirant relationship with Griffin Lane.

Cerise's throat tightened.

Don't go there. Don't think about Griffin.

The banging on the door quieted. Was Richard getting tired? Cerise jabbed the keypad's buttons in frustration. Why wasn't ES answering?

"Hello," a man's voice behind Cerise said, making her jump. She scowled. "Damn, you scared—"

As she turned her head toward him, the words died on her tongue. She had to look up to see his face, which almost never happened. Dark blond hair spilled over broad shoulders. His bare chest was scarred, but wicked beautiful. Incredibly, inexplicably, the light seemed to fracture around him, as though he were made of crystal instead of flesh.

"Who are you?" she demanded.

"I'm not available for conversation. I'm looking for my friend."

She cocked a brow.

A slow smile curved his lips. "You smell like oranges." He took a step back, pushing the hair away from his heartbreaking face, then he frowned and shook his head. "Which is actually an unwanted distraction." For a moment, he lapsed into a language so ancient, she couldn't translate fast enough to follow what he said. Returning to English, he managed, "My friend Merrick might be with a muse named Alissa."

Of course, he's beautiful. He's one of them, she thought furiously. She didn't even have a weapon to defend herself. "So you're Merrick's friend, huh? It's illegal for ventala to be in the Etherlin. It carries a death sentence. Did you know?"

He shook his head. "Laws made by men are—"

She lunged and grabbed the knife sheathed at his hip. He caught her wrist and launched himself forward, slamming her against the wall and pinning her body with his.

"Get off me," she said, shoving his shoulder with her free hand.

"You're strong and soft," he murmured, staring at her mouth. "An unusual combination—which I don't have time to contemplate." He grabbed her left wrist and forced it up against the wall so both her arms were pinned over her head.

"Let go," she snapped, trying to knock him off balance. When her forehead banged against his chin, he jerked his head back and then spun her body so she faced the wall and was crushed between it and him.

His cool breath blew against her ear, matching her own ragged breathing.

"You smell too good to be part demon, so you're not my sworn enemy. Calm yourself," he said.

She was still for a moment, waiting for her chance to throw him off, but his muscles never relaxed. She exhaled hard, frustration thrumming through her.

"You attacked me without cause," he said. "You should ask my forgiveness."

"You can kiss my ass."

His knee rose to nudge her butt. "Be careful what you demand. Someone may accommodate your request."

"You son-of-a-bitch!" she snapped, whipping her head back to slam it against his face.

A moment later she was free, and she spun to face him. He was several feet away, rubbing the swollen corner of his mouth.

"I don't have time to teach you a lesson, but your ferocity deserves one."

"You're trespassing."

He smiled, and she hated that it had a devastating impact on the part of her that noticed beautiful things.

"You don't own the world," he said. "I trespass where I

please." He turned. "Now I need to find my friend before he gets himself killed." He sprinted down the hall in a blur of speed that left her breathless.

Who the hell was that?

Cerise shook her head, trying to decide whether she should warn Etherlin Security that a friend of Merrick's was also inside. Poor Alissa. It looked like her bodyguard would turn out to be a ventala in disguise.

The thumping on the wall resumed, and Cerise jerked her head toward the door. "Okay, Richard. I'm coming."

She hurried around the corner and heard alarms ringing. She sprinted down the corridor toward ES's central control area. Her pace slowed at the sight of a bound guard on the floor. The main holding cell's door was thrown wide open, its handle broken. She glanced into the room. Debris peppered the floor. Merrick had broken out.

Cerise's muscles tightened. Where was Alissa? Had he taken her? And where was Dorie? Merrick might want revenge.

Cerise dragged the gag off the officer's mouth.

"He's out! Alissa North helped him escape," the guard said.

Oh, Alissa, no. What the hell are you doing?

"Can you get the keys and uncuff me, Miss Xenakis? I need to warn Director Easton and the rest of the officers that he's loose."

Cerise rushed into the control room and found a ring of keys. When she returned to the guard, she asked, "Where are Troy Rella and my sister?"

"I don't know."

Cerise bent over him, unlocked the cuffs, and took them off his wrists. "Richard North's locked in an interrogation room," Cerise said. "He's banging on the wall. I want you to open the door and let him out. I'll take responsibility for him."

"Richard North's not in an interrogation room. Director Easton took him out of there a while ago."

"Took him where?" Cerise asked.

"To the crime scene I think."

"Why?" Cerise demanded.

"I don't know! I'm sure he had a good reason!"

Cerise cocked a brow at the guy's defensive tone. "Easy," she said, trying to make her voice soothing.

"Sorry," he said in a lower voice, "but I don't know. Miss North also asked why Director Easton had taken him outside, but that doesn't really matter at this point," he said, scrambling to his feet. "Richard North's better off with Director Easton than here where his daughter and that guy would've found him." He hurried into the control room.

"If Alissa's bodyguard's out and Richard's not locked up, then who is? Someone's banging on the wall."

"I don't know," he said, grabbing a walkie-talkie. "Director Easton, do you read me?" he asked frantically.

She walked to the monitors. The outdoor lights blazed, and ES officers sprinted across the snow-covered ground. Examining the screens that showed the rooms inside the building, Cerise finally found the occupied holding cell.

"How did *they* end up locked in there?" Cerise murmured as she watched Dorie and Troy bang on the interrogation room wall. "At least they're safe," she added, somewhat relieved.

Now where's Alissa?

Had Merrick's blond friend caught up with them? And, if so, was he making the situation better or worse? Cerise had a feeling she knew the answer.

Trouble often comes in attractive packages.

Chapter 1

Despite the scandal that had rocked the Etherlin six weeks earlier when Alissa left the new retreat center with a cold-blooded ventala assassin, the Etherlin Council was determined to pretend that life in the Etherlin was perfect and unchanged. To that end, they were throwing a lavish party. Cerise would have skipped it, except that it was being held at her house. Her father, the Etherlin Council president, was the host. With her mother out of town, Cerise was the de facto hostess and was doing her duty by smiling on cue, until she saw the text message from Jersey Lane.

The message made Cerise freeze as if she'd been doused in slush. The sounds of the party receded as she stared down at her phone.

Can't face people after last night. Plz don't blame yourself for not being able to help, Cerise. I can't keep it together without Griff, either.

Cerise exhaled through pursed lips, chilled as if it weren't late spring. Two of Cerise's secrets were thinly veiled in Jersey's message, but seeing them displayed wasn't what concerned Cerise most.

Cerise slipped the phone into the pocket of her gunmetal gray silk pants as she glanced around. She forced a smile when she made eye contact with friends, but her gaze didn't linger. She searched until she spotted Hayden Lane slouched against the wall. He was laid-back and shy, unusual for a rock star, but he'd been poured from the same mold as his older brother, Griffin. Pain skewered Cerise's chest and tightened her throat. His name alone could still ambush her. But this wasn't the place to get emotional about Griffin, and it definitely wasn't the time.

Cerise tipped her chin up a fraction as if daring fate to sock it again. She strode across the room, weaving through people and reaching Hayden a few moments after Dorie did.

Dorie's new nose and pencil-thin brows had transformed her cute face into something vaguely plastic. Her hips, however, continued to betray her despite a diet completely devoid of everything that tasted remotely decent. If their parents let Dorie get body-sculpting liposuction as a teenager, Cerise would be sick. Of course, the blame wouldn't rest solely on their shoulders. One of Cerise's assistants had described Dorie as a Machiavellian princess in the making. Cerise had fired him, but later there'd been moments . . . Cerise could understand lying to steal a little freedom. All the muses did that from time to time. But lying to hurt another muse? Ever since seeing evidence of that at the retreat center, Cerise hadn't felt the same about Dorie. And Dorie, who seemed to sense it, had been trying too hard. Tonight though, Dorie glued herself to Hayden, which gave Cerise a bit of peace. But also didn't. Hayden had already been through a lot.

"Hayden, I got a text from Jersey. She's not coming," Cerise said.

"I figured."

"What happened last night?" Cerise asked.

Hayden shuffled his feet. "All week she kept forgetting lyrics in rehearsals so she was a nervous wreck last night. She decided to have a drink to calm down, but on an empty stomach . . ."

Cerise grimaced. Already petite, Jersey had lost weight since Griffin's death and was probably all of ninety pounds at the moment.

"She got wasted off two vodka cranberries," Hayden said, frowning. "She slurred her way through 'Sympathy, Too' and went word salad on 'Burn It Down.' I jumped in even though I don't have the voice to do it. People were pissed. They started yelling for her to get offstage." He shrugged lean shoulders. "She did."

"It hasn't even been a year since Griffin died," Cerise whispered.

"I know, but drunk people get annoyed."

"She's torn up inside," Cerise said, knowing that feeling all too well.

"Everybody misses him. You. Me. Jersey. But so do the fans, and we can't charge people money and then fuck up his songs 'cause we're too wasted to sing."

"You're right," Dorie said. "Griffin wouldn't have wanted that. She should respect his memory."

Cerise didn't spare Dorie a glance. Her sister, the sudden expert on Griffin Lane, had met Griffin for a sum total of about twenty minutes.

"Where is she?" Cerise asked.

"At the apartment."

"Griffin's place here in the Etherlin?"

"Yeah."

"Let's go check on her," Cerise said.

"Oh, come on," Dorie said. "You guys can't leave the party now. Dinner's about to start. How would that look to the council, Cer?"

I don't care what the Etherlin Council thinks. Haven't for years.

"Besides," Dorie continued hastily, probably at the sight of Cerise's stony expression. "Jersey will never pull herself together if everyone gives her a ton of attention every time she screws up. If she's going to sulk, ignore her."

Cerise turned a frigid gaze on Dorie, who blanched, then Cerise glanced back at Hayden.

"I'm worried about Jersey," Cerise said. "I have a bad feeling."

Hayden's shuffling ceased, and he straightened. "Okay, let's go," he said.

Dorie fell in step with them. "Considering that you and I are the only Etherlin muses here tonight, if you're gone, they'll probably hold dinner till you get back. So it won't matter if I go out, too."

Neither Cerise nor Hayden said anything.

"I'll come with you," Dorie added.

"No," Cerise said.

Dorie narrowed her eyes. "Why not?"

Because I don't trust you. "Because this isn't your business," Cerise said.

Even while not dancing, Cerise's fluid movements seemed to recall her ballet training, Lysander noticed. Her fingers extended gracefully as if reaching for something beautiful. Like a stolen moment.

With the beat of massive wings, Lysander rose from the tree bough that overlooked Cerise's house. Her scent didn't reach him that far up, but it didn't need to. He remembered it too well, along with the warmth of her body and the fierce way she'd fought to free herself when he'd restrained her.

She's nitroglycerin wrapped in the softest skin, he thought as he swooped across the sky, skimming the treetops of roof gardens. Cerise's wild passion had awakened his own.

Enough.

Enough of watching the girl. Enough of thinking about her.

The more a preoccupation is fed, the more powerful it becomes.

The prophecy—the one that pertained to his only chance for redemption—contained several parts, including a warning that getting involved with a woman could make him fail. He'd never risk that, no matter how beautiful she felt or smelled or danced.

He flew over the Etherlin, so named by her kind, the descendants of the ancient muses. They were the only remnants of the lofty society of the Olympians, the superhuman creatures who had once been caretakers of the world. Until their hubris and their manipulation of mankind had led to their exile from earth.

Exile.

Lysander knew all about exile. But he was hoping to make his own a distant memory.

Movement below caught his eye. *There's a child on that roof.*

A little girl. Eleven or twelve perhaps?

With an unsteady gait she wobbled across the concrete.

It's dark. Why is she there alone?

She climbed onto the ledge. Bare feet shuffled over the faded artwork that someone had painted. He hovered in the clouds.

"Be careful," he whispered.

She rubbed her arm and swayed.

He held his breath. Archangels weren't allowed to consort with humans. As an *arcanon*—a fallen angel—Lysander wasn't barred from it, but he avoided people out of habit. He also avoided them to resist the temptation that beautiful women presented.

The girl teetered.

She's not my responsibility. I've let myself get too entangled with human beings lately. I shouldn't—

She pivoted too fast and stumbled, her eyes wide with shock and terror as she fell.

He dove, a torpedo through the air, until he caught her. Her eyes rolled back and her head hung toward the concrete street that would have destroyed her skull.

She's unconscious and barely breathing, he realized.

Opium-scented breath emanated from a fragile body. She was small, but not a child after all. He landed and laid her on the doorstep under a large awning.

"Opium tastes like heaven, but isn't," he said, resting her head gently against the step. Her bleached hair fell away from an unlined forehead. Under cherry lipstick her lips turned dusky blue.

She goes, he thought. "You'll see the difference soon."

The click of heels in the distance made him look over his shoulder. He recognized the cadence of those footfalls.

Cerise.

Lysander straightened, very tempted to stand his ground, to wait for her to arrive. No law forbade him from talking to her.

The scuff of other shoes was paired with her heel strikes.

There's someone with her.

Who? A man or a woman?

He ducked around the building into shadow and waited.

From a roof's edge, an icicle hung like a dagger ready to fall. Spring had arrived but then receded, like a virgin clambering under the covers on her wedding night. Two days of freezing rain had claimed the Etherlin, but a new warm front was steadily melting the ice.

As Cerise walked with Hayden, she drew her shoulders forward, huddling against the chill.

I'm so cold. Why is it always like this when I think about Griffin?

Memories of him gushed like a flood . . . Griffin's sandy brown hair and the crooked smile that could transform his expression from angelic to devilish in an instant. The collection of vintage rock T-shirts that he and Cerise had shared between them. The "morning" coffee they'd drunk upon waking at 6 p.m.

Cerise dug her nails into her palms. *He's been dead almost ten months. You have to deal with it and move on.* The problem was she couldn't.

The final night with Griffin was a hazy blur that haunted her. And the holes in her memory stretched back insidiously. She couldn't remember the songs they'd worked on. She couldn't remember their last fight, though she was sure they'd had one.

Worst, and most important, her magic had been damaged. The power she used to inspire people had melted like so much snow. She'd been faking it since then, kept expecting it and her memory to return after the pain receded, but they never did. After ten months, she felt worse than ever.

Some of her aspirants suspected, and it was only a matter of time before the council realized, too. If only she could unlock her mind. If only she could review the steps she'd used to tap into her power in the past.

I need Griffin's missing songbook. I need to see the flow of ideas, to relive the way the magic worked. The missing pieces are on those pages. I know it.

Instincts more powerful than any she'd ever felt outside of her muse magic were driving her to find the book. She dreamed about it constantly.

Unfortunately, she and the band had been searching for Griffin's songbook since they buried him. The journal had contained all the songs that Cerise and he had worked on during his last year. There were thirty-seven songs in total, including several that Cerise had known would be number-one hits.

After Griffin died, Cerise couldn't remember a single lyric or melody from all that work, which had left Griffin's band, the Molly Times, without their lead guitarist and unable to record new material. They'd begged Cerise to work with them, to inspire them, to come to rehearsal and jam with them. But without her magic, Cerise couldn't help. It broke her heart. Hayden and Jersey had lost their brother; they should've at least had his final musical legacy. Cerise couldn't even help them retain that much.

"I don't know what's going on with Jersey. She *knows* the songs," Hayden said as they walked. "She hears a lyric once and remembers it. Always has. Do you think she's screwing up on purpose?"

"No."

"Not even subconsciously? As a way to get back at him for dying?"

Maybe, Cerise thought and flushed. Hayden wasn't only asking about Jersey now. "I don't know. I'm not a psychiatrist."

"I wish she'd let me take her to one. She needs to talk to someone about how she really feels. It might help."

"Maybe," Cerise murmured, reflecting on her own failed experience. She'd seen a therapist in secret, hoping that through hypnosis the woman would be able to unlock Cerise's memories and free her muse magic. For a few moments of their session, Cerise had seen a glimpse—a very unsettling glimpse—of the past, but then it had deteriorated and Cerise had been back in the dark and more troubled than before.

Cerise pressed her fist against the side of her thigh. When Griffin had died at twenty-seven, he'd deprived Cerise of more than her favorite aspirant; he'd been the guy she was crazy in love with, the one with whom she'd been having a secret affair.

That Griffin's death might have been partly Cerise's fault was a detail that no one knew—except Cerise, who could not get over it. She never let on how much she still hurt, but the pain was there, just below the surface.

"I've been writing," Hayden said.

"That's great. I can't wait to see what you've been working on."

"Yeah, sure . . ." He paused.

"What?"

"Dorie's cool. I thought maybe I'd show my songs to her."

Cerise's gaze slid to him. He wanted to replace her with Dorie? Cerise's blood ran cold. "Is that right?"

"Well, she's a muse, too. And I thought—"

She raised a brow, but said nothing. He flushed and clenched his teeth. She might have admired the way he was trying to assert himself if he hadn't been stabbing her in the back in the process.

"Look, we can use all the help we can get right now. Things are falling apart. You and Griffin were amazing together, but talking to you doesn't light my mind on fire like it did his. If anything, it brings me down and makes me feel—I don't know, exhausted. Kind of like I'm hungover or something."

The words crushed her, but before she could respond, she spotted Jersey's body. Jersey was the same blue color Griffin had been that morning at the bottom of the ravine. Cerise recognized it as the color of death.

Chapter 2

To distance himself from the frenzied attempt to save the girl, Lysander had flown to the roof. He stood at the edge looking down, unable to tear himself away. The girl's death was bringing Cerise pain, which made him want to comfort her, to touch and reassure her.

Don't interfere.

He stepped down from the ledge so he wouldn't be able to see Cerise any longer, and in doing so noticed the graffiti. There was very little of it in the Etherlin, but the place where the girl had tread so unsteadily was covered with elaborate artwork. The white ledge had been painted with the tangled green of a woodland scene. He studied it and within the tendrils of vines, he spotted a blackbird. He froze for a moment, unable to believe . . . But yes it was there.

He flapped his wings and rose, hovering above so he could see the entire thing at once, could stare at the swirling patterns, and he spotted what was buried. A message woven into the vines. The letters emerged in one long string.

Sadly talks the blackbird here. Well I know the woe he found: No matter who cut down his nest, For its young it was destroyed. I myself not long ago Found the woe he now has found.

The verses were from a ninth-century poem called "The Deserted Home." Lysander knew who and what had inspired it. Reziel.

Lysander's muscles locked, and his gaze darted side to side as if expecting his former brother to appear. But of course Reziel wasn't lurking nearby. Lysander would've known, would've felt him. Still, there was the message . . .

Had the demon invaded the dreams of an artist? Or maybe one of Reziel's followers lived in the Etherlin. It didn't matter how Reziel had accomplished it. What mattered was that it was part of the prophecy: *Watch for a sign. The message left by your betrayer marks the beginning of the end.*

With stunned triumph ringing in his ears, Lysander thought, *This is it. After thousands of years of waiting, the prophecy has finally begun.*

The largest tombstone in Iron Heart Cemetery was also the newest. Twelve towering feet of carved marble announced that Cato Jacobi had been laid to rest in the fresh grave. No one mourned him more than his sister, Tamberi.

A vicious kick launched the flowers that lay at the base of the headstone. Cato couldn't have cared less about dead plants, and Tamberi didn't want anything touching Cato's grave that she didn't put there herself.

From her tote bag, she extracted a one-of-a-kind Venetian vase, created nearly a hundred years ago. She clenched her jaw and flung the vase against the headstone. Shattering, its shards rained down like multicolored tears and joined the pile of fragments from what had once been Tamberi's quarter of a million-dollar Italian glass collection. Since she'd buried Cato, she'd smashed a piece each day against his headstone, marking time, creating a testament to the fact that nothing else mattered except that her brother was food for worms.

Tamberi shoved her bangs back from her eyes. She liked to keep her black hair buzzed to an inch or two long, but she'd vowed not to cut it until her brother's death was avenged.

She snagged a half-empty bottle of bourbon from the wet sod. She swigged deep, then while she caught her breath between swallows, she poured a generous amount onto the grave.

"Do you think the third time's a charm?" she asked, splashing drops of bourbon over the headstone. "A new demon contacted me," she whispered.

The sound of a throat being cleared startled her, and she went still and silent. She inhaled and recognized the cologne.

"So you're the one who's been killing the grass," his voice said.

She didn't bother to look over her shoulder at the interloper. "Hello, Dad."

"I've left you a lot of messages," he said, his voice low with fury. "Given the mess you and your brother made, I'm under a lot of pressure. Invading the Etherlin? You must have been out of your minds. At least you were hopped up on morphine, but what the hell was Cato thinking?"

She turned slowly, her eyes narrowed to slits. "He was thinking that Merrick was never going to bring us that muse that we needed for the syndicate's plan—your plan—to work. Cato was thinking that we'd go in and get the job done ourselves."

"And he got himself killed."

"Yeah, he did. But at least he had the balls to try to get out from under their thumb."

Victor glowered, his lips retracting to show his glistening fangs. "If you don't want to get thrown in a fucking cell, you'd better straighten up. And I've already told you there cannot be a blood feud. Not now. So Merrick and that bitch muse are off limits until everything quiets down."

"I wanted the rock-and-roll muse. If you'd agreed to let us snatch Cerise Xenakis, the wrong portal never would have been opened. Cato would still be alive."

"The North girl was the smarter choice. She was more isolated. And Cato would still be alive if he hadn't gone off halfcocked into the Etherlin."

"That plan worked," Tamberi hissed. "We slaughtered every Etherlin Security officer that we came in contact with. There are no living witnesses to prove we were there."

"The choppers were seen."

She shrugged.

"And Alissa North could testify."

"Not if she dies before she gets the chance."

"I'm so fucking sick of fighting with you about this!" Victor snapped. "It's like you're deaf, and—" The words that would've followed choked and died on his lips as two V3 bullets ripped through his heart.

"I heard you. Every time," Tamberi said as he crumpled backward, clutching his chest. She slid the gun she'd whipped out back into the pocket of her coat.

She walked behind the headstone and grabbed the sword whose blade was buried to the hilt. She unsheathed it from the earth, sending clumps of dirt flying.

She stalked to her father. Victor's eyes were wide with shock, his bloodless lips moving silently.

Her jaw was set. "I'm tired of fighting about this, too," she whispered. "You think it's only about Cato, and it mostly is about him. He's dead, so they need to be dead, too. But it's also about something that started a long time back. And I can't afford to have you or anyone else getting in my way anymore. You always said you can tell how committed someone is to a goal by what he's willing to give up for it." She swung the sword and didn't let herself blink as her father's head rolled free of his body. The bullets probably would've killed him, but decapitation was certain.

She swallowed hard and retrieved the bourbon bottle she'd dropped on the ground. She swiped the dirt away and took a burning swig, glancing up at the overcast sky. After a moment, she forced her gaze back to where blood pulsed, then trickled, and finally oozed from her father's severed neck.

"I have a goal," Tamberi murmured. "And I am *completely* committed to it."

Cerise tightened the belt on her purple trench with shaky hands and walked toward the side door of the urgent care center where they'd stabilized Jersey Lane. An ashen-skinned Hayden was at Jersey's bedside, so Cerise stepped out for a moment to escape the bleach-scented air and the sight of Jersey's tiny body covered in wires.

Jersey's alive. You got there in time, Cerise told herself, trying to stop her heart's frantic pounding.

But she was blue. We had to do CPR. What if she's brain

damaged? What if she ends up a vegetable? When we got her back, it seemed like we got to her in time, but maybe we didn't. Maybe I was too late to save her. Just like I was too late to save Griffin.

In a flash, she recalled Griffin's lifeless body, and that image was followed instantly by one of Jersey dead on the doorstep. Cerise's stomach churned. She swallowed gulps of air and squeezed her eyes shut.

Do not get sick. Do not.

She spit out excess saliva and slowly eased herself down the bricks to sit on the ground, her back against the wall.

In the early days after Griffin had died, the pain had been so bad she'd started to meditate, focusing all her concentration on her next breath. She did that now, listening to her breathing, clocking the beat of her heart as it throbbed in her temples.

Just breathe.

Her heart slowed, and her stomach settled.

She rested against the wall until the door opened, and Hayden called her name.

"I'm here," Cerise said, shooting to her feet. "Is she worse?"

"No," Hayden said, and a lopsided grin claimed his face. "She's awake. The little brat." He grabbed Cerise in a fierce hug and nearly sobbed. "If you hadn't said we should go—"

"It doesn't matter now."

"Yeah, it freaking does. And it always will." His bony fingers tightened against her back. "I was so stunned when we found her. If I'd been alone, I might have just stood there in shock."

"No, you wouldn't have."

"The way she looked—I don't know if I would've thought to try to save her. If you hadn't been there, she would've died. I'll never—I'm sorry about what I said earlier. The Molly Times only works with one muse. *Ever.* No matter what happens we're with you and no one else."

Her eyes misted, but she blinked away the tears and swallowed against the tightness in her throat. "We'll figure things out," Cerise said. They'd gotten a second chance with Jersey, and Cerise wasn't going to lose her. Cerise would find a way to help the Molly Times again even if it killed her. "Everything's going to be okay."

Hayden nodded with a wobbly smile.

"Let's go back in. I don't want her to be alone," Cerise said.

"Yeah, c'mon." Hayden's hand clung to her arm, and Cerise wondered if that was to steady her or to steady himself. Maybe both.

They walked down the sterile-smelling hall to Jersey's room. Cerise braced herself with a deep bleach-scented breath before she opened the door.

Inside, Jersey looked like a little doll whose makeup had been applied by a child. Smudged black eyeliner haloed her light eyes. Smeared scarlet lipstick at the corner of her pale mouth looked almost like blood, as though she were a tiny blonde tribute to the undead.

"Sorry, Cerise," Jersey said. "I'm so sorry. I just wanted to sleep and forget about everything. I guess—" Jersey had a clear high voice that could be mesmerizing when she sang. Even wavering as it did now, it was irresistible. "I guess I took too much."

"I guess you did," Cerise said, sitting on the edge of the bed and clutching Jersey's hand. "You almost killed yourself and us along with you. You scared us to death."

"Sorry."

"How do you feel?" Cerise asked.

"I'm okay." She tried and failed to stifle a yawn. "Tired."

"I bet."

"When I was dying, I saw an angel, and I heard Griffin."

"You did?" Cerise asked, brushing the platinum hair away from Jersey's face.

"Griffin said, 'I'll tell you where it is. Songs among the rafters. In the falling playground above the stage.' Something like that," she murmured. "Isn't that crazy that I heard his voice? It was nice though to hear it again." Jersey's lids drooped. "I miss him."

Cerise ran a shaky hand through her hair. She continued to watch Jersey, but her thoughts were elsewhere. In the last six months of his life Griffin had been obsessed with heights, climbing them or avoiding them depending on his mood. He'd been fixated. "The farther it is to fall, the more I love it, Cherry. And the more I hate it," he'd said to her.

Griffin's mood swings had upset them both. Cerise hadn't

probed into the cryptic things he'd said because he'd been a powder keg of emotions. She'd tried not to pressure him because questions set him off. She'd thought he would talk to her when he was ready. But leaving him alone had been a mistake; his struggle ultimately consumed him. Now he had plenty of space to brood. And she and the Molly Times had plenty of space to grieve.

Cerise shivered, withdrawing from those thoughts. Instead, she concentrated on what Jersey had said.

Songs among the rafters. Above the stage.

Griffin had sometimes written music in one of the top boxes in the performing arts center that was named for her mother. He'd liked the place's outstanding acoustics.

Could he have left his songbook there? But if he had left it in a box, someone would've found it and turned it in. Or kept it and sold it. The kind of money collectors and fans would pay for a journal of Griffin's would be a serious temptation for most people.

Cerise frowned at the thought of someone trying to profit from that book when she and the Molly Times needed it so much. It was the last piece of Griffin they'd ever have.

Griffin wouldn't have left his songbook lying around in plain sight for someone to find.

If he'd left it in the auditorium at all, he'd have put it someplace where no one would stumble across it. He would've hidden it.

I have to check.

Cerise rose. "She's asleep again."

"Yeah," Hayden said with an affectionate roll of his eyes. "She nearly gives us heart attacks and freaks me out so much I may not get a good night's sleep again ever, then five minutes after she wakes up, she's out again like she's got a clean conscience. How's that for irony?"

Cerise smiled and gave his arm a squeeze. "You watch her. There's something I need to do."

He nodded. "Sorry about you missing your dinner party tonight."

"No worries," she said, walking to the door. *That celebration party was a sham anyway.*

Chapter 3

The trees lining the walkway were strung with small blue and white lights. Grecian colors, Cerise thought. From the outside, the Etherlin appeared to be all things pearly and bright. Home to women who had descended from the ancient muses. Women who were inspiration made flesh as the saying went. Maybe the fact that Cerise spent a lot of time with rock stars who were subversive and athletes who battled for their bread made her harder to placate, harder to control. She didn't see the Etherlin as a glittering Garden of Eden. Like all things of great power and beauty, it had a dark side. Ambition and the quest for perfection made people dangerous even if they lived in the Etherlin.

And, of course, some darkness came from the shadows cast by the Varden. It was just outside the Etherlin's walls and home to the ventala. One of the Varden's fallen creatures had recently seduced a muse and the community was still reeling in the wake of her defection. Some couldn't accept that Alissa had been seduced. They believed she'd been taken.

Cerise was sure her former friend had left voluntarily, but sometimes women loved men who later caused them endless pain. Alissa was in the hands of one of the most dangerous men in the world. If Alissa decided she wanted to leave him, would Merrick let her go? Cerise doubted it. And that was a thought that kept her awake at night. What if Alissa regretted her choice? Did she think the Etherlin Council would never let her come back after what she'd done on the night she'd left?

Cerise planned to talk to Alissa. She couldn't cure her of an attraction to the wrong man, but she could make sure that one of the most talented muses in the world knew that she had the support of the other one. If Alissa wanted to come home, Cerise would fight to make that happen.

Cerise approached the Calla Xenakis Center for the Performing Arts. It was a building of alternating blue and white glass with reeds of silver in between. Musical instruments and notes were etched into the frosted panes, making it playful yet elegant.

When Cerise unlocked the door, music floated down to her, and she slowed as she stepped inside. The building was dark. There were no scheduled performances or rehearsals. Sometimes students or staff musicians requested use of the building, but Cerise hadn't wanted to run into people tonight, so she'd checked the schedule and had been glad to find it bare.

She ventured deeper inside and opened the door to the main auditorium. The dark stage was empty, but light drifted down from above. She stepped inside and looked up. The illumination was very faint. From a candle or small lamp? In one of the upper boxes? Why would anyone be playing up there?

It's him, she realized. *The Etherlin's version of the Phantom of the Opera.*

For months, there had been rumors of a performer who some of the staff called the young maestro. They claimed he played the guitar as well as Hendrix and Clapton, that on sax he was sublime and on violin unparalleled. She knew it had to be an exaggeration, but it made her curious.

The music always came from the upper boxes, and initially, some of Griffin's fans thought it was his ghost, but Griffin had only played guitar and never as well as Hendrix or Clapton.

So who was the young man who turned up out of nowhere and left the same way, never tripping the building's alarms? He was suspected to have fixed a hole in the roof caused by a lightning strike. There'd been water all over the floor, but when the workmen went up to patch the leak, there were new shingles nailed in place.

His presence had been confirmed as real rather than fantastical when the center's director had found a cash-filled donation envelope midstage during the center's annual fund-raising drive. The note had been done in writing that was more calligraphy than cursive. It read: "The welcome this space offers to music is admirable. A visiting musician offers compliments to the designers and builders of this place."

After the note, the hunt for the center's young phantom had redoubled, but he was more slippery than ever according to the students who sometimes hid in the upper boxes in hopes of spotting him and getting to listen to him play for more than a few moments. They caught glimpses of him and said he was tall and blond, but they couldn't tell much else.

Knowing the sound of her boots against the stairs would travel, she sat and removed them. Setting them aside, she ascended in stocking feet. Three flights up, his playing stopped her. In his hands, a violin was more than a violin. It was the voice of countless generations. It was the soul of the whole world. Beethoven's Fifth transitioned to Bob Dylan's "Hurricane," which gave way to "Rock You Like a Hurricane." She crept higher into the building and opened the door. She closed it silently and didn't dare move farther because she would rather have fallen down the stairs than have him stop playing.

She recognized Steppenwolf's "Born To Be Wild," which turned into Nirvana's "Smells Like Teen Spirit." Then a blazing "Flight of the Bumblebee" transitioned into "Dance of the Goblins." She cocked her head. His lightning speed had such clarity and precision that her jaw dropped. She slid down the wall to sit on the floor. Closing her eyes, she followed the music, not bothering to identify any more songs.

When the music stopped, Cerise had no idea how long she'd been sitting on the floor. And she didn't care. She uncoiled her limbs and rose. This mystery man was the most talented violinist she'd ever heard, and she wanted him for an aspirant. No sound that pure and amazing should be played for an empty auditorium. The world had a right to hear it. She would make him understand.

She followed the soft glow, enjoying the smell of sandalwood. She was surprised to find that the candle wasn't in a box. It was in the middle of a girder. And lying next to it was a book she recognized. There in the center of a steel beam several stories above the stage was Griffin's lost songbook.

She heard water slosh and turned her head sharply. When she did, she froze. The tall shirtless blond creature drinking from a jug of water was stunning in a host of ways, not the least of which was that she'd met him before.

The meeting had been on Alissa's last night in the Etherlin when the ventala had infiltrated the muses' retreat and had murdered ten members of Etherlin Security including its director, Grant Easton, whose body had never been recovered.

She should have been afraid of the blond intruder, but she wasn't. No sixth sense warned her to retreat. She actually wanted to crowd him, to challenge him. In was an inexplicable instinct.

"It can't be you," Cerise said, staring at him.

He quirked a brow. "It can be me. In fact, it can be none other." He finished off the gallon of water, his skin glowing from the ferocity of his earlier playing. "And hello. How have you been?"

"I've been fine. How did you get in?" she demanded.

His gorgeous smile widened. "I'm not obliged to answer your questions and choose not to."

Oh right. Now I remember. He's impossible. "You're an incredible musician."

"I know."

She fought not to scowl. He might be an arrogant jerk, but for a talent like his, allowances would have to be made.

"Thank you for the compliment," he added, sliding a large duffel bag from the shadow of a corner and putting the empty water jug into it.

"Where did you train?"

"Many places, and the sound quality here rivals them all."

"What school? Who was your teacher?"

"Ah. I've not had instruction. I teach myself."

Of course you do, you bastard, she thought with an inward sigh.

He wrapped his bow in a worn cloth before putting it in the bag. His violin joined the bow after being covered with a frayed towel.

"You need a violin case. An instrument like that deserves better protection."

"The violin has never complained," he said as he zipped the duffel. He looked up through strands of dark blond hair and added with a slow smile, "Which is why it makes better company than some people." He looked so young and heartbreakingly handsome that her heart thudded in her chest.

She noticed the Crimson logo written in bloodred script on the side of the bag.

Crimson is Merrick's bar.

"What's your name?" she asked.

He shook his head. "It's better if I don't even give you that much. It'll only make you want more."

She laughed. "You are so full of yourself. I've met rock stars who were more down-to-earth than you."

"That's certainly true. Being down-to-earth is not something to which I aspire."

Aspire. She'd been determined to make him an aspirant. Was she still? He had the talent, but he would be a nightmare to work with. Still, his playing . . .

"I'm Cerise Xenakis." When his expression remained blank, she rolled her eyes. The fact that she was world famous could not have escaped his attention, especially when he was in the Etherlin for God's sake. And how was he still inside? When he'd smiled, she hadn't seen fangs. Was he ventala or not?

"I'm the Etherlin muse who inspires musicians."

She waited for him to respond, and he finally said, "Congratulations?"

She scowled. "This center belongs to the Etherlin community."

"It was built for great music. That's what I bring."

She held out a hand. "I know. I'm not going to give you a hard time for trespassing. You clearly deserve to be here. I want to talk to you about your aspirations. What do you want to do with your music?"

"Play it?"

Smart-ass. She smiled. "Nothing beyond that? C'mon," she said. "You could've snuck into an auditorium anywhere in the world. You chose one in the Etherlin. Wasn't some part of you hoping to be discovered by a muse? By me?"

"Definitely not," he said flatly. "I chose this place because it's the best place to play that's close to where I live."

"Close to where you live? Where is that?"

"Will you excuse me? I should go."

"So go." She had no intention of leaving him alone. She wanted to see how he was getting in and out.

"I need to snuff the candle. To leave it burning would risk a fire."

His turn-of-phrase seemed odd at times. Where was he from originally? Not the Varden. His speech was too precise and too archaic to have been born of its mean streets.

"I tire of waiting," he said.

She glanced at the girder. The drop was dizzying. She didn't blame him for wanting to avoid any distractions when he walked out there to get to the candle, but what idiotic impulse had caused him to put the candle there in the first place? Maybe he'd gone onto the girder to look at the book?

"Sorry, but I'm not leaving," she said. "I came to retrieve the book that's sitting next to the candle. Since you're getting the candle, it would be cool of you to bring me the book. That way both of us don't have to walk out there."

"Step aside," he said.

She glanced at the end of the beam. There was plenty of room for him to get to it without her moving out of his way. "I'm not going to touch you," she said.

"Of that I'm certain." He ran a hand through his hair, adding more chaos to locks that already defied a style. "Nevertheless," he said, with a gesture for her to move.

She held out her hands in surrender and backed up. "Take all the space you need. I'll wait here. You can just drop the book as you go past."

He turned and strode out onto the beam without a moment's hesitation or fear. She glanced at his legs and noticed for the first time that his feet were bare. She also noticed the scars on his back. There were a lot of them. Mostly thin lines where bladelike cuts had been made, but also two thick vertical lines just inside his shoulder blades that didn't look like the other scars. They weren't flat and shiny white as the others were. They looked like golden brown grooves. The tops and bottoms of the vertical scars came to points that were unnaturally perfect.

What the hell are those marks?

She studied them and then her eyes lingered on his waist

and down to the seat of his leather pants. He had an athlete's butt. Griffin had been good-looking, but he'd been somewhat androgynous. This mystery musician had a stunningly beautiful face, despite its scars, but there was nothing pale or fragile about his body. He could probably play a piano; he also looked like he could lift one. The appeal of that combination was not lost on a muse who inspired great athletes as well as great musicians.

She watched his sure footwork as he turned and strode back toward her, candle and book in hand.

"Do you dance?" she asked, her gaze fixed on his well-defined stomach muscles.

"Often and well."

"Is there anything you don't do well?" she asked dryly.

"I don't lie well. Sometimes it would be convenient if I did."

She glanced at his face. "You're odd."

"That's the other thing I don't do well."

"What?"

"Blend."

He walked to his duffel bag.

"Hey," she said.

He glanced over his shoulder.

"You forgot to give me the book."

"No, I didn't," he said, zipping the duffel over the candle and Griffin's songbook.

"What the hell?" She rushed toward him, but he shouldered the bag and sprinted away. Her socks slipped on the floor, but even if they hadn't, despite being able to run a five-and-a-half-minute mile, she wouldn't have been able to keep pace with him.

By the time she rounded the corner, he'd disappeared. She looked around and up. She heard a rustle of wind, but by the time she raced back to where she thought the sound had come from, he was gone. She checked the stairwells, but there was no sign of him.

Where the hell did he go?

She swore in frustration. Griffin's songbook had probably been sitting on that beam unattended for almost a year, and on the night she'd finally seen it, she'd had the bad luck to run into Merrick's eccentric friend. The other bizarre thing about the night was that for the twenty minutes she'd spent talking to him, despite being aware of the songbook, she hadn't thought about Griffin or been pained by his memory.

That still didn't mean she could leave the songbook with the mystery musician. She needed to read it and then she needed to turn it over to the Molly Times.

Cerise put a hand to her forehead and grimaced. The only thing she really knew about the phantom musician was that he was a friend of Merrick's. It looked like she would be talking to Alissa sooner than she'd intended.

Cool air grazed Cerise's cheek, and she glanced heavenward. Suddenly, everything slammed into place.

The children of men will not recognize him for what he is unless he reveals himself. They will look, but not see.

"In the rafters," Cerise murmured. "Not: in the *falling* playground . . . In the *fallen's* playground above the stage."

Ventala don't have scars, and they don't have vertical grooves on their backs that could conceal wings.

Merrick's friend is a fallen angel.

Chapter 4

Tamberi stood at the front of the crowd in the partitioned area of the warehouse. Rebel ventala stood shoulder to shoulder. She shrugged out of her coat and tossed it aside. She didn't need a bra and wouldn't have worn one if she did. Most ventala were male and the points of her nipples against her silk shirt would help focus their attention on her.

"So you know what my position is," Tamberi said in a voice loud enough to flatten the chatter. "The syndicate has gotten more and more corporate, and I've been as responsible for that as anyone. But we're not a company. We're not a city government. We're not politicians or lawyers or fucking bankers!"

The volume of disgruntlement rose in agreement.

"I say we're not meant to be respectable citizens. We can look that way to the outside world, but to put ourselves on leashes? What are we? Goddamned dogs?"

There were shouts of agreement.

"Merrick used to be a badass, but he's decided he wants to set up house with a muse. I don't begrudge him that. She's a really beautiful piece of ass. But when he turns his guns on his own like he did a few weeks ago, he's not one of us anymore."

The room was more subdued and it wasn't because they didn't agree. It was because taking on Merrick was the last thing anyone wanted to do.

"My father put a kill order out on Merrick but then rescinded it because he was afraid of the heat it would cause. This morning he went to negotiate with Merrick, and when things didn't go well, Merrick shot my father and took his head."

The room went dead silent.

Tamberi nodded. "Over the past few months, I've buried a lot of ventala. My brother. Twelve members of the syndicate hit squads who hunted our enemies and helped bust our way into the Etherlin—the supposedly impenetrable Etherlin. Now I've got to bury my goddamned father, too.

"I'm getting fucking sick of funerals. Even I don't have that much black in my closet." She looked away, feigning emotion, blinked, and looked back. "Merrick's not an easy kill, and I don't expect anyone to go for him out of loyalty to me or my family. I wouldn't take him on out of loyalty to any of you bastards." Her mouth curved into a small smile, and there was a bit of answering laughter. "So let's get down to it. A two-and-a-half-million-dollar bounty. Each. Bring me Merrick dead and Alissa North alive."

"Then what?"

"Then you get paid," she said smoothly.

"Is the syndicate going to put a hit on him, too?"

"Probably, but they don't pay as well as I do."

"You broke from the syndicate?"

"I have no intention of interfering with the syndicate, but I plan to do things my own way. That may mean pretty soon there will be a hit squad after me, too." She shrugged. "So be it. This dog is done with the leash. I want revenge. And I want this world under our fangs again. If I get an Etherlin muse, I can use her blood to bring forth enough true vampires to overrun the world. That's why we went into the Etherlin. And the mission almost succeeded. It's worth it to try again, I promise you," she said, walking through the men to a large temporary wall that hid the remainder of the warehouse. "Some of you might not be able to imagine what a world full of vampires would be like. If you're not old enough to remember the last Vampire Rising, I thought you might like a taste." She kicked the partition, toppling it and revealing a spectacle worthy of a Roman orgy.

Tables overflowed with food and drinks. Naked women were sprawled over couches and mattresses. Some were chained in place. Others had been chemically restrained. Heroin and valium worked wonders.

The ventala shoved their way past her. "The muses and their supporters made it against the law to feed off human beings. Even the willing ones," she called as the ventala descended on their human prey. "I say if they won't let us use the willing, we'll take whoever we want." There were screams and cries mixed with grunts and groans. "Yeah, go ahead," Tamberi said. "Drink and feast and fuck like it's the end of the world as we know it. 'Cuz it is." Tamberi's smile widened as the first girl died, her skin turning marble white as she was drained dry. "That's right. We're not playing politicians or lawyers or fucking bankers anymore."

With her phone in hand, Cerise dropped into her bedroom's window seat and contemplated what to say to Alissa when she reached her. After Alissa had left the Etherlin, ES had tried to recover her, but at first she'd been completely off the grid. Then the famed Muse Wreath, which Alissa had reportedly stolen on the night of her disappearance, was returned with a detailed letter about the night's events. The letter to Cerise's father, Dimitri, had been kept confidential, but the security team had been recalled.

There were those who were concerned that Alissa had been kidnapped and was in fact still being held prisoner by the ventala syndicate's most deadly asset, and Cerise had wondered sometimes herself, but one thing made her skeptical that Alissa was being held prisoner—she'd sent Cerise a message inviting her to meet in the Sliver—the small slice of neutral territory between the ventala territory called the Varden and the muse world of the Etherlin. Cerise could believe that Alissa might be pressured into pretending to have chosen to go with Merrick of her own accord, but she didn't believe that Alissa would lay a trap for another muse. No matter what leverage Merrick or the ventala had over her, Cerise didn't believe Alissa would betray her. She'd known Alissa her entire life, and once upon a time they'd been best friends.

Cerise scrolled through her contact list to the fake name she'd entered for the number that Alissa had written in her message. Cerise pressed the button and waited as it rang.

"Hello?" Alissa said, but before Cerise could answer, her

mouth went dry. In the background, she could hear a blazing guitar solo. Her spine tingled. Was that him again? The angel?

"Hello?" Alissa repeated.

"Hey. Sorry. It's Cerise."

"Hi!" Alissa said. "Give me a moment. It's loud here," she said, and then in answer to a deep voice that asked where she was going, she added, "Just to the lobby."

The music dampened, and Alissa said, "Hello. How are you?"

"I'm okay. Where are you?"

"At Crimson. It's a club . . . in the Varden," Alissa hesitated on the last, which wasn't surprising since the muses had been raised to believe that they'd never survive a night in the Varden. Tempted by their blood, the ventala would consume their last drop of life. Had that just been propaganda? A scare tactic to keep the muses in line?

"Are you safe there?" Cerise asked.

"It's Merrick's club. He's with me," she said, as if that answered the question.

"And you're okay with him?" Cerise asked skeptically.

"Yes, I'm very well. How are you? How are things there?"

"They're all right. You're missed."

"Oh, that's—It's nice of you to say."

"When you first answered the phone, I heard music playing. What song was that?"

"Nothing you would have heard before. Merrick has a friend who's a musician, and he wrote it."

"I think I've heard it before."

"You do? I can't imagine. It's called 'Paradise Lost' because some of the lyrics are from Milton. As far as I know it's never been recorded. Unless someone made a bootleg. The guitarist from the band that usually plays weekends here cut his hand, and we convinced Lysander to come down and play a set with them. But he's only been onstage for about twenty minutes."

"Lysander," Cerise said. "Tall? Blond? Leather pants and lots of scars?"

"You *have* seen him," Alissa said, her surprise evident.

"Speaking of being seen, you wanted to see me. Let's do it tonight."

"Tonight?" Alissa asked. "You'll never get Etherlin Security to clear an impromptu trip to the Sliver at eleven thirty at night."

"Let me worry about ES. Can I visit you tonight or not?" Cerise said. She didn't like the fact that Alissa had more freedom of movement than she did.

"Of course. Do you want to meet in the Grand Hotel or at Clarity?"

"Neither. I want to come to Crimson. You're safe there. I would be, too, right?"

"Well—yes, of course, Merrick wouldn't let anything happen to you in his club, but are you sure you want to come into the Varden?"

"Can you arrange for my safe passage from the Sliver to the Varden and back?"

"Yes, if that's what you want. Merrick and I will pick you up. Where?"

"I'll wait in the lobby of the Grand. I can be there in thirty minutes."

"All right. We'll be there."

"Great, and one other thing?"

"Yes?"

"Don't tell Merrick's friend that I'm coming."

When Alissa didn't respond, Cerise added hastily, "See you soon," and she ended the call before there could be more discussion. She slid the phone into her pocket. She passed the mirror and gave herself a brief inspection. Dark hair with its black cherry hue curled softly around her face and shoulders, kohl rimmed her eyes, and wine-colored lipstick accented her full lips. She wore a tailored shirt with a maroon scarf and black leather pants. She went to her closet and pulled on high-heeled boots that would take her from five foot ten to well over six feet. Then she opened a large jewelry box and took out a couple of bangle bracelets and a 9 mm filled with vampire-killing bullets. She tucked it into the back of her leather pants and covered it with her shirt. She shoved a thousand dollars, her ID, and a tube of Black Honey lipstick into her pocket.

On her way out the bedroom door, she almost bumped into her sister.

"Hey," Dorie said. "You're going out? Can I come?"

"No," Cerise said, not breaking her stride down the hall.

"Why not?"

"I'm going to a bar to hear a band."

"So? If I'm with you they'll let me in. Like they did—"

"That was a one-time thing for your sixteenth birthday," Cerise said, hurrying down the stairs.

"What's your problem lately?" Dorie snapped.

Cerise shrugged.

"Look, I didn't make up what I said. Alissa stole the Wreath, and she locked Troy and me in that interrogation room," Dorie said.

"Alissa returned the Wreath."

"Yeah, but she still took it! And she hooked up with a filthy ventala who practically tore my throat open."

Cerise glanced pointedly at Dorie's unmarked neck. Dorie flushed.

"You act like you don't even care about that!" Dorie snapped. "You act like you blame me for her being gone. She wasn't even your friend. I'm your sister. Plus we still don't know what happened to Grant Easton. Everyone just walks around here like that night never happened."

"Alissa sent the Etherlin Council a letter of explanation. Whatever she says happened that night must have proven true when they investigated because they're leaving her alone."

"Bull! They might be leaving her alone so there's no scandal. What about the fact that Grant Easton, Alissa's boyfriend, disappeared on the same night she took off with a ventala? I think she and that ventala killed Grant so they could get out of the Etherlin. And Dad and the EC are letting her get away with it."

"There were pools of blood in fourteen different spots in the woods. We all heard the helicopters. If those were ventala helicopters and we were under siege, why didn't they come for us? I think Merrick and his people stopped the ventala syndicate from doing whatever they had planned. There have been rumors that Merrick's broken off from the syndicate."

"Who cares!" Dorie yelled. "Who cares about a vampire half-breed? I want to know why you're always defending her."

"Because I don't think she did anything to hurt anyone but herself."

"But you do believe she went off with him willingly. That

taints the whole community. And when the media catches on, it's going to be a huge scandal that reflects badly on all of us."

Cerise rolled her eyes. "You're spending too much time with Spinmaster Troy. All of life isn't about getting good press." Even though Troy was a friend of Cerise's, too, she knew how single-minded he could be when it came to preserving the muses' moneymaking brands. The memory of Griffin's last night crept across Cerise's mind. Troy, who usually discouraged the muses from drinking too much, had bought two rounds of shots. There had been something off about the way Troy had behaved that night at the bar. Cerise's brows drew together.

"Troy cares about the Etherlin," Dorie said, breaking into Cerise's thoughts. "He cares about it more than Alissa North ever did. And Alissa's certainly not going to be able to live up to her responsibilities as a muse while living with a bloodsucking murderer. He's probably drained her dry by now."

She sounded just fine on the phone, Cerise thought, but she did feel a small twinge of anxiety. It was somewhat insane of her to tread into the heart of the Varden—ventala territory. But Cerise was the muse of rock stars and world-class athletes. She inspired the bold and considered herself one of them. To fully be who she was though, she had to get her power back. There was no way she was leaving Griffin's songbook with a fallen angel or anyone else.

"Nothing to say to that, huh?" Dorie clucked her tongue. "Well, if he does kill her by drinking all her blood, it's her own fault."

Cerise clenched her teeth, knowing that she'd be similarly blamed if her reckless behavior led to trouble, and she wished that for once her drama-dredging little sister would just shut her mouth.

"It's not a good idea," Merrick said, running a thumb across his handsome jaw. Alissa's vision was still a bit blurry at times from an injury to her eyes, but her mind filled in what she couldn't completely see.

"She expects me to be there," she said as her heart beat quicker.

"It could be a trap. Etherlin Security might be there to take you back."

"You know I won't go with them."

"They might not give you a choice."

Alissa stepped forward and put her hands on his face. When her mouth was close to his, she whispered, "You'd never let them take me. And if they managed to, I'd escape and come back to you or you'd come in and get me." She pressed her lips to his and the kiss was as sweet as ever. "I promised Cerise I'd be there. It means so much to me to see her."

Merrick sighed. "You'll stay in the car with Ox while I go in to get her."

"That might be—she might not be comfortable leaving the hotel with you if I'm not there."

His jaw tightened. "Then she'll stay in the Sliver."

"James—" she implored.

It was his turn to take her face in his hands. His thumbs brushed outward from the corners of her eyes, the light touch saying what he didn't; he wouldn't risk her being hurt again so soon after she'd been blinded and had almost been lost to him forever. James Merrick could walk without blinking into a battle with creatures so deadly they were kept caged in hell. Risking his own life had never been a problem, not since a brutal childhood. But he did care about one thing, and Alissa was lucky enough to be that one thing.

"You'll stay in the car, Alissa," he said softly.

"All right."

He brushed his lips over hers, and she whispered against his mouth, "I love you."

The kiss deepened until time stood still.

Finally remembering they were in a public lobby, she drew back. "Anything more than that and we'll have to charge money for the show."

"Mmm. How will you spend your half?" he asked, stealing another quick kiss.

She chuckled. "We have to go."

"If you say so," Merrick murmured, but he didn't hesitate to raise his phone and call his bodyguard, Mr. Orvin, whose unfortunate but somewhat appropriate nickname was Ox.

After that call, Merrick slid a small earpiece into his ear

and pressed a button on his phone. "Tony, how do the cameras look?" Merrick paused to listen.

Ox lumbered forward with purpose, causing a large potted palm to sway in his wake. He didn't walk so much as advance like a linebacker, unconcerned with grace or style. He had an objective and obstacles in his path had best move lest they be crushed. Despite his bodybuilder bulk and severe ice blond crew cut, he had a nice smile that he never failed to offer her.

Alissa returned his smile. "Sorry to pull you away from the music, Mr. Orvin. Lysander's an amazing musician."

"I was ready for a little air," Ox said with a shrug. "I'm tone-deaf. Besides, I can't get anywhere with the cute new waitress with him onstage. All the girls' eyes are glued on him like they just saw their first diamond."

"Oh," she said, wrinkling her nose. "Well, if it's any consolation, he's not really competition. I'm sure that when he comes offstage, he'll disappear without talking to any of the women."

Ox shrugged again. "Whatever. So where are we going? Last night I told the boss you'd probably like the new Spanish restaurant that opened down the block. Couple of the boys and me went there for dinner Monday night. Never had paella before. It's good as hell."

"That would be really nice, but actually we're going to the Sliver to pick up a friend of mine."

"A friend of yours?" Ox said, his voice rising with interest. "A muse friend of yours?"

Merrick held out a hand to stop their conversation, and Ox immediately fell silent and looked around the lobby to be sure no one was close enough to be listening. Into his phone Merrick said, "Yeah, Tony, we're going out. I want two sets of eyes on the monitors until I say otherwise."

Chapter 5

Convincing an aspirant to smuggle her out of the Etherlin in the trunk of his car had not been a problem, but it did leave her hair pretty mussed. Cerise finger-combed her waves while trying to stay out of sight.

"Oh my God. It's Merrick," the girl at the front desk said to her coworker, who paled.

Cerise glanced at the front door. Sure enough, clad in sunglasses and a fifteen-thousand-dollar suit, the notorious ventala enforcer-turned-seducer-of-an-unattainable-muse strode into the lobby like he owned the place.

The way he moved reminded her of someone else from his side of the wall.

No wonder they're friends. They both move like they could edge out lions as the biggest predators on the block.

Merrick spotted her, and he walked to her. Her heart pounded a little faster. She might be armed, but she didn't have any illusions about which of them would be able to draw blood first. His skills were legendary. She had faith though that Alissa wouldn't have pulled her into a trap. If Alissa trusted Merrick, it was a safe bet that he wouldn't attack Cerise.

"Where's Alissa?" Cerise asked.

"I'll take you to her," he said, glancing around as if he thought someone might be lying in wait. She didn't blame him for that. If Etherlin Security had been with her, they might have shot him on sight. She wasn't sure what their orders were with regard to Merrick, which was exactly why she hadn't brought them along. Well, that and the fact that they would never have let her go into the Varden to see her mysterious musician.

"Lead the way," she said. He cocked a brow above the rim of his sunglasses, clearly surprised that she didn't act skittish. Well, she'd come this far. She didn't intend to lose her nerve at the last minute. And she didn't intend to show she was nervous. Rule number one of being a superstar . . . never let them see you sweat.

"The moon too bright for you tonight?" she asked as they crossed the lobby.

"You're the rock-and-roll muse. I expected to be blinded by your sequined jumpsuit."

She grinned.

Bright spotlights lit the hotel's front walk, and she suspected that those lights were what his eyes actually objected to.

She had to admire his icy cool. Her veins were pulsing full of muse blood, but he'd barely given her a second glance. Her stride slowed. Shouldn't it be more of a struggle for him? What if he really was keeping Alissa prisoner and feeding off her? What if he'd forced or tricked Alissa into baiting a trap for Cerise? Alissa wouldn't willingly have done it, but torture made people do what they normally wouldn't. Alissa's voice had been smooth and cool, but all the muses had had media training. They knew how to seem calm under duress.

Cerise slowed and slid a hand under the back of her shirt. She gripped the gun.

"You're quite a departure from Alissa's usual type," Cerise said. "She spent most of her life on the arm of Dudley Do-Right for a reason. How long do you think you can keep her in your world?"

He turned and stared at her.

"She'll last a lot longer than you will if you decide to raise that gun."

Cerise's heart thudded. How had he known? He'd been facing the other way when she reached for the gun. She'd slid the safety off soundlessly.

He lowered his sunglasses and locked eyes with her. His eyes were glacial cold.

"You have ten seconds to hand it over, or I'll leave you on the street."

Her fingers tightened their grip. There was no way on earth she was getting into a car with him unarmed, especially with the bloodless stare he had trained on her.

The window rolled down and a huge man with white blond hair looked out. "Everything cool, boss?"

Merrick's eyes never left Cerise. "Ms. Xenakis is trying to decide whether she wants to see Alissa or not."

"It's not personal. I always carry a gun," Cerise said.

"I don't blame you," Merrick said, getting into the car and rolling up the window.

Cerise realized they were going to leave her on the street. She exhaled slowly. Maybe it was for the best. One look into Merrick's eyes, and she'd had second thoughts about crossing into the Varden with him. She'd figured if Alissa spent time there, it couldn't be all bad, but she'd changed her mind about that.

Cerise took a step back toward the hotel. She'd check into the Grand and get someone to smuggle her back into the Etherlin in the morning.

Except the car didn't drive away. Instead the door opened, and Alissa and Merrick both got out.

Cerise was used to Alissa's skin being like a sliver of moonlight, but she had a light tan and the normally sleek hair that skimmed her shoulders had grown longer and hung in loose waves. She looked as beautiful as ever, but much more relaxed and approachable. Even her Tom Ford lace dress flirted with ease, and she pulsed with strong magic that was enviable.

"Let me hold your gun," Alissa said.

Cerise shook her head sharply, noting the way that Merrick stood with his body slightly blocking Alissa's. Would the heartless ventala actually step in front of a V3 bullet for Alissa?

"No offense, but there are two opinions on your leaving the Etherlin. First, that you were abducted and are still being held against your will. In which case, I'll keep my gun. The second: that you lost your mind and went willingly. In which case, I'll keep my gun."

Merrick moved in a blur of speed. Cerise's arm throbbed where he'd yanked it forward.

Her mouth dropped open at the sight of her gun in his hand.

"Enough standing on the street. Alissa, get in the car."

"I—Merrick, you can't," Alissa protested, but Merrick didn't answer. Instead he tapped the roof, and the blond bruiser emerged.

"We're going," Merrick said, and the big guy plucked Alissa off the ground and reentered the car with her.

Cerise started to back away, but Merrick grabbed her and pulled her forcibly into the car. The doors all closed and the instant they did, the car pulled away from the curb. Cerise's heart pounded.

"For God's sake, Alissa," Cerise spat. "You let me walk right into this? I trusted you."

"It's not like that!" Alissa said, and she grabbed Merrick's arm. "You can't do this."

Merrick popped the clip from the gun, removed the bullet from the chamber, and then dropped the gun on Cerise's lap. He slid the bullet and clip into his pocket.

"The girl behind the desk got on the phone the second she saw me," Merrick said flatly. "You wanted to talk to Cerise. When we get to the penthouse, I'll leave you guys alone in the guest room. When you're done talking, I'll drive her back to the gate."

Cerise's brows rose. "What the hell? Are you a prisoner or not?"

"Not," Alissa said firmly.

"He just kidnapped me off the street."

"He was worried that your security detail was lying in wait. Or that you'd come armed yourself to do something to me. Also, there's a problem between us and the ventala syndicate. We shouldn't spend too much time out of Merrick's territory."

"Paranoid much?" Cerise said, looking at Merrick. "I brought the gun for protection, not to shoot Alissa or you."

"You don't need a gun for protection. Your protection is sitting right there," Merrick said, nodding to the seat across from them.

"How do you figure?" Cerise said, glancing at the bulky blond bodyguard who looked as though he could bench a semi.

The blond guy smiled. "Not me. Though I'll be happy to step in if you need something. He meant her," the man said, cocking his head at Alissa. "Nothing will happen to you because you're important to Mrs. M."

Cerise's jaw dropped.

Mrs.?! What the hell?

"Alissa, no!" Cerise lurched forward, grabbing Alissa's arm. Cerise raised Alissa's elegant left hand, and there on her ring finger was the damning evidence. A flawless antique diamond ring and accompanying band. The onetime face and unblemished image of the Etherlin had married a ventala assassin.

"So it's true then," Cerise murmured. "You have lost your mind."

Lysander spotted the madman he'd become fond of in the Crimson's doorway. Alissa's father, Richard, wore navy drawstring pajama pants and a white T-shirt with a terrycloth robe and house slippers. Richard's pockets bulged with scraps of paper and pens, and the man still wore the pair of Merrick's sunglasses he'd donned upstairs. The sunglasses were to shield his eyes during their poker games, but since they were no longer playing poker, nor was there any significant light source to speak of in the ridiculously dark nightclub, the sunglasses seemed an odd addition to his already odd outfit.

Lysander glanced at the table closest to the stage where Merrick and Alissa had sat before they'd left thirty minutes earlier. He'd thought their departure strange since it was Alissa who'd asked him to play, but once he'd started playing, he was hard-pressed to stop until the end of the set. The human musicians had passable talent, and the energy and care they put into their music was admirable.

The club bouncers watched Richard closely. Lysander's fingers worked the strings with fierce precision despite the distraction. Did Merrick's men all know that Richard was Alissa's father? And if the bouncers tried to block his entry into the club, how would Richard react? In general the silver-haired man wasn't violent, but he was given to explosive monologues on occasion, which the bouncers were unlikely to tolerate.

Richard shuffled into the club, which was filled with a sleek and stylish crowd who looked like they'd never been rumpled in their lives. Richard bumped a table as he meandered toward the stage. A top-heavy glass fell over and crashed to the floor. A frowning bouncer started toward the ambling author.

Where the hell was Merrick? If he was going to keep a mad novelist as a houseguest, he needed to keep a better eye on him.

Oblivious to security's approach, Richard took a circuitous route to the stage. It really wasn't Lysander's business if Merrick's bouncers dragged Richard out, but he and Richard were in the middle of a game of chess that Lysander wanted to finish.

Lysander frowned and held out a hand to hold off the pursuing bouncers. Richard stood at the edge of the stage tapping his foot. After a couple of moments, Richard walked up the stage stairs in time to the beat. Lysander continued to watch him, and so did the audience. Weaving between them, Richard ambled across the stage, his feet catching on amp cords, which made him stumble. The crowd gasped, but Richard managed not to fall or rip any cords free.

For a moment, the other musicians lost their place and Lysander snapped a finger to draw their attention to recovering the beat. Richard went into the wings where Lysander would have preferred him to stay until the song ended. Instead, he returned with a saxophone.

Lysander raised his brows, waiting. He'd allowed Richard to wander and trip across the stage, but there were limits. When Richard played the first few notes, however, Lysander realized that the lauded author was a madman of varied talents; Richard North was a sax man. The audience applauded heartily.

Richard shuffled to a mic and played hard, like he didn't care if he put his last breath into the mouthpiece. Lysander smiled. When angels had invented music this was the way they'd intended instruments to be played.

Lysander paused, letting Richard solo, then feeling the rhythm, anticipating the timing of every note, Lysander melded his guitar's music with Richard's sax's, the notes fusing.

Just there. Flawless!

There was something more than human to Richard at times. As if in madness, he transcended human consciousness. Maybe that was why Lysander could tolerate his company so well.

With unerring timing, Richard played on. Lysander leaned back, guitar resting against his hips and loins, music vibrating through him. For several suspended moments, Lysander felt his body warm to the temperature it had once claimed before he'd fallen. Ribbons of grace edged his body, making him the closest he'd been to touching heaven in many millennia. Lysander sank his teeth into his lip, straining, holding his breath.

Closer still.

He closed his eyes, knees bent, body bowing back till his hair skimmed the floor and memory skewered his heart. He offered the music up, louder and harder.

Let the chorus hear. Let the riot in my heart be known.

Sinking to the floor so his shoulders were supported by the wood's grain, his body stretched like the strings.

At the song's end, the audience thundered to its feet, applauding wildly. Lysander panted, raising his torso from the floor. The spotlight fractured around him prismatically, but a few shards of light touched him, highlighting the steam curling from his skin. Lysander's smile stretched to his heart.

A rarer than rare moment found in the unlikeliest location. Among fallen creatures, bent on pleasure and sin, hope still trickles. The well is almost dry, but not quite. Not yet.

Lysander held out a hand to acknowledge Richard's contribution to the moment. The audience shouted their appreciation.

Locks of Richard's silver hair fell away from his face as his gaze turned momentarily to the ceiling.

Does he feel a glimmer of grace? Might he hear an echoing chorus that I'm barred from hearing?

Lysander's heart thumped. Richard lowered the sax and glanced at Lysander.

Speak, man! If you felt heaven's rush, tell me.

Lysander held his breath and waited, would have waited all night.

"The black-haired bitch's army is advancing," Richard said.

The moment's divine nature fled. Lysander's skin cooled, his hope and excitement draining away.

"Our champions are behind enemy lines. They don't realize it yet, but—" Richard tipped his head down, and his pale eyes looked over the top of the sunglasses, locking with Lysander's. "They're trapped."

Chapter 6

"Do you hear that?" Alissa asked.

"What?" Cerise said, and then everyone went silent to listen. Cerise didn't hear anything over the motor, but Merrick's gaze turned westward and he nodded. He rolled down the divider between them and the driver.

"How's it look?" Merrick asked.

"Clear streets, boss," the man said, but the sharp movements of Merrick's eyes poked holes in Cerise's calm.

"Don't take Milano. Go up a block and take Bacci." Merrick's thumb slid over the surface of his phone and he made a call. "There's a chopper coming from the west, Tony. Turn the tower cameras and see if you can get eyes on it."

Merrick pulled out the earpiece and put his phone on speaker so that Ox and the driver could hear what the man on the other end said.

"Boss, two sedans just came out of the Jacobi tunnel. They've got reaper plates," Tony said.

Cerise grimaced. *What the hell are reaper plates?*

"They won't catch us. We're only six blocks out. Check the sky," Merrick replied.

Cerise's breath caught as she heard the blades' distinctive chop. Her heart thudded in time as she looked up. Etherlin Security had four helicopters, but they wouldn't come from the west. The west was more of the Varden. The part of the Varden where the ventala syndicate was located.

"Boss, a semi just blocked Milano."

"Have we got a camera that shows Bacci and Pisa?" the driver asked.

"No," Merrick said, "but it'll be blocked, too. Ox, under the seat."

Merrick opened the sunroof and stood to look out. The helicopter noise got markedly louder.

Merrick ducked back inside and closed the sunroof. There was a pinging sound, like hail hitting the car.

Cerise tensed. "Was that gunfire?"

Merrick ignored the question and instead said, "Tony, there's one chopper on top of us. Any others?"

"Not that I see, boss. Want me to send a guy to the roof now with binoculars?"

"No. I want the guys sent to Milano. Whichever street we choose, it's going to be a battle to get through. I want men on the other side waiting for us. If I can knock the eyes from the sky, I'm gonna go east. Send someone to Crimson for a quiet word with Lysander."

"We're on it."

Alissa moved to sit next to Cerise so Ox could raise the bench cushion they'd been sitting on. From within the seat, he lifted a very large weapon that was in pieces. He put it together quickly. Cerise leaned forward and saw the ammunition. Rockets.

"I have weapons training," Cerise said. "All the muses do. Alissa and I should be armed."

"Cerise is very good," Alissa added.

"Give Alissa a gun, Ox," Merrick said, handing the clip for Cerise's gun back to her. He pointed to the corner. "I want you guys there." Cerise and Alissa moved to the designated spot.

Merrick took the assembled weapon just as an explosion rocked the limo. Merrick kept his footing. The driver yelled curses.

"Boyle, I want quiet." Merrick's voice was low and calm, and the driver immediately fell silent.

"Sedan with reaper plates a block back and closing fast," the driver announced.

"Then move this car. Make a right."

"We'll be heading right by the tunnel, boss."

"Make a right," Merrick repeated. He opened the roof and followed the gun through the hole. The blast from his weapon was followed by a deafening boom. Within seconds, a ball of fire hit the ground.

Merrick ducked inside and held out a hand. Ox slapped another rocket grenade into it.

"The chopper's down. Turn us southeast. I'm going to clear you a path," Merrick said to the driver in a tone so mild he might have been a weatherman forecasting clear skies.

Moments later, there was another explosion that rocked the car. Merrick waited for a few moments and then dropped back in and closed the roof.

"It's flash, not substance," he told the driver. "I want you to punch it and hang to the right as you blow past."

The car sped forward.

"Tony, you there?"

"Still here, boss. Lysander had already left Crimson so he doesn't know, but the guys are on the way."

They crashed through flaming debris, and Alissa clutched the armrest as the car jerked. Cerise tightened her muscles to keep herself from falling from the seat.

"Any more sedans with blackout glass come through the tunnel?"

"Haven't seen any. There were two though," Tony said.

"I know."

"Did you take out one or two on your end?"

"One," Merrick said, gaze swiveling from the windshield to the various windows and back. "Brake," Merrick said.

"I'm clear," the driver said and within the strain, Cerise's muse ears detected a waver that felt like treachery.

"Merrick—" Alissa and Cerise both said at the same time.

"Brake!" Merrick snapped, but the driver hesitated. Merrick yanked a handgun free and pointed it at the driver's head, but dropped his arm just as quickly. "Too late," Merrick murmured, surging forward to wedge himself between her and Alissa.

Alissa sucked in a breath. Cerise clamped down on her lip. Merrick shoved their heads down, and Cerise's body cramped at being bent in half. She felt Merrick's arm shielding her neck.

"Ox, hang on," Merrick said.

Suddenly, the tires didn't grip the road anymore. Instead

they popped, and the car careened sideways and spun like a top until it rammed something hard, bounced off, rammed again, and slammed to a stop. It knocked the breath from her, rattling her teeth and bones.

As Merrick's arm across the back of her body disappeared, Cerise heard the pop of gunfire. *In the car.*

Cerise sat up sharply. The driver was slumped over the steering wheel, bleeding from the back of his head where Merrick had shot him.

"I don't understand," Alissa said, staring at the driver's body.

"There was oil and a puncture strip on the road. He saw it," Merrick said.

"He was working for the syndicate?" Alissa asked.

Merrick nodded, trying to open the smashed door that was farthest from the street, but the door was jammed.

"Ox, we're a powder keg." Merrick nodded at the partially shattered window. Ox went to work bashing out the remaining glass while Merrick raised the phone. "Tony?"

"Here, boss."

"In about thirty seconds, we're on the move on foot."

"The guys are in a gun battle with the truck at Milano. At least two syndicate hit squads worth."

"Keep eyes on Milano. Some of them will bug out when they get word we're on foot. I want to know how many and which way they go," Merrick said, replacing the earpiece and shoving it into the phone, taking Tony off speaker.

Ox dragged himself through the opening of the smashed door and window. He ignored his bleeding cuts as he said in a low voice, "Careful, Miss Xenakis." He put his arm over the sharp frame so she could slide out unscathed.

Merrick glanced out the window. "Take them to that deep doorway, Ox."

Ox nodded, but whispered, "Incoming, boss."

Cerise jerked her head and spotted several armed ventala about a hundred and fifty feet away and advancing.

"Hang on, Liss," Merrick said, coming out the opening in a flash. "Get her, Ox," Merrick said before he moved to the front of the car.

Cerise crouched, following Merrick.

Merrick stood, drawing the fire toward him. From one knee, Cerise squeezed off several rounds. Between them, they dropped four assailants. The hail of returning fire made her drop to the ground, using the car for cover. Merrick was behind a tree and fired from either side. He was smooth and fast.

"Cerise," Alissa hissed.

"Right with you," Cerise murmured without taking her eyes from the street.

"Cover me," Merrick said.

Pleased that he'd asked, Cerise rose slightly and squeezed off several rounds, not as accurately as she would've liked but well enough to cover Merrick so he could dive back behind the car.

Blood dripped from his left sleeve.

"You're hit?"

"Paper cut," he said. "Get to the doorway before they swarm." Merrick held out a hand to prevent her from responding, and she knew he was listening to Tony. A moment later, he said, "If you decide to call Etherlin Security, I won't hold a grudge."

"It'll be over by the time they could get here, won't it?"

"Maybe, but for you they'll come pretty fast. They can pick you up from the roof," he said, nodding to the building.

"Can I take her with me?"

"If I'm not there to object, you should."

Her expression softened. "When I get to the doorway, should I send your man back to you to help hold them off?"

"No, he stays with her."

"Good luck," she said.

He nodded. She crouched and ran for the doorway. She heard the pop of gunfire and felt a stinging pain in her calf. Inside the doorway, she checked her leg and found a small scratch. She flicked off the fragment of ricocheted bullet.

"Merrick wants us to go to the roof," she told Ox and Alissa. They looked up as they heard a series of explosions.

Ox didn't hesitate. He slammed his body against the heavy door, popping it open, and ushered them inside. Cerise pulled her phone from her pocket, but couldn't get a signal in the dark stairwell.

They hustled up the stairs. The door to the roof was locked, but Ox, a one-man battering ram, busted it open.

She checked her phone again, but there was still no signal. She held the phone up, waving it over her head. "What the hell?" she mumbled.

"They took out the cell towers," Alissa said, pointing. Cerise spun and saw the columns of smoke where the cell towers in the Sliver were burning.

"Shit," Cerise said. "We have to go back down. Right now. There's nowhere for us to go from here."

Two more explosions from the street drew their attention. Cerise jogged to the edge of the roof and looked down.

Merrick abandoned the rocket launcher, grabbed something from the limo's trunk, and sprinted to the doorway of the building whose roof they were on.

"He doesn't realize the towers are down," Cerise said, grabbing Alissa's arm and dragging her toward the stairwell. "He meant for me to call ES to come get us."

By the time they reached the door to the stairs, Merrick burst through it.

"They took out the cell towers," he and Cerise said at the same time.

"We have to go down," Cerise added.

Merrick shook his head, dropping to a knee and opening an enormous black duffel bag. "Ox, secure that door," Merrick said, tossing him a handheld welding torch.

She raised her brows. "Eagle Scout were you?"

"Exactly," he murmured with a thin layer of sarcasm.

"Cerise, I'm so sorry I let you come," Alissa said with a bereft expression. "I thought we'd be out and back before anyone ever realized that we'd left Merrick's territory. I should have warned you."

Cerise squeezed Alissa's arm. "It's okay."

Merrick quickly assembled something that looked like a harpoon gun.

Several shafts of light moved over the roof like spotlights, and Cerise jerked her head up, expecting to see a syndicate assault team dropping from the sky. Instead there was an enormous shadow. A moment later, she could make out a winged man.

Lysander.

"You're here?" the angel asked Cerise upon landing. "Why are you here?"

"This is Cerise. My friend," Alissa added when Lysander took a step backward. "I'm so glad to see you, Lysander."

Lysander glanced once more at Cerise, then walked over to Merrick.

"You know what's interesting?" Lysander said to him.

"Your timing's excellent as always, Lyse. I want you to take the women up into the clouds for cover and then fly over and drop them in the Etherlin."

"No," Alissa said. "Drop Cerise in the Etherlin and drop Alissa at the penthouse."

"What's interesting," Lysander said, "is that Richard told me what was happening here. I'm not sure if it's a sixth sense or if he has premonitions that precede actual events by a very small increment of time."

"Yeah, interesting, but not a priority discussion at the moment," Merrick said. "Do me a favor, and get Alissa off the roof before Victor and Tamberi Jacobi send another helicopter with heavy artillery."

Lysander, who could've been having a cup of tea for all the emotion he betrayed, glanced at the cable Merrick was unspooling. Lysander walked to the edge of the roof and looked down. "Switching rooftops is a good idea. How much cable have you got?"

"Enough for two moves and then down."

"Why don't I take you and Alissa? Your bodyguard can take Alissa's friend over and down. I'll come back and help them reach the Etherlin gates, then bring him home."

Cerise's heart slammed inside her chest. The bastard wanted to leave her in the middle of a war zone?

To his credit, Merrick shook his head instantly.

Cerise's mind raced, almost not able to process how insulting and frustrating his attitude was. She was a muse, used to being the center of attention in her circles, used to being surrounded by Etherlin Security officers whose sole purpose in life was to protect her. To be made so acutely aware that to an archangel she meant absolutely nothing cut her. Especially since he intrigued her, and if their roles had been reversed, she wouldn't have agreed to leave him. She'd never have risked the loss of his talent.

"Or I'll take your bodyguard and Alissa, and I'll come back and help you escort the girl back to the gates."

I have a name, you prick!

Merrick looked sharply at Lysander, then he strode to Cerise, grabbed her arm, and leaned toward her, inhaling.

"I don't smell it," Merrick said.

"Smell what?" Cerise said, trying to snatch her arm from his grip.

"That's ridiculous," Alissa said. "Cerise is not a demon. We grew up together."

"I never said she was a demon," Lysander said mildly.

Merrick released Cerise's arm. "Lyse, time's running out. What's this about?" Merrick demanded.

Lysander glanced at Cerise, then tilted his head sideways to beckon Merrick over to him. They took a few more steps away and spoke in low voices.

When Merrick turned to look at her, his smile pissed Cerise off even more. Lysander had talked about leaving her to fend for herself against armed gunmen—what could be amusing in the explanation for that?

She also hated feeling like an outsider, even though she should've been glad she was. She wasn't supposed to have anything to do with the fallen. Unfortunately, these members of the fallen were exciting and compelling, and she was drawn to them. She wanted to be part of their inner circle.

"Ox, how much do you weigh?" Merrick asked.

You have got to be kidding!

"Two-eighty . . . three hundred," Ox speculated with a shrug.

Lysander had convinced Merrick? Just when she'd started to rethink her position on Merrick, he was actually going to send his bodyguard to safety rather than her?

"What do you say, Lyse?" Merrick asked.

"You'll have to leave the gear."

"Sure," Merrick said with a shrug. Merrick grabbed a belt that looked like it belonged to Batman and tossed it to Lysander. The angel hooked it to his low-riding leather pants and cinched it around his waist. Then Merrick put another belt around himself. He hooked a length of cable between them and inserted several hooks along its length.

"Ox, take that hook in the middle and secure it to your belt and hang on to the hold. Cerise, come here."

She strode to him, her jaw still clenched angrily. He hooked cable through her belt loops.

Alissa glanced down at her dress, which obviously had no belt loops, but she didn't seem concerned. And why should she? Of course, no one would ever suggest leaving Alissa behind. As if on cue, Lysander stretched out a hand to the ethereal blonde.

Cerise stared daggers at the angel. "So now he thinks he can carry us all? When he initially wanted to leave me on the roof?" Cerise reflected coldly.

"It's not what you think," Merrick said, the corner of his mouth curving up.

"I think he's an ass."

Lysander glanced at her.

"You're an ass," she said.

In Latin to Merrick, Lysander said, "She misunderstands. Let her."

Merrick grinned and returned in Latin, "You don't want her to know that you find her dangerously beautiful? And that her skin's gorgeous scent stays with you for weeks?"

What?

Cerise's brows shot up, but she quickly covered her shock with a neutral expression.

Lysander's eyes narrowed. After a moment's contemplation, he asked in Latin, "Alissa, does your friend speak Latin?"

Alissa fought the smile that threatened. "She's a muse. Like archangels, we have the gift of tongues."

Lysander's frosty gaze settled on Merrick for a moment, then the angel moved very close to Alissa. Lysander whispered something in her ear, and Alissa's blush was evident from several feet away. Merrick's amusement faded.

Lysander's arm snaked around Alissa's waist and pulled her body against his. "This amount of weight will be a strain. You should hold on to me," Lysander said.

Alissa slid her arms around Lysander's neck. Merrick rolled his eyes.

With his free hand, Lysander wrapped the cable around his

arm and held it tight. Lysander pushed off the ground, his wings beating hard as he and Alissa rose eight feet in the air. When the cable was stretched taut against Ox's weight, she watched Lysander rise against it and lift the massive bodyguard.

"Shit," Ox murmured, holding the cable in a white-knuckled grip.

The sound of bullets hitting the roof door made Cerise and Merrick whip their attention to it.

"Can he manage it?" she asked, glancing up when Lysander's body halted midair as he tried to pull her and Merrick off the roof, too. The cable around her waist tightened as they rose a few inches above the cement.

"Hang on," Merrick said, holding her with only one arm so he could pull his gun out at the sound of impact against the soldered door.

Cerise put an arm around Merrick's neck, but with her other hand, she pulled the gun free of the back of her pants and pointed it at the door.

With a sudden upward surge, they rose another foot above the roof. She and Merrick both stiffened to keep themselves steady and their guns ready, but by the time the door burst open, they were well into the finely shredded white of the clouds.

Above them, Lysander chatted to Alissa, whose chuckles could occasionally be heard.

"What's he speaking now?" Cerise asked. "I think that's . . ."

"Etruscan."

"Wow. That's a really dead language. Do you speak Etruscan?"

Merrick shook his head with a mirthless smile.

"That's the point?"

Merrick nodded.

"Would you like me to translate? I've never been as facile with languages as Alissa, but if I concentrate, you'll have the gist."

Merrick shook his head. "Let him win the moment. Neither of them would betray me."

She arched a brow. "How can you be sure?" she asked, surprised. She would've expected someone like Merrick to be suspicious of everyone. "You barely know her, and isn't he a *fallen* angel?"

Merrick smiled, and this time it reached his eyes. He let the question lie, smoothly changing the subject by saying, "When you said you know how to handle a gun, you weren't exaggerating. That was nice cover on the street."

It was her turn to smile, and she inclined her head in return. "And you live up to your reputation. Grace under *extreme* pressure."

He shrugged.

All in a day's work for him apparently. That level of cool is attractive. No wonder Alissa fell so hard.

"So," he said, "how are you enjoying your visit to the Varden so far?"

She laughed, and, oddly, as she hung in the shredded mist, so clean and sweet, with the echo of the words *dangerously beautiful* still on her mind, she had to admit that on some level, despite the car chase and the car *crash*, despite the flying bullets and terrifying moment of finding herself without a cell signal or a way to escape, she was enjoying it a ridiculous amount.

Fresh from the shower, Tamberi toweled herself off and slid on a pair of black lace underwear. When she heard the knock on the door, she called, "What?"

The door opened and the eyes of the ventala in the doorway immediately locked onto the points of her small breasts.

"Well?" she said impatiently as she rubbed lime-scented lotion on her arms.

"Merrick escaped, but three of his guys were seriously wounded and one's definitely dead—beheaded. Merrick did down the chopper, and we lost seventeen."

We can afford more losses than he can, she thought. *If we don't get lucky and kill him during one of these firefights, we'll grind his security force down to a skeleton crew and then overtake him.*

For show, however, she frowned and exaggeratedly rolled her eyes. "Merrick continues to make fools of the ventala who train the syndicate assassins. He gets to laugh again tonight. He once told me that St. Vincent's girls' rugby team has a tougher lineup than our hit squads," she lied. "Is he right?" she demanded.

The men flushed, shaking their heads. Tamberi pulled on a knit top.

"He didn't just have Orvin and North with him. There was a second woman in the car. A tall dark-haired woman. Good with a gun."

Tamberi narrowed her eyes. "Was it Cerise Xenakis?"

"It could've been. They thought it looked like her."

Tamberi licked her lips, her pulse thrumming. Had they really been so close to capturing Cerise Xenakis? Tamberi's fingers twitched, and she closed them into fists. She wanted to kill Merrick and Alissa North to avenge Cato, and she could put North's or any of the muses' dying blood to good use, but Tamberi wanted Cerise's bare throat under a knife for personal reasons, too. "Xenakis and North aren't close friends. They're in pictures together a lot at official functions, but they don't hang out together. Especially on our side of the wall. If it was Xenakis, what was that about? And is she still outside the Etherlin? If she is, I want her. Preferably taken alive."

"We can't send another wave tonight. We need air support, and replacement choppers can't get here until tomorrow."

She glared at them. She knew if they waited they'd risk Xenakis getting back to the Etherlin where it was impossible to get to her. "Send a couple of teams into the Sliver and have them lie in wait near the Etherlin gates. If Merrick tries to take her back, we can surround his car. We'll have him outnumbered and away from his stronghold. And if he doesn't try to take her back tonight, she'll still be in the Varden tomorrow when we'll send a triple crew of assassins to storm his place."

They nodded and turned to go.

"By the way, like North I want Xenakis alive." Her fangs ached for a taste of Cerise Xenakis's blood. Wouldn't that be a sweet end to Tamberi's unfinished business with the rock-and-roll muse?

When they were gone, Tamberi slicked back her hair and poured herself a shot of bourbon. She sucked it down, and then she had a second. Dropping onto the king-sized bed, she stared up at the swirled glass sculpture overhead. As she drifted toward sleep a face that was almost too beautiful to be male shimmered within the writhing mass of glass snakes. The heart-shaped face and its accompanying waves of sepia-colored hair were familiar. She'd had a vision of him once before.

"Tamberi," the melodic voice hissed as the demon courted her.

"What?" she murmured. "I told you. Twice, I've raised demons, and twice, they haven't done much. You guys are a lot of flash, a lot of talk. The lesser demon killed a few people at a party. Gadreel blew the top off a hotel." She shrugged. "Not impressed. Why would I waste my time helping you when I can do more damage on my own?" She stretched an arm above her head. A sensation slithered over her skin, tweaking her nipple.

"Nice," she sighed. "Demons do make great lovers; I'll give you that. But for the first time ever, I don't care about getting off. What I want is to set the world on fire and then watch it burn."

A flame sparked on her hip and seared her flesh.

She slapped her hand over it, hissing in pain. "Fuck off," she ground out.

"Haven't you long wanted to add art to your body?" the voice murmured in her head.

She did regret that tattoos weren't permanent on ventala skin. She rolled up and looked at the shape of the burn. The crisp lines were perfectly rendered. A smoking skull with a stemmed cherry in its teeth leered at her. In the smoke curls were the letters *M*, *M*, and *Y*.

"Marks of a Misspent Youth"? The Molly Times song?

She narrowed her eyes, a bittersweet taste tainting her tongue. Her gaze rose to the slithering glass. The demon's face morphed into the boy's, and her heart clutched. Then the demon's face bloomed again, a dark rose opening and banishing the face she hadn't seen in a long time.

"Your name?" she asked, her voice a ragged whisper.

"You want to burn down the world. I'll provide the match."

"Do we know each other?" she demanded.

"Sure."

She tasted blood. It dripped from her fangs down her throat. She tasted the boy she'd enjoyed, bitten, and helped destroy.

The only guy she'd cared for other than Cato. Was the phantom taste of him a trick of the demon's? Or did this member of the damned really know things?

"I don't have the spell-book with the demon-raising ritual anymore. A disgustingly pure archangel named Nathaniel took it away. And you know what that means. Once the power in the page is gone, the memory of the ritual decays instantly. I couldn't raise a demon even if I wanted to."

"I don't want to be raised in the flesh, but I need a warm welcome for what I do want. I'll show you the way if you're willing."

She stared at the face with its perfect symmetry, its unnatural beauty. Heaven's lost candy. "You'd be welcome here if you're more than pyrotechnics. But come without the match I need, and you'll be the first thing I burn."

His lips curved into a glorious angelic smile that blistered the room with its white light.

"Fuck," she said, the shards of light like dagger tips poking her eyes. She flung an arm up to shield her face, but before it covered her eyes, his mouth yawned open and down his throat she saw an abyss of souls drowning in molten tar.

She could not drag her gaze away. His mouth closed slowly.

"Counted among the first, most dare not speak my name." His lips drew back in a fierce sneer. "I invented warfare."

A chill raked over her skin, the sting as sharp as frostbite. She wanted to reach for the blanket, to curl up against the bitter creeping cold, but couldn't. She struggled against invisible tethers. How could he reach across the physical world to restrain her? It shouldn't have been possible.

The menace in his whisper struck a chord in her soul, and she recoiled from the dread it wrought. Humanity had been this demon's bitch, his victim down through the ages. She wanted to scream that she wasn't just human. She could swallow darkness, too. But her voice wouldn't come. There was no way to challenge him or to doubt his power any longer.

"I invented warfare, Tamberi. *What* do you say to me?"

"Thank you," she said, gasping, hardly able to squeeze breath from her stiff chest, as if he'd already killed her and now watched her body cool and contract with rigor.

She fought the urge to beg for mercy, but finally she moaned in pain.

Just before the cold released her, she heard, "My name is Reziel."

Chapter 7

Cerise had seen many beautiful gardens, but the unexpected ones were always the most memorable. Looking down on the roof of Merrick's building as they descended, she thought it seemed the fusion of many other places: Versailles, Italy, Japan. There were geometric patches of green grass and shrubs, potted orange trees, fountains of water falling over slabs of stone, a reflecting pool, a bamboo partition, cushioned benches, and a collection of marble statues.

"So many elements. They're surprisingly well-balanced," Cerise said.

Merrick glanced at the roof, but didn't comment. His silence had stretched over the past fifteen minutes.

"Something on your mind?" she asked.

He shook his head. They touched down, and he unhooked her, sliding the cable free of her belt loops. He divested himself of the belt and rolled the cable. Ox grinned when he landed.

"Pretty peaceful up there, eh, boss?"

Merrick nodded, and Ox unhooked himself and opened and closed the hand that he'd been using to tightly hold the cable.

Lysander landed, a sheen of sandalwood-scented sweat evaporating like mist. He set Alissa down, and she touched his face briefly and murmured, "Thank you, Lysander."

He nodded, unfastening the belt. He tossed the belt to Merrick, and a look passed between them that was apology and understanding rolled into one.

"We've got spiced meat, fresh oranges, almonds, and figs. I know you must be starving now," Alissa said to the angel.

"Thank you for the offer of hospitality, Alissa," Lysander said, walking away.

"Lysander, please come in and eat."

"Let him go," Merrick said, coiling the last of the cable as Lysander stepped off the roof with a beat of his massive wings. In moments, he'd risen into the clouds and out of sight.

"Did he leave because of me?" Cerise asked, staring into the sky.

"He comes. He goes," Ox said with a shrug. "You can't take it personally." Ox strolled across the roof to the door. He waited for them, holding it open.

"Are *you* hungry?" Alissa asked Cerise.

"I could eat," Cerise said, falling in step with her. She glanced over her shoulder, wanting to see if Merrick was staying behind or would join them. She was surprised to find him only a foot away. He moved silently, like the predator he clearly was.

"So where does your friend live? And does he often take things that don't belong to him?"

Merrick quirked a brow, but didn't take the bait and ask her what she was talking about. Still, the questioning look was enough of an invitation for her to press on.

"During the hail of bullets and winged escape I forgot why I came tonight. Lysander took a book that doesn't belong to him."

"What book?" Alissa asked.

"Griffin Lane's songbook that's been missing."

"Griffin Lane's death was such a tragedy. It must have been really hard for you to lose one of your aspirants at the height of his talent . . . terrible." Alissa shook her head. "And you believe that Lysander has his songbook?"

"I know he does. I saw him take it."

"Huh. Well, maybe he wants to look through it. Lysander's a musician. I'm sure he'll give it back when he's done. Don't you think?" Alissa asked, looking at Merrick.

Merrick shrugged.

Alissa frowned. "Well, they're Griffin Lane's songs that he wrote with Cerise's inspiration. They belong to his estate. His bandmates were his siblings, right? Of course they should have his final songbook. We'll talk to Lysander about it. I'm sure when he knows the situation, he'll return it."

Cerise wasn't looking at Alissa. She was studying Merrick's enigmatic expression, which didn't reassure her. Nor had his silence when Alissa suggested that they would speak to Lysander on her behalf.

Sconces lit the stairwell, making the glossy black walls gleam as though they were covered in patent leather. The foursome descended until they reached a door that opened into a hall with alternating lengths of indigo carpet and white marble. A black-and-white photograph of a French horn seemed to float above the ground, held in place by thread-thin wires. The walls were papered in a silver geometric pattern reminiscent of gift wrap.

"Nice," Cerise said, pointing at the horn picture.

Alissa smiled.

"Ox, go to the control room, and let Tony know we're back. There's still no cell signal, so tell him to send a runner out to the guys still in the street. Have him pull everyone back."

Cerise's and Alissa's expressions turned somber. With the immediate danger over for them, Cerise had forgotten that Merrick still had people in the streets, possibly looking for them and fighting for their lives against rival ventala.

Ox went to the elevator, and Merrick stopped at a door with a security keypad. He punched in a very long code, and the pad's light changed from red to green. Merrick opened the door.

Inside the apartment, black-and-white furniture with silver and slate blue accents dominated the room. Highly polished metal end tables had an Art Deco flair. Her gaze paused on a small bronze statue of a half-naked female huntress that was beautiful and erotic. It suited Merrick, but how did Alissa feel about her bold new surroundings? Cerise glanced at the other muse, who moved smoothly into the room, apparently at home in Merrick's place.

Merrick cast the cable into the corner and walked to the bar. He moved like the world-class athletes Cerise inspired, not a motion wasted. He made himself a Scotch Lime and then mixed a yellow cocktail that he strained into a glass.

"Cerise, what's your poison?"

"I don't drink much."

"If you did, what would you have?"

"Something where Triple Sec was the main attraction."

"Right," he said, and then added in a murmur, "Working on the perfect storm."

Cerise gave Alissa a questioning look.

"Triple sec, that's orange-flavored?" Alissa asked Merrick's back.

"That is orange-flavored," Merrick confirmed without turning around.

Alissa nodded silently.

"Want to fill me in?" Cerise asked.

"Lysander loves oranges," Alissa said.

Cerise shrugged. "So do a lot of people."

Merrick mixed several liquors and added fresh-squeezed juice from small sweet oranges that Cerise could've eaten by the dozen. Once in the shaker, he gave them a good shake and strained the contents over ice.

He walked over and handed Alissa and Cerise their cocktails. By color, Alissa's was sunshine and Cerise's sunset.

"Damn," Cerise said after the first delicious swallow. It was intensely orange with a hint of something nutty underneath. "If I ever take up serious drinking, you're my bartender."

Merrick inclined his head, then returned to the bar. He drank his Scotch and poured himself another.

"Is Cerise's an Orange Scorpion?" Alissa asked.

"Yeah," Merrick said, squeezing lime into his glass and then downing the drink. He returned to them, stopping in front of Alissa. "How about something for luck?"

The smile Alissa gave Merrick was sweet enough to rival the orange juice in Cerise's glass. Alissa tipped her head up and kissed him, then laid a palm against his cheek, rubbing the five o'clock shadow in a gesture that was flirtatious and affectionate.

"Don't stay gone long," she whispered.

He pressed another kiss on Alissa's mouth. "Not possible."

As he turned toward the door, Cerise caught his eye. Without breaking stride, he winked at her, and then slipped out.

"How long have you been in love with him?"

"Five years," Alissa said with a slow smile. "But I only realized it about two months ago."

"Were you dating him in secret for all that time?" Cerise asked, shocked. Sneaking off to meet a ventala was a major security breach. How had Alissa managed it?

Alissa shook her head, sinking onto a couch and waving for Cerise to join her. Cerise hesitated, studying Alissa over the rim of her cocktail glass. She and Alissa hadn't been close for a very long time. As children they'd been best friends, but the relationship had been strained because Alissa, always so beautiful, had been everyone's favorite—even Cerise's own father's.

Cerise hadn't been a pretty child, but she'd been a talented dancer and natural athlete. When the lead in a dance recital had been given to Alissa when Cerise had clearly earned the role, Cerise had asked Alissa to turn it down. Unable to defy the adults who controlled their every move, Alissa hadn't. From then on, Cerise had frozen Alissa out of her life.

As they grew up, Alissa continued to have things come easily to her, but Cerise stopped resenting it. Alissa was kind to everyone. She never flaunted her beauty or tried to use it to get ahead. Alissa had worked tirelessly to become a great muse, and she'd earned Cerise's respect.

For her part, Cerise had developed her own talents, grown into her looks, and amassed a legion of fans. She was confident and comfortable with who she'd become. She didn't really need to rekindle a long-buried friendship with Alissa, but Alissa's recent departure from the Etherlin had shocked everyone, and Alissa interested Cerise. Breaking an incarcerated ventala killer out of a cell and eloping with him . . . Alissa was the last person Cerise would've imagined doing such a thing. Cerise admired Alissa's rebellion. It was long overdue. Alissa the child hadn't been able to stand up to the Etherlin Council over a dance recital. But Alissa the woman had walked away from the only home she'd ever known and turned her back on the security of the Etherlin to live in a raging urban area with the violent vampire half-breed she'd married. It would've been almost impossible to believe . . . if Cerise hadn't seen Merrick and Alissa together.

With a couple of swallows, warmth spread through Cerise,

easing the edge off her nerves. She sat sideways on the couch so she faced Alissa.

"Tell me what happened the night you left the Etherlin."

Alissa rubbed her eyes. "That was a long night," she murmured, taking a slow sip of her drink. After a soft sigh, Alissa let the story pour out like water through a broken dam. Cerise felt the truth of the account and raised her brows when Alissa described stealing the Wreath from its case and locking Troy and Dorie in an interrogation room to keep them out of her way.

"Merrick's life was at stake. I don't regret anything I did that night." Alissa squinted as she reached for her glass and her hand slid by it, jostling the liquid. Alissa's fingers caught the glass on the second attempt and brought it to her lips. She finished the story quickly, and Cerise realized how terrifying that night must have been for Alissa.

"Listen, I need to warn you about something. Don't trust Troy with Dorie."

Cerise's brows rose.

The Xenakis and Rella families were close. Though Ileana and Troy were almost a decade older than Cerise, they had always taken an interest in Cerise and Dorie and supported their growth as muses. At the moment, in addition to being an Etherlin Council member and the Etherlin's publicist, Troy was also the publicist for the Molly Times and some of Cerise's other bands. When she was younger, Cerise had had a crush on Troy, the then Versace model, but for years Cerise had considered him more of an older brother or cousin.

"Alissa, what are you saying?"

"Troy likes young girls. He likes their looks and likes the control he can have over them. Young girls are less sure of themselves and he exploits that. Maybe Dorie won't be easy for him to manipulate, but I wouldn't take the chance."

"What did he do to you?" Cerise asked quietly.

"It doesn't matter. I'm not interested in dredging up the past. I just noticed that he spends a lot of time with Dorie. She's what? Half his age?"

"If he raped you, you should've told my dad. Dimitri would've kicked him off the council and seen him brought up on charges."

"Let's not use the word *rape*. I was young and naïve. He

manipulated and used me, but it wasn't some violent assault. The real damage was in the way he treated me. He betrayed me and tried to break my spirit."

Cerise winced. "You never said anything."

"At the time, I felt like it was partly my fault for being pretty, for being such a temptation. Troy's very good at spinning things. It's why he's a great publicist."

Cerise frowned. Was it true? Troy could be a flirt, but she'd never seen him do anything sleazy or inappropriate. Cerise did remember Troy spending a lot of time with Alissa when Cerise and Alissa were in their midteens. And she remembered Troy later bad-mouthing Alissa. At the time, Cerise had been glad that Troy had lost interest in Alissa. It hadn't occurred to Cerise that Troy might have preyed upon her.

"You should have told my dad. He would've been furious. He would've believed you."

"I didn't need to tell anyone. I dealt with Troy myself. I used my magic and almost killed him."

Cerise's mouth gaped open. "You did?"

"Oh yes."

Cerise felt like she'd just been told that the Easter Bunny was really the Grim Reaper in disguise.

"I only bring it up now because I've noticed Dorie's spending a lot of time with him. I just wanted to warn you."

Cerise nodded.

"It probably won't come up, but do me a favor and don't mention Troy around Merrick. Merrick has an idea of what Troy did and—well . . ."

"Merrick might try to kill him?"

"He'll do more than try."

"Have you told Merrick not to hurt Troy?"

"I told him I already avenged myself, and I don't need or want anything more done to Troy on my account."

"But you don't think Merrick will respect your wishes?"

"When Merrick was a child, his mother was beaten to death, and he was the victim of his father's brutal abuse. Merrick started out pretty powerless, but at this point he's anything but. When it comes to protecting the women and children in his territory, he's liberal with the use of force, and that's for people he doesn't know personally.

"Now he's got a young wife that he loves who was exploited in her teens by an older man who continues to live a privileged life. Nothing I say will convince Merrick that Troy doesn't deserve worse than he's gotten so far. At the moment, Merrick's focused on other things; Troy's lucky he is. I think it's best not to wave any red capes in front of a bull."

"His killing an Etherlin Council member would have a lot of consequences for you both. Aren't you worried about how dangerous Merrick is? Aren't you afraid you won't be able to control him?"

"To quote Merrick, 'If you want something tame, you shouldn't keep a lion for a pet.'"

"Do you want someone wild?"

"Apparently, I do," Alissa said with a sheepish smile. "And it's not as if he and Lysander kill without provocation. They actually have the right moral compass; they're just more prone to violence than we're used to."

"But don't you think you might eventually regret this? Running away with him? Marrying him so fast?"

Alissa shook her head. "He was always going to be the one I fell in love with. I was drawn to him from the first moment I saw him. I would've ended up with him much earlier if I hadn't been afraid of damaging my magic by leaving the Etherlin and if I hadn't been worried that my dad would deteriorate if I took him away from the house full of my mom's memory. But after opening the ancient portal, my magic's stronger than ever, and my dad's doing well here. Merrick's extremely good with him. Most importantly, Merrick loves me the way I deserve to be loved." Alissa rubbed her wedding ring absently. "Home will always be the place where Merrick and I can be together."

Alissa's conviction took Cerise's breath away. Did Alissa really know what she'd gotten herself into? Was she seeing things clearly, or was she simply blinded by love's early infatuation?

"The ventala syndicate's bloodthirsty, and they won't give up. What if something happens to Merrick?" Cerise asked, thinking of the morning after Griffin had died. The devastation and the ache that had never seemed to go away. "Is it really better to have loved and lost?"

"What's the alternative when you love someone with every part of your heart? Denying that kind of feeling doesn't work. There's no place to hide from it. No way to escape. No matter what happens, I'll never be sorry that I was with him. When I fell in love with Merrick, I found myself. I'll never regret it."

Cerise stared at her. Alissa had obviously imagined what might come to pass. To know that and to choose a potentially destructive path . . . it took real strength. If Cerise had known what would happen with Griffin, she wasn't sure she could've let herself get so close to him.

"Besides," Alissa added with a small grin. "You've seen him under fire. A part of me just has faith that he's as invincible as he seems."

"If only all the guys we fell for were invincible."

Alissa raised her brows in question.

Cerise shrugged, took a drink to stall, then shook her head, exhaling audibly. "You aren't the only one who's kept secrets."

Cerise looked into Alissa's face. Hard not to trust a beauty that seemed so pure. It had to be an advantage for Alissa as a muse; how could any aspirant resist opening up his mind under that gaze?

Cerise wasn't an aspirant, but she did have a burning need to unburden herself, to finally confide in someone.

"I had an affair with Griffin Lane. He insisted we keep it a secret so that our romance wouldn't overshadow his music. We'd been together seven months and were still in love when he fell off that cliff."

Alissa's expression became pained, but she didn't utter a word. She only reached across and put her hand on Cerise's wrist, then slid it down to squeeze her fingers.

Tears swam in Cerise's eyes. "If he did fall." Cerise swallowed hard and wiped away the moisture that formed on her lower lid. "We had a fight—I think we had a terrible fight. My memory of that night is foggy." She shook her head, trying to recall the details. They wouldn't surface. She clenched her fist in frustration.

"Troy was the band's publicist, and he was trying to help his friends who'd just opened their club, Handyrock's in the Sliver, so the Times agreed to play the club to create some buzz

for it. It was a small venue compared to the stadiums they'd
gotten used to, and Griffin really got into the intimate setting.
They did an acoustic version of 'Never More' that was amazing. It would've been a memorable night even if it hadn't been
Griffin's last performance.

"Afterward, Troy had all of us drinking shots of ouzo, but
then the party sort of went to hell. Jersey had had this stomach
flu that left her sick for weeks and she'd just gotten over it, so
Griffin wasn't happy about her drinking. And Griff had an
argument with Troy about a music fest Troy wanted the Molly
Times to do that Griffin didn't. And Griffin and Hayden were
sniping at each other for some reason, too. The night had
started off great, but it really deteriorated. I remember him
grabbing my hand and dragging me out the back door with
Jersey in tow. We dropped her off, and the driver took us to the
house Griffin and I had rented. We had wine, and I guess we
got more drunk than we realized because I blacked out.

"When I woke in the morning, I had this overwhelming
feeling of dread. I knew. Just knew." Cerise licked her lips, letting the tears fall. "I searched the house, but he wasn't in it. I
started calling around, trying to find him, but inside I thought:
He's dead. I felt like I'd crushed him. He'd crushed me, too, of
course. But I was alive to see the sun, so that didn't seem as
important.

"By afternoon, Hayden was turning over rocks at the crash
pads they'd used before they were famous. I didn't want to look
for Griffin in the city though. I knew I wouldn't find him there.

"I borrowed a pair of his snow boots. I'm so tall and have
the hands and feet to match. Sometimes Griffin and I wore
each other's stuff. Naturally it fit us differently, but somehow
it worked." She smiled ruefully. "He was thin . . . such a child-
man." She sighed. "Sometimes he could be ruthless, but I'd look
at his face, so young and sweet, and I almost couldn't believe
it. That's how beauty is dangerous. It makes you make allowances that you really shouldn't." Cerise bit her lip. "When I
went out that day, I started walking and didn't stop until I found
footprints in the snow. I remember everything about those
moments. I remember tying the purple sash on my wool coat.
I remember the way the snow dust covered the tops of the ugly
green boots. I remember staring at the tracks in the snow and

realizing that the shape . . ." Cerise trailed off for a moment, her voice wistful. "From the shape, I knew he hadn't been walking. He'd been running for his life . . . or to end it. The tracks led right off the cliff. There were no other footprints in the snow. No animal or person had pursued him that night. If he ran from something it was the demons inside him . . . maybe the ones that rose from the things I said." She shrugged. "I'll never know if he was running toward the edge of the cliff on purpose. It had been pitch-black that night. He might just have been running, and the edge was there." She paused. "I only know that he didn't slip and fall the way the story's been reported. The marks near the edge where someone slipped were mine. I went to look. I saw his body, and I almost joined him at the bottom of the ravine. But I guess I didn't love him with every part of my heart because I clawed my way back up."

Alissa's small hand, warm and reassuring, held firmly to Cerise's.

"I want his songbook. Sometimes he used it as a journal. I have to see what he wrote that last week. I need to."

"We'll get it back for you."

"What if the angel doesn't want to give it up?"

"We'll get it back," Alissa repeated.

Chapter 8

Cerise woke to the sound of someone humming. She moved the arm that was across her eyes, confused for a moment about where she was until she realized she had fallen asleep on the couch in Merrick and Alissa's penthouse.

Cerise remembered that Merrick had returned after having recovered his people. Arrangements to bury the dead and to reward the living had been managed quickly, and then, after pointing out the guest room where she could sleep, Merrick had taken Alissa to bed. Cerise had lain on the couch, unable to make herself move to the guest room. Exhaustion had battled insomnia until exhaustion won out.

Sitting up now, she found the source of the humming. Alissa's father, Richard, was dressed in jeans, a cream fisherman's knit sweater, and house slippers. He set a dish of warm cranberry scones on the sleek coffee table, and she smiled at him. Cerise had grown into her looks, but before that, she'd lived through what she referred to as her ballerina troll years. She'd been graceful, but hardly attractive. Thick-browed, enormously tall, and fifteen squishy pounds too heavy for the magazine photo spreads they'd forced her to do, she'd been painfully self-conscious. Over time, her face morphed into something exotic, her body grew strong, and if not exactly lithe, at least toned and voluptuous. Before her looks had evolved, she'd suffered the usual girlhood insecurities, which her father and the council had done nothing to assuage. Richard North, however, who'd had a wife and daughter formed of blonde perfection, had been generous and kind in his flattery of Cerise, telling her she'd grow up to become an Amazon queen. She hadn't believed it at the time, but as an adult woman she did feel powerful and confident.

And the little girl she'd been would always be grateful to Richard North for the sweet prophecy that had meant the world to her at the time.

"Hi, Richard," she said.

He nodded a greeting, buttering a scone and walking back to the kitchen as he bit into it. A few bites later, he returned with a pair of mugs of hot cocoa spiced with cinnamon and a dash of chili powder over the whipped cream.

They ate and drank in companionable silence.

She glanced out the window, and the darkness revealed that it was still the middle of the night. She needed to arrange a way home. She wouldn't risk having Merrick drive her to the gates. He'd already fought enough battles for the night. Besides, he was too much of a target himself.

She'd wait to leave until it was close to dawn so the ventala would be retreating in preparation for sunrise. They were nocturnal and wouldn't try to fight their battles after first light.

She'd have to reach out to someone with a helicopter who had clearance to land in the Etherlin. That list of people was limited, and she also needed to be able to count on the discretion of whomever she called. She didn't want it getting out that she'd been joyriding through the Varden. Too many young women looked up to her and copied her every move. She'd taken a calculated risk that had nearly gotten her killed. The last thing she wanted was for young girls to follow her lead in exploring ventala territory and get hurt.

Richard offered her another scone.

She shook her head and said, "You're up early."

"Haven't been to bed yet."

"Were you working?" she asked. She knew he'd recently gone back to writing after many years of writer's block.

"Not working, but I will soon. I was playing cards. When he wins, he can play all night. If he loses, he says he's tired and needs sleep." Richard smiled, clearly not fooled by the strategy.

"Who?"

"Lysander."

She raised her brows. Alissa had said that Lysander lived in a house carved into the side of a mountain, only reachable by air. Alissa and Cerise had thought Lysander must have gone there after leaving the roof.

"Where is Lysander now?"

"In the apartment downstairs."

"What apartment?"

"Right below this one. He never used to sleep there, but he'll stay close now. He's seen the start of the prophecy, and Merrick is part of the key."

"What prophecy?"

" 'Evil comes at leisure like the disease. Good comes in a hurry like the doctor,' G.K. Chesterton said. Lysander understands that. Twice, he's lost someone. He won't wander this time."

"What do you mean, Richard?"

He put a hand on her forearm, giving it a squeeze. "Do you want peace? Or do you want knowledge?"

She frowned. "I haven't found ignorance to be peaceful. There's a night full of missing memories that haunts me like a ghost. Ignoring the missing pieces has never allowed me to rest. Answers might help or they might not, but at this point, I prefer to know whatever there is to know about things."

Richard nodded as if sympathizing, but he didn't reveal anything more about Lysander.

She leaned forward, deciding to focus on what she was most interested in. "Does Lysander have a black duffel bag in the room with him? One with the club's logo on it?"

Richard glanced down, thinking. Then he nodded.

"Do you have a key to the apartment downstairs?"

"There's no key. Only a code. Double-oh-four."

"Zero zero four?"

Richard nodded. "Tread carefully. That one—I think his control is a façade. The pain sometimes turns him wild, and despite your strength of body—and will—you're no match for him. Nothing human is."

A tremor tickled Cerise's spine, but she tightened her muscles against it. "I only want what's mine, Richard."

"No. You don't."

She flushed at his certainty. Richard had never seen her with Lysander, so how could he know what she wanted from the archangel? Lysander was right about him; Richard seemed to know things that he shouldn't have.

Cerise swallowed and cleared her throat. "It doesn't matter what I want. Lysander's made it clear that he doesn't want to get involved with me. And I'm not exactly starved for company, Richard. Once I take what doesn't belong to him, I'll leave him be."

Richard's full smile warmed her until he spoke. "When women go wrong, men go right after them. At least you'll have lived, possibly shorter than you would have, but nonetheless a little more richly."

Cryptic and laced with foreboding . . . lovely, she thought and shivered.

"I'll be back soon," she said, rising.

"You haven't the right shoes, but he'll see to you."

I don't want him to "see to me." I don't want him to notice me at all, she thought, glancing down. She wore only socks at the moment. If she put on her boots, would they make too much noise? Would she wake the angel as she snuck into his apartment? Possibly.

She left without putting them on.

The hall was cooler than the penthouse, and she hugged her arms to her chest as she entered the steel elevator. Down a floor, the doors slid open with a whisper of sound.

Butterscotch-colored walls and polished wood floors greeted her. She passed a couple of doors of what seemed to be polished copper. There were small plates of the same metal next to the doors with engraved numbers to herald the addresses.

Then she arrived at a much larger door than the others. Instead of metal, it was made of weathered wood that looked centuries old and hand carved. Next to the door the word *Allegro* was painted in gold script above the keypad.

Entering zero, zero, and four, Cerise held her breath. The light of the security pad winked green. She turned the old-fashioned brass doorknob and pushed the heavy door inward. Light from the hall entered the darkened apartment.

Entering, she felt a familiar give to the floor under her feet. It felt like a studio or stage floor.

A sprung floor? In an apartment? Can't be.

As her eyes adjusted, the apartment's unexpected décor temporarily distracted her from spotting him. Along an entire wall to her left there were built-in shelves framed with wood that someone had been in the process of hand carving. Tools and wood chips rested on a white tarp that protected the floor.

An occupied king-sized bed stood against the other wall where the headboard seemed to transition into another set of shelves with intricate woodworking. A tree-shaped lamp arched over the head of the bed where Lysander lay sprawled, possibly nude. She should have silently searched the remainder of the room rather than approaching him, but it was as though an invisible cord pulled her toward him.

The dim light shadowed the area's details until she was nearly to him. He lay bare-chested with a mocha-colored sheet and forest green silk duvet haphazardly covering his waist and below. Her breath caught as she stood over him.

His gold hair fanned out in tangled waves, and he hardly seemed real. Rather, he looked so perfect, it was as if someone had painted him. He didn't quite fit into the world he currently occupied. A creature so unaccountably beautiful belonged lying in the forest on a bed of moss or in some other wilderness that God had made.

In her stillness, she felt only the thud of her heart . . . and the compulsion of desperate attraction.

A voice that wasn't her own seemed to whisper across her mind . . .

Touch him. No one will see.

Trace that scar where it crosses his collarbone.

With a fingertip.

With your lips.

He will never know.

Dreamlike, her hand stretched toward him. Just before it touched his skin, her breath caught again and the madness of her intent revealed itself. Going rigid, she jerked her hand back.

What the hell?

Her eyes darted across his face and exposed flesh. The lust that tightened her lower body was nearly painful in its ache. She swallowed hard and tried to draw on her muse power for control.

Don't.

She exhaled slowly.

Touching will only make it worse. He doesn't belong to this world. He fell and was banished here, forced to walk among us against his will, maybe to serve as temptation. Haven't you had enough of pretty boys who bring endless pain?

Yes, she answered emphatically.

She raised her gaze and spotted the duffel he'd carried out of the performing arts center.

Resolve washed over her, sharpening her senses.

That's what I came for. I can grab it and go.

She watched him while she reached across his body; she didn't want to accidentally brush his face or shoulder, but it was hard to look at him and not be pulled back into that vortex of wonder and lust. It was easier to resist him when he was awake and provoking her with his arrogance.

The shelf was low, and the angle would be an awkward one when she lifted the duffel bag.

Hurry the hell up!

Silently, she drew in a breath and looked down at his sleeping form. She bit the inside of her mouth, using the pain to keep her focused. The dark brown lashes twitched against his lower lids, and she bit down harder.

Stay asleep. Just a few moments longer.

When the girl reached across him, she woke all Lysander's senses at once. Roused from dreams of her, it nonetheless did not take more than a second for him to know she was actually in the room with him. He'd lain down alone, regretting that they couldn't share a bed, and now as if fate had answered temptation's call, she'd arrived.

He kept his eyes closed, allowing his other senses to feast. Inhaling the scent of oranges alight over female skin, he felt his blood stir. The faint disturbance of air rustled the hair dusting his arms. The sound of the soft hitch in her breath tickled his ears. What made her breath catch? Was it temptation as strong and raw as he felt?

Not likely the same intensity, but intense enough.

Archangels in human form were more than human. Heightened senses revealed distant sounds and faint smells. They revealed the approach of an enemy, or in this case a potential lover. It was a blessing when it came to warring with demons. It was a curse when it came to being attracted to someone with whom he shouldn't allow himself to become involved.

His lids rose, so his eyes could consume her, too. His gaze locked with hers, and her arm froze for a moment, then continued its path. He wanted to grab her hand, but was wary of actually touching her. He'd be inclined to do more, to touch more. He was already drowning in lust.

He waited until she had her hand on the duffel bag, then he caught the side of the bag and held it in place on the shelf. She yanked, and his gaze went immediately to her shoulders. She had strong muscles. He wished her shoulders were bare so he could enjoy their definition as they contracted with exertion, the way they did when she danced. Watching Cerise dance put him in mind of things he'd lost—things for which he longed.

Yes, drowning in lust.

Merrick supposed that Lysander had no experience with women, which wasn't true. Lysander allowed the misconception to stand because he didn't care to reveal the details of his past. It was true that Lysander had not had a lover in Merrick's lifetime, nor for many hundreds of years, but he did know what it was to touch that softness, to feel smooth skin sliding against his. Lysander avoided the company of women because when faced with a woman that attracted him, impulse and instinct, which were often his greatest assets, became liabilities.

"You persist at your own peril," he said, his voice low. Her breasts were only inches from his chest. He could pull her on top of him in an instant.

"You're threatening me? That's rich," she said. "You took—"

"You intruded on my solitude and woke me. I've spared you the trouble you court until now—"

"Let me take—"

It was too dangerous to risk touching her while in bed, but he could get something he wanted. He could be transported for a little while. "I demand you make amends."

That brought her up short. "Amends?" she sneered, shaking her head.

Her dark eyes narrowed, the anger making color rise in her cheeks. His heart thumped a little harder in his chest.

Go ahead. Challenge me.

"I don't need to make amends. I'm not the one who took what doesn't belong to her."

Her skin's heat warmed him, made him want to lose himself in it.

"You'll oblige me," he said, knowing it would make her angrier.

"No, I won't."

He smiled. "Your compliance is compulsory. That's what makes it a demand rather than a request." He had good reason for taking the book, and if he explained why he'd done so she'd likely become more agreeable, but he was enjoying this battle of wills. Also, he wasn't bound to explain himself to anyone and normally didn't. Sharing confidences implied friendship and intimacy, neither of which could he afford to have with this spirited young dancer.

She stared daggers at him. His smile widened. Yes, she was nitroglycerin made flesh. She'd go off with a spectacular explosion. In anger or in passion.

She gave the bag a jerk, but he didn't let it budge. Recognizing that she couldn't snatch it from his grip, she released the strap and straightened. She turned to leave.

No, Cerise, it's too late for that. Pull once too often on a tiger's tail, and you won't escape being eaten.

Her stride toward the door was purposeful, but not rushed. She held her head high. He cocked his head slightly, watching her backside as she walked. She had the sort of full round bottom that was pure female perfection. Her beauty tied his insides into knots and made him ache between his legs.

When she was nearly to the door, he sprang silently from the bed. He reached the door and put a hand on it just as she turned the knob. She looked up sharply at his hand, then over her shoulder at his face.

"What are you doing?"

"Keeping you here until you've made amends."

She glared at him, turning her body until her back leaned against the door. "And exactly how do you expect me to do that?"

I'd like you to invite me to thrust the hardest part of my body into the warmest part of yours. But I won't seduce you into that. No matter how much I'm tempted—no, absolutely not. He knew better than to pursue what he would most enjoy. Such a deep connection with her could compromise his quest for redemption.

But that didn't mean she couldn't satisfy him another way.

"You're going to dance for me."

Her brows shot up in surprise. "What kind of dancing?" she asked suspiciously. "You're naked, and I don't intend to join you that way."

"Why not?" he asked with feigned innocence. When not in the company of men, angels spent most of their time nude. They weren't like human beings, who associated their nakedness with sin, shame, and guilt. And since those associations had been born when humans fell victim to the trickery of a demon who'd tricked Lysander as well, it irked Lysander that humans were still tormented by their mistake.

Cerise pointed her right index finger at him. "You understand perfectly well why I wouldn't strip for you or any other man I didn't intend to sleep with. You weren't born yesterday."

He looked down at her body, which was only about a foot and a half from his. Shadow hid his face until he looked at her through his lashes, his intensity like the sting of a whip. Her pupils dilated and she shifted, her back arching and bringing her breasts closer, likely without her awareness.

"When *were* you born?" she asked.

"In the time before time was measured. I'd like to see you perform *Swan Lake*. Or *Giselle.*"

"Would you?" Cerise said, laughing softly. "And did you just happen to choose the most technically difficult ballets you could think of?"

"No, not by chance. I chose them on purpose."

She raised her brows.

"The harder you work, the more I'll enjoy it."

Anger lit her eyes again, and she looked defiant. "Maybe I don't know them."

"Of course you do."

"How do you know?"

He shrugged, not prepared to admit that after they'd met, he hadn't been able to resist watching her and that he'd come upon her practicing in the dance studio near her home.

Unfortunately, because he'd had to conceal himself he'd never been able to watch with an unobstructed view. Also, those weren't true performances. Her only focus had been on executing the moves with precision. Often that required halting the sequences to repeat them. He wanted to see her act the roles without interruption. He wanted to watch the music and the movement consume her. Angels had invented music and dancing. Sometimes while watching a great athlete perform, he could transcend the earth's confines. For a few moments, his soul could soar toward unreachable heights. He lived for those rare brushes with the wonders of heaven.

She glanced around the room. "There's not enough space."

"There is. I'll move the obstacles aside for you."

"How very generous," she said dryly. "And I can't leave until I dance?"

"Or until you satisfy me some other way," he said in a low voice. "I'll entertain other propositions." His muscles tightened. The game was dangerous, but to be so close, to feel her warmth, and to bask in a flirtation intoxicated him. She made him remember why women fascinated him.

"Again with the amazing generosity. I can't imagine how people haven't taken incredible advantage of you over the years."

"It's to be the dancing then?" he asked, unperturbed by her sarcasm.

"It's to be nothing," she said, her tone cool. "You can keep me from leaving—for the moment. But you can't force me to dance. Or to do anything I don't want to do." She glanced around, likely calculating escape strategies.

If it was to be a standoff of wills, he could certainly outlast her, but he didn't trust himself to be alone with her for hours without falling victim to his own desires. He'd end up seducing her. It would be better to compromise to gain her quick compliance.

"If you agree without delay, I'll give you something you want," he said.

"The book?"

He wished he could lie as well as Merrick. Then he could've said yes and she would've believed him, but his hesitation cost him any chance he had of convincing her he'd trade the book for her compliance.

"No, but I'll tell you something about it that you need to know."

He could see that the proposition intrigued her. Her gaze turned intense as she looked back at the duffel.

"What could you know about it? You just found it, didn't you?"

"That's my offer. Information in exchange for you performing for me."

"Why the hell do you want me to dance for you anyway? If you want to see someone perform *Swan Lake* or *Giselle*, all you have to do is buy a ticket. There's always some great ballet company somewhere in the world performing one or the other."

"It's you in particular I want to watch."

She smiled in spite of her annoyance. "Why?"

"Because you're an exceptional dancer." *And because you're the woman with whom I'm infatuated.*

"I couldn't do it justice. I don't have pointe shoes."

He walked to the closet and produced a pair of her custom plum-colored ballet shoes from within.

"What the—I accidentally left those behind at the studio. When I went back they were gone. I assumed some dancer thought she'd get additional inspiration from wearing a muse's shoes. Did you—how did you get them?"

He handed them to her without answering and walked away, listening for the sound of the door handle turning. If she bolted, she wouldn't reach the elevator or the stairs before he retrieved her, but he wasn't interested in giving chase. That would only stoke temptation's fire. Chasing a woman, capturing her, carrying her back . . . afterward he'd have a very hard time just watching her dance without going further. And this could only go so far.

When all the furniture was along the wall, some of it tipped onto its side to allow maximum floor space, he turned to her.

"I require one other thing."

She still leaned against the door and a brow rose.

"You won't dance in those clothes. You don't need to be nude. Your undergarments are acceptable."

"Acceptable to you maybe."

He rolled his eyes. "If I can't see the way your muscles move, it will detract from my pleasure in watching you."

"How unfortunate for you. Life is full of disappointments."

"It is, but this won't be counted among them. The apartment's warm. With the exertion of dancing, you'll be more comfortable in less clothing. And you don't need to be modest; I've already seen you nude."

Chapter 9

Suppressing the urge to gape at him, Cerise clenched her jaw. "Is that so? You're quite the Peeping Tom. Nothing better to do with your time? Had to turn to voyeurism?"

"As you like," he said with a shrug.

She narrowed her eyes. "I don't like. I'm never outside in the nude. No skinny-dipping or nude beaches for a muse when there are paparazzi with long lenses, which means that you must have engaged in some creepy stalker behavior in order to see me naked. Care to explain?"

"Not particularly."

"Well, do it anyway."

"I decline, but I will get dressed if it makes you more comfortable."

As he slid his pants on, she flashed her middle finger at him and turned to the door.

"Wait," he said as she jerked the door open.

She looked over her shoulder and added angrily, "You stalked me, so you owe me an apology for invading my privacy, too. As I see it, we're even. More than even. I didn't drag off your blanket to ogle you naked."

"No, you ogled me with the blanket in place," he said with an amused smile.

"Asshole," she snapped.

"And for the record, I wouldn't have cared if you had

removed the linens. I'm not shy and have no concerns over being seen in only my skin."

She stalked out of the apartment and down the hall. When she reached the elevator, his hand was there, covering the buttons so she couldn't summon it.

She grabbed his arm with both of her hands and yanked. His forearm muscles clenched, and his hand didn't give way.

"Let go!" She slapped her right palm back against his chest and shoved. He didn't take a backward step or even bobble. He was flesh-covered granite, which despite her current fury was, on some level, appealing.

She spun, but her foot caught on his ankle and with the force of her movement, she stumbled. He caught her arms, which kept her from slamming her knees onto the wood floor, but she still ended up kneeling.

Staring directly at his groin, she was glad he'd donned pants. She couldn't help but notice though that he seemed to be well made *everywhere*.

She clenched her eyes closed, shaking her head.

"Interesting position. Have you a new proposition, Cerise?" he asked.

She couldn't help it. She smiled.

When a moment passed, he said, "Open your eyes."

Her lids rose, and she saw his chest. He'd lowered himself to one knee. Her gaze met his eyes.

"You agreed to dance for me. I won't allow you to renege now. It means too much to me to watch you perform, but I acknowledge your point regarding my trespassing on your privacy," he said. "I wasn't spying on you to watch you undress, but my vantage point allowed it to happen. For amends, I'll dance the male role tonight. I can still stand back and watch you during the sections where you don't have a partner. During the couples sequences, I'll perform, too."

"Dancing with me, that's your idea of making it up to me?"

"For certain," he said with a nod. "I'll be the best partner you've ever had."

She stared into his eyes and felt her muscles tighten in anticipation. She loved to dance, but at nearly six feet tall and built like an Olympian herself, she wasn't exactly lithe.

"You know the steps?"

He gave her a look that said it was a ridiculous question.

She sighed, not sure she should go along with anything that would put her in his iron-hard arms.

"The best partner I've ever had, huh?"

"Absolutely."

She bit her lip. "All right. Show me."

He rose and held a hand out to her. She took it and returned with him to the apartment.

"You still have to shed some clothes. Your arms must be bare."

She appraised him. She accepted that her clothes were too restrictive to dance in, but she wasn't particularly comfortable with stripping in front of the poster boy for physical perfection, even if he had seen her naked in the past. So though it made her annoyed with herself for falling prey to old insecurities, she stalled.

"First put the music on and show me what a great dancer you are."

The corners of his mouth turned up, but he didn't protest. Instead, he executed a flawless combination of leaps, rising so high and spinning so fast that it was like he'd bounced off a trampoline or been shot from a cannon. And despite all that power, his arms and feet were perfectly positioned. He landed noiselessly.

Fucking hell. Does everything have to be so beautiful? Considering he's fallen, it hardly seems fair. And as a dancer, how am I supposed to walk away from someone who can move like that? Not possible.

Without a word, she drew her blouse off and tossed it aside, and the pants joined it.

She walked to him. "Start the music."

He smiled and did. When he returned from the stereo, she didn't hesitate. They launched into the choreography they both knew inside and out. And from the first moment that he lifted her, so completely solid and confident, she let herself go. Eventually classical music gave way to modern, but they didn't stop dancing. Without choreography, they found their own moves.

It might have been two hours. It might have been four. When

she finally sat on his bed, glowing with perspiration, she watched him with a bemused expression.

"You didn't lie."

"I rarely do." He sat next to her, more it seemed to be companionable than from fatigue. "As I said, I don't have the way of it. You're a very talented dancer, but your greatest talent is singing. When you sang the Christina Aguilera song, I realized how impressive your voice is."

"It's the muse magic. There's a vibration that enters our voice. It stimulates the human brain, inspiring creativity and activating a lot of usually dormant parts."

"Hmm. I'm not able to fall under its sway, but almost wish I could. Your voice . . . the way you sing and dance . . ." He leaned back and stared at the ceiling. "It reminds me of home."

So that was why he'd been so determined to get her to perform. That her dancing brought heaven to mind for him was flattering. Really flattering. "You miss it."

"Of course. As was intended."

"Why did you rise up? Was it really ambition?"

"I didn't rise up. I wasn't part of the insurrection."

"But you're fallen."

"Yes," he said bitterly. "I broke a law of heaven, but never with the intention of turning against God or a brother angel. I'm fallen, but I'm not damned."

"The difference being that you live on earth rather than in hell?"

He nodded and added, "The difference being that redemption is possible for me."

"How will you redeem yourself?"

He opened his mouth, but closed it before answering. The pause stretched on until he finally said, "When the critical moment comes, I'll do whatever heaven requires."

She glanced at him.

"As you saw earlier tonight, Merrick and your friend are in danger," he said. "They may need my help again soon, but they won't need yours. So if only one of us can stay, it should be me. Go home. Having you here complicates the situation."

She frowned, irritated at having been dismissed again, especially after what they'd just shared. "So sorry to complicate things."

The corner of his mouth twitched up. "I don't think you're sorry. Alissa works hard to keep the peace, but I don't believe you're inclined that way."

"No," she said and smiled. "Peacekeeping isn't my job. I'll tell you what though. I'll go home and leave you alone if you give me back Griffin Lane's songbook."

"It's amusing the way you think you can bend me to your will."

"Suit yourself. I'll just hang around and be as disruptive as possible."

She didn't anticipate the movement. One moment, they were lying side by side, the next he'd rolled so that he lay right next to her, his torso above hers, skin touching skin. Her breath caught, her body warming. He lowered his mouth to just above hers, and she inhaled his cool breath, which held traces of mint and spice. It tantalized her.

"Cerise, I am fallen, but I'm an angel still. You're no match for me. I can kiss your lips until you'll want nothing to touch them but my flesh. I can bring you to your knees with a word or a look. I warn you one last time. You're a distraction I can't afford. Please go home. I like you. I don't want to hurt you."

She clenched her jaws. She wasn't as weak-willed as all that. She was a muse. One of the four most powerful in the world. She'd been given a divine gift just like he had. He might be an archangel, but he was still only flesh and blood. Beautiful flesh, but not tempting enough to make her lose her mind. No one was *that* beautiful.

"You think you could break me?" she scoffed. "With your fists, sure. But with a kiss? No. Never." She caught a lock of his hair and closed her fist on it, tugging hard, drawing him until their lips brushed each other. "Go ahead and try."

"You challenge me?" he demanded. "You're a fool," he said and, exhaling, he added in a whisper. "And so am I."

A cool hand descended to her belly, and, against her will, her muscles clenched in anticipation. His gaze lowered to where her breasts threatened to spill out of the plum cups of her bra.

"It's not an accident that women's bodies are round," he whispered, his hand sliding up along her ribs, his thumb skimming the undersurface of her breast. "Round and soft like the curves of a cloud. Bursting and ripe like fruit. Breasts. Hips. Buttocks." His hand slid down, raising gooseflesh. He squeezed the curve of her hip, and her heart thumped in her chest.

"Even between your legs," he whispered. "Plump and succulent." He licked his lips as if tasting her. "At first, women were conceived as companionship and comfort for men." He looked through his lashes into her eyes. "But then we were carried away by the dream of you. With exertion, your skin tastes like the sea. With lust, your bodies grow juicy with arousal." A slow smile curved his lips. "Nothing was accidental."

On the last word, he bent his head and sucked her lower lip into his mouth as if to consume her.

"You were made in the image of what we most want to devour."

A touch, a lick, and then a tangle of mouths and limbs. His breath was cool, and she drew it in like the morning mist. Her heart hammered, her muscles contracted, and she twisted her fingers through his hair and held tight.

She'd never tasted his like and very quickly, she wanted to consume him, too. Her arms locked around him, pulling him closer until they were pressed together. It was the dance all over again, but with less control.

He sprung the clasp on her bra and pushed it aside. The stroke of his tongue pebbled her nipple. His fingertips hooked the lace of her panties and dipped inside as the strands of his hair trailed over her, a silky caress against aroused skin. It all drove her onward with a pounding heart.

He sucked and teased with his teeth until she writhed, until her body was desperate and hungry. Then he slid down, dragging her panties off, and pushed her thighs to the sides of his broad shoulders, spreading her open.

True to his word, his intent was to devour her. And he did.

Her body clamped around his thick tongue as it thrust into her. The rake of teeth and thumb between her legs was excruciating. And exquisite.

An orgasm wracked her body, and he continued until the sensations became so raw, the rest of reality fell away.

When he rose above her and she felt the smooth head of his cock seeking entry, she gasped, "God, yes."

He shoved forward, stretching her pulsing flesh around him.

The aching hunger built, her womb cramping in anticipation, beating like a second heart.

He closed his eyes. "Warm and wet and welcoming," he whispered. "I can taste heaven in your heat." He pulled back and thrust forward, making her body a conquest. Hungry to be claimed, she met him, joining a frenzied rhythm.

Then without warning, he withdrew. She cried out, her body screaming a protest.

In an instant, he was off the bed and backing away.

Her voice was deep, melodic, and sensual. Infused with passion and magic, she said, "I want you."

He paused, rigid and still. "I know." He clenched his jaws, straining to resist his own need. "And I want you with a force that rivals hurricanes, but I . . ." The intensity of his gaze seared her skin.

She held out a hand.

"Don't," he whispered hoarsely and then swallowed. "I almost didn't stop. Almost couldn't."

Still burning for him, her voice was laden with seductive promise. In that moment, she would've done anything he asked to have him. "Come back to me."

He took a half step forward, but then shook his head. "I'm sorry. I did warn you."

She realized too late. By the time she lurched up to grab him, he was out of reach. With inhuman speed, he burst out the balcony doors, wings erupting from his back and, in a flutter of turbulent air, he was gone.

Lysander sat on the stone ledge at the southwest corner of Merrick's building, cursing and battling the urge to return to her.

The girl was remarkable. He'd sensed it from the first. Fierceness of will. Strength and softness of body. He twisted, restless in his skin. Being inside her, being pressed against that warm, radiant flesh, he'd nearly lost himself. He'd never meant to get so carried away. He'd left her aching and confused, and there was no excuse for that. Consummating their relationship could've put her in danger and could've compromised his chance for redemption. He'd had no business sitting next to her on that bed. He *knew* better. He should've enjoyed the dance and let her go.

Especially considering that the release from sex would've created only temporary warmth and satisfaction. Still, he'd wanted it. So badly. To meet someone whose company he wanted to bask in was rare. He hadn't wanted to leave. Of course he hadn't. Being exiled from heaven meant an endless aching chill. It meant he could never get warm or be truly at peace. The demons likened it to a drug being withdrawn, and they should know. They'd created the chemicals that could simulate the feeling of lightness of soul and which when withheld created a gnawing desire for their return. Demons suffered their banishment from heaven and visited that same kind of suffering upon mankind. Spite. It was a term, an idea, that had not existed among angels before the uprising and the fall.

Lysander licked his lips, wanting a lingering taste of her. He swallowed, knowing that he needed to stay away from her, but he was already nostalgic about their time together. He ran a hand through his unruly hair, thinking of the soft, very dark waves that had framed her face like a dusky halo. He shook his head with regret. A great and dangerous beauty. Better never to have met her.

He rubbed his arms against the chill that seemed worse than usual. Then he felt a sharp pang in his chest that he recognized. He looked to the sky. Dark. Silent. Still. He glanced around and down, not really seeing, focused instead on the quiet. He felt a vibration, a wave of malignant energy, then another sharp cramp in his heart.

Demons.

Some fool had opened a gate.

Chapter 10

The ache lingered. Longing had never been so intense. Using muse magic on herself wasn't strictly legal, but Cerise couldn't move, couldn't focus. She had to try to use her gift to overcome the effects of his. With a slow exhalation of breath, she gathered strength.

"You don't need or want anything. Or anyone. You're content." The magic washed over her. She drew in a fresh breath and exhaled trouble. Angels were so addictive. She hadn't known. Now she did. The way she wanted him was unnatural and should have made her want him less, but didn't.

The longing faded, muscles unfurling, mind spooling away from the orgasm she'd had and the one she hadn't. She forced herself up and she dressed, all the while recalling the slide of his body over hers. She shuddered, then clenched her teeth, awash in emptiness.

Time ticked by, and gradually she remembered why she'd originally come to his apartment. Her gaze slid to the duffel. She wouldn't have admitted to Jersey or Hayden that if given the choice she would've chosen Lysander's body over the opportunity to get the songbook, but lying to herself wasn't an option. Some people were good at it, but she'd never been that lucky.

Cerise pulled on the bag's strap, and it dropped with a thump on the pillow. She unzipped the duffel and removed the book from where it had been tucked next to his violin. She glanced at the shelf, empty now, a lonely shadow stretching from it.

She rose and glanced at the middle of the bed where the open duffel rested, big and black like a giant beetle against the sheets. If it wasn't the first thing he saw when he walked in, she'd be surprised.

He'd open the bag and know she'd taken the book back, that she'd gotten at least one of the things she'd wanted from him—a thing he hadn't wanted to give up.

Good.

As she left, a feeling of restlessness kept her company.

Retrieving the book is enough, she told herself. *Because it has to be.*

Strange company, Cerise thought upon entering Alissa's apartment. Merrick had returned from fighting the rival ventala, and he and Richard played poker in the low light to the hum of their murmured mock barbs and chuckles. Their rapport was as easy as if they'd been friends for a lifetime. She glanced at Richard's mountain of chips, then to Merrick's sharp eyes. Richard was taking Merrick for all he was worth? *Not likely.* Amusement curled through Cerise at the thought of Merrick letting Richard win at cards. *He's very good with my dad,* Alissa had said. Apparently so. Merrick, ruthless to a fault by reputation, indulged his father-in-law for his wife's sake. Cerise felt envy's kiss. Griffin had loved her, but not that much. Not enough to tell the world. Not enough to stay with her. And Lysander . . . well, he was quicksilver through her fingers, too. She couldn't hold on to him.

Merrick looked at her speculatively. She knew she'd been gone a long time, but Merrick didn't ask where she'd been. In fact, he said nothing at all. Had Richard told him she'd gone down to Lysander? If so, she was surprised Merrick hadn't come after her. Or maybe she wasn't surprised. Merrick didn't seem the type to butt into business he didn't consider his.

"We trust in plumed procession, for such the angels go. Rank after rank, with even feet. And uniforms of snow," Richard said. "It's a shame Emily Dickinson never met Lysander. I'd like to have heard the verse she'd have written for a lost angel."

Merrick's brow quirked as his eyes slid to the songbook in

Cerise's hand. She'd held it to the side and slightly behind her, not exactly hiding it, but wanting it to go unnoticed. Her grip tightened at Merrick's interest, but he gave no indication that he'd try to recover it for his friend.

"Where's the closest helipad in your territory?" Cerise asked.

"There isn't one, but if you're arranging a ride, we'll block the nearest intersection and the chopper can set down in the street. You thinking of calling Etherlin Security?"

Bringing Etherlin Security to Merrick's front door and tempting them to try to recover Alissa from him didn't seem fair payment when Merrick had saved Cerise's life.

"No, but I have a couple of friends who owe me favors or who would like me to owe them one. I just need to make some calls."

Richard leaned forward toward Merrick and whispered, "Have a care. Mighty things fall from the sky."

Merrick's eyes narrowed.

Richard cocked his head, his silver hair catching the light. He glanced at Cerise with a soft expression. "Interesting company is the most valuable. Brooding and passionate, it consumes."

"Are you saying that I should stay? That if I try to leave by helicopter it will crash?" she asked.

Richard shook his head. "But what I told Lysander two nights ago while we played cards still holds true. Look to Basil King, I said. I had a full house and won the hand, so he accused me of using the quote to mislead him into not folding so I could build a bigger pot." With an impish smile, Richard shrugged. "When I mentioned King's advice, I wasn't speaking of cards. I never claimed I was."

She laughed. "But you let him think you were? Clever. I wish I'd been there to watch you beat him," she said. "What was the quote?"

Richard gave a vague wave of his hand.

"King's famous quote was 'Be bold and mighty forces will come to your aid,'" Merrick said.

"Yes, roughly," Richard said.

"You're a fan of quotes, too?" Cerise asked Merrick.

Merrick winked.

"He doesn't collect quotes for his own sake," Richard confided. "He does it to better converse with me, which scores points with Andromeda."

"Andromeda?" Cerise echoed.

"Yes, my daughter, Andromeda."

Cerise glanced at Merrick, who shook his head and rolled his eyes in an "it's a long story" expression.

Richard whistled low and soft. "Cerise, when you need a key, find it in the hollow at the base of the purple trellis and look to the spring equinox." Richard glanced at Merrick. "It won't be long now. Let's finish the hand."

Cerise saw Richard deal a card from the bottom of the deck. Merrick saw it, too, of course, but kept right on playing as if he hadn't.

"You should wake Andromeda," Richard said. "She doesn't like confrontations, which is why she'll be needed."

It was clear by Merrick's frown that he disapproved of the idea of disturbing Alissa. Cerise smiled. It was sweet the way that Merrick was about Alissa and Richard. She liked him for it.

Cerise called a music exec who lived in the Sliver and arranged for him to pick her up by helicopter. He promised he could get her back to the Etherlin at dawn, and she hung up satisfied.

Cerise walked to a corner reading nook next to a large bookshelf. She flipped on the lamp and dropped onto the seat of a velvet-cushioned chair, putting her feet up on the matching ottoman. She bet that, as a muse to writers, the chair was Alissa's favorite spot.

Cerise leaned back and opened Griffin's journal. In an instant, the room seemed to suck the air from her lungs and she was transported back. She saw him, clear as day, standing on the edge of a stage, singing "Marks of a Misspent Youth" over the excited screams of forty thousand fans. Then she and Griffin were alone in the living room of the rented house. He laughed and kissed her. A darkness like smoke blurred the room's edges, and she saw a hand over her wineglass. Crushed powder sank and disappeared into the Merlot. She squinted.

What was that?

She gripped the book and flipped the page, forcing her eyes

to focus. In the margin there was a drawing of an eerie tree limb from which a bird's nest was falling.

The only things she'd ever known Griffin to doodle were musical notes. She stared down at several illegible lines written in handwriting that wasn't Griffin's. Her eyes narrowed, trying to make out the words. The tiny letters crowded together as if hiding.

Had one of the other musicians used the book when it was lying around in the studio? She tried to remember what Hayden's and Jersey's writing looked like. Jersey's was loopy. It looked nothing like the tiny scrawl. She didn't think it was Hayden's, either.

She turned pages and stopped at more writing that wasn't Griffin's. Handwriting gone gothic, the calligraphy had been done in jet ink by fountain pen and half the words were curses and slithery phrases about sex and bondage.

What the hell?

In a flash, crushing fingers gripped her throat from behind, choking her. Her own hands strangled pewter-colored sheets as she struggled, trying to wrench free, unable to breathe. A rush of adrenaline. Panic. A body pressing against her. She tried to scream, to fight—

Sharp as a blade, the memory receded. Cerise's harsh breathing and pounding heart were all she could hear for a moment. The book lay at her feet, apparently having fallen from her lap.

What the fuck?

She touched her throat, which still tingled and throbbed like someone had been choking her.

Then she flushed, remembering she wasn't alone. She looked up and found Merrick and Richard staring at her.

"Tea with milk and honey. Even warrior queens once and again need soothing," Richard announced, rising.

Merrick said nothing. His eyes, dark with midnight shadows, watched her silently.

"I'm okay," she said, reaching down to retrieve the book. She set it on her lap, studying it warily. It pressed against her legs like a thousand pounds of unwanted weight. What had happened that night? She struggled to unbury more of the memory, even while dreading what she might see.

When Richard came from the kitchen, Merrick intercepted the mug and put a shot of whiskey into it.

Cerise's fingers stretched over the book's cover like spiderwebs, trapping it closed. Merrick set the mug within the reach.

"Thanks," she said, preparing herself to open the book again. Her stomach knotted a protest.

I have to . . .

"You know," Merrick said. "Lysander's mercurial, but not random in what he does."

"Meaning?"

"He kept the book even after you told him it was yours. There's a reason."

As if on cue, the balcony door opened and air gusted in as Lysander's wings folded backward and disappeared. He filled the doorway as he entered. Cerise slid her hands to the edges of the book so she could grip it tight.

"Timing perfect enough to break the heart of a Swiss watchmaker," Merrick said, stepping in front of Cerise.

Lysander waved Merrick aside. "Did you feel it? Demons rising. A fight before dawn I think."

"Did you come to get one for luck?" Merrick asked.

"One what?" Lysander said impatiently.

"Another kiss from the girl," Merrick said.

Cerise flushed. How had Merrick known they'd kissed? She licked her lips wondering if they were more red or plump than usual.

"When it's time for me to account for my actions, you won't be in attendance, Merrick. Nor can I imagine why you'd want to be."

"She's Alissa's guest."

Lysander shrugged. "I like your wife, but I don't dance at her pleasure."

Merrick folded his arms across his chest. "Are you here for the girl or the book?"

"Surely you know."

"If you didn't want her to take it, you could've put it out of reach."

"I've not had the opportunity because I've been detained here, carrying human cargo across the sky at your request."

Merrick inclined his head in acknowledgment. "You've got

a reason for keeping the book. Tell her what it is and convince her to give it to you."

"On the whole, you understand plenty, but sometimes you know less than you suppose, Merrick. I'm not inexperienced with women. And for your information, this one doesn't need your bodyguard posturing to put her at ease."

"When have you ever known me to posture?" Merrick asked with grim amusement. "It's her book."

"In point of fact—"

"Lyse, according to Alissa, it's her book. In this apartment, it's her book."

The angel let out an exasperated sigh. "Merrick, if a woodsman pointed out a poisoned berry, would you eat it because your wife asked you to?"

When Merrick didn't answer, Cerise smiled, and Lysander threw his hands up in frustration.

"You were the most hardened, most practical boy I ever met. You realize you had more sense at fourteen than you have now. Step away and let me speak to her."

Merrick moved aside, but put a hand on the back of the chair, clearly hovering. Lysander towered over her for a moment, then dropped to a knee.

She raised an eyebrow as if to say . . . this should be good.

"I got the message you left so I'm here."

"I didn't leave you a message."

The corner of his mouth turned up. "The open bag on the bed was very clearly a message. You sought to provoke a response. Here it is. That book contains more than the music and lyrics of a young man. He crossed paths with someone evil. I wouldn't be surprised if it contributed to his death."

Surprised, her jaw dipped open. "What do you mean evil? What makes you say that?"

"I would no more tell you that than let you keep the book."

Her grip tightened. He set his right hand, palm up, on her knee. He glanced at the book, then at her face. His moss green eyes shone with sincerity. "You have cause to be angry with me, but I hope you won't let that cloud your judgment. I ask you to release that book for your own safety."

"I don't want protection. I want answers."

"Not the ones contained in this book, Cerise."

"Listen, these songs belong to his band."

"I'll copy the songs and give them to you."

"It's not just the songs. I need to read what he wrote."

"Richard, what are you doing?" Merrick asked.

Cerise looked up and spotted Richard going down the hall.

"Don't knock on that door," Merrick said.

Richard's fist stopped just before it rapped against the door. Richard gave a short nod to acknowledge what Merrick had said, then he grabbed the knob, turned it, and proceeded inside.

Merrick frowned. "I meant don't wake her up," Merrick muttered. "And despite how crazy you are, you knew exactly what I meant."

"No," Cerise said as Lysander put traction on the book. "Griffin and I were involved, and I need to find out what happened on the night he died."

"You loved him?"

"I did."

Lysander shuttered his expression. "Which will make you dangerously determined to unlock doors that should stay closed." With a small jerk, he plucked the book from her hands. She grabbed his arm.

"Lysander," Merrick warned. "Free will, remember? You've warned her. That's enough."

Lysander stared at Cerise's face. "Obviously, she thinks I haven't done enough. She's had more of me than anyone has for a thousand years, but she's not satisfied."

Cerise flushed and glared at him, but he looked away to glance at Merrick.

"If the evil that brushed against the pages of this book realizes that she means anything to me, it won't rest until she's destroyed. I speak from experience."

"What do you say, Cerise?" Merrick asked. "He doesn't lie. If he says the book's deadly, it is."

"I won't open it again until I'm back in the Etherlin."

"A demon has attacked in the Etherlin before. Etherlin Security wasn't particularly effective if you recall," Merrick said.

"Enough of this," Lysander said, standing up.

"Hang on," Merrick said, putting a hand on Lysander's shoulder.

Lysander jerked his shoulder back. "Don't do this, Merrick. Even you can't win against me."

"If you and I dance, no one wins."

"Wait. What's happening?" Alissa asked, striding toward them.

"Stay back, Alissa," Merrick said in a low voice, and she slowed.

"What's going on?" she asked, walking directly to their sides. She put a hand on each of their arms. "Tell me."

"We're arguing over the songbook," Merrick said.

"Oh," she said. "Why do you want it, Lysander?"

Lysander pulled free of Alissa's grip. "Dawn is coming, Merrick. There's no time to go through it again. Do we fight each other? Or do I fight what really needs to be fought?"

"Fight each other? Of course not," Alissa said with a gasp.

"Alissa," Merrick said, moving her aside. "Stay out of the way."

Lysander stalked toward the balcony.

"What do you say, Cerise?" Merrick asked grimly.

She wasn't sure she could be at peace with things now that she knew there was a great deal more to the book than she'd ever realized. But she didn't want to destroy Alissa's happiness, and she didn't need Merrick fighting her battles. "Let it go."

Alissa bent down, kissed Cerise's cheek, and whispered, "Thank you."

"This isn't finished, Lysander," Cerise called as he flew off the balcony.

Alissa sat on the edge of the ottoman in front of Cerise. "Now fill me in."

"It doesn't matter. Just remind him that he promised to copy the songs. I want to give those back to the Molly Times. The rest I'll take care of myself."

Alissa's brows rose. "Let us talk to him. He's stubborn, but—"

Cerise shook her head. "I'll talk to him myself when I see him again."

"Are you sure you will?"

Cerise nodded. She wasn't sure how she knew it, but she did. That she and Lysander would cross paths again felt inevitable.

The sound of chopper blades made them all look up.

Cerise rose. "I think that's my ride."

"Oh," Alissa said.

"Speaking of things being dangerous here, you should come home to the Etherlin," Cerise said.

Alissa's mouth opened to protest.

"Not forever. Just until Merrick ends his war with the syndicate." She looked at Merrick. "You know it's only a matter of time before they storm this place. Do you really want her trapped here when they come?"

"You going back to the Etherlin for a couple of weeks is not a bad idea, Alissa," Merrick said.

Alissa hugged Cerise and then took a step back. "It was so good to see you. I'm sorry the evening was so violent and terrifying. And please tell Dimitri I'm sorry I didn't get to say good-bye before I left."

With that Alissa turned and walked back to their bedroom, her hand trailing along the wall as if to steady herself. Cerise tilted her head.

"Is she okay?"

Merrick nodded. "Except for the target painted on her back."

"The council's voted. In a couple of days, they'll crown me Wreath Muse."

Merrick's expression was carefully blank. "Congratulations."

Cerise shrugged. "It should have been Alissa, but she chose you. A council decision had to be made. It was long overdue. The Wreath should be in the hands of a muse, not in some glass showcase. It does mean one good thing for Alissa though. Once I have the Wreath, I'll have extremely powerful leverage over the council. And unlike her, I'm okay with confrontations. If she and Richard ever need to come to the Etherlin, I'll make sure it's a safe haven for them."

Chapter 11

Fifty minutes after Cerise Xenakis left the Varden without incident, Merrick and Alissa were in bed when the entire building shook. Merrick's head snapped up. Something had hit the roof.

He flung the covers back, got out of bed, and dressed. Alissa followed suit.

"Is it the syndicate?" she asked.

"There's no room for a chopper to land up there, but it could hover while guys jumped out."

"Would they make so much noise?"

"Not on purpose," Merrick said, walking out of their room to his desk. He tucked a gun into the back of his pants and then flipped open his computer and entered his passwords to bring up security camera views of the roof. There was no one near the door. His eyes scanned the other views, including the one looking straight up at the sky. No helicopter, but there were moving shadows high above.

"Damn." *Literally.* "Call Ox and tell him to come up. I want him in the apartment with you and Richard."

"What is it?" Alissa asked, squinting at the screen. Her vision always worsened when she was tired. He wanted her to be able to rest.

He kissed her softly on the mouth, and her tongue caressed his, sending the same message to his heart and groin that a kiss from her always did.

No matter what it costs us to be together, it's worth it.

"I think Lysander's up there fighting a demon. Let me see if he needs a hand."

"Be careful," she whispered.

Another vanilla-soaked kiss from her, and he crossed the room in long strides. He grabbed the blade cured in angel's blood from behind the O'Keefe painting, then flung the door open. He took the stairs two at a time and punched in the code to unlock the door to the roof.

His eyes skimmed the rooftop garden and courtyard. An empty pedestal and toppled marble statue made his muscles clench in anticipation of a bitter battle. As he moved closer, he spotted the darkness dripping from the corner. He inhaled. *Blood.*

He glanced at the black clouds overhead, drawing his gun. Things that fell from the sky were notoriously hard to kill. If he could wing them, they'd drop and become close enough for him to use his knife.

He stalked slowly past the orange trees in massive terra-cotta pots, his gaze swiveling, ears straining. The smell of blood grew stronger. He rounded a corner of eight-foot hedges and saw a pair of demons bending over something. The creatures had skin the color of scorched tomatoes, and their hands and mouths dripped bright blood.

What do they have?

He saw the edge of a sepia wing, and realization dawned like a nuclear explosion. Merrick pulled the trigger, emptying the clip.

They screeched and turned, the bullets bouncing off them. He dropped to unsheathe his knife, but not fast enough. They were on him.

Talons sliced his side and he rolled, trying to drag himself free by slamming their bodies against the paved stone. One had his neck, but in the next instant, the other was ripped free from its hold on him. He swung his blade as the clawed nails sunk into his throat on either side of his windpipe. He pitched backward and drove the blade into one of the demon's eyes.

One of his eardrums popped at the screech that issued forth from the demon's mouth. Merrick twisted the knife, and silence reclaimed the roof. He pulled the knife free and sprang to his feet.

There!

He lurched forward, his breath ragged, and he followed the trail of his friend's blood. Around the hedges and trees, past the cracked stone bench, past the toppled, broken marble statue of Andromeda, and around the deep groove of crushed paving stone where Lysander had crash-landed. Merrick grimaced at how massive the impact must have been. Only an *arcanon* could survive and rise minutes later from that kind of trauma. And only an *arcanon* had the kind of discipline it took to ignore the pain of shattered bones in order to continue an unfinished fight. But even an *arcanon* wasn't invincible.

Merrick heard heavy breathing and ran, crashing through the hedge, but there was no fight to join. Lysander was sitting on the edge of a terra-cotta pot, under the tree's canopy. A dead demon lay at his feet, slowly turning to ash.

Lysander's left wing hung limp and broken, the feathers of the lower edge brushing against his ankle.

"How badly are you hurt?" Merrick asked grimly, his throat aching from the wounds that pulled as he spoke. He could see numerous wounds on Lysander's chest and arms. Clots had stopped the blood loss, but part of his torso bowed inward, like a dented car.

Lysander took a deep breath, and the indentation popped out. Lysander's face contorted with pain and his shoulders sagged, sweat streaming from his face and chest.

Merrick knew Lysander could seal and heal almost any wound. But there was one type of injury that could not be left to mend itself.

Merrick slowly circled, his eyes searching. The telltale blood streamed down Lysander's back from where the demons had tried to rip the left wing out.

"Can you draw your wings back in?"

Lysander remained silent, which, of course, meant no.

"Then they have to come out. Lie on that bench," Merrick said, pointing to the smooth stone table a few feet from them.

"No."

"You don't have a choice."

"I do," Lysander said.

A chill ran through Merrick. "Better to lose your wings than your life. If you die before you're redeemed, they'll pull your soul into hell. Better to have your body survive."

"I can't ascend without my wings. I'd be trapped on earth forever."

"Better to be trapped here than in hell, Lyse. Down there you'd be at their mercy. You've been killing them for thousands of years. You know what they'll do. Eternity's a long time to be tortured."

Lysander swayed, grasping a tree. "I'll never give up my wings."

Merrick heard the finality in Lysander's voice and was at a loss for an argument that would work on a creature who probably hadn't changed his mind about anything since the Dark Ages.

"All right. Let me look. Maybe I can force it back in."

Lysander knocked Merrick's hand away. He said a few words in some dead language that Merrick didn't speak. Then Lysander switched back to Latin. "Go away. I need to stand watch."

Merrick glanced up at the sky. "Why?"

"There were six. That's the most anyone's ever been able to get through. Maybe there will be more tonight."

Six. Merrick winced at the thought. "Did you kill them all?"

"No, you killed one."

Merrick smiled. So literal. "Come inside. No one's powerful enough to open a second gate in one night."

Lysander rubbed a hand over the tree trunk, looking up at the branches.

Sensing what he wanted, Merrick said, "There's always a bowl of oranges in the guest room. Come with me."

"No," Lysander growled. "You think I don't know your mind, Merrick? You're transparent. You'll wait until I pass out, then you'll rip out my wings."

"No, I won't," Merrick lied. He would try to get the wing back inside and splinted first, but if that didn't work, then yes, he'd do what had to be done.

"If you don't leave me alone, I'll throw you off this roof," Lysander said.

Fully restored, there was no doubt Lysander could do

exactly what he threatened, but he wasn't at his best, so Merrick might be able to drag him to the stairs. Still it wouldn't be easy, and Merrick couldn't afford to be seriously wounded with more fights with the syndicate looming, but the alternative was to let Lysander bleed to death, which Merrick would never do.

"Come and try," Merrick challenged.

Lysander bent his head, his hair falling forward to shadow his face. This did not bode well. If Lysander was too weak to answer a direct challenge that could only mean terrible things about how much damage and blood loss his body had sustained.

Then Merrick felt the air shift just before Lysander moved. Merrick jumped, but not quickly enough to block Lysander, who dashed past him in a blur of speed. Merrick spun and watched Lysander vault off the edge of the roof. He sailed over the chasm, but couldn't glide on the air without both wings outstretched so he crashed on the roof of the nearby Chase Tower building.

Merrick jogged to the edge, judging the distance to it. *Too far.*

Lysander stood at the edge, swayed, and looked across the distance. "If I never see you again, know that I loved you as well as any angel of the brotherhood, and better than many."

"Lysander—"

Lysander looked to the sky. "If they succeed in pulling me down to hell, any demons that rise will be drawn to the next strongest source of heaven's ether. Guard your wife." Lysander's labored breathing wheezed through the misty air. "I'll leave my knife for the other muse."

Merrick's brows rose in surprise. Lysander's last act on earth was going to be to leave a gift for Cerise Xenakis? That didn't sound like the archangel Merrick knew. Very far from it in fact.

"Tell her to look for it under the cherry blossom tree. I hope she won't need it. She has no real chance against a demon, but she's fierce. With that warrior's spirit and my knife, she might get lucky." Lysander sank to his knees, trying to reach the spot where blood flowed in a crimson river.

"For God's sake, Lysander! You won't make it to the Etherlin. Stay there. I'm coming over. If you die, I promise I'll make sure she gets your knife, but first let me try to help you."

"I won't stay here. I know you, Merrick. You'll take my wings to save my life. I won't give you the chance." Lysander dragged himself to his feet. "Ask Alissa to tell Cerise . . ." Lysander shook his head and shrugged. "Tell her that when she dances she's better than what we dreamed."

Lysander turned and ran to the far edge of the roof. He leaped into the air with his wings outstretched. He glided in a crooked arc toward the Etherlin.

Merrick raced across the roof and yanked the door open. Leaping to the landing, he stalked to the penthouse door and jabbed the buttons to enter the code.

"Alissa!"

"Yes?"

"Call Cerise for me. Tell her Lysander's wounded. He's trying to make it to the Etherlin. If he gets there, she'll find him under the cherry blossom tree in your backyard. If he's still alive when she finds him, she needs to cut out his wings. It's the only way to keep him from bleeding to death."

"Oh my God."

"He'll try to stop her, but she has to do it."

She winced, but snatched the phone from its cradle. She felt the buttons and positioned her fingers over the pad so she could dial blindly.

"Do you need help?"

"No, I have it," she said softly.

"If she gets there and there's only a knife and a blood trail, he's gone." Merrick paused. "Tell her to keep the knife. He wants her to have it."

"He—wait. Where are you going?"

"Out to look for him. If he makes it to the Etherlin, I can't help him; I'll never be able to break into the city fast enough to get to him in time. It'll be up to Cerise. But I don't think he's strong enough to fly all the way to the Etherlin. If he crashes somewhere in the Varden or the Sliver, I'll find him and rip his wings out to keep him from being sucked into hell."

"It's almost dawn. What about the syndicate? If you leave your territory—"

"I know," Merrick said. "If I don't make it back, go to the Etherlin and stay close to Cerise. She'll protect you." Merrick kissed her. "I love you."

She grabbed his hands and squeezed them. "I love you, James," she whispered fiercely. "Save him if you can, but no matter what happens come back to me." Her voice was full of persuasive power that was so charged with muse magic, it nearly rolled him under her spell.

He pulled her to him in a crushing hug, kissed her temple, and struggled against his own resistance to let her go. After several moments' hesitation, he did.

And he left the penthouse, concerned that for Lysander it might already be too late.

Cerise's friend had dropped her off on one of the Etherlin's main helipads. Eventually she'd have to answer Etherlin Security's questions about where she'd been and about the unscheduled touchdown of a chopper, but for the moment Cerise had cited exhaustion, and after seeing the music exec back off, she'd gone home and made it into her own bed.

The ringing of her cell phone dragged Cerise to consciousness just as she began to fall asleep. As Alissa's words penetrated her groggy brain, she rolled from bed and stumbled to her dresser to grab clothes.

If Lysander fell into the Etherlin, ES would be all over him. What if he fought and they shot him? Already wounded, he wouldn't survive. Assuming he was still alive. The thought of him dying upset her more than it should have. Adrenaline poured into her veins as she yanked on her clothes.

Once dressed, she rushed down the stairs and shoved the door open. She sprinted away from the house along the lakeside path until she reached Alissa's lawn. She raced across it to the tree.

His body lay bathed in moonlight.

With a hammering heart and twitching muscles, she dropped to the ground next to him. His right fist was closed around the hilt of a dagger. Skin that was alabaster pale testified to the fact that he was nearly bloodless. The bone root of his wing partially skewed his back where there was a sucking chest wound.

"Oh my God," she said with a gasp.

His lids rose a fraction, and he squinted as though his vision wasn't clear. "Don't," he rasped. "You mustn't touch my blood, Cerise. Back away."

"Shut up," she said and shoved the heel of her hand over where wine-colored blood leaked from his back. A shot of ice surged up her arm, knocking her back.

"You shouldn't have done that," he growled, panting and struggling. "You are so reckless. So beautiful, but so reckless."

"Save your breath," she snapped, grabbing the cocked wing and yanking.

He roared and a hand shot out, knocking her back. "No!"

"I have to. It's the only way to save you."

Eyes the color of ferns implored her. "I would rather die."

A rush of pain slammed through her. His pain, she realized.

She shuddered, unsure of what was happening. How had she felt that? Another wave hit her, and all her muscles locked. Keeping his wings was a need so deep she'd felt it vibrate through her soul. Nothing would ever convince him to give them up, which meant . . .

She watched the red pool spill over, crimson rivulets streaming down his side. She pressed down on the hole to stanch the flow, but the blood ran under and over her hands, making her palms and fingers slippery with it. Tears welled in her eyes.

"I'll stay with you till the end," she whispered.

"Help me."

"Tell me how."

"Push the wing in."

"I can't. The flesh is closed around it."

"Cut it open. Please. I want it straight."

"The bones are cracked."

"Please, Cerise," he whispered.

She swallowed against a tight throat. She tugged his fingers away from the hilt of the dagger and pulled the blade from the earth. She wiped the dirt off and through a blur of tears, she leaned over him.

He cried out when she cut him, and she froze.

"No, don't stop! Hurry, Cerise!"

His urgency focused her. She forced the blade deeper, and blood poured from the wound.

Oh God. I'm killing him faster.

But through his groans of pain, he urged her on with a single breathless word. *Please*.

She worked quickly to slice him open, cutting deep and wide. She dropped the dagger and used both hands to try to push the wing in. It was too heavy to move. She jerked forward, shoving her shoulder against it to lever it upward so the bone angled. It gave way and she guided the broken root into the hole in his back that she'd made.

The instant that his wing's root was partially inside, his flesh clamped around it and her hands, trying to close the wound. She gritted her teeth till she thought they'd shatter. She held the bone and forced the rest inside with the strength of her entire body. Her muscles cramped and wailed. Sweat dripped from her brow as she tried to pull her hands out. Only the left slid free of his body.

With a sucking sound, his back muscles knitted themselves around her right wrist. She cried out at the pressure. It was like his flesh was a tourniquet strangling her arm.

She couldn't pull her hand free.

No! Oh no!

She jerked and wrenched until her shoulder muscles felt like they were ripping from the bones. She screamed in pain and panic. She couldn't get out.

She grabbed the dagger, hesitating only for a second. There was no help for it. She cut into his back, dragging the blade in a curve around her wrist, nicking her arm. She threw herself backward with all her might.

She landed hard on her back, jarring every bone. Except her hand.

Gone!

I tore off my hand!

Crying, she held up her arm. There, still attached, was a dusky blue hand.

Not gone! It's not gone!

She sobbed. It was so numb, she couldn't feel it at all. She shook her arm and the hand flopped limply. She couldn't take her eyes from her useless fingers. Gradually, pins and needles began to sting her wrist and crept outward. The pain sharpened, and her hand turned an angry red.

I feel it! Pain is good, she thought, shaking with relief.

Slowly sensation returned, and she moved her fingers gingerly. The pain eased as normal color returned.

She crawled to Lysander, whose skin was ashen and cool. She was relieved to find he was still breathing. She needed to get him in the house. With a bone-crunching sound, his wings folded and smooth slits opened in his back. There was no bleeding as the wings collapsed inward and were absorbed into his flesh with a soft sucking sound. He exhaled a sigh.

A bobbing light in the distance moved along the lakeside path. *Etherlin Security.* She knew their feelings on fallen creatures. She remembered the way they'd locked Merrick up when he'd infiltrated the Etherlin.

"Lysander, can you stand? We have to get you out of sight."

He lay still as a corpse. She lurched up. If she could get him into Alissa's house, she'd have a little time. She could try to arrange for a blood transfusion, though she wasn't sure she could trust an Etherlin-affiliated physician to keep Lysander's presence a secret. If the doctor told the council, ES would take over.

She glanced at Alissa's house, which was dark and presumably locked tight. If she broke a window, ES might hear.

She needed a key. Instantly, she remembered Richard's advice. She rushed to the purple trellis and knelt. Reaching into a hollow at the base she felt a smooth cold piece of plastic nestled among the dirt. She removed the plastic object, finding a fake gray rock. She flipped it and popped it open. A key lay inside. She extracted the key and rushed back to Lysander.

The lights were almost close enough to spot them, and the hazy orange of sunrise crept over the horizon.

His skin was frosty cold, but his chest moved more forcefully as he breathed.

She grabbed his arm and pulled, but he was much too heavy to drag, especially with the pain in her shoulder from where she'd wrenched her muscles.

She jabbed him with the key. "Lysander," she whispered fiercely.

He stirred, and his eyes opened to small slits.

"C'mon. You have to get up. The security guys are coming."

He moved, and she helped him roll onto his side. He panted from the effort, his lips pursed and bluish.

"I can't stand yet."

"You have to. C'mon. Try," she said, pulling on him.

He took her hand and rose partially, then toppled, knocking her down with him. She gasped in pain. There was no way she could lift him. If he couldn't stand, it was over.

Her gaze darted from side to side. She spotted the gardener's shed. She jerked to her feet and ran to it, careful to avoid the motion sensors. It was lucky that she'd come across the property so many times before on her clandestine escapes.

She pulled the shed door open, wincing at the creaking sound. Finding a wheelbarrow, she hurried back to him.

It took two attempts to get him half into it and then she rolled it back to the shed, closing the door. She held her breath and peered out a small hole. The ES officers were nearly silent as they combed the grounds. If they got close enough to the tree, they'd see the blood. And, shit, find the dagger. Her heart thumped. She imagined herself trying to explain what she'd been doing in the shed concealing a mostly bloodless fallen angel.

They scanned the area and a beam of light ran over the ground at the base of the tree. She froze.

Damn it! We're done. When they see the knife and the blood, they'll search every inch—

But the flashlights moved on.

What the hell?

Her heart banged inside her chest. Moments passed, and she couldn't believe it, but they didn't close in on the shed. Why had they ignored the knife? They moved farther away.

Cerise turned her attention to the rising sun. She didn't have much time before it was full light. Her only chance of getting him inside without anyone seeing was to move him immediately.

She turned and bent over the wheelbarrow where he was draped with the edges of the barrow cutting into his flash.

"Hey," she whispered. "I have to move you, and you have to help by staying absolutely silent. Can you do that?"

He didn't move a muscle. She put a palm above his nose and felt cool misty breath against it. *Still alive. Just unconscious.*

She opened the door, which creaked. She winced, gritting her teeth, but there was no sign of ES returning.

It's now or never.

Cerise pushed the door wider and then lifted the wheelbarrow and pushed it. She bit her lip against the ache in her shoulder and wheeled him to the back door, keeping a steady watch. The lights weren't far.

Don't look this way.

She unlocked the door and stepped inside. She entered the date of the spring equinox on the security pad, and the light on the alarm pad turned green.

Thank you, Richard.

She returned to Lysander's inert body and with a heave, tipped the wheelbarrow sideways. He rolled out and landed with a thud.

She shoved his body so it slid over the tile, then wheeled around and returned the empty wheelbarrow and closed the shed. She couldn't resist veering to the cherry blossom tree to retrieve the knife. She noticed the blood was gone, as though it had been completely absorbed into the earth.

Not a speck on the grass? That's a little . . . miraculous?

She returned swiftly to the house and closed the door. Once it was locked, she slid down to sit next to Lysander, trembling from the exertion and the adrenaline rush.

We made it, and he's alive. At least for now.

Chapter 12

Cerise's head ached from lack of sleep, but she couldn't simply cover Lysander and leave him lying on the cold hard tile. Her sore shoulder complained when she rolled him onto a blanket and then held the edges in her fists and dragged him across the floor. It was tougher to slide him when the blanket hit the carpet, but she kept pulling and then rolled him the rest of the way. Finally, she dropped onto the carpeted floor alongside him and covered them both with the blanket.

She opened her phone and called Alissa and Merrick's landline. Alissa answered immediately.

"It's me, Liss."

"Are you all right? Merrick just got back. He looked for Lysander in the Varden and the Sliver, but he wasn't there. Did you—?"

"Yes, I found him."

"Thank God."

"He's alive, but he lost a lot of blood. I got him inside your house. I'm going to call Dr.—"

"Did you remove his wings?"

"No."

"Is he still bleeding?" Alissa asked, alarmed.

"No. I put his broken wing back inside his back, and the skin sealed over it."

"Oh good," Alissa said, exhaling in relief. "Don't call anyone. If he's taken to the hospital who knows what they'll find in his blood or on his X-rays. ES considers fallen angels the same as ventala. The minute they hear what he is, they'll try to take him into custody, which would be a disaster when he wakes up and decides he doesn't want to be in custody."

"He's cold, Alissa. *Really* cold."

"He'll survive. Just keep him warm."

"I don't know."

"Look, call if you feel you have to, but I promise he'll be all right."

Cerise stared at the ceiling, and moments ticked away. Alissa would never risk Lysander's life. "If he's going to stay here to recover, no one can know. I notice your house is shiny clean and smells of Pine-Sol."

"That's Mrs. Carlisle and the maids. She wants everything ready for us to come home. I'll call and inform her that you're house-sitting and working there. I'll make sure no one comes to the house."

"That would be good." Cerise paused, rubbing the bridge of her nose.

"Cerise, thank you for helping him. It means a lot."

"You're welcome."

"You must be so tired. Try to get some rest. Call me when you wake."

"I will." Cerise closed the phone and let it drop onto the carpet. Her eyes burned as the lids closed over them. She moved closer to Lysander, putting an arm around his cold chest. His muscles twitched, and she pressed against him, shivering at the chill.

"Alissa and I are just becoming friends again," she whispered. "If you die, I won't be able to forgive her or myself for not calling you a doctor. So that'll be on you." She put her cheek against his neck. "Better if you survive."

She woke slowly, the smell of sandalwood and earth filling the air. She breathed deep against the pressure on her chest. She opened her eyes. Tangled strands of dark gold hair blocked her view. She brushed them away and took in the state of things.

Lysander's hand held her hip, his head rested on her chest,

and his body was pressed to hers. The intimacy of their positions made her skin tingle and tighten.

He'd warmed, or her body had chilled to match his. She stretched her shoulders and the lack of stiffness seemed a good sign.

Her fingers combed his hair, then rested on the back of his neck.

"Are you awake?"

"No," he murmured. "I'm dreaming."

She smiled. "How's your dream?"

"Soft. Sweet. And smooth."

She traced his neck muscles to where they met his shoulders, then her fingers kneaded his flesh. His exhalation of breath ruffled her T-shirt.

"No hands ever felt better on my body. Not even when I was in love," he said. "I wish this was a dream; I'd pray to never wake up."

"When were you in love?" she asked, aware that the jealous pang in her solar plexus was unwarranted. This closeness was only an illusion.

"I'll tell you about it, but before that there are other things that need to be said."

Her hands stilled at his grave tone. As if her body's stiffening were his cue, he raised himself to a sitting position. He twisted slowly, and a hiss of pain escaped his lips.

He extended his arms toward the ceiling, but jerked to a stop with a grimace. "The root of the wing is still cracked." His pursed lips were pale, but not blue as they'd been the night before. "I'll have to modify my movements to let it heal. It's a miracle that you managed to—" He looked at her. "I owe you my life. And an apology."

"An apology for what?"

"For creating the circumstance where my blood was under your hands." He rubbed his jaw. "I shouldn't have come here, but Richard's house is empty. I didn't expect anyone to find me. I thought to leave you a gift."

She put an arm behind her head to prop it up as she watched him. "Why is it a problem that I touched your blood?"

"An old tradition. An old law." He studied her, pausing as if trying to decide how to explain. "Through the ages, men have sworn blood oaths and have scored their hands to mix their blood as a testament to their brotherhood and loyalty to each other. It was once thought that all maladies were found in the ill humors of blood and that draining away bad blood would be curative or at least therapeutic." He licked his lips. "The human preoccupation with blood comes from the angels. When we took on the flesh of mankind and saw that wounds bled— that we could share a part of ourselves—we made the first oaths. And it became law that to touch an angel's blood or to carry his blood inside one's body was to become bound. That's why when I made love to you I didn't complete the act even though I wanted to. If you would've become pregnant and carried my blood inside you, we'd have been bound and I didn't want that."

She frowned.

"I would never have tied your fate to mine on purpose," he continued. "I'm fallen, and that's a dangerous state of being. I have no brotherhood to stand with me against my enemies— which are numerous—and no sanctuary within which to leave a lover. I belong nowhere. Unfortunately, now neither do you."

Her stomach clenched, dread building, and she sat up. "What do you mean? What does that mean?"

"We're connected."

"Permanently?"

He inclined his head.

"I didn't agree to that."

He smiled ruefully. "Your agreement isn't required. You acted on impulse, but there are still consequences."

She pursed her lips. That couldn't possibly be how things worked.

He must have sensed her skepticism because he pressed on. "Imagine you're in your kitchen and you bump something which then falls from the counter. Instinctively you grab it. It turns out to be a butcher's knife that you caught by the blade. The fact that you didn't have time to consider your actions doesn't protect your fingers from being cut. You bear no blame, but there are still consequences."

As this logic penetrated, her mind raced. She couldn't have changed her whole life in that instant. She was one of the four most powerful muses on the planet. She had a special destiny—a divine gift of her own. She wasn't just a trophy human to be dragged along by an angel. "My life is my own."

"Yes, and now it's tied to mine. My blood marked you and sealed my obligation. I'll defend you to the death. And until your soul is delivered to heaven or hell, you're mine."

Her pulse pounded like the feet of runners in a dead sprint. *Hold on.* She took a deep breath, trying to slow her racing heart. *He could be lying to trick me into doing what he says. Demons would do anything to have a muse's ability to influence people. Maybe an almost damned angel would, too. Everyone knows the fallen can't be trusted.*

"I live here in the Etherlin where no fallen creature is welcome."

"I did warn you not to touch me." He rose to his towering height. "At the time, I wasn't strong enough to stop you. But you saved my wings, so I can't . . ." He paused with a pained expression. "I can't completely regret that I wasn't." He tapped his fist against his leg.

She stared at him. He had warned her. In fact, he'd hesitated to get involved with her all along. Unless that had been an act—a really convincing one. She narrowed her eyes. Con men and tricksters often did things to draw their marks to them. They pretended reluctance to make the mark more eager. Could that have been part of his ploy to draw her in? No, he really had been bleeding to death. That definitely hadn't been a ruse. But what did she really know about him? Only that Alissa cared about him because he was Merrick's friend.

"You didn't answer my question."

"I didn't hear one," he said.

"The implied question," she said, scowling. "I live here. You can't. How will you act as bodyguard under the circumstances?"

He walked to the doorway, glancing briefly over his shoulder at her. "I'm sorry your life changed without your consent, Cerise. When you're done grieving your loss, come to the kitchen. For now, I'll leave you with your thoughts."

Lysander diced tomatoes with the kind of speed usually reserved for master chefs. She watched from the doorway, admiring the way he moved even while she was swamped with doubts about him and about her own future.

When he reached up into a cupboard with his left hand, he stopped sharply and brought his arm down to his side, using the other.

"You need a sling to remind you not to use that arm."

"A sling," he said, glancing down as if one might appear. "That would be a good reminder of many things. Like how close I came to losing this body. Again, my thanks. I think it wasn't easy work getting that wing back inside."

"No, it wasn't."

"I'm lucky you're stronger than most people. And that you had the fortitude to cut a wider wound. Many could not have brought themselves to do it."

"Tell me more about what us being tied together means."

He ran a hand through his hair, his fingers catching on the tangles. "I've explained it as well as I can. Fate will reveal the rest."

She studied his face, unease rippling through her. He knew more than he was saying. Things she probably wouldn't like and wouldn't want to accept. "I want more information."

He shook his head and turned away.

"Lysander?" she said, infusing her voice with persuasive power. She felt a rush of exhilaration at using her magic. She realized it was the second time she'd been able to—the first had been when she'd talked herself out of the grips of over-whelming lust when he'd left her.

"Do you like French toast?" he asked, apparently unaffected by muse magic. That grated, her joy melting away momentarily. She wanted her divinely instilled power to be as strong as his.

"About us . . ."

"Maybe eggs."

She glared at his back. "Lysander, I deserve the most detailed explanation you can give me. I expect that much considering that I saved your wings and your life."

His shoulders tensed, but he didn't say more. He crushed pistachios and flipped egg-saturated bread in them, then he dropped the bread slices into butter sizzling in a pan.

She sighed. She had to coax him to talk, to open up to her again. To reveal *more*. She needed to know everything.

"How did you fall? You said you didn't rise up during the rebellion."

"That's exactly how I fell," he said. He turned and studied her face for a moment, then nodded. "You probably should know the details of what happened since my enemies are now yours."

She shivered.

He turned back to the stove and poured eggs into a second pan. He shook spices into them. "For a time, the world was left in the care of the Olympians. Your ancestors," he said, glancing at her. "They were bright and brave enough in the beginning, but the more they involved themselves with humans, the more they became like men. They could be creative and charismatic in wondrous ways, but they were also driven by jealousies and rage, by passion and other strong emotions. They acted out of spite and made men pawns in their games with each other. Eventually the Olympians were forced to cede power."

"Forced?"

"They wouldn't go willingly. It was a battle, and many of them were more experienced in fighting and war than we—the angels—were, but," Lysander ran his hand down his chest and belly, then flexed his biceps, which rippled with impressive effect. He smiled. "Heaven has the power of creation. When we became flesh, there was nothing to match us. And we were devoted to any mission given to us. We trained tirelessly and hard. Proud of our dedication, He gifted us with what He gave to the lions."

"The lions?"

Lysander nodded. "Lions don't know fear. It's the same for us. In the moment of battle, nothing and no one can intimidate an archangel."

"Merrick has that, too."

"You noticed," Lysander said with a smile. "There's a story there. A story for another time." He flipped the bread as she continued. "Most of the Olympians were banished to another realm. Some who'd been faithful to their original charge were allowed to stay on earth, and they tried to integrate into human society. They married and had children. In the end, however, they all rejoined their own society in the other realm. With one exception. Hades built a massive underworld that he ruled. By agreement, he was never allowed to rise, but there was nothing in the original compact that prevented his interference with mankind. When there is a loophole in a law, there is someone to exploit it. I'm sure you've seen as much."

She nodded with a small smile.

"Hades raised an army of former men. He cursed them to crave human and angel blood and then released them into the world."

"Vampires."

"Exactly, but by then there was an archangel army. We kept the vampires at bay, and they receded into the shadows of caves. Over the years, we withdrew from earth and let mankind govern and protect itself. Like a child that reaches adulthood, the society of men had to make its own way. Often they gave us cause for pride and celebration. Unfortunately, not everyone was happy to see man's progress and their close relationship with heaven."

Lysander tossed shredded cheese and sautéed vegetables onto the eggs and folded them over. "Some angels, like the Olympians, lost their innocence during their visits to earth. We were warned not to interfere with mankind in a way that would cause harm. That fanned the flames of jealousy. We were the first children of heaven and had always felt ourselves most favored. With so much attention paid to mankind, some angels became bitter. When their rumblings were not well received, they hid their feelings, buried them so deep that many of us didn't understand what was brewing in their hearts."

"Jealousy is so dangerous," Cerise said, thinking of her complicated relationship with Alissa and how it had affected Cerise's relationship with her father, Dimitri.

"You're familiar?"

"Jealousy and resentment ruined my childhood friendship with Alissa."

"She must be quite changed in adulthood then. She doesn't seem given to jealousy at all now."

Cerise smiled. "She wasn't jealous of me. I was jealous of her."

Lysander paused. "Why?"

Cerise laughed, pleased that he seemed astonished. "Another time. Finish your story."

"I had taken flesh and was on earth searching for my closest brother. He'd gone missing, and there were rumors that he must've been overcome by a mass of vampires. Lucifer and I found his medallion at the mouth of a river. We smelled fresh blood on the banks and knew there were underwater caves. I dove into the water without a moment's hesitation.

"Heaven's trumpet call sounded and I surfaced. There's a law that at the sound of heaven's trumpet, all angels return home and form ranks. There hadn't been a call in many hundreds of years. Lucifer looked up and said, 'We're being called back to get orders for this. They know he's in trouble.'

"I should've leapt from the water and taken flight for home. Instead, I looked up at the stormy sky and thought he must be right. There were no Olympians left, and no creatures but vampires were ever foolish enough to challenge us, so what else could the call have been for?

" 'They've dragged him down. These may be his last moments. Why don't you go in? I'll return to heaven and tell them where you are. We'll rejoin you,' he said.

"Lightning streaked the sky, and the trumpet sounded again. I should have risen. Instead I listened to Lucifer and dove underwater."

Lysander's hands rested on the counter, and he hung his head, his hair shielding his pained expression.

"While I slaughtered vampires and searched the underground caves, Lucifer and Reziel, for whom I was searching, and their band of malcontents rose up against our brothers. They tried to overtake the kingdom of heaven in a bloody battle. Many of the best warriors fought with Lucifer. Victory was a very near thing, but the hand of God stretched out with gusting winds and storms of flame. Heaven was emptied of angels. Even in the darkest caves, I felt the earth rumble and quake. Realizing something was terribly wrong, I rushed back to the surface. I shot from the water into the air. The sky rained bodies, but I didn't let that distract me. Heaven was under siege, and I raced to get there to defend it.

"I arrived too late. Much too late. The gates were locked. I rattled the bars and shouted, but no one came. I returned to earth and found a spritely angel named Toibel that I'd trained.

I lifted him and his blood flowed like a river over my hands. His wings had been ripped out, his back shredded."

Lysander's voice was a ragged whisper when he said, "With wide eyes and his dying breath, Toibel asked, 'Lysander, where were you? They could never have killed so many if you'd been there to fight.'" Lysander put his hands over his ears as if to block out Toibel's voice echoing in his head.

Cerise's throat tightened and she stepped forward, but he put out a hand to block her from touching him.

"Never offer me comfort for that mistake. I earned this pain."

"They tricked you."

He nodded. "Which is why I'm fallen, not damned." He glanced up a moment, lost in difficult memories, then continued, apparently determined to tell it all. "The earth cracked to reveal the underworld, and tornadoes of flames swept the damned downward. Lucifer tried to drag me along, taunting me, saying that I was barred from heaven like the rest. He swore they would make a paradise of the roiling underworld, that it would be greater than heaven. I was on my knees with despair, and Reziel, whom I'd loved as a favorite brother, put a hand on my shoulder. 'I knew you would be torn. I spared you the pain of the choice. It's over now,' he said, gasping from the pounding pressure and flaming gusts that were forcing them down. 'There will be no angels left here, and you can't rise. You have to come join us so you won't be alone.'

"I shoved him away, but he grabbed me and held on. 'I won't give you up. I told Lucifer, I'd never give you up. I wouldn't raise a blade against you. Come with me. You must!'

"I swung my blades and severed his wrists. He fell backward, screaming with pain, shocked and enraged. He shouted, 'You cut me? You cast me off? Curse you, Lysander! A thousand curses! We're brothers no more!'

"When the crater closed and the storm ended, I was alone here—the enemy of everyone I'd ever cared for."

She grimaced.

"And so I would remain for thousands of years, chilled to the bone for the lack of heaven's light and warmth." He licked his dry lips. "I fight for a chance to redeem myself so I can return home. Seven hundred years ago, Gabriel told me that I'd earned a chance. He delivered the pieces of a prophecy, the shreds of hope."

"Such a long time," she said.

He shrugged broad shoulders. "Many of heaven's faithful were lost during Lucifer's uprising. My neglect puts their blood on my hands." He drew his thumb over his lower lip as if to rub away the difficult words that passed them.

"I've never shirked my duty since." Lysander's gorgeous eyes narrowed. "When demons rise, I race heaven's archangels to reach the damned first, to fight and slash and kill, to force them back down. heaven won't claim me, but I wage war in its name. And of heaven's ranks, I'm the deadliest soldier of all. Still." Lysander's mouth curved into a smile. "They curse my name in hell."

The fierce gleam in his eyes intensified and his icy smile widened, making him glorious in the way reserved for warriors.

From betrayal comes the ripped and deadly poster boy for retribution. Beware the fallen angels.

He inclined his head as if agreeing to the thought she hadn't voiced.

"It's my one satisfaction in this world," he said. "I'm the bane of hell."

After breakfast, Cerise took a shower. When she pulled back the curtain, Lysander was bending over the sink brushing his teeth. She quirked a brow.

"There are probably ten bathrooms in this house."

"Yes, but your naked body was in this one," he said. His gaze perused her curves, hotter than the steam smoking the mirrors.

"Considering the way things ended the last time you had my naked body at your disposal, you're not invited to join me when I'm naked." She snapped a finger and pointed to the towel she'd left on a shelf.

He lifted it and held it out, but didn't release it. A sexy smile curved his lips. "That was then."

She arched a brow and tugged. His hand opened, and she took the towel and wrapped it around her.

Noticing the packaging in the wastebasket, she glanced at the sink's drawer. "Are there more new toothbrushes in there?"

He rinsed his mouth, set the toothbrush down, and turned, leaning against the sink and blocking her hand's reach for the drawer. "There are. Not unexpectedly, Alissa and Richard are good hosts."

"So give me one," she said, turning up her palm. When he didn't move, she frowned at him. "What's your deal?"

"Not precisely a deal—wait, you were using a colloquialism. I'm not always familiar. Unlike demons, who follow the lives of humans and mimic their language so they can better communicate and interfere, I don't normally fraternize. Before I befriended Merrick, it had been about seventeen years since I'd conversed with anyone."

"Nice hermit life."

He shrugged. "I prefer things now. Angels aren't suited to solitude, but I've needed to be wary of building connections here."

"Well, don't let me stop you from going your wary way. It's a very big house."

He smiled and shook his head. "We're bound now, so there's no reason to separate myself from you anymore." His gaze dropped from her mouth to the place where the towel was knotted above her breasts. "I can get as close as I'd like."

Her brows rose. "It's not only about what you'd like."

His eyes met hers. "Of course not. I can also get as close as you'd like."

She was tempted, but couldn't help recalling what he'd said. The fact that Lysander hadn't intended to help Lucifer's uprising had spared Lysander from the full consequences of being complicit. Intentions counted. She may have touched Lysander's blood and somehow tied herself to him, but how much tighter and more unbreakable would heaven consider their bond if she took him as a lover?

"At the moment, I'm not sure what I want," she said. "Why don't you—?" She flicked her fingers toward the door.

He pushed off the sink, towering over her. She wasn't used to having to look up at anyone, and it punctuated the strange seductiveness of his size.

"I have some things to investigate, Cerise. It'll be easier with your help and I intend to exploit that advantage. It seems only right that you should be allowed to exploit any advantage this arrangement affords you, too." He leaned close, his minty breath sweet against her lips. "I'll need my body for fighting when there are demons to put down, but the rest of the time . . . you're free to use it for your pleasure."

"My very own supernatural stud service. What more could a girl ask for?" she said dryly.

"Have a care, Cerise," he said, his grin widening. "If you challenge me to strip the derision from your tone, I'll rise to the occasion."

"Wow," she said, putting her palm in the middle of his chest as he crowded her. "What's that in your veins? Distilled testosterone?" Her hand shoved against him. "Back up."

"May I have a kiss first?"

"Obviously if I'm telling you to back off, then no." Her heart thumped hard in her chest. In no way did she trust herself to stop things if he kissed her.

"As you like," he said, stepping back. Then without so much as a warning, he shucked his pants. Ignoring her slack-jawed expression, he walked past her and stepped into the shower.

As asses go, that one's perfect. She looked away and shook her head with a frown. *Tread carefully. He's in a rush to leave this world and you're not. The last thing you can afford is to be drawn into the battles he and Merrick fight. That would be way too dangerous.* She glanced at the fluttering shower curtain where beating water tempted her toward its warmth and toward his hard wet body.

Get out while you have the chance.

She snagged a toothbrush and the toothpaste and fled the room. She wandered until she found Alissa's dressing room. Most of the designers sent Alissa sample sizes that could be worn by models who were a size four like Alissa. Stretch fabric would be required for Cerise to fit into anything found in Alissa's closet. She flipped through knit dresses, finding a loose jersey style that looked like it would serve.

Pulling it on, she glanced down to where her thighs emerged from under the fabric. "Not meant to be a minidress, but it'll have to do." She ran her fingers through her hair and tossed the wet towel in the clothes hamper before going off in search of Richard's room.

The last thing she wanted was for Lysander to wander around with all those buff muscles unclothed and close at hand. She needed to cover as much of him as possible.

Searching Richard's closet, she didn't find much that a seven-foot-tall angel could wear. She settled on a charcoal knit sweater with short sleeves. The pants were hopeless. He'd have to make do with his own leathers again.

"Nice stems."

Startled, she jerked, then looked over her shoulder. He'd come into the room so silently, she hadn't known he was there until he'd spoken. She quirked a brow as he stared at her legs.

"Did you say 'nice stems'? Did we time travel to the 1950s and no one told me?"

Lysander smiled. "Merrick used to say that occasionally as a boy."

"Merrick's nowhere near old enough for that to be his turn of phrase."

"I think he picked it up from an old guard when he was incarcerated. Merrick's appreciation for the female form is boundless. When he was young, admiring and pursuing it was his highest priority. At sixteen, he told me that if I wanted to learn to flirt with women, I should watch him."

She and Lysander laughed.

"It was well meant. He never lacked for female company and I always did. He couldn't fathom that my solitude was by choice."

Cerise forced her eyes to stay on his face rather than dropping for a glimpse of his nude body. She reached into the closet and grabbed a thick bathrobe and thrust it at him. He shrugged into it without comment.

"You mentioned you'd been in love. Tell me about her. Or him," she ventured.

"Her," Lysander said, unperturbed by her implication that the lover might have been male. "Felice." He glanced away, and the amusement lighting his face disappeared. "I'll share that story sometime, but not now. It'll make me melancholy, and I'm in the mood to be—not melancholy. Shall we go out? I want to show you some artwork. A demon's trespassed here. Not in the flesh, but through the mind of someone artistic."

"Lysander, you can't go out. Not until it's dark when you can fly out of the Etherlin undetected."

"Fly?" He shook his head. "My wing will take time to heal. It's the only sort of injury from which I don't immediately recover. And I'd never risk more damage to it by trying to fly before it's fully mended."

"Then you'll be a bit of a shut-in here, because as a member of the fallen, you're persona non grata in the Etherlin. We can't risk you being spotted and caught. You can tell me where the artwork that you want me to see is located and I'll go and have a look. *Alone.*"

He smiled. "Alone? Without my protection?" He shook his head. "You're bait for demons now, and the last thing I'd ever share with them is a girl who's mine."

"Yours," she echoed in a pavement-flat tone. "I haven't agreed to that, so I'd appreciate it if you'd stop repeating that we're hopelessly bound to each other."

"Silence on a subject doesn't make it less true."

"I have a few things to take care of on my own. I'll come back for you after dark."

"No."

Her jaw tightened. "Why not? There are no demons on the loose at the moment, are there?"

"Pay attention," he said, his voice going cool and hard, "because just as you tire of me repeating myself, I tire of it, too. Someone opened a window to hell last night. More demons escaped to this side than have ever come through before at one time. They almost took my wings. Whoever opened that portal will try again because Lucifer and Reziel will promise them anything to do it. I am hell's worst enemy. They'll never stop hunting me. And now that you're important to me, they'll never stop hunting you, either. You are not safe."

"How would they even know I'm important to you?"

"You've been anointed with my blood, with my essence. When close enough, demons will smell it. Some of the more powerful demons will be drawn to it from miles away."

"What if I don't intend to take your word about this? I need proof that there's no loophole that I can climb through to get my life back to the way it was before I touched your blood."

He made a dismissive hand gesture. "You'll have your proof if demons capture and kill you," he said. "Trust me, you don't want proof."

"Listen, it's not quite dusk. In the past, haven't demons always been raised at night?"

"Often, but there's nothing that prevents a daytime ritual."

"Of course there is. Fallen creatures are nocturnal and if one is going to raise a demon, that's better done under the cover of darkness, isn't it? When there are fewer witnesses to see them take to the skies? The law of probabilities says that the next time someone raises a demon it'll be at night. I promise I won't be gone long."

"You're not a poker chip, Cerise. I don't gamble with things I'm not willing to lose. I'll go where you go, whether you like it or not, because you can't stop me."

She offered him a look of pure ice. "We'll table this discussion for now, but don't kid yourself. If you do something that proves you can't be trusted, I'll rid myself of you one way or another."

He inclined his head with a wicked smile that tugged at the deepest reaches of her body. In a low voice that was both dangerous and seductive, he said, "I look forward to seeing you try."

Chapter 13

As daylight faded, Cerise and Lysander walked the wooded path toward the Etherlin's center. At her request he'd brushed his thick hair and secured it in a rubber band, which allowed her to study his handsome face.

"If you can heal any wounds other than those to your wings, why do you scar?"

"When the wounds are fresh, I could heal the skin if I wanted to."

"Why wouldn't you want to?"

He shrugged. "They're battle scars. The trophies of my victories. Also, I believed the scars would make me less appealing to human beings. I thought it would be easier to avoid people if they shunned me."

"How'd that work out for you?"

"Why ask if you already know?" he said. "Your pupils double in size every time you look at me."

She frowned, knowing he was right. Maybe if he'd had worse scars on his face it would have worked, but for some reason she found his face and body more compelling with them. It was almost as if he'd have been too beautiful without them.

She rolled her eyes. "Poor you. You were trying to turn people off with your scars and it didn't work. You think it's tough being gorgeous? Try not being gorgeous sometime. That's what's tough."

"How would you know?"

"I was an ugly kid."

His gaze slid to her. "Truly?"

She nodded. "By conventional standards of beauty, absolutely."

"And it was difficult?"

"Alissa was freakishly beautiful from birth. I learned very early on that no matter what I did or how much I primped, in any comparison to her, I would always lose. You see it all the time in famous families. The good-looking kids get all the media attention. They're perceived as more interesting and talented. It's the way things work. At a photo shoot when I was twelve, I overheard the stylist and photographer discussing a long list of my physical flaws. It was like having birds pick the flesh from my bones. Thank God for dancing. It was the one thing that gave me confidence."

"It must have been a relief when you became beautiful."

"I'm still not beautiful, but I don't mind if you think so," she said with a sly smile. "The thing that was a relief was growing up and showing myself the important things I could do with the incredible gift I'd been given. Crowds of thousands upon thousands hold their breath when my athletes perform and when my musicians rock a stadium. The thunder of the applause is deafening. The spectators cheer and sob and clutch the people around them; that tide of human emotion is unstoppable. Whenever I see and feel it, I know I have something more powerful than beauty. It probably also helps that I'm not modeling side by side with Alissa anymore," she said wryly.

"Alissa's kind, and at moments, I see evidence of her power. She can certainly slay Merrick with a word or a look, which is no easy feat. But I can't imagine how she could've ever overshadowed someone like you."

"Come on. You can't deny she's stunning."

"She has a lovely face," Lysander conceded. "But she's slight. To me, she looks fragile. A blown-glass ornament for the shelf. I don't know how Merrick doesn't shatter her with one rough kiss."

Cerise laughed, but shook her head. "Alissa's perfect. If you didn't have freakishly huge archangel proportions she wouldn't seem small at all."

"She could never have bloodied my lip with her forehead. She couldn't even have reached it."

"I probably couldn't have busted your lip, either, if I hadn't launched myself."

The corner of his mouth curved up. "Exactly. You've got long powerful legs and a will to match. No matter how rough the kiss, you wouldn't shatter."

"The funny thing is how you think that's a compliment," she said, amused. " 'That Cerise, she's built like a prized bull with a temper to match.' Just what any woman longs to hear."

They rounded the corner of a tall building, and he dragged her with him into the shadows and pushed her against the bricks. His mouth came down against hers without warning, cool and demanding. He bruised her lips, and she shoved her fingers into his hair, pulling. He pinned her against the wall, his knee pressing between her thighs, causing a stab of lust where he touched. She bit his tongue and his lower lip. As the kiss roughened, they ground their lower bodies together until she throbbed and longed for him to thrust inside her.

The noise of shuffling feet stirred her, and she dug her nails into his back over the site of his wounded wing. He drew back, his mouth coming away on a gasp.

"We have to break this up. Someone's coming. It could be ES," she rasped and panted to catch her breath.

He still crowded her against the wall, and light danced dangerously in his wild, tawny eyes. *He gifted us with what He gave the lions,* he'd said. Yes, she could see that. Her heart pounded and her body still thrummed with wanting more of him.

Lysander licked the swollen corner of his mouth where she'd bitten him hard enough to draw blood. "That you can't be broken with a kiss suits me. That you're human and almost a match for me makes you remarkable. Never doubt that."

"Or you'll be forced to prove it by shoving me against a wall?"

"Did you like being shoved against the wall?" he asked in a low voice, deep and sexy.

"No," she lied.

He flashed her a smile and stepped back. "Yeah, I felt how

much you hated it. Come, let's go before you provoke me into seeing what else you'd hate for me to do to you against a wall."

The shuffling footsteps drew closer, and Cerise spotted a pair of teenage boys. They whispered to each other and approached.

"Hey, Cerise," the taller boy in the Hollister jacket said.

"Hello," she returned.

"New aspirant?" Hollister asked, and both teens turned their heads to study Lysander.

It was always big news when a muse took on an aspirant, and Cerise hadn't chosen anyone new to inspire in more than a year. She would've enjoyed the distraction of engaging someone fresh, but her powers . . . Although her ability to persuade had emerged, her power to inspire hadn't. She couldn't feel the internal spark she needed to light a fire in someone's soul. Her mind hopped to Griffin's songbook. She'd had so many dreams about that book and had felt so compelled to find it. Would reading his journal help her recover her magic as she'd believed? Or was there another very different key? She glanced at the angel standing silently at her side.

The boys still waited for an answer about whether Lysander was a new aspirant. That was better than the alternative explanation she decided. Anything was better than admitting that she'd taken up with a fallen angel.

"We'll see," she said.

"Basketball player?" the smaller boy with inky hair asked.

She shook her head. "Gladiator. We're thinking of building a new coliseum over at Park Casabel."

They laughed. "So there'll be job openings? I could use some part-time work."

"Sure. Someone's going to have to clean out the lions' cages."

Inky continued grinning. "Really though, what kind of athlete?"

"He's a musician," she said. "A violinist."

"C'mon," Hollister said, waving off her answer.

"How long have you guys been going out?" Inky asked.

So they'd seen the kiss. Cerise shook her head. "Just friends."

"I'd like to be one of your 'just friends,'" Inky said with a wink. He looked at Lysander to see if he'd have a reaction. Lysander was an oak. "Doesn't speak English? Figured as much. The hair was a dead giveaway that he's not American."

"Where's he from? The Netherlands? Germany?" Hollister asked.

In perfect German, Lysander said, "Are you going to spend the night conversing with children? Or can we go and investigate how a demon infiltrated your walled city?"

"Told ya," Hollister said and bumped fists with his friend.

"Good night," Cerise said to the boys, whose smiles slipped a bit. To their credit, they didn't stall. They simply nodded and shuffled away.

"Terrific," Cerise murmured when they were out of earshot. "By morning the whole Etherlin will be abuzz with the fact that Cerise Xenakis was making out behind a building with some long-haired giant dressed in a stolen coat."

He glanced down at the sleeves that stopped several inches shy of his wrists and he strained against the fabric, which tried to constrict the movement of his shoulders and back. "It's too small, but that doesn't automatically make it stolen. Richard would certainly have loaned it to me if I'd had the opportunity to ask him for it."

"Well, it's certainly yours now that you've ripped the seams of the right shoulder."

He smiled. "You felt that? You don't miss much. Another admirable quality."

They crossed the street.

"My hair makes me look foreign?"

"Usually it makes you look disheveled."

"You dislike it?" he asked. "It has grown wild. I don't pay attention, but I do cut it when I can't pull a comb through it after a fight."

"You cut it yourself?"

He nodded.

"That explains a lot. Like the fact that it's uneven. What do you use on it? A weed-whacker?"

"You can cut it when we return to Richard's."

"*I* can? I'm a muse, not a hairdresser. What makes you think I can cut hair?"

"Faith." Then he grinned and shrugged. "It's only hair."

Her smile echoed his. "Maybe I'll buzz it all off."

"As you like," he said.

She quirked a brow, but the fact that he offered to let her do whatever she wanted was charming. "You don't go to a hairdresser because you avoid people?"

He nodded.

"You do realize that I'm a world-famous muse who never met a crowd she didn't like?"

"Then being with me will be an interesting change for you."

"Likewise," she said with a laugh. "I don't intend to go into hiding."

"Archangels don't hide."

"Well, whatever you call your life of solitude. It's not how I live," she said, her voice full of challenge.

He glanced at her and paused before answering. "I can suffer a crowd for you, Cerise, if you need them."

Her muscles relaxed. She couldn't imagine that he compromised much in his life. "Thanks."

"Here," Lysander said as they rounded another corner. Her heart nearly stopped. Lysander walked to the doorway where she and Hayden had done CPR on Jersey.

Griffin's apartment building.

"What are we doing here?" she asked, her voice tight with emotion.

"The artwork I want to show you is on this roof." He tried the door handle, which was locked. He raised his elbow, poised to break in.

"It's not necessary to bust the lock. I have a key."

"Why?" he asked. "This isn't where you live."

She didn't bother to ask how he knew that. "I used to stay here a lot."

"Why?"

Raw emotions threatened to engulf her, making questions unwelcome, but he'd been willing to tell her about his past, so she felt obliged to reciprocate. "This is where Griffin lived."

Lysander glanced up at the building, frowning. "I won't ask you to go inside if it would be painful for you."

She closed her eyes and ran a hand through her waves, pushing them back so she could feel the cool air on her face. She inhaled deeply and blew out the breath, her lids rising slowly.

"He died almost a year ago. It's been long enough." She swallowed and stole a glance at Lysander.

He didn't move or encourage her; he simply waited with the patience of someone who'd lived lifetimes. His consideration of her feelings made it hard to believe that he was a ruthless nearly damned creature. It might have been an act, but the sweetness rang true. It struck a metaphysical chord in her muse sense and the power lit through her, stronger than it had been in so many months. It felt amazing.

After a moment, she realized that Lysander was still waiting for her to open the door. She glanced around, then extracted her keys and stepped forward. Forcing the key into the hole, she clenched it and her jaw, bracing herself for the memories.

Lysander's hand, heavy and reassuring, rested on her left shoulder and his right hand slid along her forearm and closed around her fist.

"I've got it," she said.

"I know," he said, but the hand on her shoulder kneaded the knotted muscles. She exhaled, resisting the urge to lean back against him. It would be easy to do, but she didn't.

They turned the knob together and pushed the door open. Entering, she smelled the familiar amber and vanilla scent. She raised the lights and glanced around the lobby. Rose paint, honey-colored wood, and a large stone fireplace. The plush seating arrangements conjured memories of nights when she and Griffin and the band had come back from a gig or a club, shared a bottle of wine or something stronger, and Hayden played acoustic guitar until dawn. She could almost see the others: Griffin next to her on the couch across from the fireplace, his long fingers tapping the cushion and surreptitiously trailing across the back of her neck. She shivered.

"Your mother's been away for quite a while?"

She blinked and turned her head to look at Lysander. "What?"

"It seems that your mother's been away for a long time. Why is that?" he asked, ushering her to the elevator.

She realized that he was trying to distract her from her memories of Griffin. It was a strange change of topic. "She has. She's making a statement."

"What statement?" he asked.

"Why do you ask about her?"

"The music center where I found Griffin's songbook is named for her, isn't it? I overheard someone talking about how hard she worked to see it completed after the first builder embezzled the funds."

"Yes. The council didn't want to fund its completion, and she had to fight to see it done."

"It's a wonderful place. Worth the fight."

"The muses founded the Etherlin as a place for them to pool their power and use it to the maximal effect. Over the years, they became more and more focused on using their gifts and let others take control of their money, their schedules, the running of the community. It started out well because the muses couldn't do everything themselves, but later several of them came to regret how things evolved. My mom is dead set against the council selecting which muse gets the Wreath. She feels that decision should be left for the most powerful muses to decide, even though it's created conflict in the past. She thinks it's our responsibility to choose a leader and to settle our differences. She left in protest of the competition the council puts us through. The council felt it was the most fair and systematic approach to choosing the Wreath Muse, and they fought to keep control. It's a big source of conflict between my parents—my mother the dissenting muse, my father the Etherlin Council president."

"Whose side do you take in the debate?"

"Hers. Because she's right. And for . . . other reasons." She scowled. Another bleak topic.

Lysander raised his brows in question.

"My dad and I don't have the best relationship."

"Why not?"

She sighed. "Because when I was growing up, he always made me feel like I wasn't enough."

"Enough what?"

She shook her head, dismissing the topic. "I thought you changed the subject to make me feel better."

"I did."

"Thank you. Try again."

He glanced around the lobby as if it would offer a subject for conversation. When it didn't, he beckoned her onto the elevator. She almost pressed the button for Griffin's floor, but Lysander reached over and pressed the button for the top floor. She leaned back against the wall, looking at the ceiling.

"Who do you think has been the most important influence on modern music?" he asked.

"On rock and roll? Probably Led Zeppelin."

"Your reasons for choosing them?" he asked, ushering them into a discussion on the history of music. He was well versed and mentioned several artists whose influences weren't widely recognized.

The elevator doors opened and they stepped out onto the roof, but she stopped and stared at him in wonder as he continued. He confessed that he'd haunted the recesses of Tin Pan Alley during the twenties, set himself in the path of a gangster outside the Cotton Club to keep intended violence from becoming dangerous to Duke Ellington and his band, and how he'd opened a door on an Indiana college campus so jazzman Hoagy Carmichael, who was drunk and wandering home when seized by a tune he was afraid wouldn't survive the night unless he played it, could have access to a piano on which to compose. Carmichael wrote "Stardust," which would establish him as a songwriter.

"You protected the American blues and jazz movement."

He shrugged. "It was an important moment in the evolution of music. I was enjoying it and didn't want anything to interfere with their progress."

She fired off a slew of questions to suck the memories from him. She peppered in her own anecdotes, and they realized that they'd both been in the stadium when the Rolling Stones played Wembley in 2003. Him up above, away from people. Her backstage. They talked about Robert Johnson, Duke Ellington, Eminem, Nirvana, and Mary J. Blige. He told her about the greatest concerts he'd crashed through the ages.

"Nothing compares to the view from heaven, but being earthbound has had its sublime moments."

She beamed at him as they crossed the roof, feeling buzzed from being able to connect with him so deeply over music.

"Lysander," she said, catching his arm.

He paused.

She fisted his sweater and pulled him to her. She pressed

her lips to his and kissed him soundly, feeling his body respond. She gave his lower lip, which had already healed from the last time she'd bit him, a gentle tug with her teeth. His hand tightened on her hip.

"You're a decent distraction. Not much else ever has been, so thank you," she said and attempted to back away. His hands held fast to her hips.

"I guess I'm a pretty decent distraction, too," she said with a smile. "We're up here for a reason, remember?"

"The ledge isn't going anywhere. If you want to divert my attention some more, do your worst."

"No, not right now. It's my turn to shove you against a brick wall, but there isn't one around."

The corners of his mouth quirked up, and he let her step away. "Something for me to look forward to then."

"As you like," she said, echoing him again. "Show me the artwork."

He turned and walked across the roof. She strode with him and heard the low curse he muttered. He darted to the ledge and dropped to a knee. As she joined him, she could see the tar-black paint dripping down the sides of the ledge like blood. He pressed his fingertips to the paint and lifted them. It was still wet.

She looked around at the empty roof. They must have just missed whoever had painted over the images. She shook her head.

A scent wafted through the air. Soot and something spicy. Her head turned toward it and so did his. She walked along the edge, and the scent became stronger. She bent. There was a broken glass vial, like the kind used for perfume samples. She touched the black liquid and, for a moment, she was somewhere else, standing on the bank of a black river, steam and sulfur rising, flames licking her heels. A rush of heat swallowed her. Then she was in the rented house where she'd spent the final weekend with Griffin. She saw a wineglass on the bureau and her hand on the glass. She felt breath against her neck. "Drink up. It goes down like nectar." The liquid was smooth then icy cold as it washed down her throat, coated her insides. There was a strange aftertaste and she felt dizzy. Really dizzy and scared. She couldn't breathe. Flashes of memory like a strobe light. Struggling to get away. Someone behind her, hands on her throat. A harsh voice, not Griffin's. Her heart slam-dancing in her chest, the air too scarce, her body heavy, lids that wouldn't open. Struggling and struggling. Too weakly.

Stop! Let go!

Please stop . . .

The world went as black as the tar-colored paint.

Chapter 14

"Cerise?"

She swam toward consciousness. "What the hell?" she groaned, jerking to an upright position from where she'd been lying with her head on Lysander's lap.

"All right now?" he asked.

"I—Did I faint?"

He nodded.

"Bullshit," she snapped, more at herself than him. "I don't faint. I've never fainted in my life." Her hands went to her head, and she touched it experimentally. "You caught me?"

"Of course. You almost stumbled over the ledge. I said your name, but you didn't seem to hear me. The look on your face . . . what did you see before you passed out?"

"Memories from the night Griffin died—a lot of hours are just gone . . . or I thought they were." She looked at Lysander. "There was someone in the house that night. I don't know what happened—what was done to me." She shuddered, and dread and fear gave way quickly to fury. She slammed her fist against her thigh. "Damn it! I have to remember. It's there—" She raised her fist to strike again, but he grabbed her wrist and held it.

"No."

"I feel—I just want to hit something."

"Hit me."

Her eyes widened.

"You can't hurt me, and if you did, I'd heal in under an hour. Your flesh takes longer to recover; have a care with it," he said gently.

She shook her head. "You're the last person I want to hit right now." She tugged on her arm and he released it.

"What did you see?"

"I don't want to talk about it. Let's go. Let's get off this roof. It reeks of paint and worse." She shot to her feet and marched across the concrete.

"What do you smell?" he asked, keeping pace as she hurried to the stairwell door.

"I'm not sure."

"Describe it."

She jogged down the stairs with him close at hand. Entering the top floor hallway, she strode to the elevator and jabbed the call button. Lysander grabbed her arms and whirled her to face him.

"What did you smell? Tell me," he said.

"I don't know. Soot. Spices. Something sulfurous, like spoiled eggs."

"Yes. Have you smelled it before?"

"I don't know."

"Concentrate."

The elevator dinged, and the doors slid open. She tried to turn, but he held her arms and shook his head.

"Not yet. Think back," he said.

"I don't want to think! Not now. Not with you right on top of me. I want to be alone with it." She tried to jerk free, but he held on. "All right!" she said, and he let her go. "Yeah, it seemed familiar. It triggered a memory just like Griffin's journal did at Merrick's. I think—I think someone slipped something into my wine that night. But if I remember that, I must have seen him do it, so then why would I have drunk it? I don't do drugs. I never have. I'm beginning to think that whatever was in that drink is the reason I can't remember what happened. And maybe why I couldn't defend myself if someone attacked me."

"Who attacked you?"

She shook her head. "I don't know. The memories are all jumbled. I need to figure out a way to sort them out. I need to look at Griffin's songbook somewhere safe—maybe on a bed where I can't hurt myself if I fall. I need to do a guided mediation using my magic or something," she murmured, thinking out loud. She turned to him. "Let's get the book."

"It's out of reach."

She opened her mouth to snap at him, but he cut her off.

"I put it in my house before I went to fight the demons, but I can't get to my house until my wings heal."

She scowled at him.

"Tell me everything you remember about your last few days with the musician."

"No."

"This is my fight. I won't be dealt out of it," he said.

"It's not your fight! It happened months ago. Long before I met you."

"Yes, but you're mine, and any trouble that's yours belongs to me, too."

She shook her head sharply, but he continued, "Yes, Cerise. That scent on the roof was from the ash of a slain demon mixed with fresh blood. You might have smelled it tonight because we're bonded, but then any memories that were triggered should've been mine. Instead you say it uncovered your own missing memories. Are you sure?"

Her mind reeled. "Yeah, I think—yes, I recognized the house. The one Griffin and I rented. And when I looked down in the vision I saw my body, my hands. Are you saying a demon broke in that night?"

"Did the smell trigger the memories?"

"When I touched the blackness from the vial that's what triggered it."

He frowned. "Why would you have been a target before we even met? Had you ever taken part in a black magic ritual? Tried to call dead spirits or a demon?"

"Of course not!"

"Then someone else marked you somehow. And whoever that is has been serving the demon for months." His narrowed eyes looked out the window and scanned the horizon. "What is he doing?" he murmured. "And how is it being done? No demon can enter the world without me sensing it. I feel it instantly."

"Maybe there are some demons that you can't feel?"

He shook his head. "Even the lowest-ranking demons make my senses scream. That ash you smelled came from one of the most powerful demons in hell. It came from *him*. From Reziel."

"He's here?"

"No, but someone uncovered his ashes. It's been a very long time since he was flesh. No one could've found traces of his ashes without being guided to them. Reziel's in close contact with a human being. The thing I don't understand is if someone has his ashes and if Reziel can instruct them so clearly, why haven't they done a ritual to raise him by now?"

Of course he didn't expect an answer from her, which worked out since she didn't have one.

"When your wings heal, you'll show me the songbook, right? You wouldn't let me look at it before because you worried it would draw demons to me, but that's moot now, isn't it? Being tied to you makes me a target?"

"It does."

"So we'll look at the book together. Maybe there's something in it that will give us a clue as to how Griffin and I came into contact with Reziel's representative."

He nodded.

"Can't we get to it some other way than by flying? There's no road access?"

"None."

"Helicopter?"

"It's on the shear face of a mountain. There's nowhere for a helicopter to land."

She rolled her eyes in frustration. "So if you'd lost your wings, you could never have gone home again?"

"If I'd lost my wings, losing my earthly possessions would've been the least of my concerns."

She sighed. "Let's go to Griffin's apartment. I doubt we'll find any evidence of the demon there since we're in the Etherlin, but it's worth a try."

"And if there's blank paper, I can try to recreate the artwork from the ledge. Especially the end where there was a symbol that might have been the artist's signature."

They stepped into the elevator and descended. Emerging on Griffin's floor, the bland hall with its uninterrupted beige soothed Cerise. When she'd spent a lot of time in the building, she'd been annoyed by the dull halls, but at the moment even an explosion of color would've been an assault on her frayed nerves.

She braced herself at the door. The apartment had been Griffin's, but so much of how it looked could be attributed to the purchases she'd made. Andy Warhol prints, the lotus blossom wall tattoo, the funky blown-glass chandelier, and the cranberry velvet chaise longue were all her choices.

When the door opened though, she wasn't assaulted by a barrage of memories. The thing that hit her immediately was the smell of food. Her brows rose, and she strode into the apartment.

Propped against a mountain of pillows and wrapped in a blanket on the chaise, Jersey Lane looked like a ghostly little doll.

"Hey," Cerise said with a smile. "Hayden's last text said they weren't letting you go till tomorrow."

"I'm okay, so they let me go this afternoon," Jersey said with a crystal clear voice as lovely as the best-tuned instrument. Then Jersey's eyes widened and she sucked in a gasp, pressing back into the pillows like she wanted to disappear through them.

Cerise glanced over her shoulder at Lysander, who wasn't doing anything more menacing than being seven feet tall.

"It's okay, Jerz, this—"

"It's him. He's the angel I saw when I died."

"The what?" Dorie asked.

Cerise whipped her head toward the kitchen, and her heart sank at the sight of her younger sister coming out with a bowl of soup.

"What are you doing here?" Cerise demanded.

Dorie's full attention was glued to Lysander. "I called Hayden to check on how Jersey was doing. He needed someone to stay with her."

He should've asked me, Cerise thought furiously.

"I wasn't busy, so I came and made with the pillow-fluffing and soup-making. Cream of broccoli with yummy garlic croutons," Dorie rambled. "Who's this, Cer?" she asked, never taking her eyes off Lysander.

"He's a friend," Cerise said. "And now that we're here, you can take off."

Dorie set the soup on a tray next to the chaise and then put the tray on Jersey's lap. "Eat up." Dorie circled the chaise and walked straight to Lysander, thrusting out her hand.

"I'm Dorie Xenakis. I'm a muse, too."

Lysander folded his arms across his massive chest and gave her a look that could've blistered the paint from the walls. Dorie took a step back. "Do you speak English?"

He continued to stare at her with an expression so filled with fury that it raised the hair on the back of Cerise's neck. She crossed the space to her sister in three long strides and grabbed Dorie's arm.

"You need to go," Cerise said.

"What's going on?" Dorie snapped as Cerise propelled her toward the door.

"Just go. I'll call you later."

Dorie's furious expression rivaled Lysander's. "You'd better call me in like ten minutes."

"Or what?" Cerise said.

"Or I'm calling Etherlin Security. They'll get right to the bottom of who he is and what he's doing here."

"Are you threatening me?"

"Not you," Dorie said, clucking her tongue and tossing a glare back at Lysander. "If he's so dangerous that you have to run me out of the apartment, he doesn't belong in the Etherlin or anywhere near a muse."

"Just stay out of it."

"No, I won't. We've already lost Alissa to that bloodsucker, Merrick. I'm—"

Cerise sucked in a breath.

"What?" Dorie asked, eyes narrowing. Her gaze darted back to Lysander, and she whispered in a hiss, "Don't even tell me he's one of them! Some friend of Merrick's who's managed to sneak in. What are you doing with him? Why haven't you called ES already?"

"I'll talk to you about it later. Do *not* call ES or anyone else."

Cerise yanked the door open and walked out with Dorie.

"Cer, wait! I'm not just going to—"

"I'm not Alissa," Cerise said, her voice low. "If you cross me, I won't forgive you. Not ever."

Dorie blinked. "Listen—"

"No, that's all there is to say," Cerise said, stalking back into the apartment. Once inside, she closed the door and locked it. She scowled at Lysander. "Congratulations. We have no time."

"She tried to get Merrick killed by falsely accusing him of attacking her. She's not a demon, but she might as well be."

"Merrick's ventala and a killer for hire. Dorie shouldn't have lied, but she did think she was protecting this community."

"Merrick kills things that need killing. And what's between him and Alissa is not your sister's business."

"Things aren't exactly that simple. Ventala have raped and murdered muses in the past. That's why there's a wall to keep them out."

"*Vampires* raped and murdered one muse."

"Are you claiming ventala aren't dangerous?"

"I'm saying Merrick wasn't a threat when he infiltrated your retreat center. And anyone who tries to kill him is my enemy."

Cerise put out a hand. "There's no point discussing this now. I have to get you out of the Etherlin."

Lysander seemed to contemplate her words as he glanced around the apartment, but when he spoke again, it was on a very different topic. "Now that the soup's cool, do you know what I smell?" he asked, looking at Cerise. "Paint."

She swiveled her gaze from Lysander to Jersey, who was sitting silently against the mound of cushions. "Jersey, did you go up to the roof and paint over a mural on the ledge?"

"No," Jersey stammered as Lysander stalked to the balcony and yanked open the door. He held up a paint can with telltale black smeared on its rim. "I didn't do the painting. Hayden did, because I asked him to."

"Why?" Cerise and Lysander asked at the same time.

Jersey bit her lip. "You'll be pissed."

Lysander moved toward Jersey, but Cerise waved him back and sat on the edge of the chaise. "It's really important, and we don't have much time. I'll only be pissed if you don't tell me everything right now."

Jersey swallowed and stole a nervous glance at Lysander.

"Hey," Cerise whispered. "It's me. No one is going to hurt you. Just tell me."

"I was supposed to—I just wanted to be numb for a while. Life's been so screwed up; I needed to forget about everything. Just for a little while," Jersey whispered to her soup. Cerise moved the tray and sat closer, taking Jersey's hands in hers.

Cerise infused her voice with persuasive power and felt a surge of triumph when the magic coursed through her as she said, "You're not afraid. You know that no one will be upset with you. You want to tell me everything."

Jersey's lids drifted to half closed. "I called Griffin's dealer."

What the hell? Griffin had a dealer? Cerise's pulse quickened. Griffin told her he'd tried a few recreational drugs, but that he'd never used regularly. While they were together, he'd sworn he wasn't taking anything except his prescribed Klonopin. She'd asked about it because of his mood swings, but she'd never come across any paraphernalia in the apartment . . . And he'd sworn up and down.

He swore on his music.

Had he been an addict and too afraid or ashamed to confide in her?

"Was he using while we were together?" Cerise asked.

"I don't know," Jersey said, but Cerise heard the hesitation in Jersey's voice. She knew. She just didn't want to trash Griffin's memory.

"So what happened when you went to meet the dealer?" Cerise asked, trying to keep the anger from leaking into her voice.

"When I went to meet him, *she* was there. That scary ventala woman with the short black hair. And she said—she said Griffin owed her money. She'd only let me buy if I did something for her. I said I'd made a mistake. I told her to forget it, and I tried to go, but she wouldn't let me." Tears welled in Jersey's eyes. "They held my arm and shot me up, made me drink something."

Assholes! Don't tell me some of the ventala aren't dangerous fucking criminals! And who's the black-haired ventala woman? Tamberi Jacobi? The daughter of the syndicate leader? She's rumored to be more predatory than any animal on earth.

Cerise held tight to Jersey's hands.

"I don't remember how I got back here," Jersey continued. "I just remember the roof. There were a thousand whispers in my head. I had a vial clutched in my pocket, and I was supposed to break it over the blackbird. I climbed onto the ledge and walked along. I saw the painted blackbird, but I didn't want to do what she said. I felt like I hated her and hated the whispering voices. I didn't want to help them. So I just stood there, feeling dizzy and tired and sick. Then I lost my balance," she cried. "Lost my balance and fell. I couldn't breathe, and then I saw these facets of light, like I was looking through a diamond. He had giant wings. He caught me and a bunch of blond hair hung down around his face and mine like a cloak. I heard a low voice, not vicious like the whispers, just peaceful. I felt myself dying, but I wasn't too scared because the angel was holding me, and I remember thinking that I'd finally get to see Griffin again. Even when my heart stopped, the angel stayed with me so I wasn't afraid." Tears trickled down her cheeks. Jersey stared at Lysander. "Thanks."

He nodded, and Cerise had to blink away her own tears and swallow against a throat so tight it burned like a thousand flames. If she'd had any doubts left regarding Lysander, they evaporated in that moment. No demon would've hovered over a dying girl to ease her fear. Lysander might be fallen, but there was still goodness in him.

"I told Hayden about the vial. I thought maybe I'd dropped it on the roof. He went up there and smashed it on the ground, not near the picture of the bird. I don't know who painted that ledge or why, but I know it's bad. I didn't think we should leave it, which is what I told Hayden. He got the glossy black paint you guys used on the trim in the teal bedroom and went up to the roof and painted over the picture."

Cerise nodded. "You guys were probably right to do that, but I needed to see it. Are you sure you don't know who painted it? Could Griffin have done it?"

"No way. Griffin couldn't draw like that."

"Have you ever seen artwork that looks like it?"

"I think the painting on the fourteenth floor looks kind of like it. When you get off the elevator you turn right and go to the end of the hall and around the corner. There's a big mural."

"The top floor. Right under the roof," Cerise said, exchanging a look with Lysander. Cerise leaned forward and pressed a kiss to Jersey's forehead. Infusing her voice with power, she said, "Rest now."

Merrick has definitely gone soft, Tamberi thought, sitting at her desk whose top was made of recycled cut-glass windows and whose wood was stained with varnish infused with blood, à la *The Red Violin.*

By now Merrick had certainly heard that she'd been telling everyone that he'd killed her father. He should've offered a swift denial and attempted to put a bullet in her brain by now, but there'd been only silence from his patch of the Varden.

She'd heard it had taken him all night to mop up the casualties and hunker down. *Let's see how he manages a battering again tonight,* she thought. With Merrick there could be no middle ground even if she'd wanted that, which she didn't. She wanted him headless, heartless, and permanently dead.

She'd heard that Cerise Xenakis had gotten back to the Etherlin by chopper. That pissed Tamberi off, but she had to keep the big picture in mind. Taking Merrick out and working with Reziel would be game-changers. She wouldn't let temporary setbacks distract her.

She looked over the maps again. She really wanted to blow up Merrick's building and reduce it to rubble, but getting someone inside would be tough. The word was that the place was completely locked down, and there were rumors that he had an underground bunker with a separate exit. Of course that might be bullshit. Everyone gave him too much credit. No one could plan that far in advance. If he had, why would he have set up house in his apartment with his muse girlfriend and her derelict father? He could've taken them anywhere in the world. Only a moron would've sat around waiting for Tamberi to come for revenge. Unless Merrick hadn't been worried. Unless he'd believed his own press and considered himself invincible. He wasn't. No one was. And she was just the bitch to prove it.

When her phone rang, she answered by demanding, "What?"

"It's Lane week."

She licked her lips. "The little girl's back for more?"

"No, the brother. Hayden Lane would like to know how much money his brother owed you."

Tamberi laughed. "Tell him fifteen grand."

"Shit, that guy was into you for fifteen grand worth of smack when he died? No wonder you were pissed when they found his body." *Griffin Lane didn't owe me a fucking cent when he died or I'd have gotten paid long before now.*

"Tell the kid he has to deliver it in person."

"Will do."

Tamberi replaced the receiver. There now. Things were getting easier all the time.

Chapter 15

Cerise boarded the elevator with Lysander, but her mind wasn't on the mural they were going to examine. Her racing pulse was driven by the muse magic that still flowed through her. Her power was definitely getting stronger. She subdued her smile, but couldn't keep the rush of excitement from her step.

There were two elements to muse magic. The first was the power to inspire, which was the most important skill, the one they all tried to cultivate and hone. The other was the power to influence people outside the realm of creativity. All of Cerise's magic had been extinguished by Griffin's death, but since the night in the retreat, she'd felt her power of persuasion returning. It hadn't been strong enough to be of consequence until she used it on herself after Lysander left her alone and burning for him.

Her magic was being slowly restored to her, and the catalyst for its restoration seemed to be contact with a seven-foot angel with stormy green eyes and a mane of tangled gold hair.

"Lysander, is it possible that when I came into contact with Reziel's follower, he or she did something to impair my memory?" *And my muse abilities?*

"When a human being comes into contact with an angel or demon, their memory is affected. People are not supposed to have access to the other side until their lives are over. We're part of that other side, so we can influence what's recalled. And heaven can influence it. For example, the rituals for raising a demon fade from memory. They have to be written down and carefully preserved. Even the ink or blood that those spells are written in degrades faster than it would normally. Hell-bound demons must work extremely hard to raise themselves to conscious thought in a human mind. They do it with one goal in mind. To be brought forth in the flesh."

"What happens when they become flesh?"

"They can do whatever a human being can do and more. Many of them have wings and the knowledge of ages behind them."

"Could they interfere with a witch's magic? Steal it or suppress it?"

"If the witch raised the demon, then yes. Entering into a pact with a demon strips a person of heaven's protection. Any supernatural power, any divine gift, including the soul, is forfeit and the demon can claim it at will."

"What if one met a demon and didn't know what it was? If a person helped a demon unknowingly and without breaking any divine law, would that still make them vulnerable?"

Lysander shrugged. "I'm not sure. To forfeit the soul, a pact must be entered into knowingly. The law is absolutely clear on that point. But whether someone's supernatural abilities could be hijacked without some kind of compact . . . I can't say I know. There are so few people with true supernatural gifts that I don't imagine it comes up very often. I'm not a demon nor was I in heaven when the laws that apply to demons were laid down, so I don't know all the restrictions that bind them." As they exited the elevator, he added, "How long have your abilities been gone?"

Obviously her questions had been too thinly veiled, but there was no one in a better position to provide her with information than Lysander. As far as most of the muse scholars were concerned the only way to amplify a muse's magic was to commune with other muses or to wear the Muse Wreath. Neither thing had helped where her missing magic had been concerned. "My power isn't gone," she said.

"But you've had trouble using or controlling it?"

"For a time I did."

"When?"

Until I met you. "It's not important," she said.

He caught her arm and stopped her progress toward the mural. "It could be. We're trying to discern with whom Reziel has made contact. If the person who's helping him impaired your ability to inspire your aspirants, maybe we can pinpoint when you met him and who he is."

"Maybe he wasn't someone we knew. Maybe he just broke into the house Griffin and I rented."

"You remember that? You remember a burglar?"

She held out a hand. "As I said, my memory of that night is very vague, but I get flashes of terrible memories. Something was done to us . . ." She trailed off as she resumed walking.

"When I saw Griffin's tracks in the snow, I had this strong feeling that he'd been running from someone, but there were no other footprints. What if it was Reziel in the flesh? With his wings, Reziel could've flown through the woods without ever touching the snow and chased Griffin right off that cliff." She stiffened as a feeling of dread coursed through her.

"It's possible. I've battled most of the demons who've risen, but there's another archangel of the flesh who could have vanquished a risen demon before I got to it. It's more likely that there was no demon, and the musician fled the house to escape Reziel's human follower."

Cerise rubbed her hands together to warm them. "Even a person under demonic influence must be monstrous. Griffin must have been terrified."

"He was a coward."

"Hold on—"

"By running, the musician abandoned you. The malignant force could have returned to the house where you were alone and incapacitated. If he loved you, he should never have left you."

"Griffin's not you, Lysander. He wouldn't have stood a chance against a demon."

"Whether he could've won is not the issue."

"We don't know what happened. Maybe he left to draw the danger away from me. Unless I can remember more of that night, there's no way of knowing. And why don't you ever use Griffin's name?"

Lysander's jaw tightened.

"Lysander?"

"I don't respect him."

"God didn't give men the courage of lions, Lysander. You can't expect everyone to stand and fight. Especially in the face of something really terrifying, like a demon."

"Would you have run? Would you have left your lover to face a demon alone?"

"I have no idea what I would have done."

"Yes you do, and so do I. You wouldn't have deserted him or anyone you cared for. You would have stayed and died if necessary. He wasn't worthy of you," Lysander said with such contempt it made her wince.

"Don't say that. Don't attack him when he's not here to defend himself. I think Griffin might have left the house because of something I did or said that night. We had a fight. Maybe I kicked him out, and some kind of evil was lying in wait. Maybe it's my fault."

"Maybe he deserved what he got."

"Lysander!" She stopped walking and scowled at him.

Lysander stopped, too, and she noticed his hands were balled, like he wanted to put a massive fist right through something or someone.

Clenching his jaws hard enough for her to see his muscles working, Lysander stood rigidly still. Then after a deep breath and a moment of silence, the tension seemed to ease and his hands opened.

"There's perhaps another reason that I despise the mu—that I despise Griffin Lane. As I mentioned when I told the story of how we fell, archangels aren't immune to jealousy."

She cocked her head.

"The closer you and I become, the less I like hearing about your feelings for him."

Because he looked sweetly dejected, Cerise stepped forward and put her arms around him. She grazed his cheek with her lips, hugging him.

"It's all right for you to have a little humanity in you. If you didn't, I don't think I'd be able to relate to you. Or that you'd be able to relate to me."

His arms snaked around her, creating a fierce embrace. Being pressed against his rock-hard body, which smelled so delicious, made things low in her body tighten. She felt her resolve cracking. It wasn't just Lysander's beauty and strength that drew her. They shared the same philosophy about love and friendship and loyalty, the same feelings about music and dance and who knew what else? At moments, she felt like her soul was a lock to which Lysander might hold the ultimate key, and all he needed to do was to slip it inside and turn it to open everything she was. She didn't know whether that strange impression came from them being bound by his blood or if they really were just that well suited to each other. No matter the reason, it scared the hell out of Cerise.

You could back away . . .

She didn't move.

Or not.

Moments ticked by, her body heat rising. She tightened her grip even as she murmured, "We should probably look at the mural."

His breath ruffled her hair in the most intriguing way, and her own breath caught. She wanted a kiss. And much, much more.

He brushed his lips over her temple. Blood pounded through her veins.

I want—

No! You can't have him right now. You're in a freaking hallway!

She sucked in a breath and twisted her upper body, struggling against his grip and against her own instincts.

"You were going to tell me what happened to your magic," he said, clearly stalling.

She smiled. So he was burning, too. Well, at least they were in lust together.

"Yeah, but I can walk and talk at the same time as you may have noticed."

He released her. She stepped back, tingling with unsatisfied cravings. She licked her lips and straightened her shirt, and all the while he watched her with an "I want to devour you" look that pleased her and made her wary.

"There's not much more to tell," she said, walking farther from him. "After Griffin died, my magic wasn't the same. At first, I thought it was grief, but that wasn't the problem. Even when I started to recover emotionally, my magic didn't."

He lengthened his stride and kept pace with her. "You said you've had a return of your powers though. Since when?"

She hesitated, flushing. He raised his brows in question.

"I'm not sure exactly when."

He cocked his head and looked faintly amused. "But you have an idea," he pressed.

"It seems to have started to really come back since we were alone in the apartment. Maybe when we danced."

"Or maybe when I made love to you?"

She shrugged.

His lips curved into a smile. "You're welcome," he murmured.

She rolled her eyes. "All right. If it is because of you, then I'm glad. And grateful."

He nodded and added smugly, "So my supernatural presence trumps whatever evil Reziel visited upon you. I'll remember to tell him that when I face him next. Right before I cut his throat and force him back into that sewer they call hell."

His mix of righteous fury and icy menace awed her. She couldn't take her eyes off him and paused without realizing it.

"Here, Cerise," Lysander said, striding the rest of the way down the hall. He stood in front of a brightly colored mural of writhing vines. It was a tree house in the middle of the rain forest. "This is the same style. And here," he said, nodding. He crouched down to the lower right corner. "This is the same symbol that was on the ledge mural. I think it's how the artist signs his work."

She studied the logo of intertwined letters, *I* and *R*. "Her work," Cerise said a little breathlessly, drowning in dread.

"You know it," Lysander said triumphantly, but his expression turned grim when he looked up at her face. "You know it," he repeated, his tone flat.

"I do. It's Ileana Rella's logo. Ileana's the fourth Etherlin muse, and she's a friend."

Tamberi licked Hayden Lane's blood from her lips. Waifishly pretty in a geek-boy way, Hayden hung by his arms, which were secured to the ceiling by a rope. His head lolled forward toward his bare chest. She gave his body a push and his toes skimmed across the fifteen thousand dollars scattered on the floor.

She was in the midst of running a sharp nail over his nipple to rouse him when an explosion rocked the floor. She spun and ran to the window.

The south warehouse, which had been her headquarters, was a ball of flames.

She screamed curses as she rushed to the phone. Another more distant explosion rocked the world again.

"What the fuck?" she yelled, grabbing her silk robe and flinging it on.

Merrick! That son-of-a-bitch. While my teams were mobilizing, he was already here planting bombs.

She tied the sash and shoved her feet into shoes, reaching for her loaded gun.

Thanks to her plan that had knocked out the Varden's cell towers, her own communications were limited. She swept out of her office and down the hall. There were snipers on all the rooftops surrounding the syndicate headquarters building, so she didn't have to worry about Merrick strolling in. Unless he'd disguised himself in some way. Would he expect her to be at syndicate headquarters? Probably not. She'd been running things from the warehouses. She was lucky she'd come in for a meeting and had decided to stay and play with Hayden.

She heard footsteps in the stairwell, and she pulled the door open. "What's going on?" she called, spotting a plump figure with fuzzy brown hair waddling down the stairs in pumps.

"Merrick's blown the tunnel and the south warehouse. He sent a message that he's wired two other syndicate buildings to blow," her father's secretary Sylvia said. "He's claiming that he didn't kill Victor and can prove it, but that if the syndicate prefers to be at war with him, he'll play."

"Motherfucker. I am going to cut off his fucking head," Tamberi said, tasting blood and ash on her breath. She licked her teeth.

"Why would he say that he can prove he didn't kill Victor? Merrick's too smart to believe that he can get away with a bluff."

"Of course, he's going to lie. He has to lie, Sil. He's fucking under siege. The syndicate just needs to keep gunning for him. The teams will take him out tonight."

"Haven't you heard? The east warehouse's team is dead. Merrick had dozens of snipers lying in wait. A group at Bella Cera and Scavolini took out the whole team."

A scream of pure rage wailed from Tamberi's lungs. That sneaky son-of-a-bitch!

An icy hand stroked her neck and she shivered. She swiped the air, trying to ignore Reziel's invisible presence.

"I'm leaving. This could be one of the buildings that's rigged to blow," Sylvia said. "And we'd all better hope Merrick's proof satisfies the syndicate because this isn't a war anybody should want."

"He has to die. Can't you see that? No single ventala can be allowed to become more powerful than the syndicate. He has to be put down. No matter what it takes."

Sylvia waved a disgusted hand and clattered down the next flight of stairs.

"They'll cave. They're such a bunch of pussies. I wish they were all dead."

She felt slush wash over her brain. "You're right," she said, exhaling. "This wasn't the main event." She grabbed her bangs in her fist and yanked, the pain helping to center her. "I can be patient. As long as you keep your promises, I'll keep mine."

She backed out of the stairwell and glanced around. Was it time to lie low for a few hours and regroup? Things were already in motion. Yeah, let Merrick finish his offensive and get tangled up with syndicate negotiations. And then she would strike again . . . with more force than anyone in the Varden had ever seen.

She strode back to her office, keeping a sharp eye for any signs of movement. She raised her gun as she reentered. Empty ropes hung from the ceiling. Had Hayden been playing possum?

Sneaky little fuck. Good for him.

She narrowed her eyes as she stalked around the room. She didn't find him crouched behind any large pieces of furniture or under her desk.

It didn't matter. Playtime was over anyway.

"Let's go, Lysander," Cerise said as her phone rang again. She'd turned the phone on so she could text Ileana, but hadn't gotten a response from the other muse. That wasn't unusual. Ileana wasn't as tied to her cell as the rest of the world. She often left it setting somewhere out of hearing distance for hours.

Cerise scrolled through her own text messages. She'd been getting them all day from the new ES director and from her dad, but she hadn't answered. Now both Dimitri and Dorie were calling her. Cerise let the calls go to voice mail, but could almost feel security officers being called together for a briefing about a fallen angel being discovered in the Etherlin.

She jabbed the down arrow on her phone and called her voice mail to listen to her dad's message. She pictured him, stout and powerful in a black suit, pacing holes in the living room carpet while he tried to reach her. He would not be happy.

"Cerise, your father here. I've just heard from Etherlin Security that explosions have destroyed the main tunnel and several buildings in the Varden. This is clearly a continuation of the gang war that erupted last night. We're locking down the Etherlin. I'm told that you haven't passed the checkpoints and are safely within the Etherlin. I need that confirmed. Call and let us know where you are."

Good girl, Dorie. Her sister hadn't called her dad or ES. At least not yet.

As Cerise and Lysander left the top floor, she sent a text to her dad.

Am okay and in the Etherlin. Am at Griffin Lane's apartment visiting his little sister who was sick last night. Sorry I missed your texts earlier. Battery was dead. Will call you later.

Then Cerise called Dorie.

"It's me," Cerise said. "You can come back and stay with Jersey."

"No, I can't. Dad wants me home. He wants you here, too."

"When Hayden asked you to stay with Jersey, did he say how long he'd be gone?"

"He thought a couple of hours. He should be back any time, but ES is locking down the Etherlin. If he doesn't get here soon, he won't be able to get inside. There are bombs going off in the Varden. I hope he didn't go there. He said he wasn't, but he seemed nervous about whatever he had to do."

"I'll text him about the lockdown."

"I already did."

"Did he text you back?"

"No, but ES said the cell towers are down in the Sliver. In the Varden, they're killing each other in the streets. Can you even imagine? They're like a bunch of wild animals. Thank God for the wall. And speaking of the fallen, what are you going to do about *him*? Is he gone yet?"

"He's leaving now."

"He'd better. When will you be home?"

"Soon. I have to go, but I'll call you back in a little bit." Cerise ended the call, powered the phone off, and turned to Lysander. "Things have gotten more complicated. Because of the unrest in the Varden, there will be a lot more Etherlin Security officers on patrol. We can walk to Ileana's house from here, but we need to do it without being seen, because if ES spots me, they'll insist on taking me home. My father's orders."

"You needn't worry. I won't allow them to take you anywhere."

She held up a hand. "I don't want there to be a confrontation. If we see any guards coming our way, we'll duck into the shadows."

"I'm an archangel, Cerise. I don't hide. As I told you, on the ground or in the air, if there's a fight, we hold our positions. We never run."

"You transported us away from the fight when the syndicate was attacking us."

"That wasn't my fight. They hadn't attacked me. If ventala had engaged me personally, I would have stayed to fight."

"But at the moment, you can't take to the air. So what happens if Etherlin Security spots you and tries to take you into custody?"

"I won't be taken."

"Meaning you'll fight and kill men who are just doing their jobs?"

"Angels are bound by instinct and by law to defend themselves. So yes, anyone who attacks me will have a deadly fight on his hands, be he human or demon."

"There won't be just one. There will be a lot of them."

"One man or a legion of men, it makes no difference to me."

If an entire army were marching toward him, would Lysander really stand his ground? She looked him over and decided he probably would. He was proud, unapologetic, and decidedly male.

He's right. He's like a lion.

She loathed that about him. And loved it.

His crazy mane of golden hair had come loose when the rubber band broke. It was somewhat fitting, but Cerise didn't want him to look quite so wild when she introduced him to Ileana. They needed information from her. "That hair," she murmured regretfully. "I wish I had time to cut it—"

He grabbed his hair in his fist and in a blindingly fast motion drew his razor-sharp dagger through it. Tousled waves fell to his shoulders, and he tossed the mass of cut hair aside. He sheathed his knife and ran his hands through his remaining hair. "Better?"

"Much." She glanced at the ground where a gust of wind blew the fallen strands, scattering them even as they became powdery gold. She bent to touch the glimmering dust that gilded the ground.

"Someone will wonder what this is," she said.

"No one will notice it. The earth and the air will absorb it in moments. Even if they did not, human beings would pass it by. The aspects of an angel are hard for them to see."

She looked up at him. "Is that why ES didn't see your dagger? When you were wounded, I took you into the house, but I forgot the dagger at first. The ES officers shined a light right on it but didn't seem to notice."

Lysander nodded.

"Could you become completely invisible to them?" she asked.

"Not while I'm flesh."

"Too bad. That would certainly make things easier."

Lysander couldn't fly, so if he entered into a conflict with ES officers, it wouldn't come to an end until someone had won. No matter who that was, she would lose. She walked to the door and looked out at the street. He didn't know the way to Ileana's so she could take whatever circuitous route she wanted, but there was no route that would ensure that they wouldn't come across a patrol. She needed his cooperation. "If you want to meet Ileana, you need to agree to take whatever route I choose to get to her house."

His mouth opened a fraction and then he closed it. "I agree to follow your route . . . within reason."

"Okay," she said, peering outside again.

"But if at any point you decide to dive into the bushes for cover, don't expect me to join you. I won't be," he said, sounding faintly amused.

She appraised him coolly, looking him up and down. Her gaze paused at his groin and then slowly rose to meet his eyes. "If you'd been willing to roll around in the bushes with me, I would've made it worth your while, but . . ." she trailed off with a shrug and turned back to the window.

She felt him at her back, his breath cool and sweet near her ear.

"If I had a purpose for lying in the grass, it couldn't be considered hiding."

She turned her head so she could see him out of the corner of her eye. His beautiful jaw was within reach of her tongue. It tempted her in the most maddening way.

"I'll tell you what," she whispered. "If we make it through the Etherlin without anyone seeing us, when we get back to Alissa's house and we're alone, you can shove me against any wall you want and do whatever you'd like. Within reason."

His voice was husky and rough and unapologetically male when he said, "Let's go."

Chapter 16

Cerise felt like a creature of the night herself. They strode through the shadows and wove through the trees. They didn't speak, didn't make much of a sound. Sure-footed and silent, she held his hand and gave it only the smallest press or tilt to indicate a change of direction. It was like dancing with him had been. Their bodies were very close as they moved, and yet there was no awkward bumping into each other, no tangling of feet. At moments, she felt as though she could close her eyes and walk blind, following only her instincts and the sway of their linked hands.

As the dark deepened, it tested the way they moved, but they never faltered.

Yeah, I'm the lock and he's the key.

Twice there were officers patrolling and three times there were civilians nearby, but she and Lysander weren't spotted even when a young couple passed within a few feet of them. Cerise leaned against a tree and pulled Lysander against her. Content to have their bodies pressed together, she and Lysander tasted each other's mouths while the couple walked on without their gaze ever being drawn to where a muse and an archangel silently kissed.

When they reached Ileana's, Cerise paused at the edge of the house. She glanced down to where their fingers were still intertwined, not ready to let go.

"You rival the air," he whispered.

She tilted her head. "What does that mean?" she whispered back.

He shook his head, hesitating. "To fly, to glide, to fall through clouds . . . To be surrounded by nothing but air, whether the whipping winter wind or the stillness of a hot summer night, it can almost feel like being in heaven. Just walking with you, the way you move beside me, as if you were gliding on the same slipstream . . . I didn't know it was possible for a woman to rival the air."

She smiled and stepped forward, putting her free hand on the back of his neck and drawing him down. She pressed her mouth to his in a soft kiss.

"Come on," she said. "The sooner we talk to Ileana, the sooner we'll be done talking to Ileana and can find a wall someplace private."

He flashed a smile as they strode to the door. She rang the bell and waited. There were lights on in the second story rooms facing the street, and within moments the foyer light blinked on as well.

When the door opened, however, it was Troy rather than Ileana Rella who stood in the doorway. Troy was effortlessly handsome in his black trousers, snakeskin belt, and burgundy knit shirt. His black hair gleamed like patent leather and was perfectly styled as always.

"Hey, Cerise," he said with an easy smile. Then his gaze settled on Lysander and the smile faded. "Who's this?"

"He's a friend. May we come in? I need to talk to Ileana about something."

"Actually, she's not here."

Cerise nearly began asking questions about where Ileana was, but didn't want to have the conversation while she and Lysander were standing on the stoop where any ES patrol that marched by could spot them.

"That's a shame. Can we come in anyway?" She didn't wait for a response. Instead, she opened the screen door and pressed forward.

Troy stepped back to let her inside, but his focus remained on Lysander.

"This is Lysander. Lysander, this is Troy Rella. Ileana's brother."

"Hello," Troy said, nodding at Lysander, then he returned his attention to Cerise. "Can I get you something to drink? Coffee? A glass of wine?"

Lysander closed the door gently behind them.

"No thanks," Cerise said, looking at Troy's hands. Could they have been the hands that had put something in her wine? After Alissa's warning and knowing that Troy had links to the Molly Times and to Ileana, both of which had encountered Reziel's subject on earth, she found herself scrutinizing him in a way she never had before. "If Ileana's out, why are you here?"

"I stopped by to water her plants."

Cerise's head tilted forward, a ball of unease forming in the pit of her stomach. Ileana rarely left the Etherlin. "Is she out of town?"

He nodded.

"Where is she?" Cerise asked, keeping her tone light.

Troy's dark eyes slid sideways to follow Lysander, who had walked to the living room coffee table to look at the books of architectural photo commemoratives featuring the work of Rella aspirants through the years.

"Who is he?" Troy whispered.

"He's a musician."

Troy narrowed his eyes. "He's more than that."

"Troy, where is Ileana?"

"She's with a new aspirant. Promising young guy she met at the architects' expo we sponsored in Denver a few months ago."

"Did you meet her new aspirant? What's he like?"

"He's talented and a pretty big flirt from what I gather. He's too young to be more than a fling, but they seem to be having a good time together," Troy said with a brief smile.

Lysander walked to the stone fireplace.

"Have I ever met him?" Cerise asked.

"Who? Ileana's new aspirant?"

She nodded.

"Why would you have? You don't travel in those circles."

She heard something in his voice that stiffened her spine. *He's lying.*

"Has he been to the Etherlin? Maybe stayed overnight at Ileana's building at Ionic and Temple Boulevard?"

Lysander moved the iron fireplace grate aside.

"I doubt it. I don't think she's even applied to get him clearance."

Lysander leaned down, stirring the ashes with a poker.

"What are you doing?" Troy asked. When Lysander didn't answer, Troy scowled. "Hey, Lysander is it? Do you mind?"

"Sorry. He's a little eccentric. Do you have a number for Ileana's new aspirant? I need to talk to her, and as usual she's not answering her texts," Cerise said with an indulgent smile.

Lysander straightened, setting the poker in the stand and moving the grate back to its original location.

"I don't have a number for him. You'll have to wait until she calls you back."

"It's important that I speak to her. I'll have ES contact her security detail with a message. It'll be easier to reach her that way. What's the aspirant's name by the way?"

"Listen I've got a lot to do tonight. I was just about to lock up. Why don't you take your strange friend and go?"

"Sure, of course."

Troy's shoulders dropped, relaxing.

"Before we go, I wonder if you and I could talk for a couple of minutes about the night that Griffin died."

Troy stiffened again. "Another time would be better for me. I've got some conference calls set up with the West Coast."

"Yeah, I'm not sure another night will work for me." She glanced at the clock. "How long until your conference calls? It's quarter after seven. We've got at least fifteen minutes?" she speculated. "Or forty-five?"

Troy's face hardened, but he nodded. "Listen, I don't like that guy, Cerise. I want him out of Ileana's house," he said in a low voice. "Ask him to wait outside and I'll be happy to sit down and have a conversation with you. I'll be in the kitchen brewing some coffee. Meet me there when you've dealt with him."

Troy stalked out of the room. Cerise crossed the living room to join Lysander, who was sifting through a bowl of spicy-scented potpourri.

"Smell any demon ash?" she whispered.

"Not so far. He didn't give you the name of the man the other muse is spending time with," he pointed out.

"I know. You're a distraction. Why don't you go upstairs

and look around? I'll make Troy think you're gone, then I'll use a little muse magic to persuade him to tell me the truth about Ileana's aspirant."

Lysander nodded, strolling to the stairs and padding up them silently.

She walked into the kitchen and found it unoccupied. She looked around, eyes narrowing, and strode to the door. She opened it and glanced into the small television room off the kitchen. Had Troy stepped out of the room? Or out of the house?

Cerise went to the back door and pulled it open. The lit walkway was empty, but hearing a car engine, she jogged outside and around the house in time to see Ileana's town car speed away.

"Oh, Troy, what the hell have you done?"

She yanked her phone out and powered it on. As soon as she had a signal, she called Troy's cell. He didn't pick up. She hadn't expected him to.

When the call went to voice mail she said, "Hey, Troy. Not sure what's up with you. Why don't you call me back when you get wherever you're bolting to? We have things to discuss, like the bad company you and Ileana may be keeping. And like what you were doing with Alissa when she and I were teenagers. Yeah, call me back. Or very soon I may not be the only one asking you questions."

She hung up, tucked the phone in her pocket, and hurried back into the house. Ascending the stairs, she called out for Lysander.

"Here, Cerise," he said.

Inside the enormous master bedroom, Lysander cut open a custom couch cushion. Stuffing erupted from the gaping slice as he tossed it aside and looked through the contents of a plastic packet he'd pulled from it. He dropped photographs and folded paper onto the carpet until he came to something that interested him. She moved next to him for a better look. He unfolded a sketch and raised it to his nose, inhaling, then frowned. Lowering the paper, he studied what appeared to be a charcoal sketch of a blackbird.

He ran a thumb tentatively over the sooty wings. "The dark smudges of the bird's eyes were done with demon ash. And the signature on the piece." He held it out to her.

She glanced at the letters in the corner, which were oddly geometric. She cocked her head, deciphering the name.

"John . . . Leizer. I don't know—"

"Leizer," he said. "Reziel spelled backward."

Frowning, she paused a moment, then murmured, "Oh Ileana." She had hidden the sketch. Did that mean she knew whom she was involved with? Cerise's mind rebelled against the thought. Surely not.

Cerise's eyes darted around the room and down to the pictures and papers scattered over the carpet. They could be clues to where Ileana had gone and who she was with.

Cerise crouched to gather them, but her phone rang. She pulled it out and looked at the display.

"Troy, the lying brother," she announced before she answered the call on speaker. "Hi, Troy."

"I can't believe you brought a member of the fallen into Ileana's house."

"I'd say a member of the fallen is the least of your worries. Ileana's had contact with much worse lately."

"What are you talking about?"

"Is her new aspirant named John Leizer?"

"I don't know. She kept his last name a secret even from me."

"She's in trouble, Troy. Really serious trouble. Where are they?"

"Ileana's fine. She has ES with her twenty-four-seven. And so will you soon enough. You can tell that fallen angel you're with that he'd better fly away while he's got the chance. On my way down the driveway I called the new ES director and warned him who you've got with you. Officers should be arriving any minute."

Cerise bolted to her feet. "You asshole."

"And as for that lying bitch Alissa, she's about as reliable as the fiction she inspires. Who do you think people are going to believe these days?"

"Tell me a couple of things, Troy: Did you slip something into my drink on the night Griffin died?"

"What? Of course not!"

"Did you introduce us to a demon?"

"Have you lost your mind?"

"Answer the question."

"Good-bye, Cerise."

"One more, did you seduce my little sister?"

His end of the line went silent.

"Troy?" When there was no answer, she nodded grimly and turned off her phone. "Yeah, you better run if you did those things, you bastard. If you did them, Merrick will have to get in line to kill you."

Lysander watched as she shoved the papers and photos into her purse.

"Ready to go?" she asked, hurrying from the room.

"Cerise, did you mention to him that I'm a fallen angel?"

"Of course not. He guessed."

Lysander nodded. "So then he's been knowingly affiliated with Reziel—either as his follower or as a contact of Reziel's representative here."

"How do you know?"

"Because he knew me for an angel," he said as they descended the stairs. "Most men couldn't reach that conclusion without me revealing it."

"Troy has his ear to the ground. He might have heard rumors that Merrick has a fallen angel friend named Lysander. I'm not saying he's not directly involved, but we can't jump to that conclusion yet."

"Let's go to his house. I liked your plan to use your magic to persuade him to tell us what he knows," he said as they crossed the kitchen.

"He won't go directly home," she said. "He'll avoid the places I'd expect him to go until he knows you're out of the Etherlin or that ES has you in custody. We need a place to wait things out," she said, striding out the back door. "Alissa and Richard's is only a block away." If they could reach it and kept the lights off once they were inside, they might be able to escape notice for a little longer . . . long enough for her to come up with some sort of plan that didn't involve a showdown between Lysander and ES.

She headed toward the lake where the woods would offer some sporadic cover, but suddenly flashlights were trained on them.

So much for avoiding a confrontation.

"Lysander," she said softly. "I'd really appreciate it if you didn't kill anyone."

He reached down for his knife.

She grabbed his arm. "Don't draw it yet. Just stay close to me. We're trying to avoid a confrontation."

He fingered the dagger's hilt. "I won't use it without cause."

That's what I'm afraid of.

A pair of ES officers—Pinter, who was young and solid with a mop of brown curls barely subdued with gel, and Rawlins, who was just over forty with hard edges and ruthless eyes—appeared on the path with their weapons drawn.

Cerise attempted to move in front of Lysander, but he said, "Absolutely not," and blocked her with his arm.

"Can you see me well enough to tell who I am?" she asked the officers.

"Step away from him, Ms. Xenakis," Rawlins said.

"No, you lower your weapons," Cerise said. "He's with me."

"We can't let him roam the Etherlin without clearance," Pinter said.

"I'm taking him to meet my father. Dimitri will arrange for his clearance," she said, though of course that was pretty unlikely.

"The director can contact EC President Xenakis and ask him to meet us at headquarters. I'm sure we can sort this out there," Pinter said, taking his handcuffs from his belt.

Cerise frowned. Going to headquarters would require Lysander to allow himself to be taken into custody.

"You know, maybe it's a better idea for Lysander and I to leave the Etherlin. I'll arrange for clearance before he comes inside again."

"We're on lockdown. It's not safe for you to leave right now," Rawlins said.

"Since I'm not a prisoner, I'll decide what's safest for me."

"Let's speak to your father and ask him to help sort the situation out," Rawlins said calmly. She was glad at least that the ES officers didn't seem trigger-happy or likely to lose their cool. She glanced at Lysander. His stance was casual, but lurking in his eyes was an unmistakable danger.

She turned on her phone. A series of message alerts sounded. She ignored them and called her home phone number.

Her father answered immediately.

"Hey, it's me. I'm outside Ileana's house with a friend, and

ES won't let us pass. I'd like to bring my friend to meet you. Can you call the director, and have him call off his officers?"

"Who's with you?" Dimitri asked sharply.

"A new guy I'm involved with. See for yourself. Let me bring him to the house to meet you."

"Stay where you are. I'll be right there." The connection died.

"Sublime," she murmured sarcastically. She glanced at the officers and added, "My father's on his way."

Several minutes passed, and she had to give the guys credit. All men of action, they managed to remain still and unruffled. She'd almost begun to relax as she scrolled through her text messages until she opened the one from Jersey.

Can u call me? Am worried about Hayden.

Cerise's brows crowded each other. "Jersey's brother Hayden is still gone," she murmured to Lysander. "I need to call her back and find out if she knows where he went." She sighed. "Why the hell did he have to go out in the middle of all this?"

"I could ask you the same question." Her father's voice was gruff, like the rest of him despite the polish of his expensive suits. Thick black brows brooded over his eyes, and his stocky body looked like even a hurricane wouldn't stand a chance of toppling it.

Lysander, towering tall and golden, seemed the opposite of Dimitri at first glance, but the dangerous glint in his eyes and his broad build echoed her dad's.

With a small hand gesture, Dimitri indicated that the ES officers should lower their weapons, and they did.

"Hello," Lysander said. He stepped forward and extended a hand. "I'm Lysander. I'll welcome your hospitality if you extend it."

"Let's not get ahead of ourselves. Who are you? And how did you get into the Etherlin?"

Lapsing into Etruscan, Lysander asked, "How much do you want me to reveal, Cerise?"

She thought her tongue would tangle on Etruscan, so she answered him in German. "We're in uncharted territory. Just follow your instincts," she murmured. She glanced around at the other ES officers who were sprouting like weeds and spotted Dorie, who'd crept up and was hovering a few feet behind her dad.

"I fell into the Etherlin," Lysander said.

"Do you make a habit of that? Of falling?" Dimitri's dark eyes bored into him.

"Not a habit, but it has been known to happen."

Dorie approached with mincing steps and stood at their father's right side. She whispered something to him.

"I told you to stay at the house," he said brusquely.

Dorie frowned and continued to whisper to him.

"I have reason to believe that Ileana's in trouble," Cerise said. "Lysander and I came to talk to her and discovered some troubling things. We should talk to you about them privately."

"Maybe Lysander knows there's a problem because he caused it," Dorie said, folding her arms across her chest. She stared at Lysander, who didn't acknowledge her accusation or her presence.

"What kind of trouble?" Dimitri asked.

"We think she's with someone who's colluding with a demon," Cerise said, covering Lysander's silence.

Dimitri scowled. "There hasn't been a demon near the Etherlin in years, and the ones that have been raised are little more than horrific monsters. They're not capable of conspiring."

"Those lesser demons are driven by hunger and rage and enter the world in a frenzy of bloodlust, but just as legend tells us, the higher demons in hell are cunning. They're capable of complex trickery." She glanced at Lysander, who nodded his agreement. "I suggest that you use all the Etherlin's available resources to find Ileana. I'm helping Lysander conduct his own investigation, and of course we'll share any information that could lead to Ileana's safe recovery—" Cerise broke off as Lysander gave her a small push away from him. His head was turned toward an ES officer who was slowly approaching them from behind.

"Don't do that, Collins," Cerise said, her eyes narrowing. "Back up."

Collins, a middle-aged man who usually had a cheerful expression on his face, was all business now.

"Stand with your father," Lysander said in German, giving her a gentle shove. "When it begins, you mustn't get in the way of their bullets."

"He's getting ready to fight," Dorie said. "He wants Cerise out of the way so he can attack."

"That's not what he said," Cerise snapped and ground her teeth together. She stepped closer to Lysander and put a hand on his back, locking eyes with her father. "If they attack him, he'll defend himself and it won't end well. I'm asking you to make them back off."

"No one wants to hurt him," Dimitri said. "Lysander, take out your knife and lay it on the ground. Security will escort us to ES headquarters where we can talk."

"We can talk here," Lysander said, his gaze slicing through the darkness, keeping track of the positions of all the men.

"Dad, don't make me regret calling you. This is me trying to reach out."

"He's a member of the fallen, Cerise. How do you not see what a massive mistake it is to harbor him?" Dimitri asked, his voice low and harsh.

"All the fallen are not the same. You claim the ventala aren't capable of control around muses, but Merrick has saved Alissa's life more than once. Draining muses dry of their blood seems to be the last thing on Merrick's mind."

Dimitri's shock registered instantly. "What do you know of Alissa's present situation?"

"I know she accused the former ES director of kidnapping and attempted murder."

"There's no evidence of that. The former director's missing and presumed dead. He makes an easy target since he can't defend himself."

"All I know is that Alissa's been with Merrick for six weeks and she's still alive. In fact, she's the happiest I've seen her look since her mom died."

"The happiest she's looked? When did you see her?"

"I visited her."

"In the Varden?" Dimitri asked, horrified.

"And I'm still alive to tell the tale," Cerise said.

"You're crazy! You're out of control and crazy," Dorie cried. "Dad's right. We should all have twenty-four-hour guards on us. I'm willing to deal with it if it'll keep the rest of you out of trouble."

"They're not going to use V3 ammunition on Lysander, Cerise. They'll just tranquilize him," Dimitri said. "Move away from him."

"Don't do this," Cerise snapped. "Lysander's an archangel. No one's better trained than ES, but they're only human. The cost of trying to take him into custody will be too high. Open the gate and let him out. No one has to get hurt."

"If he wants to leave no one will stop him."

Cerise slid her hand along Lysander's side, looping their arms together and gripping his forearm. "Let's go."

"Not with you!" Dorie said.

"No," Dimitri agreed. "He can leave alone."

"I'm not a prisoner! I'll leave if I want to."

"No." The finality in her father's voice made her heart clench. She knew he was worried about her, so worried that he wouldn't listen to reason.

"What the hell is your deal?" Dorie demanded, stalking forward.

"Don't," Cerise said, trying to shove Dorie away. Dorie grabbed Cerise's arm with both of her hands and yanked with all her might. Cerise jerked forward a step, then pulled back, widened her stance, and planted her feet.

They struggled. "Let go of him," Dorie yelled, red-faced and furious. Cerise yanked her arm out of Dorie's grasp and used it to push her away. Dorie charged forward.

"Get the girls out of the way," Dimitri ordered, and the officers surged toward them.

Time seemed to slow and in a frozen moment, Lysander whispered in Etruscan, "Before battle, Merrick takes a kiss from his muse. A ritual I think I'd relish."

Her eyes widened as Lysander turned, dipped his head, and brushed his lips over hers. Then she and Dorie fell because Lysander's leg swept theirs out from under them.

"Stay down," Lysander said as a dart whizzed through the air. He caught it by the shaft and then he was in motion, and it was like nothing she'd ever seen.

He charged and with a vertical leap he sailed over the heads of the guards, taking himself out of the closing circle.

He toppled them like bowling pins, weaving and spinning and jabbing them with their own tranquilizer darts.

Dorie screamed, Dimitri shouted, but Cerise watched him in silence. He didn't dance. There was no flourish or showmanship. It was ruthless efficiency. It was moves that defied gravity. And it was all over in moments.

When the last of the guards lay unconscious on the ground, Lysander strode to her.

"None is dead. You're welcome," he said with the flash of a dark smile. He pulled her up from the ground and clasped her hand over his thundering heart. "Not easy to overcome instinct. Reward me later."

For a moment, she only stared at him with her own heart hammering.

Realizing she was stunned, he said, "Everything's all right now. Killing averted." He nodded to reinforce his words.

"Thank you."

"I don't want words," he said in Etruscan. He bent his head to whisper in her ear. "Later, I want a physical reward."

She continued to stare at him, her body traitorous and perfectly ready to be the reward he had in mind.

Dorie tried to get a hand on them, but Lysander swatted away her grasp and pulled Cerise out of reach.

"Cerise," her father said. She looked at him and sympathized with his shocked expression.

Still a little dazed herself, Cerise opened her mouth, but words failed her. What could she say? That she was going with Lysander because the way he moved was unbelievable and he deserved a reward for such a sublime demonstration of nonfatal ass-kicking?

"Dad—" she began haltingly, but Lysander shook his head, cutting off the beleaguered exchange.

Lysander's voice carried through the clearing, over the bodies that were strewn like fallen trees after a storm. "Once victory speaks, nothing more need be said."

Chapter 17

Soot-covered and crusted with dried blood, Merrick would've liked a shower before Alissa saw him, and he could've had one in the building's gym, but the gym might be in use and he wasn't in the mood for any company that wasn't his wife's.

He'd been in Jacobi territory and had waged war until Tamberi's men had been beaten and forced to retreat. In the wake of his bombings, the syndicate had accepted a temporary stay of aggression, so he could afford to return home for the night.

He punched the code into the security pad of his place and entered, finding Alissa, Richard, and Ox all awake.

Alissa sat in a chair, making notes with a purple gel pen on a manuscript that had come by FedEx. Her aspirants weren't aware that the Varden was at war . . . or maybe they didn't care. If Richard was anything to go by, authors could be so obsessive about their work that they were oblivious to the state of the world at large. Since working would distract Alissa from worrying about Lysander and Cerise and about the syndicate, Merrick was glad the delivery had reached her.

Ox stood. "All right, boss?"

Merrick nodded. "There'll be a cease-fire while Victor's death is investigated." Merrick tilted his head toward the door, indicating Ox could go.

"I'll be around. Let me know if you need me to do anything." Ox strode out, waving good-bye to Richard, who was discussing novels with an empty chair presumably occupied by either his wife's ghost or his delusion of her ghost.

Richard's deep purple bathrobe was embellished with a garish gold logo and stitching that made it look like it belonged in the closet of a royal or a drag queen. Under it, Richard wore battered slippers, a white cotton shirt, and frayed khaki pants like safari wear gone wrong. They looked absurd with the bathrobe.

"Nice outfit," Merrick said.

Richard slid his reading glasses down and looked at Merrick over the top of his frames. "You feel in a position to criticize? I admire that unflappable confidence of yours. I also enjoy it when I'm not the only madman in the apartment."

Merrick smirked and went to the bar. He mixed himself a Scotch Lime and drank it down.

Richard pushed his glasses back up the bridge of his nose. "Is there a grocery market open this time of night?"

Merrick paused, glancing over his shoulder at Richard. He was used to the non sequiturs from his father-in-law, but he knew better than to ignore them. "Why? What do we need?"

Alissa stepped close, smelling like pears and vanilla. His abs tightened. More than a shower, he wanted his wife's skin under his mouth.

"You smell like smoke. Are you burned?" she asked.

"Nowhere that counts," he murmured as she kissed his jaw. "But I need to scrub off the war before I'll be fit for those lips."

"That's not what you promised."

"What do you mean?"

"The spirit of the vows covered all eventualities. Sickness. Health. Rich. Poor. Battle-bloodied or scrubbed clean, you're mine no matter what shape you're in."

He smirked. "No arguments about me being yours, sweetheart, but we'll have to throw out the mattress and the sheets if you don't douse me in some soap and water before you take me to bed."

She laughed softly. "Give me a kiss while I think it over."

The silk lace trimming her neckline was as pristine as her luminous skin, so he clasped his hands behind his back to keep the grime off her. Still, he couldn't resist bending his head and capturing her mouth in a deep kiss.

When the kiss ended, Richard was still reading pages from the working draft of his novel and chatting with the chair.

"Richard, what do we need from the grocery store?" Merrick asked.

Without looking up, Richard murmured, "The duke of Edinburgh said, 'Champagne and orange juice is a great drink. The orange improves the champagne. The champagne definitely improves the orange.'"

Merrick smiled. "Our friend the angel will be back soon."

"With trouble in tow."

"Trouble for us?"

Richard shook his head. "All his."

Merrick shrugged. "He knows his own prophecy better than anyone."

"No doubt, but when fate offers an Amazon warrior queen with sable hair and plum-colored lips, no man stands a chance. Not even an archangel."

Alissa sighed. "I'm concerned for both of them, but selfishly I can't help but be pleased that she'll be here again soon."

"The barn's burned down. Now I can see the moon," Richard quoted.

Merrick and Alissa both laughed.

"Nothing wrong with reaping the silver from the lining," Merrick said to Alissa, leading her toward the hall. "Why don't you and your optimistic outlook come wash my back for me?" Over his shoulder he added, "And Richard, you better check your powers of perception. We don't get oranges from a store this time of year. There are orange trees on the roof."

Richard mumbled something that even Merrick's superior hearing didn't catch. Merrick would've asked him to repeat it, but Alissa's fingers trailing along his throat raised ideas for better uses of his time.

Cerise decided that even though they probably wouldn't find Troy at home for questioning, they should check his house for evidence of his involvement with anything demonic. She'd also decided that she didn't want to see Lysander's restraint tested in another confrontation with ES. Now that she wasn't trying to conceal Lysander's presence in the Etherlin, driving seemed a better idea than walking where they might cross paths with ES foot patrols. So they headed to Alissa and Richard's to borrow a car.

She glanced at Lysander frequently. With shorter hair, he looked less like Tarzan straight from the jungle. His face was young and handsome, but the way light fractured around him still marked him as more than human. And his scars spoke to his dangerous nature. Cerise didn't mind. She enjoyed his looks and that threat of wildness. Cerise understood Alissa's move to the Varden better and better.

The whipping wind made for turbulent waters as they walked the cobbled path along the lake. He had an arm casually around her shoulders, affectionate and intimate. Young lovers on a stroll. Except that their topic of conversation was darker than midnight.

"After I trained Merrick to fight demons, I gifted him with a pair of antique blades that were forged with my blood. When we return to his building, I'll ask him to give you one of them, and I'll show you how to use it."

She'd always loved martial arts training. To be able to fight with a fraction of Lysander's skill would be incredible. "I look forward to that."

"I warn you though: you're talented physically, but fighting should never be your first strategy if you encounter a demon. Even with training, you'll only be able to kill one if you take him by surprise. We—angels—move too fast. Even in the flesh, we're too powerful for a human to defeat. You understand? I'll teach you as a precaution . . ." He cast a sideways glance at her and smiled. "And because I think I'll enjoy challenging your body to reach its peak performance."

"You will, huh? How does that work with the law about defending yourself? Come to think of it, on the night we met I busted your face with my head. If you're bound to defend yourself, why didn't you break my neck?"

"I defended myself. If you recall, I subdued you."

"Subdued, yes. Injured, no."

"Well, bare-handed you weren't a serious threat. And . . ."

"And?"

"You're a woman, so my instincts don't dictate a violent

response." His smile widened. "In a physical confrontation, my urge isn't to kill you. You may have noticed."

"I could be your Achilles' heel then."

His smile faded. "Yes, that's always the biggest threat to me. Allowing someone I care for to get close enough to betray me."

She stopped and turned to him. "I wouldn't do that. I might fight with you or try to get rid of you, but I won't do it by lying or stabbing you in the back. I'll tell you to your face that we're over. You can't count on me to be easy to get along with, because I'm not, but you can count on my honesty. I'll never betray you, Lysander. You can rely on that."

He stared at her for a moment and said, "I believe you."

"So Reziel," she said. "What does he want with us?"

"With muses? I couldn't say."

"Does he think we could help raise him? What does that entail?"

"Blood. For a demon of Reziel's stature, a multivictim human sacrifice would be required. And the ritual would have to be performed by someone who's studied and is skilled in black magic."

"Ileana would never perform a black magic ritual. Even if she wanted to, she wouldn't know how. Could she be used as one of the sacrifices? Alissa said the ventala were going to use her as a sacrifice to open a portal to bring forth vampires, so the ventala syndicate must have some knowledge of black magic."

"Yes, the female ventala, Tamberi Jacobi. Merrick said that she had an ancient grimoire that was used to raise lesser demons. But an archangel, Nathaniel, recovered and destroyed it, so she shouldn't be able to raise them anymore. Unless—" He paused, rubbing his lower lip thoughtfully. "If Reziel's had contact with her, he might be able to reach her to instruct her on how to raise him. He would need a tight bond with her. I can't see how he could've achieved that. It would've required close contact like sexual intercourse. To have that kind of interaction with her, someone would've had to raise him in the flesh first. I would've felt his presence in the world. I didn't."

Lysander looked over thoughtfully, then continued. "But if

he is somehow communing with Tamberi Jacobi, it could be
with the objective of furthering her plan to bring forth a vampire apocalypse. She and her syndicate tried to sacrifice Alissa
to open a portal for the shapeshifting species of vampires to
return. That would appeal to Reziel. The last time vampires
came through in droves, they slaughtered millions. If there was
a way for him to assist in keeping the portal open, the world
could be overrun. And recently, someone opened a hole that
allowed several lesser demons to come through. Ileana Rella
may have been sacrificed to allow for that."

Cerise paled. "So she may already be dead." She swallowed
hard, stunned by the thought that her friend might have been
slaughtered when none of them had even realized she was in
trouble. "It can't be true," Cerise mumbled, her mind racing.
"When a muse is out of the Etherlin, her security detail reports
in every two hours. If they'd lost contact with her bodyguards,
ES would know Ileana was in trouble. She's still alive. She
must be."

The thought of Ileana being sacrificed made Cerise's stomach knot. "Isn't there anything else a demon might want with
her? To use the power of Ileana's voice to influence people? To
manipulate them into starting wars or doing other destructive
things?" Cerise asked as they reached Alissa's house.

"Perhaps, but then she would have to knowingly cooperate.
Would she?"

"I wouldn't have thought so, but given how much I didn't
realize about Alissa and Troy, I'm not sure I really know what
any of my friends are capable of."

Jersey was making tea when she heard the key in the front door.
She gasped in relief. "Hayden!"

But when the door swung open it didn't reveal her missing
brother. Instead the smooth and devastating Troy Rella walked
into the apartment. She stiffened. Despite his good looks, for
Jersey there was nothing appealing about him anymore.

"What are you doing here?" she asked, supporting herself
against the counter.

Troy looked her over. She was so glad she'd showered and

dressed. Even in a thick sweatshirt and jeans, she felt as raw and vulnerable as sushi.

"I could ask you the same," he said, walking down the hall to the bathroom. He closed the door and she heard him opening and closing the cupboards under the sink.

"So," Troy said when he returned. "Why are you here?"

What the hell was he looking for?

Her gaze moved to the front door. Should she bolt?

No. No way. He's the one who needs to go. Tell him to get the hell out.

"It's Griffin's apartment. The rent's paid until the end of the year," she said, pushing the damp bangs back from her eyes and tucking the fringe behind her ears. "What are you looking for?"

"Where's Hayden?" he asked, opening the desk drawers and pawing through them.

"He'll be back soon. How'd you get in? I know Griffin didn't give you a key."

"I was his publicist and one of the few people he knew in the Etherlin. Why do you think he wouldn't have given me a spare key?"

Smudges of heat spotted her cheeks. "I just don't believe he did. You're Ileana's brother, and it's her building, maybe you got a key from her . . . or took one."

He closed the desk drawer and turned slowly. His dark eyes narrowed, but his voice was mild when he spoke. "I'm sorry that things didn't work out between us, Jersey, but it's been over such a long time. Are you going to mope around and give me wounded looks forever? Don't you think it's time to grow up and move on?"

She shouldn't have given a damn what he said, but it still stung. She turned off the burner under the kettle. "I *was* over it until I found out what you did."

"What are you talking about?" he asked impatiently as he walked to the tall bookshelf and ran his hand over the top. She wondered again what he was looking for. Whatever it was, if it was valuable or important he wouldn't find it. She and Hayden had searched every inch of the apartment for Griffin's songbook. There wasn't anything hidden left to find.

"I talked to your assistant, Courtney, a couple of weeks ago."

"My *former* assistant Courtney. The one who's extremely angry that I fired her," he said casually, but Jersey noticed how rigid he went at her mention. "No one smart would believe anything she has to say about me these days."

"She has a pharmacy receipt. The date was the day after you asked me to get an abortion and I said no. You told her the abortion pills were for Ileana, but Courtney never believed that. She thought it was strange that you flew out to see us in Phoenix when you were in the middle of Etherlin Council meetings. She wanted to know why I had to be rushed to the hospital after the show. She'd heard I'd had the stomach flu and dehydration, but wanted to be sure."

His jaw hardened. "And what did you tell her?"

"Maybe I didn't tell her anything. Or maybe I told her the truth. That I had a miscarriage and almost bled to death."

"Are you asking me if I poisoned you, Jersey? Can you really accuse me of such a thing?"

"Yeah, I can," she said, glaring at him. "Griffin was planning to fire you. Why? I never told him anything about you and me. I never told anyone. I always kept it a secret like I promised to, but Griffin said he had to get you away from us. Those were his exact words. He said there were too many shadows around you. I didn't know what he meant, but something must've happened to make him not trust you. What was it?"

Troy folded his arms across his chest, glaring at her. She gripped the counter next to the stove, holding herself steady. She knew she should stop talking, but now that she'd started she couldn't bottle her fury anymore. She had to confront him.

"I died last night," she said. "Right before I did, I met an angel, and the light around him was like looking through a diamond. Ever since I woke up, I've seen shadows and light surrounding people." The darkness around Troy blackened further. "You're all covered in muck, Troy. Your skin looks almost gray."

His pursed lips turned white with rage. It was satisfying to see him upset, but as an oily film slithered outward from him across the floor and toward her, her muscles locked and her breath caught.

"During your near-death experience, you must have suffered some brain damage," he said coldly. "Let's hope you recover."

"Get out of here, and stay away from us."

He eased toward her, the darkness advancing with him.

Air chilled her skin, raising gooseflesh.

Don't let it touch you!

She backed to the other side of the kitchen. Her breath fogged the air in short bursts, fear twisting her belly. She kept her eyes locked on him. He did the same. For a frozen moment, neither of them moved, then he sprang forward. She spun and darted away, but his palm slammed between her shoulder blades. She fell, crashing to the floor. The impact drove pain up her arms and knocked the wind from her. She scrambled to escape, but his hands on her throat strangled her and a knee in her back crushed her against the floor.

She strained to reach up and back, clawing at him as her eyes bulged and tongue thickened. He banged her head on the ground, and pain shot through her head in a blinding fury. She smelled licorice and rotten eggs, retched against a closed throat, and then ceased to hurt anymore.

Chapter 18

"Feel it?" Cerise asked with her right hand over Lysander's left on the gear shift.

He nodded and shifted.

"Perfect. See? No one with your reflexes and coordination should drive an automatic."

"When I said I didn't know how to drive a manual transmission, I didn't mean that I drove the other kind. Normally, I go the way of the wind. If I need to travel by car, I'm driven."

"Like a child," she teased.

He rolled his eyes. "Like someone born before there were cars."

"What about horses?"

"Yes, before those, too."

She smirked. "I meant, did you ever ride horses to get around?"

"Occasionally."

"You don't want to keep up with the times?"

He shrugged, shifting again. "I follow mankind's progress. Sometimes I take advantage of it. I have a computer."

"Do you use it?"

"I download music."

"Do you have an email account?"

"I do," he said, then laughed. "And a website that Merrick created for me when he was a teenager. Get-me-out-of-here-dot-com."

She barked out a startled laugh. *That's hilarious.*

"The email username was Fallen_guy."

"Subtle."

Lysander nodded. "And after soliciting a promise that I would check the account, he proceeded to send me pages of junk mail."

"Did you get pissed?"

"No, I got even. I filled his shower with sand."

"Sand?"

"To the top. He had a date with a girl he'd been pursuing. He opened the door and the sand spilled out."

"Wow. The shower must have been unusable."

"It was."

"Did he miss his date?"

"No, he got ready elsewhere, but he was late. And afterward he couldn't bring her back to his place."

"There must have been sand in everything for weeks. Did he have to hire a plumber to fix the shower?"

"Certainly."

"Did he stop sending you spam?"

"No, he sent twice as much. But then it only made me laugh because I knew how mad he was when the sand came pouring out. He cursed at me in three languages, including one he doesn't speak."

She smiled, charmed by the thought of the pair of hardened killers participating in a lighthearted one-upmanship.

He shifted gears. She glanced at his hand.

"It's a crime for this car to be sitting in Alissa's garage with no one around to drive it. And she needs her own car. Cars are freedom."

"She can't drive it," Lysander said. "Her sight was damaged when she opened the portal to your ancestors."

"I *knew* there was a problem with her eyes. What's being done about it? Has she seen a specialist?"

"I don't think so. Her vision's returning slowly. It was fully restored with the Muse's Wreath, but she wouldn't keep it. She felt the Wreath would better serve the world from the Etherlin."

"What would serve the world best is if one of its most powerful muses brought her magic back to the Etherlin. Do you think Merrick would move to the Etherlin if things there were different? If there was no risk of him being imprisoned? Or does he like being a mob boss in his own territory?"

"I believe what Merrick liked about his territory was its proximity to Alissa. Now that she stays with him, I doubt he cares where he lives."

"Then why is he in the Varden when they're being hunted by the ventala syndicate and that bitch Tamberi Jacobi? If they're not going to be in the Etherlin, they should live in New York or the Florida Keys or Paris. Some writer-friendly place for Richard and Alissa's aspirants."

"They can't leave the area yet."

"Why not?"

"Because Merrick has an obligation to fulfill."

"What obligation?"

"His promise to fight with me when the time of the prophecy comes."

"Ah." Cerise paused thoughtfully as she parked in front of Troy's house. "Actually, Alissa may have the right idea anyway."

"About what?" he asked, making no move to get out of the car.

"About leaving the Etherlin. I don't know what our grandmothers would think of the Etherlin these days. They created it as a community for them to live and work together, to enhance each other's powers of inspiration by their close proximity. And this spot was idyllic with its snowcapped mountains and icemelt lakes, evergreens and cherry blossoms. It's stunning. Each generation of muses became more powerful and world famous, but as we got more focused on our work and only our work, the Etherlin Council sucked up more and more control. The community needs money to keep it running. Since money can be a corrupting force when it comes to creativity, the muses signed over their earnings to the Etherlin trust. There were stalkers and vampires and ventala to contend with, so Etherlin Security had to become more protective and more formidable. Now between the EC and ES, we're like dolls living in a dollhouse, flanked on all sides by men who want to protect and control our images and our lives. So much has changed in a couple of generations. *Too much.* The muses a few generations back were fiercely independent. Maybe they didn't accomplish as much in as short a time as we do, but they also didn't live their lives in some sort of weird perpetual adolescence. They weren't prisoners in their own homes." She glanced over at him. "They had affairs with whomever they wanted."

"I can think of no one better suited to follow her own instincts than you, Cerise. And I don't only say that because it's in my interest for you to decide to have an affair with someone your community deems unsuitable."

"I've played the rebellious teen for way too long. I'm closer to thirty than nineteen. It used to be simpler to keep secrets than to face resistance and EC scrutiny. And Griffin wanted our affair to be kept secret, so I'd sneak out of the Etherlin like a teenager climbing out her bedroom window. But this isn't a game, and it's time for all of us to grow up.

"The community and my family in particular have been on edge for weeks. Ever since Alissa left without warning or explanation. There was speculation that Merrick was controlling her somehow or had abducted her . . . seduced her into doing something she would later regret. But he didn't. I know Alissa feels like she can't come home. And we've been made to feel it'll never be safe to visit her and that she somehow betrayed all of us by getting involved with Merrick, when in fact all she did was fall in love and be true to herself. That can't be wrong," Cerise said. "Now Ileana's out there with someone dangerous. If she hadn't tried to keep her relationship with the guy concealed, maybe one of us would have realized what he was." Cerise shook her head. "I don't owe anyone blind obedience, and they'll never get it from me. But I do owe them the truth, even if it leads to an exhausting fight that costs me plenty."

He smiled at her. "I admire in you the same things I admire in Merrick."

She raised her brows in question.

"Consequences cannot deter you the way they would deter lesser men and women."

She smiled. "The consummate warrior approves of us fighting. What a surprise."

He laughed softly, grazing his knuckles over her forearm, raising gooseflesh. "Heaven may not have given men the courage of lions, but what it put in mankind's heart is just as noble. Perhaps more so, since fighting must be chosen."

She liked that perspective, liked everything about him. Her gaze fixed on his mouth for a moment, temptation curling through her. "There's no time right now for me to fully reward you for your restraint against the ES officers, but there's time for a kiss."

"Good," he murmured, leaning closer. "Take one."

She traced his lower lip with the tip of her tongue, mingling their breath. Moments stretched along with their bodies. When she finally lifted her face, he looked at her with eyes the color of the murky depths of the sea.

"I'm glad I never kissed you before last night."

"Why's that?" she asked, her heart tattooing a beat against her ribs.

"Because if I'd known how you would suit me, I would've been tempted."

"Tempted to?"

"To always have you this close." His mouth curved, wicked and sweet. "Becoming bound to you might not have been the result of an accident. I'd have considered seeing it done on purpose."

She pressed another kiss, hard and rich, onto his mouth. Drawing back, she added, "Careful. If you spend too much time around human beings, you'll become as reckless as we are."

He sighed ruefully. "That is a danger."

After a quiet moment, she exited the car. He followed suit and they went to Troy's front door. About to slam his shoulder into it to force it open, Lysander stopped short at the sound of Cerise's ringing phone. He tilted his head.

"Check who that is," he said.

She cocked a brow, but pulled the phone out. "Amazing instincts," she murmured when she saw Alissa's name displayed.

"Hey," Cerise said when she picked up the call. "Are you guys all right?"

"We're fine," Alissa said. "Merrick negotiated an end to the violence. At least temporarily. How's Lysander?"

"Alive and kicking."

"I never doubted it. My father wants to tell you something. He insisted that I call. Do you have a moment to speak to him?"

She glanced at the door, wondering how long it would be before ES marshaled its forces and made another run at Lysander. "Sure. We're a little busy, but we can make time for Richard."

Lysander nodded in agreement.

"Okay, Dad, Cerise is on the phone." There was a pregnant pause and she heard Richard speaking in the background.

"What?" Cerise asked.

"Sorry," Alissa said. "He's talking something over with himself. Dad, Cerise and Lysander don't have much time. Can you please talk to her now?"

"Hello?" Richard asked.

"Hi, Richard. There's something you wanted to tell me?"

"Zelda said, 'Nobody has ever measured, not even the poets, how much a heart can hold.' "

"Uh—"

"The Montblanc pen Helene gave me on our first date is inside a copy of *The Great Gatsby* on her desk. Bring it with you when you return."

"I'll see what I can do."

"And her notes on my last novel. They're in the closet next to the bamboo plant. My wife thinks I'd benefit from rereading her comments on that book. And my own. The margins, you know, we make use of them."

"If Lysander and I go back to the house and have time, I'll see if I can locate it. Listen, I have to go now—"

"I know. You've got to go back to the high-rise."

"The high-rise?"

"Yes, and hurry. He's breaking your doll."

Chapter 19

For a split second, Cerise froze, but the next instant she grabbed Lysander's arm and jerked it to indicate that he should follow her as she hurried to the car.

"What doll, Richard? What high-rise? Are you talking about Griffin's little sister?"

"A bird in the air is better than two in the cage."

"Richard," she snapped as she hauled the driver's door open. "Are you talking about Jersey Lane?"

"Possibly. Don't forget the manuscript."

"Gotta go," she said, ending the call and shoving the phone into her pocket. As Lysander pulled the passenger door closed, she related what Richard had said.

The car roared through the Etherlin, and Cerise slammed her foot on the brake to jerk the car to a stop in front of Griffin's building. She leapt from the seat and ran to the front door. Lysander kept pace.

The elevator ride was brief, but felt too long. Cerise sprinted to Griffin's apartment door and when she pushed it open, she was assaulted by the one Molly Times song she hated. "Sympathy, Too." Its eerie violin bow against guitar strings opening and the ode-to-death and self-destruction lyrics turned her stomach.

Razor-ending zero, I endanger lives.
Taken all at midnight, Black berries done all right.

"Jersey?" Cerise screamed, rushing through the apartment. "Jersey?" Cerise flung the bathroom door open and gasped. The sight of so much splattered blood left her breathless. Troy lay on the floor in a black cherry pool, one side of his throat gaping open like a startled mouth.

In the formerly white tub, a tiny naked Jersey sat with her knees clasped to her chest, blood dripping down her calves.

"What happened? Are you bleeding?" Cerise stepped over Troy to reach the tub. Jersey sat in a few inches of pink water. It gushed from the tap, but the plug lay sideways next to the drain with its old-fashioned chain hooked over Jersey's foot.

"I woke up when he cut my wrist. I grabbed his head. I meant to bang it against the tub I think. Not sure—" Jersey stammered, looking up at Cerise with wide eyes. Without makeup she looked about fifteen. "The knife jabbed into his neck."

Cerise glanced down at the bloody butcher's knife whose blade could just be seen under the claw-footed tub. Cerise grabbed Jersey's arms to examine them. The gash in her left wrist pumped bright blood and Cerise pressed her fingers over Jersey's pulse to stop the bleeding.

"He choked me till I passed out," she said through chattering teeth. "He could've killed me right then. He didn't have to put me in the bathtub naked. Didn't need to slice me up." She paused and swallowed. "He took off all my clothes, left me with nothing," she spat, her small shoulders starting to shake.

"He was staging it to look like a suicide," Cerise said grimly.

"He left me naked on purpose. Fucking asshole," Jersey said in her high clear voice. "I'm cold, Cer. Really cold."

Lysander lifted a T-shirt that was wadded on the floor. He ripped a strip of fabric from it and held it out. "Here," he said. "Bind the wound."

Cerise fashioned a tight bandage around Jersey's wrist.

"I'll get her. You find something to wrap around her," Lysander said.

Cerise nodded, standing and moving past him. When she returned with a blanket, Lysander lifted Jersey by her upper arms and held her aloft. Cerise wrapped Jersey in a tight cocoon of fabric and Lysander swung her into the cradle of his arms. He carried her out to the living room and laid her on the chaise.

"With Troy dead, we won't get answers from him," Cerise murmured.

Straightening, Lysander shrugged his brows. "That which is most precious or secret is kept nearest."

Taking his meaning, she returned to the body. Still warm, but cooling rapidly, Troy's body resisted movement. She tried to avoid the pooled blood as she knelt next to him and emptied his pockets. She set his wallet and keys on a patch of dry white tile. From his other pocket, she removed a pill bottle with a yellowed pharmacy label. It was Griffin's prescription for Klonopin. He'd taken them for seizures. Had Troy put them in his pocket so they'd be handy? Was he planning to force a few down Jersey's throat as part of the suicide scene?

Lysander's large hands yanked Troy's bloody shirt open, buttons popping free like popcorn. Lying against his black chest hair was a gold chain and from that hung a jump drive, a small three-pronged lightning pendant—the symbol from a Molly Times CD—and a small smoked glass and pewter vial. Lysander snapped the chain and spilled the pendants into his hand.

"Take the technology and the charm," he said. After she obliged, he uncapped the vial. The smell of the blood on the floor was overpowered by the scent of licorice and rotten eggs.

She coughed, and Lysander recapped the vial. "There's human blood mixed with the aspect of a demon in this vial. Rella wasn't only under Reziel's influence. He made a covenant with the demon, a blood oath. Tell the girl never to regret sending this man to hell. The world is well rid of him."

The words were like a hammer against her skull, and Cerise's mind was jarred between the present moment, kneeling on a blood-soaked floor next to the corpse of an apparently evil man and her memories of Troy, of the many times they'd shared as friends while working together to promote the bands she inspired.

She stared down at Troy's handsome face, as familiar as her own. "I knew him my whole life. He was like family." She felt ill. She swallowed, sweat dampening her temples and the nape of her neck.

"I considered Reziel my brother once. A close association

doesn't always reveal an underlying character defect. If anything, it can make it harder to fathom."

"Then how can we prevent ourselves from being taken in?"

He shrugged. "I'm not certain we can. The only true defense
is to trust no one."

She frowned. "I couldn't live that way." The nausea ebbed.
She grabbed a length of toilet paper and dabbed her forehead.

"Few people could. In lieu of that, I recommend keeping a
blade close at hand and training yourself to move automatically
in self-defense. In a fight to the death, there's no room for sen-
timent or hesitation."

"Great," she mumbled as she stood. She went to the sink
and turned on the taps. Cupping water in her hands, she brought
it to her mouth, sucked it in, and swished. She spit the water
into the sink and rinsed again, feeling a little better. "We should
call ES about what happened here, but if we do that, they'll
take Jersey into custody and we won't get a chance to talk to
her about why Troy tried to kill her. She'll also be stuck here
where demons have apparently been hanging out with the
highest-ranking members of Etherlin society."

"No police. With demons involved, we should handle this
ourselves."

"If there's anything incriminating on this flash drive, it'll
be encrypted. Does Merrick have a computer guy on his pay-
roll? Someone who could get past Troy's security?"

"Likely he does, and Merrick could be helpful in finding
Ileana Rella's present location."

"He could?"

"Certainly. Merrick's job as an enforcer required him to
hunt creatures all over the world. Some were quite cunning in
their evasive tactics, but Merrick always tracked them down in
the end."

"Alissa said Merrick has arranged for a temporary truce, so
he's got things under control in the Varden for the moment. We
can go there."

Her cell rang. "It's my sister," she said, wanting to ignore
it. She looked down at Troy's face and thought of Alissa's warning. For six weeks, Cerise had pushed Dorie away and possibly

right into Troy's grasp. Had Dorie's recent malicious behavior toward Alissa stemmed from Dorie being a victim of Troy's manipulation?

"I'm going to pack a few things for Jersey and me. I'll be back in a minute," Cerise said, walking out of the room. When she was out of earshot, she answered the call.

"Hey," she said.

"I'm sorry about earlier. I know you're mad, but I have to tell you—" Dorie's voice caught.

"Tell me what?" Cerise asked.

"It's a mess, Cer. It's a terrible mess. Ileana's gone. She's missing. We don't know for how long. ES thinks—" Dorie's voice broke again and she started to cry. "They believe that someone else has been holding the cell phones—hers and her security detail's—and sending the text message check-ins. When the ES director tried calling and insisted on voice communication, there were no more texts."

Cerise's heart sank.

"They're sending a team to Denver where they had their last voice communication, but they say if her security detail didn't call in after losing their phones, it means her bodyguards must be dead and that someone's taken her." Dorie paused, choking on emotion. "Is that fallen angel still with you? If it was a demon who took Ileana, you know he could be involved. Please tell me you're by yourself and safe," Dorie said through tears.

"Hush. I'm 100 percent okay."

"Come home. Please come home right now. I'm scared for you. For all of us. They're patrolling the outer wall, talking about how they'll handle it if the ventala try to blow a hole in it."

"Calm down. No one is going to try to blow a hole in the Etherlin walls. The ventala are fighting with each other. Period. It's nothing to do with us." Except for Alissa.

"Will you come home?"

"Yes."

"Now? Right now?"

"Soon."

"You have to. Dad's so worried. We both are. I tried calling

Troy, and he's not answering, either. He's going to freak out when he hears. You know how close they are. How close we all are. Ileana's been like another big sister to me. I can't believe this could happen."

Cerise bit her lip. "I have to go for now."

"No, don't! Stay on the line with me. Please. I need to hear your voice."

"I'll call you back soon. I promise. Right now there's something I have to do."

Dorie sniffled.

"Everything will be okay." As Cerise pulled a suitcase from the closet, she noticed bloodstains on the knees of her pants. She grimaced. "I'll call you back soon," she whispered and hung up. Resting her forehead against the closet door, she closed her eyes, feeling close to tears herself. She fought the urge to break down.

"Are you all right?" Lysander asked, his voice close. She didn't answer. His arms slid around from behind her and pulled her back. She leaned against him, her muscles tight. She couldn't relax.

"My sister's really upset, and I hung up on her."

"Do you think she's safe where she is?"

"Yes."

"Is there anyone other than you who can offer her emotional support?"

Cerise nodded. "She's close to my dad. She can lean on him." She took a sip of air through pursed lips then blew it out. "But it feels like I should be there. I don't want to add to their worry and pain, not when Troy's body's going to be discovered soon and when Ileana's been officially declared missing."

"So it's official."

"Yeah," Cerise said and filled him in.

"I think we'll do the most good by going to the Varden without delay, but if you want to see your family first, we can stop there."

She shook her head. "Seeing you with me will only upset them more. If we can find Ileana and return her to the Etherlin, it'll go a long way to proving to them that you're not in league with demons."

* * *

They returned to Alissa and Richard's house to swap Alissa's sports car for a town car. With Jersey dressed in sweats and wrapped in a blanket in the backseat along with the luggage, Cerise drove to the gates and they forced the ES officers to let them pass.

The drive through the Sliver and the Varden passed without incident. Cerise and Lysander questioned Jersey gently about what had driven Troy to try to kill her. Jersey's flat-voiced explanation about her secret relationship with Troy and how it led to a near-fatal miscarriage left Cerise speechless and chilled to the bone. Had Griffin realized what Troy had done? Was that why he'd been getting ready to fire him?

As they pulled up to Merrick's building and saw the line of people waiting to get into Crimson, Cerise murmured, "Wow. It was a war zone last night, tonight bombs exploded, yet here they are."

She pulled into a parking spot and got out of the car. She and Lysander retrieved the suitcases, and Jersey trailed behind them. As they passed the gathered club-goers, Cerise glanced at the women in slinky dresses and men in slick suits. "I guess if it's the end of the world as we know it, dancing and drinking isn't a bad way to finish things off."

Lysander clasped her hand and drew her close as they went inside.

The security guy on the platform nodded at Lysander and said, "You got a haircut. Looks good."

Lysander passed the counter without responding. "Thanks," Cerise said for him.

They boarded the elevator and ascended to the penthouse. Lysander tried the door, but found it locked and frowned.

"Isn't it always locked?" she asked, surprised that Merrick wouldn't keep it that way.

"I don't know. I usually land on the balcony. That door's often left unlocked."

"For you, sure. This many floors up, who else is going to use it?"

She rapped on the door. After a couple of minutes, Merrick

opened it. His wet hair curled over his collar and his dark eyes assessed the pair of them.

"Hall door?"

"My wing's healing. No thanks to you," Lysander said, shouldering past Merrick to gain entry. As he still held her hand, Cerise joined him.

"Glad it worked out," Merrick said mildly. He glanced at their intertwined fingers.

"Apparently as a reward for saving his life, I have to keep him," she said, nodding at Merrick's bemused expression. "Sort of the way if you rescue a stray kitten from a tree, you become a cat owner. Of course with cats there is the alternative of the Humane Society. You don't happen to have a number for Archangel Control, do you?"

Merrick smirked. Lysander rolled his eyes, but gave her hand a squeeze before he let it go and went into the kitchen. A moment later, he announced, "You're out of oranges."

"Yeah, been busy with a syndicate war. You remember where the roof is, right?" Merrick said.

"Doesn't matter if I do. The trees are empty by now. You've got a bat infestation."

Merrick's brows shot up. "Since when?"

"I noticed them last night. There were almost no oranges left."

Merrick rubbed a thumb over his lower lip. "So that's what Richard was talking about."

"Richard," Lysander said thoughtfully. "He went to the roof?"

"Not as far as I know."

Lysander cocked his head, glancing up at the ceiling. "If Richard's sixth sense was attuned to the presence of those bats, there must be a reason. There's nowhere on the roof for them to roost, so they migrated there from another location. Did they discover the fruit by chance? Or were they drawn to those trees for another reason?"

"Got a theory?"

"I touch those trees. Didn't you tell me some time ago that in the past Tamberi Jacobi raised demons in bat-infested caves?"

"Yeah, I did."

"Maybe the bats from those caves, tainted by black magic, became sensitive to supernatural energy. Bats are an animal form that supernatural creatures have taken in the past. Vampires," Lysander said.

"Those weren't vampire bats. If they'd been attracted to blood, they would've attacked Alissa and Cerise. Muse blood is magical and potent," Merrick said.

Lysander nodded. "I still wonder why they chose your fruit trees. There must be berries and other fruit in the woods closer to their caves."

"True," Merrick said.

"Perhaps something drew them or drove them from their cave toward this area. Do you know which caves Jacobi used to perform human sacrifices to raise demons? Perhaps we should look at them."

Merrick leaned against the back of the couch. "Tamberi had a grimoire, but it was confiscated and destroyed. I thought without the book, she wouldn't be able to raise any more demons."

"A copy?" Cerise said.

"Only a real witch should have been able to effectively copy the spells," Lysander said. "Maybe she's ventala and part witch. Or maybe someone else is active. We know that Reziel has been in contact with people in this area."

Alissa emerged from the bedroom in a cloud of spicy vanilla-scented perfume and a pale gold dress and matching sandals. She approached them, trailing a hand over the furniture as she advanced.

Her vision's faded again, Cerise thought. *Sometimes it's good enough for her to read. Others she must barely be able to see. What causes that?*

Alissa clasped Lysander's forearms and squeezed. "I'm so glad you're all right." She turned to Cerise and gave her a tight hug.

"Thank you," Alissa whispered. "Thanks for helping him."

She's changed. She doesn't hold anything back now, doesn't guard her emotions. Being with Merrick really has set her free.

"You're welcome," Cerise murmured, emotions banging around in her throat.

Jersey stood just inside the door, unspeaking.

"Before we get further into things, this is my friend Jersey. She's had a rough night," Cerise said. "Troy Rella tried to kill her, but he's the one who ended up dead. She needs some stitches."

Jersey stared down at her bandaged wrist.

Alissa strode forward and put an arm around Jersey's shoulders, her voice melodic and soothing. "It happens that Merrick has a surgeon on retainer. She's very good. The stitches won't hurt, and you'll hardly have a scar." Alissa looked in Merrick's direction. "Where should she stay? In the apartment two doors down from Lysander's?"

"That's Ox's place now. What do you say, Ox?" Merrick asked. "Mind staying on four for a while?"

"Yeah, no problem. I wasn't planning to move my stuff for a few more weeks anyway," Ox lied. "You want me to take her down there? Get her settled in and call the doc?"

Merrick nodded.

"All right," Ox said, holding the door open.

"Jersey," Merrick said.

She looked at him.

"I probably don't need to tell you that Rella got what he deserved."

"Most people won't think so. I left the scene. I'll be in trouble for sure," she said softly. "But I couldn't just let him kill me, could I?"

"Course not," Ox said.

Jersey glanced at Cerise and murmured, "I still think I'll be in trouble eventually."

"No, you won't," Merrick and Cerise said at the same time.

Ox put one of his big paws between Jersey's thin shoulder blades. "You're covered. You don't have to worry about it anymore." He ushered her toward the hall.

Jersey turned back. "Cerise, don't forget about Hayden."

"I won't. Get some rest. I'll come tell you as soon as I hear from him." Cerise turned to Merrick. "Her brother went to see Tamberi Jacobi. With the Varden cell towers out of commission and the Etherlin on lockdown, we haven't heard from him. Could you make some calls? Find out if he's still in her territory?"

"Yeah, no problem."

"See," Ox said, guiding Jersey out. "The boss will take care of everything. Now I gotta admit I'm a fan. And I'll tell you who's nuts for your music is my little sister. Maybe after the doc patches you up and you get some rest, you can sign a couple of autographs . . ."

Alissa's worried expression softened. "She'll be all right with him. Wounded women and children are Ox's specialty."

"Then Jersey's perfect since she's a little of both," Cerise said.

Merrick poured himself a drink, and Cerise noticed the tightness around his mouth. Alissa crossed to Merrick. "What's wrong?"

"That kid looks pretty torn up. Rella was on my list. I wish I'd gotten to him sooner."

Alissa's expression turned grave. "If that's anyone's fault, it's mine. I didn't speak up when I could have, and I asked you to leave him alone."

"You didn't know he'd turn killer," Merrick said.

"Yeah, Liss, don't blame yourself. Troy probably started to unravel because he thought Lysander and I were closing in on him. I threatened him and set him on edge."

Lysander rolled his eyes. "The blame for Rella's actions belongs to him. From what I gather he liked to prey on young girls. That a tiny teen girl turned the tables on him is poetic. What's more, the demon who keeps his soul for a pet in hell will torment him with that fact. So much the better."

Lysander cracked his knuckles. "Assuming her character is good, when the shock wears off, the girl will do well enough."

"She's not an archangel," Cerise said.

"Clearly," Lysander replied.

"And because she's not," Cerise continued impatiently, "she might not take to killing demons' minions like a duck to water. She's just human, which is why the rest of the *humans* in the room are concerned about the effect tonight might have on her."

"Will worry or regret change anything?" Lysander asked casually, making Cerise glare at him.

"Lysander's right," Alissa said and gave Merrick's arm a squeeze. "Let's move forward." She walked to the couch and sat, waving a hand to the other seats. "Why don't you guys sit down and fill us in."

Cerise rolled the small suitcase over and took a seat across from the couch. As she started to relate what they'd discovered, she bent and unzipped the bag. She pulled out the Montblanc pen and set it down with some CDs she'd grabbed from the house.

"These are Richard's," Cerise said. "I couldn't find the manuscript he wanted. There were dozens of boxes in the closet and we didn't have time to sit around while I went through them."

"Of course not," Alissa said.

Lysander raided the refrigerator before joining them in the living room.

"Anyone hungry?" he asked. They all shook their heads, and Lysander sat, putting a tray of bread, cheese, and fruit on the table. Cerise stared at the gallon of milk that he set in front of him. Apparently he planned to drink it all.

Cerise blinked, not wanting to get distracted by him. She unzipped the suitcase's inner pouch and emptied its contents.

"What's all that?" Alissa asked.

"Some of it was hidden inside a couch cushion at Ileana's and the rest Troy had on him."

Merrick lifted the pill bottle. "Klonopin?"

"Griffin and Hayden were in a bad wreck when they were teenagers. Afterward, Griffin had seizures. Not the full-blown kind where you fall on the ground and shake, but the kind where he'd stare into space and not realize what was going on around him."

"Any idea why Rella had the pills?"

"No. I thought maybe he wanted to use them on Jersey to add to the suicide scene he was staging. I figured he was keeping them handy in his pocket until he needed them," Cerise said.

Merrick uncapped the bottle, rattled the pills and sniffed them. "Pungent."

"Let me see," Lysander said, taking the bottle. He waved it under his nose. "Smells like a plant extract." Lysander closed his eyes to concentrate and then nodded. "Not demonic despite its name. It's devil's trumpet."

"Jimsonweed?" Merrick asked, then sniffed the bottle again and nodded, smiling faintly. "When I was in juvie as a kid, we used to have to pick up trash in the fields as part of the work furlough. Jimsonweed grows about five feet tall and the seeds are a hallucinogen. Every time we got a new guard that didn't recognize the plant, at least one or two kids had to be taken to the hospital for tripping on it."

Cerise took the bottle and inhaled. "I don't smell anything."

"The odor's pretty faint."

"Why should the bottle smell of anything?" Cerise poured the pills into her hand. They were stamped in the usual way. Clearly pharmaceutical grade, they'd been manufactured and dispensed through a pharmacy. She dumped them back into the bottle and closed it. Had Griffin stashed drugs in the pill bottle? Or had someone else adulterated his meds? Troy? If so, why? To make Griffin more dependent on the people managing his career?

"Here's the flash drive that was around Troy's neck," Cerise said. "I plugged it in to one of Alissa's laptops at the house, but as expected, it's encrypted." She slid the drive across to Merrick. "Lysander thought you might be able to get into it." Merrick took it without comment. Alissa picked up the bird sketch, bringing it close to her face for examination. Merrick's nostrils flared and his hand shot out, pulling the paper away from her.

Alissa looked up through loose blonde waves and raised her brows in question.

Merrick glanced at the sketch, folded it, and passed it to Lysander. "When you wash your hands, sweetheart, add a few drops of bleach to the soap."

"Now?"

"Now."

"What was on that sketch?" she asked, rising.

"Demon ash."

Alissa frowned, but said nothing as she went to the kitchen.

"You can hardly expect to keep her out of things when she's living here," Lysander said, breaking off a hunk of bread and spreading some goat cheese on it.

"Try and keep up, Lyse," Merrick said mildly. "We already discussed the fact that demon-hunting's best left to the professionals."

"Even so, she's in this. You married her."

"Doctors marry lawyers. Lawyers don't moonlight in the operating room, and doctors don't try cases. Alissa's working to inspire a breakthrough that could make taking the salt out of ocean water feasible. I couldn't help a scientist with that and neither could you. Like us, she's got rare skills. I leave her to her work, and she leaves me to mine."

Finishing off the milk, Lysander said mildly, "Scientists are unlikely to attack the penthouse."

"Neither are demons if we take the fight to them."

Alissa returned to her seat. She leaned back, resting her shoulders against Merrick's arm, which was stretched out on the back of the couch. She folded her hands on her lap.

They're certainly cozy, presenting a united front.

"So Merrick, you'll see what you can discover about Ileana Rella's current whereabouts?" Lysander asked.

Merrick nodded.

"I'm going to put Cerise through some training exercises. Afterward, we'll rest if she needs it, then we'll see if we can locate Tamberi Jacobi. That female ventala seems to be at the center of the demon-raising activities and needs to be dealt with," Lysander said, breaking off more bread.

"You think it's a good idea to parade a muse and her magical blood through the Varden when Tamberi's bent on vengeance? Why don't you search alone and leave Alissa's friend here?"

Lysander chewed and swallowed. "Cerise stays with me. My claim to her trumps all others, including Alissa's."

"Which one of you was in the tree again?" Merrick asked.

"Exactly," Cerise said dryly. "The arrangement seems a bit off, doesn't it?"

Lysander swallowed, unperturbed. "The last time I had a lover and let her out of my sight, Reziel murdered her. Felice left me because we weren't the right match, and I didn't pursue her." He shook his head. "She was alone, but she was nephilim. She should've been able to recognize Reziel for a demon and should've had a chance of defending herself from his attack." Lysander shook his head again, his features turning granite hard. "Things were done. No part of her was spared. When he finished, he displayed her broken body." He clenched his jaw.

"When I caught up to him, I made him sorry. I showed him

what it feels like to be beaten without mercy." Lysander exhaled slowly. "Even now that fight's darkness is slime on my soul. He earned my wrath and felt it, but I know him. Living underworld has twisted him. He'd kill again and do worse to spite me. Especially if he finds a woman whose company suits me hand in glove, the way his used to before we fell. His jealousy will be as black as charred earth. Reziel's not risen now and doesn't take the flesh lightly, but I'm sure rising is what he intends. Am I likely to leave a woman I'm responsible for undefended? No. Never."

"Undefended? I suggested you leave her here."

"Reziel's many ranks higher than the demons you've fought, Merrick. You're a credit to your training, and I'd give you decent odds against anyone, but killing demons is never a simple thing, and I wouldn't trust you to protect Cerise before the other muse in this apartment. Reziel would spot that weakness in an instant. Cerise stays with me." He glanced at her for signs of protest.

Cerise studied him, the slant of his cheekbones, the slashing scars, the set of his jaw. "I enjoy arguing, Lysander, but you haven't really left me an opening. Reziel's been mucking about in my world, and I want that to end as much as you do. You're interested in keeping me alive; I'm interested in staying alive. What's there to fight about?"

"Wise beyond your years," Lysander said, his shoulders relaxing. "Also, you couldn't desert me yet even if your life weren't at stake." He rose and collected his dishes.

"Why's that?" she asked.

He set the dishes in the sink and turned, scorching her with a look. "You owe me a reward for my earlier restraint."

She smiled.

Lysander turned to Alissa, skinning the sweater from his chest and setting it on the coffee table. "I borrowed one of Richard's sweaters and a jacket. They couldn't stretch as far as I needed, so I damaged them. I'll pay for replacements."

"Not necessary. But speaking of that, I have something for you," Alissa said, rising and proceeding to a nearby closet.

Merrick was next to her in an instant. He opened the closet door. "I've got it."

Alissa turned as Merrick set a couple of large shopping bags on the couch. "Let's see," Alissa said, digging through the first bag. "There's this," she said, holding out a knit shirt to Lysander.

Cerise looked at the hanging straps and said, "What is that?" Cerise took it and examined it. The chest and sleeves were a black knit stretch fabric, but there was no back. There were suspenderlike straps hooked at the neck and waist horizontally.

"It's backless. Because of your wings, you're often shirtless, but in the winter it's freezing. I had Merrick's tailor make this as an experiment. I also designed a coat that has a back panel with a cord. You pull it and the back will pop open. I know normally you just wrap yourself in blankets and sit by the fire when you arrive somewhere, but even in spring your skin's incredibly cold after flying."

Cerise looked at Lysander, who was staring at Alissa. "Warmth is a true gift to a fallen angel. Did you know it's part of what we lost? When a portal opens, many demons try to rush through, but the opening is too small. Only the lesser ones can escape into the world. And the reason they're all in such a frenzy is the earth's heat. They'd tear each other to pieces to enter the world of men because when they're flesh, they feel warmer and closer to heaven. The chill, it's the ache that never ends."

He pulled the sleeves onto his arms. "That's part of the reason, besides the natural male instinct, that we feel compelled to make love to human beings. You're warm."

"The fallen are always cool-skinned?" Cerise asked, realization dawning.

"Yes, and the damned are like ice inside. Hence the rumored fires in hell. No matter how intense the heat, it's never quite enough." Lysander tried on the one-sided shirt, pulling the straps to tighten them, then moving experimentally. "The fabric yields well to movement. It's a brilliant design." Lysander took Alissa's hand and kissed it. "You honor me with your thoughtfulness. Thank you."

She smiled. "I'm glad you like it. I was thinking maybe goose down for the coat, but that might be too bulky. We'll see."

"What else is in the bag?"

"More of these shirts and some pants. Denim and leather. You left a worn pair in the guest room, so I gave them to the tailor to copy."

208 ❖ Kimberly Frost

"Very nice." Lysander glanced at Merrick's dubious expression and smiled. "Merrick's offered me the use of his tailor a hundred times."

"I know you haven't taken him up on it, but isn't that because you like to keep your circle of acquaintances small? You don't like meeting new people."

"Exactly."

Alissa shrugged. "This way you don't need to. We can take care of it. It's no problem."

"That suits me. Thank you." He turned to Merrick. "I concede that sometimes it's convenient for you to have a wife."

"I still don't care what you think," Merrick said.

Lysander rolled his eyes. "Alissa and Richard understood my reservations. You almost got yourself killed on their account."

"And would do it again."

"Which involves me since you have an obligation to fulfill."

"One doesn't exclude the other. You still intend to fulfill the prophecy, don't you?"

"Of course!"

"But you've taken on the responsibility of Cerise's safety."

"I have, but that's different."

"Is it?"

"Of course. I didn't have a choice. She's been forced on me by circumstance."

Stung by his admission, Cerise took a step back.

Merrick shook his head at her as if to reassure her. "Yeah, by the circumstance of you flying into the Etherlin with your blood gushing out of your back, so there was no way for her to avoid it."

"I didn't intend for her to find me alive. I only planned to leave her my knife."

"Sure, you did."

Lysander scowled. "You accuse me of lying to you?"

"I accuse you of lying to yourself."

Lysander waved him off impatiently. "Speaking of knives forged in archangel blood, Cerise needs one. I can't get to my own home while my wing is still healing. Give her one of the daggers I gave you until I can replace it."

"We can use the gym for her training," Merrick said.

"Just give her the dagger. Her training is my concern."

Merrick smiled. "So it's okay for you to share my wife, but you're going to keep Cerise all to yourself, huh?"

"Now you see the way of it," Lysander said coolly as he walked to the door.

The corner of Merrick's mouth curved higher as Lysander stepped outside. "Yeah," Merrick murmured, "it was all forced on you by circumstance." Merrick winked at Cerise and said, "Come on, beautiful. Let's get you a knife."

Chapter 20

Dressed in black stretch pants that molded to her lower body and a white V-neck Hanes T-shirt that was as transparent as tissue paper over her lace bra, Cerise stood in the middle of a mat, dagger in hand, and waited. Lysander studied her with a predatory look in his eyes.

A headband held the hair back from her face, and she studied him with an intent expression.

"If you can cut me three times before you're too exhausted to fight, I'll consider the session a success," he said. "Stretch and tell me when you're ready."

She waved the tip of the dagger toward herself in a "bring it on" motion.

He smiled. "You don't want to stretch?"

"I stretched when I changed clothes. Come on."

In the next hour, she landed on the mat so many times, she thought her rattled brain might ooze out her ears. He showed her moves and maneuvers that she would never have dreamed a human body could manage and yet she did. She cut him four times in all before she was too spent to stand.

"Good, Cerise. Very good," he said, taking the dagger from her limp grip and setting it aside. He sat next to her on the mat and rubbed her hands, working the tension from her fingers. He bent forward and took her leg, rubbing the muscles then lengthening them in a series of slow stretches. Gastrocs, hamstrings, and gluts. She gave no resistance when he rolled her onto her stomach. She sighed as he drew her shoulders back, stretching her shoulders and pecs. Then he worked her back, easing the strain, massaging in slow firm circles till she felt about as solid as a bowl of warm pudding.

"I'm going to sleep here," she murmured, closing her eyes.

She woke later when he moved her.

"I'm up," she mumbled, pulling loose of his grip and running a hand through her hair as she rose. "Any idea what time it is?" she asked.

He glanced at the window. "Early morning. Three or four."

She nodded, rubbing her arms where the salt of dried sweat tattooed her skin. "I need a shower and a strong cup of coffee." She walked to the table where her cell phone rested. There was a signal.

"Finally! They've managed to get at least one of the towers repaired." She scanned through the texts and found one from Hayden. She opened it.

Am okay and crashing at friend's place. Will come back to Etherlin tomorrow.

She tried calling, but went straight to voice mail.

"Hey, it's Cerise. I'm glad you're okay. Where are you? Give me or Jersey a call. Something happened to her tonight—it's too long for voice mail. Just call when you get a chance."

She ended the call and joined Lysander, who waited by the elevator.

"The girl came down to check on you. She looked better by the way."

"Oh good. Had she heard from Hayden?"

"I'm not sure. I asked her some more questions about what happened. She said that Rella didn't come to the apartment to confront her. He was looking for something."

"Did she have any idea what he was looking for?"

"He started looking in the bathroom for whatever it was."

"Maybe the pills then," she said as they boarded the elevator. "A lot of people keep their prescriptions in the medicine cabinet above the sink. Griffin kept his in the kitchen." She tipped her head up to stare at the roof of the elevator. "Troy wouldn't have just happened across that prescription to use for the suicide staging. I think he came for the bottle." She narrowed her eyes. "Griffin's behavior was erratic the last couple months of his life. What if Troy ground up some jimsonweed and dusted it over his pills?"

"To what end?" Lysander asked as they ascended.

"If it gave Griffin more seizures or made him think he was losing touch with reality, maybe Troy would've had an easier time controlling him. There were days when Griffin was a control freak about the music and his career and the band's image. Other times, he would've signed anything anyone put in front of him. On the night Griffin died, he and Troy had an argument about a music festival that Troy wanted the Molly Times to play. Besides it being a lot of money for everyone involved, if the Times had signed on, Troy could've gotten a couple of other new bands he was promoting on board, too. Troy bought us a couple of rounds of shots, which he normally wouldn't have been in favor of me drinking. Maybe he did it to soften Griffin up. Maybe he came over later to get Griffin to sign off on the paperwork. I wouldn't have let Griffin sign if he was out of it, but maybe Troy expected me to be passed out. He could've slipped something into my drink to be sure I would be unconscious. But was Troy's endgame really just about making money? Or was he involved in something else? Something bigger?" she wondered aloud.

Inside Lysander's apartment, Cerise stripped and showered and wrapped herself in a thick blue towel. Lysander showered, too, and emerged from the bathroom naked.

Water dripped from his skin and his blond hair curled at the ends as he sat next to her on the bed. The dagger wounds had all healed, and the other scars in the areas where she'd cut him had faded, too. Some of his original scars were still prominent, but others were like melted wax that had been rubbed away, leaving only faint marks. His ability to heal was amazing.

She put a hand on his chest, his flesh cool against her palm. *The fallen are always cold.*

"You should wrap yourself in a blanket."

"I plan to," he said, watching her with dark green eyes. The low light in the room fractured away from him in that strangely alluring way.

She nodded. She let her hand slide lightly over his muscles, then fall onto her lap. "I've never had a casual affair."

"I never proposed that the affair be casual."

"No? You've made it pretty clear to me and to anyone who'll listen that you're stuck with me out of circumstance."

"Just because I would've resisted binding you to me out of choice because I know the risks, doesn't mean I regret what happened. Your company is a pleasure I savor. I didn't admit that to Merrick because love is the one thing that makes him reckless, and I've criticized him for it. Confessing that I enjoy being near you is information I don't choose to share. He already sees too much."

"What difference does it make if Merrick knows you want me with you?"

He paused. "Ultimately it doesn't. When it comes to emotional attachments, Merrick doesn't look to my example, nor do I look to his. But I encouraged him to behave with restraint in his passion for your friend. If I'm now unrestrained as I fall in love with you, he'll expect me to admit I was wrong when I advised him. I won't. I wasn't wrong. But I don't relish tension between Merrick and me. He won't go back on his word to help me, but when he's angry, his silence is an abyss."

"If you don't want there to be tension, you should stop suggesting Alissa would be better off if you gave her up. Anyone can see neither of them will ever agree to that."

"You're right," Lysander said. "It's Richard all over again. The man had a mad passion for his wife. Still does. Merrick and Alissa seem bent on the same reckless course, to love with such abandon that it destroys everything in its wake."

"I say good for them. Why shouldn't love be as precious as war?"

He raised his brows. "Meaning?"

"Meaning, to use a poker metaphor, Merrick goes all in. He wouldn't run from a fight, and he doesn't love in a half-assed way, either. He's all in."

Lysander flashed a smile. "Is that a challenge? An indictment of what you perceive to be a lack of romantic courage on my part?"

"I don't know if it's lack of courage as much as lack of interest. Redemption, fighting, and demon-hunting are your priorities. Anything you'd have with me would be somewhere near the bottom of your list."

"You're wrong," he said, rising and pulling the covers back.

"Am I?" she asked.

He lay on the bed and dragged the comforter to his waist. With an arm behind his head, he watched her. "One of the most difficult things about living in exile is being alone. I got used to it out of necessity. You're a gift I never expected. Even being able to form friendships was more than I hoped for, considering what happened in the past."

"With Felice?"

"Yes. And with others."

She tilted her head in question. He rubbed his thumb over her hand.

"I've been killing demons for centuries. None of those battles, not even the one I fought last night, have been enough to secure my redemption. I'm sure the fight that redeems me will be more deadly than all the others. I have supernatural instincts, and I know that time is winding down. I feel it. Merrick's destiny is tied to mine. It's not certain that either of us will survive."

"Does he know that?"

"He understands the danger."

"Alissa and Richard need him. When he made his promise to you, they weren't a factor."

"Exactly, and they still shouldn't be. It was his choice to remove her from her world. He could have waited until after the battle."

"Love doesn't always leave a person with choices."

Lysander's shoulders rose and fell. "Merrick will destroy the biggest threats to Alissa and Richard while there's still time. If Merrick dies, Alissa will have to find her own way. She's a muse. She's attractive. The rest of the world will embrace her again."

"You could release Merrick from his promise."

"I can't win without him. It's not a fight for one."

"Maybe someone else can help you."

He shook his head. "The prophecy was clear, and I recognized Merrick the moment I saw him fight. He was a young teenager living on the street. He fought several men and there was a move—a sweep and turn followed by each hand striking in a different direction. It was one of my moves."

"Who taught it to him?"

"No one. He moved that way by instinct."

"That's quite a coincidence."

"It's no coincidence." Lysander hesitated, then added, "He inherited it from me."

"Inherited?"

"Merrick's mother was eight generations descended from Felice."

"From Felice and you?"

Lysander nodded. "She made everyone believe her child died. An angel had appeared to her and warned her that the demons would come. They told her that if they found the boy, they'd kill him. She gave the child to the angel who hid him. I didn't know the truth until seventy years later."

"Did you meet your—son or his children?"

"Any involvement with me would've drawn demon attention. Anonymity protects them. I left them alone."

"Until Merrick."

"Merrick's part vampire and was in trouble long before he met me. Being descended from angels and born to a prophecy is what sets him apart from other ventala. I trained him, and killing demons has raised him from the common ranks. Heaven watches him with interest. He has greatness in him, but it competes with darkness. My influence changed the course of his life. We became friends—and more than that. We're the closest thing to family that either of us has. It's led us to where we are now and what we must do together."

"Does Merrick know he's nephilim?"

Lysander shook his head.

"Why haven't you told him?"

"I liked winning his loyalty and friendship. It was worth the earning, and his choices have done him credit."

"Why tell me?"

"I wanted you to know that I'm not just using him. He's a brother to me, and I to him. Also, I wanted you to understand what's between Merrick and me, so that when I tell you that you've become as important to me as he is, you'll understand your significance."

"As important as the warrior who could help you gain redemption? That's a little hard to believe."

He shrugged, letting his hand fall away from hers. "True, nonetheless."

"When you're redeemed, you'll be leaving. You said yourself time is running out. I've already suffered a pretty tough loss just this year. I'm not sure I could face another."

"You, of course, must decide for yourself what you're willing to risk. All I can promise is that I'll never desert you as the musician did. You won't be left in a fog of confusion and doubt."

"If you and Merrick survive the confrontation that's coming, is it possible that you'll live on earth for my lifetime or longer?"

He paused thoughtfully and rubbed his thumb over his lip. It was a gesture she'd noticed Merrick make, too. Did they realize they had that in common?

"It's possible. I've never been given a timeline."

She nodded and leaned forward to touch the gold hair fanned over the pillow. "I need you to do me a favor."

He took a deep breath in, his lids drifting down as if he savored her scent. "What favor?"

"Stop announcing that you didn't choose to be bound to me. I know it's the truth, but it pisses me off every time you say it."

He nodded. "Shall I confess a secret I've been keeping about that?"

"Go ahead. You seem to like making me the guardian of your secrets."

"If they'd given me a choice of any woman in the world to become bound to, I would've chosen you."

She smiled. "Am I supposed to be flattered? I'm probably the only woman other than Alissa that you've spoken to in the past hundred years."

"I don't need to talk to a woman to know whether she suits me. I'm an archangel. I have exceptional instincts."

"So maybe Merrick's right. Maybe the instinct to fly your dagger over on a broken wing wasn't an accident. Maybe subconsciously, you chose what happened."

He glanced at the ceiling and licked his lips. He sighed and glanced back at her with a chagrined smile. "I can't deny it's possible. My history shows that I can be reckless and ruled by emotions. Perhaps Merrick inherited that from me, too. Perhaps that's why I'm so critical of him for it. I see myself in him." His fingers tapped idly against his ribs. "I swear it was never a conscious thought to come to you so we'd be bound by blood, but whether the instinct to go to the Etherlin was born of wanting you . . ." He shook his head. "Maybe. If it was, I hope you'll forgive me."

"If it was, there's nothing to forgive."

She traced his lip with a finger, and the tip of his tongue stretched to meet it. She closed her eyes as he licked her fingertip.

"We have a lot to do," she murmured, pulling her hand away.

"I'm glad to hear it," he said in a low voice. His hand gripped the top of her towel.

"I meant we have work to do and probably shouldn't spend precious waking hours in bed."

"There's time enough," he said. With a deft motion, he unfastened the tucked end of the towel and it fell open, exposing her. The cool air raised gooseflesh on her arms, but heat quickly washed over her as he cupped her breast, his thumb stroking her nipple.

Her breath caught, and her mouth went dry.

"So beautiful," he said, squeezing her. "Warm and ripe as fruit on the vine under a midday sun. Your body is a miracle, Cerise, at once strong and succulent."

She closed her eyes and bit her lip as sensations swirled through her. His fingers tightened on her nipple, and she gasped at the stab of painful pleasure that rippled through her.

His hand released her breast slowly and slid down to her hip then to grip her thigh and buttock. His strong fingers kneaded her flesh as it had earlier in the gym, but this time it wasn't to soothe.

Trailing his hand over the slope of her thigh and nudging it outward, he whispered, "You could make me a slave to your pleasure."

She tipped her head back, panting.

He stroked her slick heat, teasing her with the tips of his fingers. Her mouth fell open, and she sucked in a breath. He ground his thumb against her, setting her on fire.

"Wait," she growled, grabbing his wrist.

His fingers stilled.

Breathless, she looked down at him through black lashes.

"What am I waiting for?" he asked, pulling his arm out of

her grasp. He licked the taste of her from his thumb with such relish, her nerve endings burned.

She dragged the sheet down and ran her hand over him. "I don't just want an orgasm. I want you."

"Then have me."

She stroked his erection and watched his stomach muscles tighten.

"We've danced together, so you know we have the strength and flexibility for any position man has dreamt of," he murmured and then groaned as she closed her fist around him. "Choose one. Choose them all. Just have mercy on me and choose quickly."

"I appreciate your offer to take me on a tour of the Kama Sutra," she said, swinging her leg over so she straddled his hips. "But I'm too impatient to get creative." She positioned him at her entrance and sank down slowly, stretching beyond comfort.

"Oh—" she gasped. Her lower body cramped and throbbed, and she gripped his arms hard enough to leave bruises.

"Do you want to—" His last words were crushed by clenched teeth as she rose and slid back down.

"What I want is to ride you like the stud you promised to be," she teased, leaning forward for an angle that promised to send her spinning over the edge into orgasm with maximum efficiency.

"If anyone can do that, it's you," he murmured, closing his eyes.

She started with a slow rhythm that he matched carefully, every muscle taut. He was ripped like the greatest athletes in the world, and she feasted on him with her eyes, watching his muscles contract and ripple as he struggled not to lose control.

Soon she didn't care about anything beyond the intense sensations that roared through her. She moved faster and harder, and he steadied her as she lost control.

An orgasm crashed over her, and she cried out. With shaking muscles, she fell forward onto his chest.

He tipped her head up and sucked her tongue into his mouth for a kiss, then rolled her over onto her belly. Snaking a hand under her, he stroked her tingling sex and entered her again, hard and fast.

"Lysander," she groaned.

"Hmm," he murmured, biting her shoulder as the weight of his body crushed her between the bed and him. She drowned in the suffocating pleasure, her face pressed into the soft sheets. She struggled to meet his thrusts and then lost her mind in another body-jarring rush.

Still seated deep inside her, he turned her over, pressing her into a wild, erotic stretch with her right leg hooked on his shoulder.

"Wait," she gasped as he brought her left knee toward her side and wrapped it around him, tipping her pelvis up. He leaned forward, not moving inside her.

She throbbed around him, barely able to breathe.

He kissed her gently, his tongue caressing her mouth. Then he kissed his way along her jaw and whispered in her ear, "Give me one more."

"I'm not sure—"

"You can."

"Go slow," she begged.

"As slow as we can stand," he murmured and bent his head. He drew the tip of her breast into his mouth and suckled her until the raw sensations turned warm and liquid again. He groaned and nipped her, making her breath catch.

"Your heat is heaven's chorus in my head. Hold me tight," he whispered.

She slid her arms around him, pressing her chest against his and loosening her thigh muscles. He felt her open and moaned with his mouth vibrating against her throat.

She was both slick and ready, and swollen and sore. She held on and bit her lip, digging her nails into his back as he thrust harder and deeper.

Light broke over the room, and her senses were overwhelmed. Hot and cold, sandalwood and orange, pleasure and pain. Sensations without mercy dragged her into one last blinding orgasm. She wailed, feeling him join her.

For many moments aftershocks rocked her body, and the world beyond the bed seemed hazy and unreal.

A thudding heartbeat and tingling flesh slowly gave way to an awareness of the room around them. Soft light. Rumpled sheets. And satisfaction so deep it almost hurt to feel it and know it would fade.

"The stamina of angels and the courage of warriors," he murmured.

"Yes," she said, pressing a palm against his low back. "You're amazing."

"I meant you," he said, his breath a sweet breeze against her neck. "I'm yours," he whispered. "For life and longer."

She smiled and turned her head to kiss his jaw. "Very romantic. Will it ruin the moment if I ask you to let me up? You're crushing me."

He laughed softly and raised himself. He moved onto his back, careful not to roll over any of her limbs. Then he pulled her on top of him. Her head lay against his chest, listening to the thump of his heart, its rate slow and strong. One of his heavy palms rested possessively on her naked buttock.

He'd promised to be hers for life. She couldn't get her head around that yet, couldn't think about whether she was ready to make any promises in return. She only knew that being with him felt more right than anything ever had.

Chapter 21

Cerise woke with a wintry chill. Beneath her Lysander's body leached heat from hers, leaving her stiff and aching. She extracted herself from his grip and rolled onto the bed, shaking. She rubbed her arms as he stirred.

She climbed from the bed and went into the bathroom. She took a very hot shower and felt her muscles start to unknot. Afterward, she towel-dried her hair and dressed in sweatpants, a sweatshirt, and thick socks. She covered him to the throat with the blankets, but he pushed them back down to chest level.

"It doesn't help," he murmured.

"What?"

He rubbed his eyelids then opened them. "If the surrounding temperature is very low, clothes or linens can help prevent my body temperature from plummeting or can help me rewarm, but indoors where the temperature is moderate, blankets and clothes don't do much." He yawned. "Body heat is the only thing that works."

"I woke up feeling like a Popsicle," she said.

"Sorry."

She took his right hand and rubbed it between hers. "Are you cold?"

"No worse than usual." His left hand rested on his chest. "Better in fact, for the moment."

She got up and gathered the things they'd taken from Ileana's. It was time to concentrate, but before she could return to the bed, someone knocked. She glanced at the door, then at Lysander.

"You can answer it. There's no danger to us."

She set the photos and papers on the end of the bed, grabbed the dagger she'd been training with, and walked to the front door. She kept the knife in her right hand and hidden behind her, opening the door with her left.

Mr. Orvin hulked in the hallway.

"Sorry to bother you, Miss Xenakis."

"It's okay. What's happening?"

"The boss got a call about Jersey's missing brother. He's just Varden-side of the Sliver, trying to buy a gun and V3 ammunition."

A gun and vampire-killing ammunition? Hayden's not violent. Cerise knew suddenly, with a lurching stomach, that that ventala bitch Tamberi Jacobi had done something terrible to him, something that could only be settled with a V3 bullet.

"The dealer's keeping him there," Orvin continued. "I'm going to swing by to pick him up. The boss thought you would want to know."

"I do. Thanks. Is Hayden okay?"

"He's trying to buy a gun, so he's on his feet. That's a good sign. Sounds like he's kind of banged up though."

"Banged up how?"

"The boss didn't say. Listen, the little songbird's sleeping. I didn't wanna wake her up yet. Thought you could stay close to her till I get back with her brother."

Cerise's brows knitted. "Hayden's hurt. I'll go with you."

"No need for that. We've got a truce on for the moment, but the peace is kinda shaky. Easier for me to go after him alone."

"We won't slow you down."

"We?" He glanced over her shoulder. "Oh, right. It's like that," Orvin said with a carefully neutral expression.

"Yeah, it's like that," she said with a half smile. *Until he's gone.* She felt a pang of dread at the thought, but pushed it from her mind. *Just live in the moment,* she thought with another glance at Lysander stretched out like a ray of sunshine before them. *It's a really great moment.*

"You can't do better than him in a fight, but I can do this quick and easy on my own." Orvin looked over his shoulder toward the other door. "She's had a couple nightmares. She might sleep through, but I told her if she needed something to knock here. Hate for her to find the place empty if she comes."

Cerise nodded. "You're right. I don't want her to feel alone."

"Great. Here's the key and the code for that apartment in case you want to check on her. I'll be back in about an hour. You need anything while I'm out?"

"Just the Molly Times bassist."

"I'll get him," Orvin said with a smile, then he turned and lumbered away.

Cerise closed the door. "Merrick's bodyguard has a crush on Jersey."

"They're an odd match. If they were mythical creatures, she'd be a pixie and he'd be a giant. They're two feet and several octaves apart."

Cerise laughed. "Sometimes opposites attract."

Lysander shrugged.

"They do both have that white-blond hair," Cerise noted.

"She uses bleach to make hers that color."

"Lots of women do. Blonde's always a popular color." She sat on the edge of the bed, lifting a photograph from the collection of papers they'd brought from Ileana's. The photos had been taken in a place Cerise didn't recognize. One of the walls was painted black and had graffiti on it. The three-pronged lightning bolt from the inside cover of the Molly Times debut CD was central to the artwork. Then she came to a skinny male body, nude against rumpled blue sheets, and she froze, recognizing the Misspent Youth tattoo on the naked flank. She squinted and could make out a Ramones' "Road to Ruin" T-shirt on the floor.

Griffin—

His face wasn't in the frame, but it was him. Her mind reeled.

"What the fuck?" she said as the blood drained from her head. Feeling Lysander's hands on her shoulders, she clutched the picture tighter, staring at the image, trying to get her head around it.

"What is it?" he asked.

"What the hell is she doing with this? Who took it?" Cerise pulled so hard the corner tore off. She looked around wildly, then at Lysander. "This is Griffin. Why would Ileana have had this? Where would she have gotten it?" She lurched to her feet and marched to her phone, then remembered that there was no way to reach Ileana. "I don't understand," Cerise barked, staring down at the picture. "Ileana barely knew Griffin. They'd met a few times. His apartment was in her building, sure, but these aren't our sheets . . . It's not our place." She raised the photo. "Cream-colored carpet with the purple swirl pattern. It's the carpet in Ileana's house?"

She thrust the picture at Lysander. He glanced down at it, frowned, then looked back at her. She snatched the picture and examined it again.

"It appears to be. Yes," he said.

"There was no graffiti in the master bedroom, but maybe she painted over it or maybe this is a guest room." Cerise's head jerked from side to side. "What the hell?" she said, her voice ragged and harsh. "I don't believe it. I would've thought a groupie maybe, when the Times were on tour and I wasn't with them, or some indie rock musician or that waif tattoo artist in San Francisco. But Ileana? No way. She was the farthest thing from Griffin's type possible."

Lysander's dubious expression made her furious.

"What? What do you have to say?" she demanded.

"Nothing if you want me to be silent."

"No, tell me. What?" she said.

"You're a muse. You were his type. She's a muse," Lysander said.

She clenched her fists. "I can't believe them. Either of them."

"Just because she had a nude photo of him doesn't mean they had an affair. Are you certain it's him?"

"It's him, damn it. His body. His tattoo. The Ramones T-shirt I bought! He wore that T-shirt for a fuck date with another woman," she said with a churning stomach. "You know I wasn't the one who wanted an exclusive relationship. It was his idea! He pushed and pushed for us—" She shook her head violently. "What the hell?"

"It's as I said," Lysander said, folding his arms across his chest. "He wasn't worthy of you."

She crumpled the photograph and flung it to the floor.

Lysander looked away with a strange expression passing over his face. Her muscles tightened.

"What are you thinking?" she asked.

He shifted his shoulders uncomfortably. "I'd rather not confess it."

She caught his chin and turned his face toward her.

"This," she said, moving her hand to indicate the two of them, "is still new. Don't hold back. I feel like that picture of Griffin turned my whole world upside down. He and Ileana lied to me and kept me in the dark. They were screwing each other behind my back, and it makes me feel like a fool. I couldn't take it if you started keeping secrets. The way you confide in me is what makes me trust you."

He ran a hand through his shorn locks. "The explanation wouldn't help. It wasn't a thought worthy of an angel, fallen or not."

"I'd imagine that not every thought you have is. Tell me anyway."

He shrugged in surrender. "You and I together, we're the right fit." He pressed his palms together, each finger the perfect mirror of its fellow. "If we'd met earlier, Griffin Lane would have been in my spot. At moments, his memory still is. I'm sorry that seeing the picture hurt you, but—in truth, I'm also not sorry you found it."

She arched a brow, exhaling through pursed lips.

"If I'm being brutally honest I'm not sorry he's dead and gone. You're mine now, and I want you to myself." He shook his head. "I know how dangerous jealousy can be, but in the end, I want you to love only me."

A wave of hot emotion crashed over her, and she found it satisfying. Jealousy might not be worthy of an angel or a muse, but the passion that inspired it was hard to resist. She licked her lips, staring at Lysander's gorgeous face, and let herself feel possessive of him.

Archangels are part of heaven's forbidden fruit, and no woman alive gets to taste this one but me. If Griffin did screw Ileana, to hell with him.

"If you ever cheat on me while we're together, I'll kill you."

He smiled. "I'll never cheat on you. It's not in me to do it."

"No?"

"Loyalty comes as naturally to me as athleticism—or pride," he said with a self-deprecating smile. "I'll never give you cause to doubt my fidelity."

The steadiness of his gaze, unflinching and open, eased something inside her. She wouldn't have thought anyone could calm her at such a moment, but Lysander could be—and was—larger than life.

The tension in her muscles loosened, and she appraised him with mock cool. "Despite your fallen status, if you continue to play your cards right, you may get your wish and turn out to be the only man I love," she said.

The corner of his mouth turned up, and he inclined his head. "I accept your challenge. I'm a great card player," he said slowly.

She clasped her hands together. She wasn't really in the mood for banter. She wanted to smash something, to sprint full-out across the world, pounding the ground into submission, or to work off her anger some other way . . . but she made herself play, to prove to herself how little Griffin's betrayal meant.

"A great card player? That's not what Richard North says."

Lysander rolled his eyes. "Richard cheats at cards, and Merrick lets him."

That truly made her smile. "Richard doesn't have a particularly firm grasp on reality, and he's Merrick's new father-in-law. It's cool of Merrick to let him win."

Lysander shook his head with a frown. "I don't object to Richard taking my money, though I can't see why he needs it when Merrick and Alissa provide everything for his care and comfort. I object to my other losses."

"Other losses?"

"Have you heard of something called 'bragging rights'?"

She laughed, almost surprised at the sound. "Once or twice."

He tapped his thigh. "My competitive nature can't abide losing and then being ribbed about it."

She leaned forward and kissed him. Lysander's mouth opened against hers, taking as he gave.

A little bit of heaven to wash away the bitter taste in my mouth.

Cerise leaned back and licked her lips. "We could go back

to bed for a while. I'm going to want to talk to Hayden as soon as he gets here. Until then we could rest . . . or do other things. Have a preference?" she asked.

"A very strong preference," he said and kissed her again, grabbing her around the waist and propelling them both back onto the mattress.

"Okay then. Make me forget him," she whispered.

He smiled, eyes dark and calculating. "For certain."

Things were slow and sweet, like drizzling syrup. They savored each other until finally, in a heap of dampened sheets, she fell into a deep and dreamless sleep.

Lysander had turned the heat up high and covered them with blankets so that Cerise wouldn't be chilled by his body being pressed to hers. Unlike when she'd slept against him before, this time she woke feeling refreshed.

She opened her eyes to study his handsome face. His lips were slightly parted, his breath sweet and cool against her forehead. She turned her head and through the window she saw late-day sun.

"Oh," she murmured, raising her head and shoulder to see the clock. Five thirty in the afternoon. "Hell."

"What about it?" Lysander murmured, pressing his face against her breast. His lips closed over her skin in a lingering and sleepy way.

"We slept all day."

He licked her with the flat of his tongue, like a cat trying to capture a drop of cream.

"Lysander," she said, catching his hair in her hand and holding his head still while she leaned away from his questing mouth.

His lids rose a fraction of an inch. "I can still reach," he said, and his tongue snaked out to lave her nipple. It sent a thrill through her that raised gooseflesh, but it was obvious that one of them was going to have to stay strong.

Her fingers twisted in his hair and gave it a hard tug. "Just because you can doesn't mean you should."

"True enough. And just because you pull my hair doesn't mean you want me to stop."

"True enough," she echoed with a small smile. "I actually *want* you to keep going, but I'm telling you not to."

Relenting, his head fell back onto the pillow. She studied his mouth, wanting to plant a kiss on it, but that would be begging for trouble. Instead she smoothed down his hair and rose from the bed.

She marched into the bathroom and took a hot shower. Thoughts of the night's revelations made her furious at Griffin again. Lysander had been an excellent distraction, but even he wasn't enough to overshadow that damned nude photo forever. Did she care anymore where Ileana was or what was happening to her? *No.*

The Rellas hadn't been her friends. They were treacherous liars. Let Etherlin Security hunt for Ileana; Cerise was done with that part of things.

When she came out of the bathroom wrapped in a towel, she was surprised to find Merrick and Alissa in the apartment.

With a casual wave of his hand, Lysander said, "Merrick and Alissa came to speak with us."

"So I see," she said.

"Oh, Lysander," Alissa said with a soft laugh. "When I said you should let her know we were here, I meant you should let her know before she came out of the bathroom from her shower."

"Why?" Lysander said.

To Cerise, Alissa said, "I'm sorry." Alissa hurried to a closet and retrieved a bathrobe.

Lysander glanced at the robe disdainfully. "The human obsession with nudity is wasted energy. And Cerise is the last person who needs to cover her body. It's superb."

When Cerise had the robe around her and fastened, she pulled the towel out from underneath it, wadded it up and flung it at him. He caught it and set it next to him on the edge of the bed.

"I see you're dressed," Cerise said dryly, glancing pointedly at his jeans.

"Merrick insisted," Lysander said with a shrug. "He left Alissa standing in the hall while I put these on."

"It's a social convention. It costs you nothing to conform and would make us uncomfortable if you didn't. Why resist?" Cerise asked.

"On principle."

"You'd get further having this argument with a rock. He's immoveable on the subject," Merrick said. "And on plenty of others."

Lysander nodded. "Would you paint over Cabanel's Venus to cover her nakedness? Do you wrap sheets in toga fashion around the sculptures in your rooftop garden?"

Merrick rolled his eyes.

"Of course you don't," Lysander continued. "The form and function of human bodies is a work of genius, of unparalleled artistry. And no demon plot will ever rob me of that perspective."

"You can be philosophically opposed all you want as long as you keep your clothes on," Cerise said. "While we're involved, I'm the only woman who gets to see you naked."

Lysander cocked his head, his gaze going to the crumpled photo. "Nakedness implies intimacy, so it's cause for jealousy?"

Cerise nodded.

"Then I'll follow convention if you want me to."

Merrick raised his brows in surprise, and then looked at Cerise. "That's some trick. You're welcome to stick around."

Lysander rolled his eyes. "You, on the other hand, can return to your apartment with Alissa whenever you want, Merrick."

Merrick smiled at the invitation to leave. "Is 'make love not war' your new motto, Romeo?"

Lysander ran a hand through his hair. "If battle is imminent, I'm ready. Until it's imminent though, I prefer her company to yours."

"Can't blame you for that," Merrick said.

Cerise cleared her throat, seeing she would have to get them back on task. "So what brought you guys down here, Merrick?"

"Hayden Lane slipped through Ox's fingers. From what I can piece together, Tamberi Jacobi told Hayden and Jersey that Griffin died owing her money. When Hayden went to settle accounts, Tamberi decided she'd rather have his blood than his money. Or, knowing her, both his blood and his money. Hayden managed to escape, but after a transfusion at the local urgent care, he seems to have decided to take his blood back from

Tamberi using the age-old method. He's gonna watch it drain out through a lot of lead-lined holes."

"Oh no." Cerise scowled. "Hayden's no match for Tamberi Jacobi. The second she sees him approach, she'll know he's come for revenge. He'll never get close enough to shoot her before she kills him."

"He's had no weapons training?"

"No," Cerise said.

Merrick's grim expression spoke volumes.

"I need to find him before he tries to confront her," Cerise said.

Lysander rose to join her.

"Merrick, any idea where we can find her? Or where we'll find Hayden?" Cerise asked.

"Tamberi's a frequent fixture at Di Vetro. It's a club," he added. "No guarantee that she'll be there tonight though, unless we bait the trap."

"What do you suggest?" Lysander asked.

"That I come along and invite her to meet me for a drink so she and I can settle our differences."

"I know she wants to kill you, but she'll have to suspect that the invitation is a trap," Lysander said.

"If I make the meeting request public enough, she won't be able to ignore it without losing face. She'll come."

"That works," Cerise said.

"I take it that you don't want me to join you?" Alissa asked.

Merrick shook his head. "You killed Cato. There's no one on earth Tamberi wants dead more than you. Not even me."

"I bet you never expected to find my name above yours on a Wanted poster," Alissa said.

Cerise couldn't help but smile. Merrick loomed dark and dangerous over his pale wisp of a wife, but there was a glint in Alissa's eyes that said she shouldn't be underestimated.

"Actually, I wouldn't say that," Merrick returned. "You've always been on the top of my Most Wanted list."

The edges of Alissa's mouth curved up. "Sometimes it's nice to be popular. As for Tamberi Jacobi . . ." Alissa tilted her head and continued in a deceptively mild tone. "She's a danger to the world. If she misses her brother so much, she should join him."

Cerise raised her brows. *Yeah, let's not underestimate Alissa.*

Alissa laid a hand on Merrick's arm and squeezed. "But no matter how Tamberi Jacobi ends the night, I expect you to come home in one piece. Do that, Merrick." Cerise felt Alissa's power pulse through the room, the scent of amber and vanilla wafting on the air. Merrick licked his lips like he'd like to take a bite out of his wife. Cerise wondered if Alissa shared her blood with him. If she did, it certainly wasn't leaving her weakened. To Cerise, Alissa had never seemed more powerful.

"I'll work on things from here," Alissa added.

"What things?" Cerise asked.

"I need to set the record straight for the EC on a couple of matters," Alissa said, trailing a finger absently over Merrick's arm. After a moment, she stepped away from him.

Setting the record straight. That was something Cerise needed to do in her own head. She thought of Griffin's songbook and the need to retrieve it from Lysander's house. Turning to him, she asked, "How are your wings healing?"

"Well," he said. He moved his back experimentally. "I think only another few hours to go. It's hard for me to exactly determine, but the pain of healing is much less than before."

"You're in pain now?" she asked. "You don't show it."

"You expect me to whimper and complain?" He smiled and shook his head. "I'm grateful for the pain of healing. Much better than the alternative."

She nodded. "And I suppose archangels aren't allowed to whimper?"

"There's no law against it," he said, "but you're right, it wouldn't suit us."

"Unfortunately, keeping silent about the pain means that you'll miss out on the comfort someone might offer," Alissa pointed out.

"In certain company," Lysander said, glancing at Cerise, "that would be a shame."

"We're quite the cozy foursome these days," Cerise said dryly.

"Yes. I'd be happy if that went on forever," Alissa said.

Cerise glanced at Lysander, who said nothing. That gave Cerise a pang. He didn't want it to go on. He still wanted to leave them behind. She frowned, unable to keep shards of ice from forming around her heart.

"Dimitri's been trying to contact us," Alissa said. "I'm going to talk to him about Troy. For the sake of everyone involved, the council needs to be aware that there was more to Troy than he let the EC see."

"Good luck convincing them of that."

Alissa smiled a distant smile, glacial in its resolve. "In this case, I don't need luck. I kept proof."

Chapter 22

From the outside, the massive multistory club Di Vetro looked like a haunted mansion. Inside, the swirled glass accents gave the club a surreal feel, as though you were sitting in the middle of a coral reef at the bottom of the ocean.

A maroon light fixture with uneven scalloped edges like it had been formed from melted wax hung from a distressed chain over the bar. Because the fixture was familiar, Cerise stopped walking. The light was similar to the ones hanging over the kitchen counter in Griffin's Etherlin apartment. His were purple and yellow, like a bruise. She hadn't liked their asymmetric shape, and Griffin's lights had an impression etched into them that looked like bats' wings, which Cerise found creepy. Griffin had denied the pattern's resemblance to bats, saying it reminded him of an umbrella. He said the fixture had come from a shop in San Francisco. If that was true, how had another piece from the same artist ended up in a Varden bar?

She stood very still with Lysander's hand pressed against the small of her back, whether just to touch her or to urge her forward, she wasn't sure. The question staring her in the face had her rooted to the spot.

Lysander asked, "Is something wrong?"

"Too soon to tell," she said, running a hand through her hair. "I'm going behind that bar."

Like blades through flesh, Merrick and Lysander cut through the fray. Cerise strode forward, inclining her head at the bartenders who were splashing liquor into glasses and passing cocktails to the raucous crowd.

"Need something?" one of the bartenders barked at her.

Merrick leaned against the bar, saying, "She's not your concern."

The bartenders jerked to a stop, looking over Merrick and Lysander.

"What can I get you, Merrick?" the bartender asked.

"The Macallan Twelve on the rocks," Merrick said. "And a pair of orange 'ritas."

Cerise stood under the light fixture examining it for a signature. Instead she found Molly Times lyrics etched on the inner lip. *Razor-ending zero, I endanger lives.*

"Son-of-a-bitch," she said flatly. She turned to the bartender who set the drinks in front of Merrick. "Do you know the artist who made this glass?" she asked, tapping it with her fingertip.

"Don't know about the artist, but it was a gift to the club's owner from Tamberi Jacobi. She named the place, too. Di Vetro means 'of glass.'"

"Did the lead singer of the Molly Times ever come here?"

"Griffin Lane?"

She nodded.

"Yeah, sure. He showed up with her sometimes."

"With who?"

"With Beri Jacobi."

What? No! With that psychotic ventala bitch who raises— he wouldn't—

The rushing sound in her ears drowned out the noise, and she felt like she couldn't breathe.

The bartender slid one of the orange drinks to her. "Need this?" he asked in a tone that was ripe with condescension.

She glared at him, but took the glass. Tipping her head back, she hoped the alcohol burning its way down her throat would make her numb.

"They came in together?" she asked.

"And they left together. And while they were here, they were *together,*" the bartender said with a smiling sneer. "He might've been your aspirant, but she owned him as sure as if he'd come with a price tag. Wore him like a hat. Don't know where she bit him, but he walked like it was someplace close to his balls."

"Is that right?" Cerise asked, her voice distant and brittle as she felt her heart break all over again. *How many other women were there? Did he ever really love me? Or was it an act to get me to help him with his music?*

No. No way. I would've known—wouldn't I have known?

Feeling humiliated, the lyrics to "Sympathy, Too" echoed in her head. *Taken all at midnight, Black berries done all right.* It seemed that as Griffin had sworn, those lyrics weren't a reference to Cerise's black cherry hair. *Black berries . . . Black Beri's done all right.* Had Griffin actually woven a reference to Tamberi Jacobi into his song?

Cerise felt sick and precariously close to tears.

God, I thought he was hurting, that he needed my support.

He made such a fool of me.

How did I not see it? Not sense it?

She slapped the fixture hard, and it swung in a long arc. Unfortunately the chain wasn't long enough for it to shatter against the wall. She passed the swinging glass on her way out from behind the bar.

Stop. Just stop.

He was a liar and a cheat. She'd given him her time, her talent, her heart . . . All those months she'd grieved for him— that she'd worried that she might have done something to make him hurt himself. She'd felt so guilty, so responsible. She'd even lost the thing that mattered most—her muse magic.

Her eyes burned and she blinked. *Don't you dare cry over him! Not now!*

"Hey, Cerise—" the bartender said, grinning at her.

"I wouldn't," Merrick said in a low voice.

At Merrick's warning, the guy shrugged. "She asked."

Merrick's stare was diamond hard. It held the promise of a painful death. She loved him for that. The remnants of the bartender's smile evaporated.

"Get you another Scotch?" the bartender asked.

Merrick said nothing. His eyes did all the talking, and the bartender ambled to the other end of the bar.

She swallowed past the pain in her throat. "There are some nights—like this one—when I'd like to be able to crush someone with a look," Cerise said. "You'll have to teach me that trick."

Merrick nodded. "Need another drink?"

"No," she said, glancing at Lysander's face and then down his chest to the flat muscles of his stomach. The archangel watched her with interest. He hadn't interfered in her exchange with the bartender, and she was glad. He had faith in her ability to take care of herself in most situations, which meant a lot to her. But she did desperately want to escape the pain and frustration she felt, and Lysander had proven himself an excellent distraction.

"You know what works better than skulking off to a corner to lick one's wounds?" she asked Merrick, her voice full of false bravado.

"What's that?" he responded.

"Skulking off to the corner with someone pretty who'll do it for you."

Merrick flashed a smile. "True."

"If a fight breaks out and you need a wingman, or woman, give a shout."

Merrick nodded toward his glass, and the bartender materialized immediately to pour him another shot.

"Take your time. I'll cover my end."

"I don't care what they say about you, Merrick," Cerise said and pulled out an expression Merrick was rumored to use, "you're a peach."

Merrick laughed and glanced at Lysander. "You're lucky I met my muse before I met yours. Things might've turned out differently."

She didn't believe that for a minute, but when her pride was in shreds on the floor, it was a cool thing for Merrick to say.

"No, they wouldn't have," Lysander said flatly. "You were right all along. She's mine, and eventually I would've taken her away from anyone she was with. Even you."

Merrick saluted Lysander with his glass.

Lysander pulled Cerise to him and tipped his head down to whisper in her ear. "The more we find out about Griffin Lane, the luckier it is that he's already dead because I probably would've killed him."

She smiled and kissed the side of Lysander's neck. "You know, you've got a talent for making me forget there's anyone in the world besides you. I wish you'd do that now."

Lysander's mouth found hers, and his hand cupped the back of her head, drawing her close. The world swirled in seductive sensations. She pressed forward so they were chest-to-chest, heartbeat-to-heartbeat.

"Come dance with me," he said.

They wove through the club and up a curled staircase to a room with cathedral ceilings and enormous metal and crystal chandeliers. The stage was set for a band, but they must have been between sets because a DJ in a cubbyhole controlled the playlist at the moment. The dim room was slightly smoky and an enormous wrought iron birdcage hung about twenty-feet overhead.

Cerise mouthed the words to Adele's "Rolling in the Deep," which roared from the sound system. People turned to stare as she and Lysander strode to the center of the dance floor. They were taller than everyone and the low light fractured around him, so he couldn't be ignored. Once they began to move in that perfectly matched, born-to-dance-together way, the other dancers formed a circle around them, swaying and staring.

Songs changed, their steps changed, but she could feel him, anticipate what he'd do and how he'd do it. When "Born This Way" pounded from the speakers, she hit a crescendo of adrenaline and endorphins. She'd danced away from him to the very edge of the large dance floor. People writhed and tapped their feet to the beat. As she rushed forward, she was one with the music. She leapt, and Lysander caught her and hoisted her. She arched her back, taking flight. Sailing upward, ten, twenty, thirty feet. Her fingers skimmed the chandelier, setting it in motion. Screams and cheers rose to meet her.

Cerise turned in the air, reversing the climb. There was a moment when her stomach clenched as she fell, but she never doubted that he'd catch her. She tossed her head back and watched the distance between her and the ceiling yawn, lights blurring, beat slamming. It was perfection.

Strong hands and arms guided, then arrested her descent. Her toes and fingers skimmed the floor to massive cheers and foot-stomping. Lysander swung her up and she curled against him, kissing that mouth before sliding down his body to land gracefully on the floor. The applause went on and on.

He glanced down at her and winked. She smiled.

Thank you.

He pulled her up against him as the next song started. The still exploding crowd finally calmed after the first chorus.

"We could charge for that show," she murmured, spinning toward him and away. Her hand lay against his naked chest, feeling his heart thud. She slid her fingers down his torso and hooked them just inside his pants. His muscles tightened.

He grabbed her arm and bumped against gyrating dancers as he led her away from the floor. She didn't ask where they were going. She didn't care.

He pulled her down a dark hall, then shoved the door to the men's restroom open.

"Out," Lysander said to a young guy who was washing his hands.

The guy raised his brows, but didn't argue. When he was halfway into the hall, he said, "The door doesn't lock, dude. Good luck."

When the door swung shut, Lysander pushed her against it and slanted his mouth over hers. He smelled of sandalwood and musk, and his skin was cool and damp and wonderful against her hot flesh. She pulled him tighter to her body. His demanding mouth crushed her lips.

He lifted her, and her limbs tangled around him, her fingers twisting into the waves of his hair, tugging now and again as they rubbed against each other. It quickly became less than enough.

Her heart pounded like the hoofbeats of racing horses. His breath turned ragged and harsh. She ground her body against his.

"Cerise?"

"Yes," she said, fumbling with her zipper.

In moments, they were naked enough. He buried his face in her hair, his lips against her neck as he thrust up and into her. He was silent and she tried to be as well, biting her lip and stifling the low groan that escaped her throat.

Their weight and Lysander's knee against the door prevented anyone from entering, though a couple of people tried. She would've laughed at the wild absurdity of it, but her concentration was focused elsewhere.

Her body reached for satisfaction, and she raced him there. Digging her heel into his back, her fingernails into his shoulder, she scratched his flesh hard enough to break the skin. He exhaled, but didn't vary his tempo.

Moments later, orgasm crashed over her. Her body tightened and wailed with joy, and she bit the inside of her cheek to keep from crying out.

"I won," she husked in his ear.

Lysander ignored the words and kept going for much, much longer, wringing pleasure from her until she shook from the exertion.

He finally came in a thundering rush. He held her for a while. She dangled from his arms, unconcerned that if he let her go, she'd melt into a puddle on the stone floor.

"Who won?" he asked, raising her, staring into her eyes. "Me, I'm certain," he said, his lips curving into a satisfied smile.

"How do you figure?" she demanded and then tapped her chest to indicate herself. "First and more times. If we're keeping score, I won. Clearly."

He set her on her feet. "A tie?"

"If you say so," she said with mock skepticism as she righted her clothes.

"I love you," he said in a casual tone as he zipped his pants.

She gazed up sharply, her fingers going still. "Is that so?"

"That *is* so," he said. He leaned forward and kissed her, then tapped his chest. "First. And most deeply." His eyes were a brighter shade than she'd ever seen them, moss giving way to forest green. "And more than I've ever loved anyone before . . . so I win," he said.

"First maybe, but most deeply? It's too soon to judge," she said, feeling dangerously happy. He'd been exactly what she needed tonight. But what would happen if he earned his redemption? Would he love her enough to stay earthbound? She wasn't brave enough to ask him.

Instead, she walked to the sink and turned on the taps. Cupping water in her hands, she splashed herself with it, then toweled off her face and neck. Her skin was flushed with evaporating heat, and underneath she felt powerful magic humming through her veins. She felt primed to inspire, primed to conquer the world.

Yeah, this feels like heaven on earth to me. Is that how he would describe it? He who's been there? Is this as good in its own way?

She desperately wanted it to be. She glanced at him in the mirror. He leaned casually against the door, coolly perfect and blindingly beautiful. And the way he looked at her, like she was a slice of heaven, too—it took her breath away all over again. How could she not fall a little more in love with him every minute?

But will it last?

A memory of Griffin onstage in L.A. flashed in her mind. How much had she loved him that night while he rocked a crowd of tens of thousands? The answer was that she'd loved him a lot. And now she didn't love him at all. He'd broken her heart, and she hated him for it. Emotions could turn on a dime.

Cerise dried her hands. "I guess we should check with Merrick to see if Tamberi Jacobi's arrived. I need to ask her a few questions." *Like how Griffin got involved with that ventala witch. And how long they were together.* Cerise wished she didn't care about the details, but a part of her did.

And I can't forget Hayden. He's the Lane I should be worried about. This night was supposed to be about protecting him.

"We can check with Merrick if you like," Lysander said. "But he'll send someone for us if we're needed. We can enjoy the music a little longer."

"I'm all for a little longer," she murmured, walking to him and catching his hand. She laced their fingers together.

When they walked out though, she felt Lysander's pace slow, his body go rigid.

"Wait," he said, narrowing his eyes. "There's danger. Approaching fast," he said, easing forward to draw his dagger. She let go of his hand and slid out her gun, her gaze swiveling from side to side. Then she saw them, black-haired and hulking, with their lips drawn back to reveal fangs. *Ventala.*

People scattered, clearing the center of the room until nothing stood between her and Lysander and the half-dozen assassins. Cerise's heart raced, readying itself.

Lysander didn't look at her. In a low voice, he said, "Stay

on my right and behind me. If any get by me, fight the way I know you can."

She tightened her damp-fisted grip on her gun. In a gym on a mat was one thing. Against murderers with superhuman speed and strength . . . ?

A chill ran through her as a massive ventala snarled at them.

"Cerise," Lysander said sharply.

Her gaze darted to the back of Lysander's golden head. He glanced over his shoulder and glared at her. "No fear."

Easy for you—

The thought died. Taking advantage of Lysander's distraction, the monsters charged.

Chapter 23

The Skype conversation between Alissa and Dimitri Xenakis had started well enough. There had been sentimental greetings. Then he'd listened carefully as she'd related the details of her relationship with Troy. He agreed to examine everything that she emailed to him.

When the business was concluded, he wanted to know where Jersey and Cerise were.

"I'm not going to talk about them."

Dimitri frowned. "Jersey will have to make a statement. You say she only defended herself, but you know that ES has to hear that directly from her."

"I'm sure an interview can be arranged—when she's ready."

"The EC got the notice that you've severed financial ties with the Etherlin and that you're going to take the compensation from the energy patents directly. Who's going to manage your fortune from here onward? The ventala?"

She simply stared at him, mimicking Merrick's ability to use silence to answer uninvited questions.

"Can we expect a notice that you're going to sue for the money you donated to the trust?"

"No," she said. "Use it well."

"Where will you live? If you stay in the Varden, it's only a matter of time before something terrible happens. Can you even walk down the street there?"

"How I live is my concern."

"I'm worried about you," he said, his voice low and sincere.

Her heart creaked. For many years, Dimitri had been a surrogate father to her.

"I'm also worried about Cerise," he said. "I wish . . ." He shook his head. "I understand your hesitation to trust the council. We've had a rigid policy against the fallen, but it hasn't escaped our attention that Merrick doesn't seem to have hurt you physically."

She held out her arms, opening herself to his scrutiny. "I'm fine."

"If Merrick and Lysander were excluded from the law against the fallen being allowed into the Etherlin, would you consider coming home? Would you meet with us here where it would be safer for you and Cerise? We might be able to come to an agreement that's acceptable to everyone."

"I don't know," Alissa said, feeling a pang of regret. She loved the Etherlin. She missed the view of the lake from the walking path, missed watching the sun rise over the mountains and her mother's trees in bloom. She missed the household staff, meeting Dimitri for lunch, and being able to sit outside at the coffee shops and cafés without worrying that she'd be attacked. Then she thought about Merrick, and all the things that she missed about her former home melted away. What she felt for him was bigger than anything she'd lost.

"Merrick doesn't really . . ." Alissa paused. "He doesn't follow rules, and the Etherlin has a lot of them."

"The Wreath and your mother's house and her memory are here. Richard's contacted me several times asking for things of hers to be sent to him."

"He has?" she asked. Alissa hadn't realized that her father had been in contact with anyone from the Etherlin.

"This community was the dream of the muses of only two generations ago. Are you and Cerise really ready to let it die? Because even if Ileana is recovered, her skills and Dorie's won't be enough to sustain it. The community will have to change dramatically."

"I think it would have to change dramatically anyway for me to come back. I can't speak for Cerise."

"No one can speak for Cerise," Dimitri said with a fond smile. "Is she all right?"

Alissa nodded.

"Will you at least consider it?"

Alissa nodded again. "I'll speak to Merrick about it. And to Cerise."

"Will you ask her to contact me? I'd like to hear my daughter's voice for myself."

"I will," Alissa said softly. "And for what it's worth, I'm sorry that our choices have been hard on you."

"That's the burden of parenthood," he said, shrugging. "But no matter what you or Cerise ever do, I'll never regret that I loved and helped raised you both."

Alissa looked down and bit her lip. She took a deep breath in and swallowed against the emotion clogging her throat. She glanced back at the screen with damp lashes. "Thank you for that." She smiled at him.

A knock on the door drew her gaze. "I need to go, but I'll speak to you soon. I promise."

"All right. Take care, Alissa."

She closed the screen and crossed the room as Ox, who was in the apartment, opened the door with his weapon in hand. Tony, one of Merrick's men, stood in the hallway.

He held out a laptop to Ox. "We got past the security on Rella's flash drive. The boss said to bring it up as soon as we did."

Ox took the computer with his left hand and nodded. Tony glanced at her and offered her a quick smile of acknowledgment.

"Mrs. M," he said as she took the computer from Ox.

"Hi, Tony. Thanks very much for this and for your help when we were trying to return from the Sliver."

"No problem."

Ox waved his gun in a "get going" gesture.

"See you," Tony said to her. To Ox, he added, "And that guy, the musician, turned up. He said he heard his sister was here and that we were looking for him."

"Hayden Lane? Where's he at?"

"Downstairs. You want me to bring him up to you?"

"No, but you can take him to see his sister, and stick around in the hall. Make sure it's a quiet reunion."

Tony nodded and left.

Ox closed the door and secured it.

"I'd like to talk to Hayden Lane," Alissa said, sitting down on the couch with the laptop.

"You think the boss will want you to look through that alone? Maybe you should wait till he's back."

She smiled, opening files. "What's next, Ox? Wrapping me in Bubble Wrap whenever he's out?" she teased.

"No, but—"

"This conspiracy's big enough that it requires the work of several people," she said, and he nodded. She looked back at the screen. Troy had kept trophies . . . pictures of teen girls in compromising positions. She didn't find any of herself and wouldn't unless he'd taken them without her knowledge. What she'd kept was a stack of emails, but the pictures would go even further toward making a case against him to protect Jersey from the ramifications of his death.

Then Alissa found a folder labeled maps. The first one she opened was titled "tunnel." It was a route from the Etherlin into the Jacobi territory. Her hand hovered over the keyboard, and she moved to the file list to check the date. He'd last modified the file two weeks before she'd been abducted from the Etherlin and turned over to the ventala syndicate. Troy had known. He'd been an accomplice to her kidnapping.

She double-clicked on a jpeg file and a map of the local area opened. There were several marks on the map. All in wooded areas. One of the marks extended into the Etherlin, near the retreat center. She tipped her head to the side.

"An unholy arrangement."

She jumped at the sound of a voice right over her shoulder. She turned to find her father leaning close, looking at the screen.

"What do you mean, Dad?" she asked.

Her father touched the screen over one of the marks and traced a path through the others. "The lines form an inverted pentacle. And look at the superimposed image."

She squinted, straining to see the faint image that was like a watermark under the map. A horned goat. She shuddered, her blood running cold. So Troy had been into Satanism, just as Lysander had asserted based on the blood in the vial around his neck. She had been skeptical, though she should have known better than to question Lysander's judgment when it came to demonology. It was just that she couldn't imagine Troy serving anyone but himself.

Alissa pushed the laptop a little farther away with a sigh. She hesitated, feeling extremely uneasy. She thought of the way Merrick had asked her to wash her hands after she'd touched the tainted blackbird sketch. She hadn't minded. In truth, she didn't want to brush against evil. She preferred to keep the energy around her pure . . . or at least well-intentioned.

"Put on the whole armor of God, that you may be able to stand against the schemes of evil," Richard said.

She looked at her dad.

"A very old literary reference," he added.

"The Bible?"

He nodded. "Ephesians."

She pushed her hair back, clasping it tight at the base of her neck as though holding it there and preventing it from falling in her eyes would allow her to see exactly what the demons intended.

She exhaled slowly. "I need to look through these files, but I don't relish it," she murmured with a shiver. All things demonic made her skin crawl.

"I think the marks on this map are caves," her dad said. "Lysander said that all the demons that have risen over the past several hundred years have done so in this area. These mountains have become dusted with demon ashes. The most powerful muses and the descendants of the vampires migrated here for a reason. There's supernatural energy in this region that makes it easier for them to gain power. And demons are drawn to angels. To our own angels," he murmured and then glanced at the ceiling and let out a hiss, as though in pain.

She jerked her head to look up, but there was nothing overhead. She turned to him. "What is it?"

"A wound."

"Who? How bad?"

"Gather some things, Moonbeam," he whispered. "We may need to leave this place in a hurry."

"Dad, who's wounded?" she asked, clutching his arm.

"Before the night's over. All of them."

*   *   *

The ventala syndicate forces kept pouring into the club. Merrick had slammed into the room on the body of a massive opponent who once fallen did not rise again. Together, Merrick and Lysander were a blur of bloodletting fury, but she couldn't enjoy the show because she had to strike out against several ventala herself. She'd run out of V3 ammunition, so she'd had to resort to her dagger.

She felt a whisper of wind behind her. It raised the hair on her neck and she spun, but was too late to stop the hand that grabbed her throat.

Jerked forward by the angular-featured female ventala, Tamberi Jacobi, Cerise's knife tumbled from her grasp. Tamberi had come from the women's bathroom. Had she been lying in wait? She dragged Cerise into the bathroom and threw her against the wall.

Cerise lurched to her feet as Tamberi stalked forward. They struggled, but in hand-to-hand, Tamberi was fast and vicious. With a sharp crack, Cerise's head hit the tile and the room became gray and muddled. She felt herself being dragged and saw Tamberi open a passage under a sink.

A passage?

Tamberi shoved her, and Cerise fell through a hole. She landed hard on the padded ground and struggled to catch her breath. Tamberi dropped and landed next to her.

Cerise turned her head. They were in a catacomb under the club.

Tamberi grabbed Cerise's hair and yanked.

"Get up or I'll slit your throat right here," Tamberi snarled.

Cerise didn't move. Her head was clearing rapidly, albeit with a splitting headache emerging in the wake of the haziness. Cerise had no intention of moving anywhere quickly. Not only because she needed a minute to get her legs to work properly. But also because she wanted one of Lysander's daggers to follow them down.

"Get the fuck up," Tamberi hissed, jerking hard enough on Cerise's arm to wrench it from the joint. Cerise screamed and slammed her fist into Tamberi's throat. Tamberi reeled, grabbing her neck and drawing in a wheeze. Cerise swung a leg out in a makeshift roundhouse kick. The bony ventala stumbled sideways, tripping off the mat.

Cerise rolled to her knees and forced herself up.

I need a weapon.

Tamberi came at her. Cerise crouched and launched herself forward, slamming her body into Tamberi. Cerise felt her shoulder grind back into its socket as they landed hard on the stone floor; Tamberi was on the bottom, and Cerise's hand dug for Tamberi's gun. The ventala bitch's fist bashed Cerise's jaw, and Cerise felt a bone-jarring crack and tasted blood.

Cerise went momentarily still, then clenched her teeth, sending a wave of nauseating pain through her broken mandible. She launched a new attack, fighting with everything she had. She lost track of the room, of up or down, of left or right. She felt only flesh hammering flesh, pain piled on pain. Then cold metal against her wrist.

Her fingers struggled to close around the gun's handle, her index finger digging into the metal loop. She fought to get her bearings and to point the barrel away from herself.

The bullet exploded from the chamber, and Tamberi screamed.

Flung off the ventala, Cerise landed hard and the weapon discharged again, the bullet ripping into the wall and sending a scatter of debris.

Tamberi clutched her lower ribs, breathing hard as blood seeped through her fingers. Cerise's left arm hung limply by her side as she walked toward the fallen ventala. She held the gun aloft. Cerise needed to put a vampire-killing V3 bullet through Tamberi's heart or to cut off Tamberi's head in order to finish her off for sure. Any other wounds, Jacobi could recover from.

Cerise pointed at the middle of the left side of Tamberi's chest.

Tamberi grinned. "Go ahead. It won't make any difference. Griffin wouldn't betray you. No matter what was done to him, in the end he wouldn't turn you over. But that doesn't mean he won't end up being instrumental in your death."

What?

Cerise heard footsteps behind her. She turned sharply and saw a figure emerging from the shadows.

His name slipped past her lips. "Griffin?" she whispered,

recognizing that gangster swagger he sometimes had when he walked onstage or into a club.

Something glinted in the darkness. She couldn't see him. She squinted and stepped forward.

A low voice that she hadn't heard in a long time said, "Hello, Cherry."

Then a gunshot cracked the air, and a stinging pain erupted into a sharp cramp in her chest. Cerise fell back, landing flat and hard on the cold ground.

"What the fuck?" Tamberi said, laughing. "I don't get you."

"No, you don't."

Cerise struggled to breathe, holding her chest, feeling blood pump through her fingers. The arched stone overhead swayed and her vision blurred. A lanky figure approached. She saw the black "Road to Ruin" T-shirt she'd bought, squinted at the man wearing it.

Griffin?

No, not Griffin.

"Hayden?" Cerise croaked.

"Not at the moment," he said, crouching, and glassy red violet eyes shone in the darkness.

She felt something hard pressed under her ribs.

"I wish we had more time together, Cherry." He cupped her sex in a crushing squeeze. She struggled to move away, then had a flash of memory. Hands on her throat. Pain between her legs. *"I wish we had more time together, Cherry."*

Her mind wailed, but her lips only moved wordlessly. Then he kissed her, forcing his tongue into her mouth. She gagged. With her wounded jaw she couldn't bite hard enough to sever his tongue. She fought to slam a fist into his back. She only had a fraction of her strength. Her body seemed to weigh thousands of pounds, and her arm felt like she'd been lifting weights for hours as she raised it to strike him again.

She clamped her jaws down through the pain, biting his tongue, tasting blood and making him grunt. He grabbed her hair, lifted her head, and banged it against the stone floor. Her jaws jarred open and he pulled his head back with a laugh and spat blood on the ground.

"Going down fighting. As always," he whispered with icy fondness.

Then pop, pop, pop, like firecrackers, three more gunshots tore through her in rapid succession.

She sank into darkness, ripped apart as much by the last words she heard as by the bullets.

"Thank you for helping me destroy Lysander. I couldn't have done it alone."

Chapter 24

Reziel, Lysander thought.

The club was flooded with the stench of demons as though Reziel were all around him. Lysander and Merrick dispatched the ventala efficiently, but then there were human aggressors who had been anointed with ash. Lysander and Merrick sifted through the men and women who smelled of hell, hunting for a flesh-and-blood demon, but they didn't find one. And they realized too late it was a distraction.

When pain cleaved Lysander's heart, he froze. His eyes widened as he felt Cerise fall.

His gaze darted around the club, searching for her.

"Merrick!" Lysander said, spinning around. "Cerise is down. Help me find—she's badly wounded."

"This way," Merrick said, stalking to the men's bathroom.

They tore the doors off to open the stalls, finding only an empty room.

"I smell her," Merrick said, looking around.

"It's a false trail. I had her in here earlier," Lysander said, then pain ripped through his guts and he dropped to his knees, gasping for breath. "God, no." He clutched his chest. "She's dying." He closed his eyes. "She can't die. If I lose her . . ."

"Where? Concentrate, Lyse, where is she? Which way?"

"Below us. She's in a tunnel below us."

Merrick grabbed Lysander's arm and yanked him up. "C'mon."

The club was hazy, and images swam through the blur. Cerise's face. Red malice-filled eyes.

Reziel stood before him, smiling. Lysander swung his dagger, but caught only air and the wall.

Not real.

"Leave her alone," Lysander snarled.

"Why? Because you did?" the demon whispered and faded away.

"Hey!" Merrick snapped.

Lysander's vision cleared, and he realized they were standing at the bar. Merrick had the bartender by the throat.

"Where's the trapdoor to the tunnel under the club?"

"I don't know," the bartender croaked, wheezing for breath. Merrick's grip tightened, and the man's eyes bulged.

"You've got ten seconds to tell me before I crush your windpipe," Merrick whispered.

The bartender's red face swelled from the pressure of Merrick's hand.

"Okay," the bartender mouthed.

Merrick's fingers relaxed enough for the bartender to croak, "All right. It's in the bathroom. The women's bathroom." The bartender struggled to draw in a breath. "False panel under the last sink."

Merrick let go, and the man dropped to the floor behind the bar.

Lysander and Merrick raced through the club and into the women's restroom. Merrick tapped the wall under the far sink and finding it hollow, kicked the panel open, splintering the wood.

"Too small for us," Merrick said, smashing every bit of the frame around the opening.

"Move," Lysander said. He ripped a sink from the wall and swung it. Porcelain shattered and plaster exploded from the blows as the hole widened.

"Good enough," Merrick said, swinging his legs through the gaping space.

Lysander followed and dropped twelve feet to land on the

floor in a crouch. He sprang forward to Cerise's body, which lay in a pool of blood.

Her hands were pale and mottled, but her face was puffy and bluish purple like she'd been suffocated.

"Christ," Merrick murmured.

"Blood in the sac," Lysander said with a desperate ache in his chest. "It's crushing her heart."

Lysander ripped Cerise's shirt open and sliced her bra. There were several holes in her chest.

Merrick knelt, leaning over Cerise with a somber expression and descended fangs. For a split second, Lysander considered telling Merrick to back away, but held his tongue. If Merrick felt himself losing control at the scent of muse blood, he could be trusted to police his own reaction.

Lysander pressed the point of his dagger to Cerise's flesh and clenched his teeth. He pushed the blade inward and filleted her chest open.

"Pull her ribs apart," Lysander said.

Merrick's fingers snagged Cerise's bones and spread them. Lysander sliced a hole in the bag around Cerise's heart and blood sprayed out.

Lysander widened the hole with his fingers and felt her heart. It was an empty muscle that had been drained of blood and compressed from the pressure in the sac.

He felt for the wound where the bullet had punctured her. Finding it, he glanced at Merrick.

Merrick was sweating, clenching his jaws hard enough to crack them, but his grip was steady.

"Lean back," Lysander said, raising his own left arm and holding it over Cerise's limp heart. With his right hand, Lysander swung the dagger blade down, hacking into his left wrist deep enough to score the bone. He turned his arm so the pumping blood shot into Cerise's chest. Lysander dropped the dagger and used his right hand to scoop Cerise's heart up and tip it toward the blood shooting from his artery. He aimed the jet directly into the wound.

"C'mon," Lysander said, rhythmically squeezing Cerise's heart. "You're strong enough. I know you are."

For moments, nothing happened, even as her heart slowly

filled. Lysander's wound closed, and he had to cut his arm twice more, the burning pain shooting up to his shoulder as his own blood throbbed out of him.

He bent his head and whispered to her. "Please, Cerise. If you die, I lose everything. My last chance. Please, try." Tears stung his eyes. Her heart twitched in his hand.

He exhaled, feeling heat radiate from a distant point. "The angels have her," he whispered, his hand stilling. "I don't have the right to drag her back to this world, but she's all I have now—" He swallowed against the tightness in his throat. He didn't want to give her up or to lose his last hope. He didn't want Reziel to win.

I'm selfish, he thought, gritting his teeth. He stared at her face, pale as alabaster. She was the one. He'd fallen in love with her like a meteor crashing to the earth, hard and fast and out-of-control, in a blaze of flames to light the skies.

He lowered his head until his mouth rested against her ear. "I know the pain of a broken body. You can bear it if you're willing. You're strong enough. Please try."

This was his fault. That someone so remarkable and rare had been cut down by evil. His guts knotted, twisting around a hollowness that threatened to swallow him alive. "I wish you would come back to me. I need—" His voice broke. "I've no right to ask, but I need you. Stay with me, Cerise."

Her heart twitched, then squeezed. He stilled, waiting, holding his breath. It squeezed again, and blood churned as it struggled to beat.

Then he felt its rhythm catch and tears spilled over his lashes in relief. He rubbed them away and swallowed.

She's remarkable and rare, for certain.

The thump of Cerise's heart quickened, beginning as a limp, then pumping faster till its walls slapped against each other at a sprinter's pace. He slid his hand out from under it gently, kissed the side of her face and whispered, "Thank you."

Chapter 25

Hayden woke on the sour-smelling ground of a Varden alley between a mangy cat and a Dumpster. His splitting headache told him that he'd blacked out again. It seemed like no matter how many of Griffin's seizure pills he popped, the blackouts were getting worse.

The last thing he remembered was heading to Di Vetro to put a bullet in that bitch Tamberi Jacobi. Merrick's big henchman had said Merrick and his archangel friend would deal with her . . . but she was slippery, like an eel. A shrieking biting sea snake was exactly the way he thought of her.

He touched the swollen bruise on his neck where she'd torn his flesh and drained his blood. She'd violated other parts of him, too. He wanted to smash her into a million pieces. He wanted to watch her die.

At moments he hesitated, knowing he was just a musician; he had no business taking on a stone-cold killer like her. But another part of him simmered with the kind of rage no man could stand. He had to try to kill her before anyone else did.

He dragged himself to his feet. Despite the blood transfusion he'd gotten at the urgent care center after escaping Tamberi's attack, he still didn't feel 100 percent. It was the seizures. Lately, they left him exhausted and aching. He worried that they'd turned into more than staring spells. The way he felt when he woke up made him wonder if he was having full-blown grand mal seizures now. Falling to the ground? Foaming at the mouth?

It turned his stomach and embarrassed him. What if it happened onstage? The late nights and flashing lights could trigger them. Or that's what the specialist had told him and Griffin. But neither he nor Griff had ever had a problem onstage. It was only offstage, in the quiet and lonely places they sometimes haunted that the blackouts hit them.

Hayden needed to hustle if he wanted to get to the club in time, but he smelled like hell. Would the Di Vetro bouncers even let him in when he smelled like a pile of garbage? Doubtful.

He stepped out of the alley and realized he was only a block from Crimson. He could get a quick shower in Merrick's building, in the apartment where Jersey was staying. He checked to be sure he still had his gun. It smelled like smoke and liquor.

He took the clip out. Jesus, there were several bullets missing. Had he fired it? His gaze darted down the alley. There was no one around. If he had fired the gun, wouldn't someone have called the cops? Wouldn't they have found him in the alley? Yeah. Maybe the clip hadn't been full to begin with. He hadn't looked closely. That must have been it. The jerk gun dealer had given him a partly empty clip. V3 ammunition was ridiculously expensive. The guy had probably pocketed a few to resell them.

Hayden heard a snapping noise and looked sharply over his shoulder. There was no one behind him. No sign of movement. He glared at the shadows then turned back to the street and picked up his pace. Not because he was afraid. He had a gun full of ventala-killing bullets, after all. He was just still shaky from the seizure and from Tamberi's attack. He'd feel better after he had a chance to rest. And after she was dead.

"She's strong," Lysander said as the wounds closed.

Merrick nodded. "Especially with your blood poured into her," he said, standing.

"These wounds were from man-made weapons. If they'd been from a demon's blade . . . a different outcome. I have to do more to watch over her during a fight."

Cerise groaned, her lids fluttering. Lysander clasped her

hand. "I'm with you. I know the pain's bad. It'll fade. Just hold on."

Merrick unbuttoned his shirt and slid it off. "She needs this," Merrick said, holding it out to Lysander.

Lysander covered her with the shirt, and Merrick stepped back, checking his cell. "I can't get a signal down here. As soon as it won't damage her to be moved, let's roll."

"You go. Walk the tunnels and see if you can find the source of the demon stench down here."

"The shooter's long gone by now, but I'll take a look."

"If you find an exit, use it. You can take the car. My wing's healed. I'll bring Cerise back to your building when it won't cause her too much pain to be lifted."

Merrick nodded and disappeared down a passageway.

When Cerise's flesh closed, her eyes opened, looking especially dark against the pallor of her skin.

She pulled her hand free of his. He glanced at her hand, which she rested near her side, then back to her eyes. She blinked away tears and cleared her throat.

"I knew . . . knew we were too good to be true. You lied."

"No, I didn't."

Her lids closed, and she took in a sighing breath. "Help me sit up."

"Your ribs—"

"I feel them," she said, grimacing.

So stubborn.

He gripped her shoulders and pulled her to a sitting position, steeling himself against the guilt that came from seeing pain contort her face.

She held her chest and gasped for breath. He resisted the urge to touch her or to lie her back down. After a few moments, she opened her eyes again.

"You lied by not telling me the most important thing of all."

He suspected he knew what she meant, but asked anyway. "Which was?"

"If you succeed in being redeemed and are called back to heaven, what happens to my soul?"

"We're bound."

"Lysander," she said in a warning tone.

"If you know now, then why ask me?"

She grimaced, holding her ribs. He reached toward her, but she shook her head sharply. "I wanted to be sure that you knew."

"Your time on earth was always transient. What difference do a few years make?"

"It makes a difference to me!" She gasped.

"Don't hurt yourself."

"I didn't hurt myself. I got shot because of you. Just the way you warned me I would."

"I'm sorry I wasn't there to protect you."

She held out a hand. "What does it matter? You're trying to get us both killed anyway."

"I am not."

"No? How do you see it? My understanding is that these bodies die. Isn't that what happens if you get your way?"

"I—yes, we leave here. But not in defeat. If demons kill me before I'm redeemed, I don't ascend. My soul is forfeit."

"And if I'm killed by demons?"

"I can't be redeemed. When Felice was killed, I swore an oath on my redemption that I wouldn't let them kill another woman I loved."

"Wasn't that an idiotic oath to make?" she asked wearily.

"Probably, but the broken body of the woman I'd made love to for seven months was in my arms. Grief and guilt are powerful emotions. And, as my history proves, when I'm under the influence of strong emotions, I'm reckless."

"I have plans for my life."

"Cerise—"

"No," she growled, then a soft sob escaped her. She rubbed damp eyes, shaking her head. "Men always act like their plans are more important than a woman's. My father's role as EC president. Griffin's role as a rock star. Yours as a fallen angel seeking redemption. Your goals may be the most important things in the world to you, but they don't have to be the most important thing to me. And they shouldn't."

She struggled to her feet with a sharp inhalation of breath. He rose from his knees.

"Cerise, wait. You haven't felt what heaven is like. When you get there, you won't regret leaving this place a few years earlier than intended."

She narrowed her eyes, glaring at him through tears. "I understand how great heaven feels. I've had you, haven't I? My soul was just surrounded by angels who aren't fallen, wasn't it? I felt the amazement. It was better than riding a wave of muse magic, and nothing's ever been better than that. Don't you think I was tempted to go with them? Do you imagine it was easy to force myself back into a dead shell of a body? Into a world of torn flesh and broken bones?"

"Then why did you come back?"

"Because you're here," she whispered. He reached out a hand, but she pushed it away. "Don't. I can't—It's already the hardest thing I've ever had to do." She swallowed, tears spilling over her lashes. She closed her eyes, wincing. "I'm supposed to make something of my life and my gift. I'm supposed to leave a legacy. A daughter."

"Is that what you saw when you died? A child who wouldn't be born?"

She nodded. "I've always known I would give the world at least one muse. I planned to do great things and to teach her to do the same. That's what heaven intended for me. It wasn't time for me to leave this world. Not today. With or without you, I have to see my life through."

Without him? She still didn't seem to fully understand. She thought because they'd shown her a version of what her life could've been, she could choose it.

Lysander took a step back and looked away. "I'm glad you're here. So glad, but—"

"And there's another reason I had to come back," she said, suddenly fierce.

He glanced at her, almost unable to look at her because it hurt so much to think about having to ruin her dreams for her life. He hadn't understood . . . She was right that he hadn't considered her gift or what heaven's intent for its use might be. He'd believed himself highest in the hierarchy and hadn't cared about what Cerise's loss would mean for the world. There were other muses. But Ileana might be dead, and Dorie was no great prize. Possibly Alissa could satisfy the world's needs, but Merrick's blood was vampire and nephilim more than human. Their daughters were unlikely to carry muse magic of any consequence. In death, Cerise had felt the truth. She might be the world's only hope for future muses. His stomach twisted in knots. Could he give her up? Let her have a child with someone else? Jealousy and pain streaked through him, every part of him rebelling at the idea. No. And even if he could bring himself to make the personal sacrifice, how could it be accomplished when they were bound together?

It wasn't possible. When he left the world, so would she. And time was running out. He felt the prophecy roaring toward its conclusion. They had days left, not years. And then she'd have an eternity to blame him for depriving her of her life. What if she turned away from him? Refused to be with him in the afterlife? He didn't think he would be able to stand it. It would be like losing heaven all over again. *Please not that.*

If she has to banish me from her presence, don't let it be forever. Don't let the world despair and fall to ruin at the loss of divine inspiration when she leaves here. Make it possible for her to forgive me. I'll wait as long as it takes, he prayed.

"Lysander," she said.

He looked at her, feeling as though all the air had been sucked from his lungs. She was meant to be his. He felt that to his core. Unless this was part of the sacrifice he had to make to redeem himself. His punishment for falling from grace and for allowing Reziel to kill Felice? Had heaven given him Cerise, the woman he really wanted, only to take her away?

"Lysander," she repeated.

"Yes?" he asked, his hands fisted tight enough to make his fingers cramp.

"The other reason I came back was because if I hadn't, Reziel would've won. I'll give you up for mankind's sake and for my daughter's, but I'm not going to let hell get you by killing me."

Lysander's smile didn't reach his eyes, but he nodded. "He underestimated you."

"I want to make him regret that for so many reasons. Not the least of which is that he took control of my friend's body in order to shoot me."

"Your friend?"

"Hayden. He shot me, but it wasn't him. The way he walked and spoke . . . his eyes—" She grimaced. "I've met Reziel before, but didn't know it," she said, stiffening. "Hayden's not the first Lane that Reziel's possessed."

What?

"A demon of Reziel's power and energy couldn't enter the world and force his way into a human body without a serious compact with someone."

"I don't know how he's doing it. I'm just telling you he is. I need Griffin's songbook. That's the key. I feel it."

"The cell tower has been repaired. I don't understand why I can't reach him," Alissa said as she and Ox waited in front of the elevator.

"He's probably in some part of the club where there's no signal. I'm sure it won't be long before he calls you back," Ox said, holding the door open for her.

"Dad, come on!" Alissa called. "Leave that bag. It's too heavy."

"Go ahead. I'll catch up," Richard said, trundling out with a massive bag that contained two manuscripts, a laptop computer, two days' worth of clothes, and a pair of reference books on the Bosnian conflict that he "couldn't work without."

He snapped his finger and pointed at the blank wall. "The pair of you shouldn't do this." He glared at the wall and began to march back and forth.

She frowned at his agitation. Just what was going on in his head? And were Merrick and Cerise and Lysander all right?

"Dad, we're not leaving until I reach Merrick. You'll have time to go back for your things."

"Man plans. God laughs," he said, getting on the elevator with them. They descended to the floor below and exited into the hall.

"Why do you think we'll be leaving unexpectedly? What did you see?" Alissa asked.

"Nothing, but that's hardly the point," he said. "I believe in what I can't yet see. How else could I write books?" He paused and dropped his bag. "No!" He shook his fist at the empty corridor. "Putting on brave faces while you break each other's hearts? You don't deserve what you've been given!" He clutched his temples, wincing. "How am I supposed to concentrate on my writing with all this turmoil in my head?"

"Dad," she said gently.

"No," he said, dragging his arm away from her. "I need some room. Let me pace."

"I don't think I should leave him out here alone," Alissa said to Ox.

"Mr. North, you gotta come in the apartment with us. You can pace in there. There's plenty of room, and if you need more, I'll shove some furniture against the wall. C'mon now," Ox said, unlocking the door.

"Orvin, wait!" Richard shouted, spinning toward him.

But it was too late.

When the door swung open, Alissa only caught a glimpse of a young man before the explosion of gunshots.

Chapter 26

Following coordinates that Reziel the sneaky bastard had given her, Tamberi climbed down the ridge. When she smelled sweat and muse blood, she smiled. She'd found the cave. She pushed aside the tree branches that covered the opening and dropped inside the hole that burrowed into the mountainside.

Tamberi clicked on the small flashlight she'd brought and drew her gun. Reziel had no reason to want her dead when she was helping him but Tamberi trusted no one, least of all a demon who'd been keeping secrets.

A frumpy, dirt-smudged woman who barely resembled the highly polished Etherlin muse lay on the ground on a stained mattress.

Loving the new digs. Must be quite a step down from her mansions, Tamberi thought, and her smile widened. *The muse of architects and designers held captive in squalor? How the mighty have fallen. Do you see this, Cato? I hope you freaking see this.*

The muse squinted at the light that Tamberi shone in her eyes.

"Leizer, please," Ileana Rella rasped.

"Who's Leizer?" Tamberi asked.

"I thought—oh, thank God! Thank God you found me. I'm Ileana Rella, one of the Etherlin muses. I've been held prisoner by Hayden Lane. He made me call him Leizer, made me keep our affair secret. He was so much younger I didn't want people to find out. I thought Cerise might interfere or be angry because he's young—but there's nothing young and fresh about him," Rella said.

Tamberi arched a brow. The woman must've been half out of her mind from dehydration and isolation to be talking so much.

Rella rattled on for several more moments before finishing with, "He's a sociopath! A monster!"

Good for him.

Rella got up slowly, obviously stiff and sore. "Are you a hiker?"

"No," Tamberi said, "but I am going to get you out of here."

The muse broke down then, loud sobs wracking her body as Tamberi unlocked the cuffs around her wrists that chained her to the wall. Tamberi rolled her eyes as she tossed the shackles aside.

Tamberi's stomach growled, wanting another sip of muse blood. She'd licked some of Cerise Xenakis's blood from her leaking wounds, but Tamberi hadn't dared to stay long in the catacombs knowing Merrick and his angel pal would eventually come looking for Xenakis.

Still, stopping to lick the wounds had been worth the risk. Muse blood was delicious and invigorating. Tamberi's wounds healed faster and her senses sharpened under its influence. The trouble with biting Rella was that her blood was going to be used for something big. Something more important than quenching Tamberi's thirst. So for the moment, Rella was safe.

"You're not Etherlin Security. Are you with the American authorities? The FBI?" Rella asked.

"We don't have time for questions, Miss Rella. Let's get going before he comes back."

The color drained from Rella's face, and she shut her sniveling mouth. *Finally!*

At least Merrick's muse and Cerise Xenakis showed a little backbone when they were under attack.

Dorie pushed her feet into her boots and tied the sash of her sweater. She glanced at the clock again and then reread Hayden's text message.

*Hey, gorgeous. Hope ur doing good. Have some stuff to tell
u in private & need ur advice. It's about Alissa North and your
sister. Can u meet me? Without ES breathing down our necks?
Don't want them to overhear b4 u and I decide what to do.*

Dorie's heart sped in anticipation. Yes, she'd talk to Hayden,
the cute and famous rock star who was offering to tell her
things she already should've been told by her own family. She
was tired of being kept out of the loop. She had just as much
right to know what was going on with the other muses as Cerise
or the council or ES. Troy had told her things, but Troy hadn't
really known what was going on with Alissa North until it was
too late.

Hayden lived in the Sliver. He was more plugged in to what
was happening outside the Etherlin, which was key at the
moment. It was so stupid of Cerise and Alissa to get involved
with the fallen.

Dorie didn't care what happened to Alissa, but Dorie had
to make sure that Cerise didn't throw her life away over some
fallen angel, no matter how good-looking he was.

Dorie's heart thumped as she went downstairs. She could
go out through the kitchen and the backyard. Part of the woods
didn't show up on the security cameras, and if she stayed in
the shadows, she could get to the spot by the lake where she
was supposed to meet Hayden.

She had to admit that even though she considered the Varden a filthy gutter, it was pretty cool that Hayden could go in
and out of it without a problem. He was street-smart from
before he'd become famous.

Of course, she wouldn't have looked twice at him if he
weren't a rock guitarist and a millionaire. No lowlife trash for
her. Muses should have some standards. Why the hell couldn't
Alissa see that? Alissa, who had always acted so elegant and
uptight. She certainly hadn't been what she seemed. Dorie was
going to watch everyone around her more closely from now
on. You just never knew what people were hiding.

Chapter 27

They'd found the catacombs' exit. On the street, Lysander held out a hand to Cerise and waited. She hesitated. She didn't want to get so close to him. She didn't trust herself to.

Dangerously beautiful, she thought.

Cerise barely kept herself from grimacing as she walked over to him and then turned so her back was to his chest. He stepped forward and put an arm around her waist.

It overwhelmed her, the feel of his muscles, the smell of sandalwood, and the desperate ache in her gut. Being bound meant they were never supposed to be separated, but she would have to give him up soon. And it was killing her.

Heaven had shown her the key to giving her life meaning, and if she fought to live, heaven would see that she had the opportunity to fulfill that promise. She also knew that, more than anything, Lysander wanted to go home.

The blood bond will have to be severed.

It was a thought that made her want to wail. She wished she could ignore the future fate of the world and hold on to him with both hands.

No, I need to do what's right.

We won't necessarily be apart forever. Maybe when I get there, he'll be waiting.

She would cling to that hope. Anything else crushed her.

His wings beat, and they rose slowly into the sky. His voice was low in her ear, his breath rustling her hair. He pointed into the distance and said, "That's where you live. See the inverted triangle of lights? It's from the paired cupolas on your house and the light on your gate."

He went on to explain why he'd chosen to live in a mountain and shared more stories of teenage Merrick who had helped him build it. Lysander was being kind she realized, filling the silence with conversation that didn't challenge her on the choice she'd made—to live her own life rather than stay with him.

He was trying to put her at ease. And that just made it harder. By the time they reached the windows of his place, she was blinking away tears and biting down on the inside of her mouth.

He unlatched the enormous hinged window and pulled it open. He set her inside and stood on the ledge while his wings folded into his back. Then he stepped down and pressed a switch.

A light blinked on, and her jaw dipped open. Like its owner, the dwelling was like nothing she'd ever seen. She walked to a wall to examine a twelve-inch-tall mural that had been carved around the entire room. It was, she realized, the story of the world. She followed it back, studying the moments from history that he'd chosen to include. Wars, of course, and tragedy, but also great buildings and inventions. Finally she reached the place where there was an image of him on his knees with another angel holding a dagger to his back. His depiction of Reziel betraying him.

She turned away and was confronted by a small sculpture of a dancer. She walked closer to the shelf it rested on, but stopped when she realized that she was the girl carved in alabaster. A sketchbook sat next to it and she opened the book, finding lots of drawings, including many of her—in the dance studio, standing in her backyard, sitting in her bedroom window seat. He'd been watching her, had been with her all along.

She closed the book and set it gently on the shelf.

"You occupied my thoughts from the moment I met you," he said. "You were never supposed to find that out." He offered a self-deprecating smile.

"I know it might have been easier if we'd never met—" she whispered.

"We had to meet. Reziel was in your life. Our paths

crossing was inevitable. And being attracted to each other . . . that was inevitable, too."

"I'm sorry."

"I'm not," he whispered.

She looked over her shoulder at him, tears prickling her eyes. She strode to him and slid her arms around his neck. She hugged him tight.

"I want you to be able to go home, but it'll be so hard to lose you."

His arms tightened around her, crushing her against him. "You won't lose me."

She bit her lip. "Okay, enough," she murmured, pulling back. "Reziel thinks I'm dead and that my death will leave you distracted and upset over the loss of your chance for redemption. He'll make his move soon. We need to know what he's planning and what he's capable of. Can he possess anyone he wants? Anyone he's met or had contact with?"

"I don't think so. The female ventala, Tamberi Jacobi, raised him. She's likely orchestrating whatever he needs done."

"Yes, but I don't think she's working alone. Troy had demon blood around his neck. Ileana is involved with some architect who's going by the name John Leizer. Tamberi could've had something on Troy and maybe she just hired some guy to seduce Ileana, but I can't help but feel that there's a missing piece. Something that I need to know . . . I keep coming back to Griffin's book and the night that he died. Was Tamberi in the rented house? Did she come alone or with the demon? I need to remember."

Lysander walked to the coffee table and retrieved the songbook. He held it out to her. With a deep breath, she took it. Exhaling, she opened it.

As soon as she looked at the words in the margins, flashes of memory assaulted her. Being choked, being forced onto the bed. She gasped, and when her vision cleared, she was on her knees and the book had fallen to the ground.

"Damn it!" she shouted.

"Easy," he said, trying to soothe her.

"Why can't I control it?" she demanded. "I want to know what happened. I have to know."

"Reziel's extremely powerful."

"So am I," she said, glaring at the book.

He smiled. "You are," he said. "And you're determined, but there's probably a reason your mind wants to avoid these memories. Also, Reziel's ashes coat the pages and that probably interferes with your recall. Let me turn the pages for you so you won't have to touch them."

"Go ahead."

He sat on the couch, and she joined him.

"Give me a minute," she said. "I want to draw on my magic to steady myself."

He waited.

"Okay," she said, gritting her teeth. "Open it." She closed her eyes for a moment, whispering encouragement to herself. Lysander set a cool hand on her knee, and it was comforting to feel her connection to him.

She raised her lids a fraction and looked over the pages as Lysander slowly turned them.

"Wait there," she murmured, studying a page with a three-pronged lightning bolt in the margin and two sets of handwriting. She leaned back so the letters were distant and only half in focus. In the back of her mind, she heard someone playing an acoustic guitar and her own voice singing.

That's it. Let it come, she thought, magic sluicing over her skin. Her lids drifted lower. She smelled liquor and licorice. Her vision blurred and readjusted.

Griffin set his guitar down and went to stoke the fire in the stone fireplace. They'd showered after returning from the club and his damp unstyled hair was adorably shaggy. Cerise sat on the bed with his guitar next to her. She plucked the strings absently, thinking about the song they'd been working on.

"Finish your wine," he said.

"My head's already full of bees," she said. "If I drink any more I'll pass out."

"So? We're on vacation," he said, draining his own glass. He kissed her, his soft insistent mouth stirring passion. He leaned back and held her glass to her lips.

She sipped the wine, which had a tart cherry note to it and a slightly bitter, but not unpleasant, aftertaste.

270 ->

The room whirled slowly, and against her ear his mouth whispered, "Goes down like nectar."

She sank into an oily darkness, music and voices echoing in her head.

My throat hurts. Can't breathe.

The room tilted, her body jarred, rocking to the rhythm of rough sex. She was facedown on the bed and he was ramming . . . who? As she woke, terror roared through her.

Her unsteady fingers clawed at the hands around her neck. She fought, scratched, screamed against a closed throat. Thrashing, she caught a glimpse of him in the mirror.

Red violet eyes narrowed, the vicious sneer on his face making him almost unrecognizable.

In her head, she screamed for him to stop. He was killing her. This version of Griffin, one she didn't know, was choking her to death while he raped her.

She fought desperately, and an endless shriek continued over and over until her mind shattered.

She woke shivering and sore in a bath of warm water. A crying Griffin bent over her, scrubbing her body with a soapy washcloth.

For a moment, she couldn't move or speak. Her head hurt, throbbing and swollen like the rest of her. The world seemed distant, as though her skull had been packed with cotton soaked in hand lotion.

A little spike of clarity stabbed her heart. Fury, black and bleak, put strength back in her arm. She slapped him so hard his head smacked the wall, cutting his cheek where it struck the ceramic tile.

Stunned, he fell back, landing on his ass.

"I'm sorry," he said. "I'm so sorry—"

She lurched from the tub and landed on him, pummeling him until she had to stop to catch her breath.

He huddled in a ball, bruised and bleeding, begging for forgiveness.

"It wasn't me. I swear it wasn't me," he cried.

She wobbled to her feet and stumbled out of the bathroom. She had to escape this nightmare.

The floor tilted and rocked like a theme park ride. She landed on her hands and knees and felt so tired she couldn't even crawl.

Out. Get out!

Her limbs didn't obey. Instead they buckled, and she collapsed onto the rug. Her heartbeat throbbed in her temples, and she struggled to hold on to consciousness. The exhaustion was too much.

This time he was calm when she woke. She was unnaturally calm as well. She lay under a throw blanket on the couch where he'd obviously placed her. She watched as he put a black cord, duct tape, and a hunting knife into a duffel bag. When he coughed she thought she smelled eggs too old to be eaten.

In the grips of a chilling realization that Griffin had a sociopath alter ego, she shifted to look around the room. The loaded gun she always carried when she was outside the Etherlin was waiting inside her purse, which sat on the table.

She sat up slowly, silently, but he still sensed or heard something because he turned and stared at her.

He swaggered toward her with his left arm hanging back behind his body.

That's not how Griffin walks. Not usually.

She rose, gripping the blanket. She would drop it if she needed to fight, but until then she didn't want to be naked. She stared at his arm, trying to see if he held anything in his hand like a weapon or something he could use to restrain her. She edged around the couch toward the table.

"You're up," he said with a smile that turned her stomach. "How do you feel?" he asked lightly.

How the hell do you think I feel?

He darted forward and caught her arm.

She jerked her arm out of his grip and widened her stance.

"I think we should go back to the Etherlin tonight," he said.

"Who are you?" she asked.

His brows rose. "What do you mean?"

She stared at his eyes, looking for the hints of red she'd seen earlier, but he'd buried the telltale signs. Still, she knew this wasn't her Griffin.

Several moments passed before she spoke, the silence stretching eerily until her blood ran cold with dread.

With a flat voice, she said, "The Griffin I know wouldn't have done what you did."

"What did I do?" he asked, the cadence of his speech slow and careful and nothing like the way Griffin spoke when he was upset.

The stranger's tone was pleased, not confused. This creature knew exactly what he'd done, and remorse was the farthest thing from what he felt about abusing her. His smile widened while she struggled to choose whether to slam a fist into his smirking face or to rush to the table in an attempt to reach the gun before he caught her.

Her heart banged in her chest, but that actually felt good. Most of the earlier haze had lifted, and as adrenaline spiked her blood, her muscles tightened.

Whether he felt her stiffen or just became impatient, she didn't know. But when he tried to take her arms, she slammed her knee into his groin and her fist into his throat. He staggered back as she bolted to the table.

Her purse was partially unzipped. She yanked it open and dug inside until cold metal reassured her. She spun to point the gun at him.

He stood massaging his crotch and throat. At the sight of the gun, he laughed.

"Your mind and body are stronger than most, I'll give you that," he said. "So now you have a gun. But if you succeed in killing this body, you'll lose Griffin." His voice was a low hiss of malice. "Or we could bargain. Would you like to save your boy toy?"

"What are you talking about?"

He took a step toward her, and her finger twitched against the trigger.

"Come even an inch closer, and I'll end this conversation." She meant it, and her hard tone told him so.

He studied her. "You just might . . . I'll let you say good-bye to him."

His eyes, momentarily red, rolled back and Griffin's body collapsed. His face contorted and a violent seizure slapped his jerking body against the floor. Bloody saliva dripped from his mouth from the cut on his tongue made by his clamping jaw. Her instinct was to rush to help him, but she never moved.

She waited, unsure whether the seizure would kill him. If it didn't, she wondered who she would be facing when he woke and wondered how Griffin had ended up with multiple personalities. Was he an innocent victim whose personality had fractured from some terrible childhood trauma? And what about his eyes?

The seizure ended, and his labored breathing slowly returned to normal. Soft groans became unintelligible words and finally mumbled phrases. She waited for what felt like hours for him to regain his senses.

When he did, he sat up. "What happened? What did he do to you?" he asked, his voice catching.

"You don't remember?"

He shook his head. "I never do," he whispered. "I wake up in strange places. Sometimes there's blood, and I never know if the person it came from is alive or dead." Tears filled his eyes. "I'm so sorry. I never meant for any of this to happen."

"What did happen? Where did he come from?"

He winced and held his head. "I have such a headache."

"Answer me, Griffin."

He looked up at her beseechingly. He seemed young and a little fragile, and it made her heart contract painfully. He wanted her to let him off easy as she often did when something upset him, but this time she couldn't.

"Tell me," she demanded.

"I never knew I would meet a muse. Never knew I'd get the help I needed to take my music to the next level. I was desperate. You know how it is for people like me. We're obsessed. We'd do anything. We can't help it. And who knows if I'd ever have met you if my music hadn't started to take off. You noticed me because the music became great."

She cocked her head. What was he saying? That he—no, it wasn't possible. "What did you do?"

He sighed. "The tattoo artist in San Francisco was a witch. We were using Ecstasy together one night. I was trying to reach a different consciousness, to find a source of inspiration that would help me write that one hit song I needed to launch my career. While we were lying there, I was running on about how desperate I was to become one of the greats, and she said she knew a ritual to get me what I wanted. I remember I said, 'I'll do anything.'"

Tears streamed down his face, and he sucked in a breath. "The next night, we summoned a demon. It was bloody and painful, but he played music that was so hard and so sweet, it felt worth losing my soul for. He told me I'd become a legend and that he wouldn't necessarily take my soul. He'd give me the option of buying it back from him. When it was over, my head exploded with creativity. It was fucking great," he said, crying.

"I didn't hear from him for a couple of years. I started to wonder if it'd even been real. But then he started to come to me in dreams. He wanted me to perform rituals." He shuddered. "At first I did. I didn't want to kill animals, but that's done all the time, isn't it? If we're not vegetarians, animals are slaughtered for us. What's the difference, right?" He shrugged. "Then you and I met and got involved. And having you as my muse . . . I could feel the difference. The purity of the way I could create with you. I wanted to be done with the demon. I wanted to make one big sacrifice to buy my soul back. But the thing he wanted would've ruined everything."

"What did he want?" she whispered.

"You." He scrubbed a hand over his face. "They all want you. The ventala. The demons. Other fucking musicians. Everyone always wants me to deliver you to them. Like I'm nothing. Like I don't matter." He licked his lips. "Maybe I don't. But I said no. I told the demon to fuck off. Ditto to the ventala and everyone else. That's where I draw the goddamned line. But he wouldn't let it drop. The blackouts I've had since I was a teenager got worse, and I started to think I was doing things . . . or my body was." He clenched his fists.

"It turns out the demon, that motherfucker, was recruiting. He was making offers to the people around me, setting up his network. He's got Troy. That sick asshole was trying to cover up something to do with young girls and the demon helped him do it, saved him somehow. Troy let things slip when he thought he was talking to the demon. That's how I found out that I'm not alone in this body. It's been a nightmare ever since.

"There's a female ventala, a real bitch, who's raised demons. I thought she might know a way I could cut him out of my life. Do some ritual to banish him. I've tried to get information, but she's cagey and I could never trust her with the truth. She'd use it as leverage. Besides if it came down to him or me, she'd probably choose him. I think he's been screwing her."

Griffin leaned his back against the coffee table. "I do love you, Cerise. I love you more than anything, more than the fame and a lot more than myself. Sometimes I think I should kill myself. He's been talking to Hayden. Now he's hurt you. I'm so fucking sorry." He swallowed. "And I can't take this," he said, his voice catching. "He owns my soul and he's got a way of smashing it into nothing, so he can use my body. I can't stop him. There's nothing I can do. I wish—I wish you'd use that gun on me."

She sat in the chair, resting the gun on her lap, and cried.

He stood and took a step toward her, but she shook her head.

"Don't come near me."

He covered his mouth with his fist and shook his head. The anguish in his eyes devastated her. She wiped the tears away with her left hand while the right held tight to the gun.

"You know I love you," he said.

"I loved you, too," she whispered. "But you got involved with me knowing your life was infected with a demon."

"If I could get rid of it?"

"I'd still never be able to trust you again."

"No, Cer, c'mon! You have to have a little faith. If I thought we were over, I couldn't—listen, there isn't anything we can't do together. You know that!"

"What I know is that you didn't warn me. You knew he was using your body and you let me get drunk and come here alone with you. He used your body to rape me."

"I never thought he'd hurt you! You're important to him. I never thought he'd do anything like what happened tonight. You have to believe that!"

"Do I? Do I really?" she spat. "He's a demon. Are you really surprised he does evil things?" She glared at him. "I think you knew something like this could happen and probably would. But you were selfish. You wanted your music and me and the life you sold your soul for. Now you expect me to say that everything will be okay if you can get someone to exorcise him from your body? How can you ask that of me after what you did?" She shook her head. "It'll never be okay, Griffin. And as long as he can take control of your body, you're a danger to everyone you know. You should be locked up."

"Do you want me to kill myself, Cerise? Is that what you want? Because I think you're saying that you're not just gonna leave me, you're going to ruin my life. If I couldn't play music—"

"That's what you're worried about?" she roared. "Your career? Aren't you afraid of what else he'll do using your body?"

He held out a hand. "No, because now you know. You can watch me. And I'll do anything you say. See a priest. Another witch. Anything to get rid of him! Just help me."

"What if there's no way to get rid of him? What if while you're trying to find a way, he hurts me even worse or hurts Hayden or Jersey? Look at the things he was putting in that duffel bag. It looks like stuff that would belong in a serial killer's bag. He could already be killing people."

"No. He wouldn't risk me getting accused of murder and having my body arrested. Murder's petty to him. He's planning something big. And as long as we can keep him from doing that, we've got time to get rid of him."

"There's no 'we' in all this, Griffin. I don't want to be anywhere near him." She shook her head for emphasis. "You should turn yourself in to the police and confess to what he did to me. If you're in jail, he won't be able to do the same kind of damage. You can try whatever you want while you're in custody. Read the Bible, pray, see a minister or a priest. Try everything."

"Are you kidding me? Get locked up? I paid for this life with my soul. Please don't ask me to give it up. I can't do that. It's not fair. I'll find a way to keep him from hurting people."

"Go," she said flatly.

"Leave? Now?"

"Right now."

"No, I'm not going. Not until you swear you won't go to the police and accuse me of something. Not until you say you'll think about this and try to help me figure a way out of it. You love me. You can't just give up on me because I made one mistake when I was twenty years old. Think about the times we've had, how happy we've been."

"Get. Out."

His eyes narrowed and his face hardened. "Listen, this isn't just my problem. He's been with you. He's marked you. He'll use that connection against you, and you're the key to whatever he's got planned. Something that'll create hell on earth."

She raised the gun. "If you don't leave, I'll help you get rid of him once and for all."

He shook his head. "So you're just going to abandon me? I wouldn't have done that to you. I would've stayed with you no matter what. I was going to marry you."

"You can't give yourself to me, Griffin. You already gave yourself to a demon."

"Are you going to the police?"

"You should do it yourself."

"And if I don't?"

She bit the inside of her cheek, staring at the face of the man she loved. Losing him would tear her heart out, but she didn't let her voice quaver when she said, "Then yes, I'll do it for you."

"Shoot me. If you want to destroy me so much, just get it over with."

She winced, knowing that she probably should, but she just couldn't. Not when he sat there quietly, staring at her with begging eyes. She shook her head. "Just leave. Haven't you put me through enough tonight?"

His eyes rolled back and his body shuddered, then red eyes stared out at her. The demon clapped his hands. "Well played. I'm sorry we won't have more time together, Cerise."

He darted forward and slammed a hand against her wrist as she pulled the trigger. The shot went wide, and the gun flew from her grip. They rolled on the floor, over and over, until the back of her head hit the wall.

He'll kill me.

Through a haze, she grabbed Griffin's hair and slammed his head on the floor. The red eyes blazed, and his hands closed on her throat.

She knocked her head into his and brought her arms up between his and forced them apart. When he lost his grip on her, she sucked in a breath and continued to batter him.

"Fucking useless mortal body," he snarled.

She slammed the heel of her hand into his chin and he fell back. They scrambled toward the gun, and she reached it first. He sprinted across the room as she fired.

He flung the front door open, and she chased him outside. Something wet and foul splashed on her face. Snow mixed with something. The world spun.

She stumbled back, trying to wipe the poison off.

The demon swaggered to the edge of the porch. She tried to aim, but her eyes wouldn't focus. She had to escape. She fell back into the house.

Lock the door!

She saw Griffin's body jerk and fall to its knees.

"Not now, boy. I swear I'll kill you," he growled.

Cerise dragged herself up and wobbled to the door. She caught the edge and swung it. When she crashed to her knees, she heard him say, "I'll be back for you, Cerise. And you won't see us coming."

She slammed the door shut and fumbled to turn the dead bolt. Then the world tilted and she slumped on the floor, fighting to stay awake.

No! Keep the gun! Stay awake. He's coming back.

Blind terror made her feel sick, but she couldn't sit up, and within moments everything began to fade. The pain of what Griffin had done. The details of the attack.

Had it really happened? The world felt hazy, like she'd been half asleep. Had it been a nightmare?

No.

Yes?

Emotions receded and with them her sense of herself. Dampened like a wet cloth had been draped over her, her life and her magic were muted, but the terrible pain was fading, too.

It was just a bad dream.

Rocked from the memory world, Cerise looked around. Sitting in Lysander's living room, everything came into sharp focus. She felt as if a veil had been lifted. Her power surged, lightning streaking along her nerves.

She also felt all the pain and revulsion she'd suppressed. She'd been in love with someone who'd bowed to a demon.

I didn't want to face it. When Reziel rolled my mind back, I was willing to let go of the truth to spare myself. I wanted so much to believe that Griffin had loved me the way I needed to be loved. I wanted to keep feeling how I'd felt when I was with him. Reziel exploited my pride, my desperation to be that girl— muse to a rock star, the great love of his life. I was used and abused. And then I forgot.

She swallowed. *A muse is no match for a demon in disguise.*

She looked up at the ceiling.

Forgive me. I protected my ego instead of protecting a divine gift. Let me recognize my enemy in whatever form he takes and I promise not to make that mistake again. Ever.

As though her soul was made of guitar strings, she felt heaven strike a chord.

Chapter 28

"Did you take a play from your lover's playbook? The silence, that's Merrick's thing," Hayden said, nodding for Alissa to climb into the helicopter.

"You'll know soon enough what Merrick's thing is," she said.

"Think he'll rescue you?" he asked, smirking as he shoved her inside with the gun pressed precariously to her ribs.

"He will, if I haven't escaped myself before then."

He laughed. "Want to try your magic on me again? It worked so well for you the first twenty times you tried it."

"What have you done to yourself, Hayden? To not feel the pull of muse magic, you must have cut yourself off from humanity."

"Well, I crowned Jersey and shot your father and your bodyguard. Don't you think that would be enough?"

"No. Even murderers have some traces of humanity left."

"I must be in a class by myself," he sneered. "Why aren't you sobbing?"

"I'm in a class by myself, too," she said coolly, though inside she felt ill.

"Not even going to mourn your father and bodyguard?"

"They're not going to die."

When Alissa had bent over her dad, his wound hadn't looked severe, though it had been hard to tell in those brief seconds. But Ox had been shot several times. At least he'd been breathing. She hoped he'd heard her voice when she whispered to him. Just the thought of the attack made her stomach knot. He'd been a loyal friend to Merrick and so protective of her and her dad ever since they'd come to the Varden. She swallowed the lump in her throat. She wouldn't cry. Not yet. And never in front of the man who'd shot them.

"They're not going to die? Why not?"

"Because I told them not to. Their humanity's intact. My magic works on them." She stared daggers at him. "They'll be found in time."

"I doubt it, but it makes no difference to me either way."

"What do you care about?"

His eyes narrowed. "Go back to being silent," he hissed.

"Why? What don't you want me to know?"

He raised his hand. She didn't flinch. When he actually did strike her, she deflected the blow fairly well, but it still knocked her back onto the metal floor.

"If you're smart, you'll shut up when I tell you to."

"If you're smart, you'll let me go before you end up like the last man who tried to kidnap me. I decapitated him."

He smiled. "You're an icy bitch. I almost hate to kill you."

"The feeling's not mutual."

They lapsed into silence for a few moments, then he said, "Merrick's Lysander's best friend. How did that happen? The ventala are beneath an angel's notice unless they attack one. Is that how they met? Merrick managed to kill a demon, and Lysander befriended him?"

"No, it was Lysander who taught Merrick to kill demons."

"Why? What was so special about Merrick?"

"Tell me why you care, and I'll tell you how they met."

"I don't have to bargain with you. I can get you to tell me your deepest, darkest secrets any time I want. I've broken the sons and daughters of angels. In five minutes, I could hurt you enough to make you promise me anything."

She narrowed her eyes. "You're not Hayden. What's your name?"

He didn't answer.

"Shall I guess?" She glanced at the gun. "You shouldn't do this, Reziel. It'll end badly for you."

His grip tightened on the weapon.

"Hayden, are you still in there? I'd like to talk to you."

She saw his hand fly toward her and jerked back to avoid most of the blow. Her cheek stung where he'd hit her, but it had been worth it to find out who and what he was.

Reziel couldn't face Lysander in a human body. There was only one reason he'd taken her. He planned to use her to open a gateway to hell so his true demon form could rise. And he wouldn't be alone. With her muse blood, he'd be able to keep the gate open for much longer than he could with an ordinary person's. He'd likely used Ileana's blood to open a portal, which was how those six monstrous demons had gotten through a few nights before. But the gate obviously hadn't stayed open long enough for him to rise himself. If her blood was more powerful than Ileana's . . .

How many demons will enter the world if I let him spill my blood in a ritual?

She would have to escape or die trying. Those were the only choices she considered acceptable.

"Cerise," Lysander said.

She turned and stared at his face.

"Are you all right?"

"I am," she said, wiping the damp from her lashes. "Reziel poisoned me. He threw something tainted with black magic on me and because I was so devastated and didn't want to live with the truth, it sapped my power and my memory. Now that I know, he won't be able to blindside me again."

"Merrick summoned me. He doesn't do that lightly. We should see what's happened."

"Let's go," she said, sitting up. "Tell me something. Can't a ritual be done to raise a specific demon? Using a human sacrifice?"

"Yes."

She rose and walked with him to the window. He slid an arm around her and plunged them into the misty air, which felt chilly, but wondrous against her skin. She tightened her hold on him and was hit with a rush of adrenaline and exhilaration as he made a swooping arc. Nothing was better than dancing with Lysander. Except perhaps flying with him.

"Griffin sold his soul to become a famous rock star. Reziel brokered the deal. They were in close contact to the point of Reziel possessing his body. If Reziel had wanted Griffin to raise him personally, wouldn't that have been an easy thing?"

"Not necessarily an easy thing. Griffin wasn't a warlock. Performing black magic is complicated, and to raise Reziel several human sacrifices would've been needed, but with Reziel's direct guidance, yes, it could've been done."

"Reziel's been trying to get his hands on me since last year, presumably because I'm a muse. Hayden was wearing the Ramones T-shirt I gave Griffin and he's the same build. It could've been him in the picture that Ileana had. I don't know if Hayden has the same tattoo as Griffin, but he might. They went to the same tattoo artist in San Francisco.

"Reziel could've been using Hayden's body to get close enough to Ileana to abduct her."

Lysander nodded.

"That three-pronged lightning bolt that's in Griffin's songbook was part of the artwork on the first Molly Times CD. It was also the charm Troy had on his necklace. Is it Reziel's mark?"

"A trio of lightning bolts converged and hit the earth just before it cracked open and the damned angels were dragged into hell. I believe that's how pitchforks became associated with demons. They turned a symbol of their fall into their calling card. It wouldn't surprise me to learn that Reziel uses a triple lightning bolt as a mark on his followers."

"The night Griffin died, Reziel and I had a confrontation. He said he would come back. He said, 'You won't see *us* coming.' At the time, I thought he meant he and Griffin would be back for me that night after I passed out."

"I don't think so. When Reziel was using Griffin's body, Griffin's consciousness—or spirit or whatever made him who he was—was gone. And I don't believe Reziel thought enough of Griffin to include him in a threat. Griffin told me he wouldn't go along with Reziel's plan to use me. I don't think he was involved in Reziel's grand scheme."

Lysander waited, thoughtfully.

"When Reziel said 'us,' it made me shudder, made me feel

a sense of overwhelming dread beyond anything I'd felt all night, even when he was actually physically abusing me."

"With your muse gift, your power to sense things is extremely acute."

"It can be. Especially with an aspirant I've inspired. Reziel was in Griffin's body and I was deeply connected to him. There was something in his voice."

"I'm sure your instinct about Reziel's feelings toward Griffin Lane is correct. Demons don't credit men with much worth. I would be very surprised if by 'us' Reziel meant himself and a mortal man."

"And I doubt Reziel's endgame is to let a dozen monstrous lower demons into the world," she said. "Even if they go on a killing spree and you don't rally to fight them, there's still Merrick and that archangel, Nathaniel, to pick them off. And if Reziel rose, they'd vanquish him eventually, too. It doesn't make sense to do something small. Griffin said Reziel planned to create hell on earth. I think letting those six demons out was a dry run. If they'd succeeded in killing you, great. But if not, it wouldn't matter because it was just a test to see what they could do using the blood of a muse."

"A test run . . ." he murmured, furrowing his brows.

"They killed me to get you out of the way. The last time Reziel was involved in a plot to get you out of his way, they tried to take over heaven. And who did Reziel conspire with?"

Lysander clenched his jaws and nodded bitterly. "Lucifer."

"What if Reziel plans to enter the world with the devil himself? What if they plan to open a gate big enough for the most powerful demons in hell to pass through?"

"Only flesh-and-blood angels can fight demons of the flesh. At present, that's just me and Nathaniel. If Reziel and Lucifer brought the twenty-five highest-ranking demons in hell with them to earth, even with Merrick and Nathaniel joining the fight, I probably couldn't stop them from taking over the world."

"Then we have to keep them from ever opening a gate that wide."

"Yes," he said, frowning. "But I don't see how they could do it. Even if Ileana's alive and Reziel spills every drop of her blood it wouldn't be enough to open a portal that large."

They swooped down to the roof where Merrick was pacing and talking on his cell phone. When he spotted Lysander, Merrick ended the call.

"That kid, Hayden Lane, shot Ox and Richard North and took Alissa. I've emptied the building of my guys. I've got everyone on the street looking for them, but Lane's probably out of my territory by now, and word is that one of the syndicate helicopters lifted off and headed north toward the Etherlin."

Lysander whirled and scanned the horizon.

Cerise jerked her phone out of her pocket and called her sister. The call went straight to voice mail. She called her father next.

"It's Cerise. Is Dorie there? Is she in the house?"

"Of course," her dad said.

"Are you looking right at her? Is she in front of you?"

"No, why? What's going on?"

"I need you to check, Dad. Right now."

She waited, holding her breath.

"Did you see Dorie go out?" her dad shouted to someone, presumably an ES bodyguard. "She's not in her room! Check the rest of the house. Do it now!" Into the phone he said, "I last saw her about two hours ago. She said she was going to sleep for a while. I don't know how long she's been missing. What's going on? Where do you think she's gone?"

"I think she might have gone to meet Hayden Lane, but if she did, it won't be Hayden she finds. It'll be the demon who's possessing his body."

"Oh, God!"

"I'll call you right back. Give me a minute to talk to Lysander and I'll call you back, Dad." She lowered the phone. "Ileana's blood wouldn't be enough, but what if they had three muses? Would the sacrificial killing of three muses be enough?"

Lysander tipped his head back, clenching his eyes shut and shaking his head in despair. "Yes, three would be enough."

Chapter 29

"What are you doing?" Dorie screamed as the helicopter lurched.

Alissa had attempted to escape twice without success. For her trouble, she had snow-soaked clothes, a sprained ankle, and a broken wrist from Reziel slamming her arm against a metal strut when she'd almost gotten his gun away from him.

Prevented from escaping, Alissa decided her next course of action would be to use magic to persuade the pilot to land immediately, before they got to their destination. The jerky descent came from Reziel interfering.

"Help me get this door open," Alissa said, the pain in her wrist wailing as she tried to unlock the latch.

"Are you crazy? What if we fall out?"

"Better that than being sacrificed in some demonic ritual. Get over here now," Alissa said.

"Wait!" Dorie yelled.

As Alissa got the door open, she felt a sharp pain in the back of her head. She buckled forward, falling as the world went black.

Multiple human sacrifices had been arranged at the four other caves that made up the points of the inverted pentacle. But the key to everything, Tamberi knew, would be the muse sacrifice at the cave of ancients in the Etherlin.

Ileana Rella had finally caught on to the fact that she wasn't being taken home, despite many promises of fabulous rewards or ransom. Now Rella vacillated between shocked silence and noisy sobbing. Tamberi controlled the latter by hitting Rella in the face whenever she lost control.

"In demon-raising, as in life, you get what you pay for. Animal sacrifice, lesser demon. Human sacrifice, humanoid demon. Muse sacrifice . . ." Tamberi licked her lips. "Well, that's gotta be a show worthy of the circus big top. Here's our stop," Tamberi said, dragging Rella out of one of the helicopters she'd stolen from the syndicate.

The dozen guys still willing to stick their necks out for Tamberi climbed out of the chopper with their loaded assault rifles. Tamberi doubted she'd need them if things went off as planned. Line the muses up and cut them down. That was what they were going to do.

Tamberi was sorry she wouldn't get to slaughter Cerise Xenakis, the woman Griffin had loved more than Tamberi, as part of the ritual. Of course, slicing Alissa North's throat would be almost as good. Alissa had killed Cato in the exact cave they were traveling to.

Tamberi hoped Reziel followed her advice and taped the bitch's mouth shut and handcuffed her hands behind her back. The blonde was crafty. If they weren't careful, they wouldn't end up with a cadre of demons. They'd end up with a bunch of harp-playing ancient muses with a blinding light that burned the skin off the bones of the unworthy.

"Where is that demon?" Tamberi said, looking at the sky. "He better not be too late. Merrick might not have wings, but you better believe that bastard won't take long to get here if he figures out where we're bringing blondie."

One of her guys got set up to hammer spikes into the mountain, and Tamberi shoved Rella toward the clearing in front of the cave.

"C'mon, Rez, get your ass here," she murmured. Then she heard helicopter blades chopping the air and she smiled. "Speak of the devil."

* * *

The muses had been strung up like animals ready for slaughter. They were at the mouth of the cave of ancients positioned in a triangular formation with a fire blazing in the center.

The sharp pain in Alissa's right wrist dragged her to consciousness. To hang from ropes that tethered a broken bone was excruciating, but the pain helped her overcome the fog of her head injury. Alissa shuddered as blood oozed down the back of her neck from the place where her scalp was torn.

Cold and sick and barely able to breathe, she twisted, trying to get her feet firmly on the ground. Hayden's eyes blazed red as Reziel read from a tablet.

Tamberi Jacobi, leering with excitement, stood next to Alissa. The ventala witch held a thin blade in her hand. The hilt looked very old. Was it bronze? The dirt on the dagger made Alissa think they might have just unearthed it from some nearby tomb.

Tamberi took the tablet and read a passage. The throbbing in Alissa's head made it hard to listen.

"Let's salt the earth to prime it," Reziel said and grabbed Dorie's leg. She struggled and kicked, but couldn't wrench free. He sliced Dorie's ankle over a vein. She screamed behind the tape over her mouth.

Alissa gagged, afraid she might vomit behind the tape and choke. Although maybe that would be a mercy. Then her heart would stop and wouldn't provide them with as much pumping blood when they cut her.

Through vision that blurred and then cleared as though she were diving underwater and surfacing, Alissa saw Reziel watching her. Was he worried she might suffocate before they finished their ritual? She might be able to use that. She had to stop them.

Reziel cut Ileana's leg. Ileana seemed to be in a state of shock and didn't even try to resist.

Blood slithered down Alissa's back in a sinister trail and dripped on the ground. She shivered, but knew that if she could get the tape off her mouth, she could use the muse blood to open a portal that would do Reziel no good at all. She arched up, making a show of her struggle. Then she heaved.

Screaming pain shot down her arm from her wrist, but Reziel stalked forward and reached for the tape on her mouth.

Tamberi stopped reading and grabbed his wrist. "Don't. You can't let her speak a single word. She'll ruin everything. Let her pass out. I'll slit her throat while she's choking to death."

Reziel watched Alissa twist and gasp, jerk and gag, but he stepped back. She closed her eyes, desperately trying to think of something, anything, to circumvent the demonic ritual, but she was bound too tightly. She tongued the tape, but couldn't loosen it enough to shout from underneath it.

Tamberi's voice echoed through the clearing and into the cave, and a foul wind whistled from it. Alissa smelled sulfur and rotting meat. Her stomach heaved, and she had to swallow the acid that rose. Sweat beaded on her neck and forehead, and waves of pain crashed over her.

Don't pass out. Stay alert!

If a chance comes, you have to be ready.

Her vision darkened, fading to black. She heard distant moans and growls. Something that was not human gnashed its teeth, impatient to enter the world.

Cerise felted weighed down by the two daggers, gun, and belt with several clips of ammunition. There hadn't been a question of whether she would go with them. When Lysander had told Merrick to give her weapons, Merrick had raised a brow, but hadn't objected. He equipped her and, in a matter of minutes, they were back on the roof. She tested a retractable blade. Lysander reminded her how to use it to the best advantage. In an aerial attack, she and Merrick would crouch, drawing the demon down and lurch up and thrust the blade. The spring-action blade would slide out in an instant to impale the descending demon.

They believed that the most likely site for the ritual would be at a cave near the muse's retreat center in the Etherlin where the ventala had tried to open a portal once before. As Merrick hooked industrial cable to a utility belt, Lysander prepped them.

"Cerise, with my blood in you, you should be harder to kill and more able to channel my skills. Use your magic to inspire yourself to move the way I do. I trained or fought many of the damned angels who may emerge. I know their weaknesses. Trust your instincts. They're exceptional."

She nodded, using a hook to link herself to the cable.

"Merrick, there are four that are more dangerous than all the rest. If possible, leave them for me. First, Lucifer. You'll know him by his horns and his manner. He'll charge forward and then drop back and flank to his left. Be wary of letting him get behind you. He's catlike when he fights; he likes to attack from the back. If he leaps, roll under and get behind him. Cross cut him through the back, right to left." Lysander illustrated a quick move. Cerise and Merrick watched. Cerise mimed the movement, but Merrick only nodded.

"Uriah is next. He has a claw mark on his right shoulder, and he fights equally well with both hands. He likes to thrust upward with his dagger as if it were a switchblade. It leaves his upper chest vulnerable. With a vertical leap, you can come down, blade behind his left collarbone, for the kill. You know the move, but you have to deflect his blade or you'll impale yourself on it when you land.

"Reziel. He'll come for me first, but if I'm killed you'll be next. In his natural form, you'll know him by his wings. They're black, but gold-tipped on the ends. He used to like to come straight overhead and the retractable blade worked well, but he's learned over the years that I know that weakness and his style has changed. When he's wounded and recovering, he returns to old habits. If possible, wear him out and bleed him down. Then he'll come from overhead. And finally Purim. He'll be the smallest. Only six feet and thinner than the rest. He moves like quicksilver. You have to move fast and don't let him anticipate you. Be unpredictable in what you do. If you can hit his face a few times or jab him in the face with your blade, he'll protect his head and neck excessively and leave his heart and wings unprotected.

"All twenty-seven are powerful and dangerous, but so are you. Use your training, your experience, your instincts. On your best day, you can defeat any of them," Lysander said, putting a hand on the side of Merrick's neck and nodding. "Today has to be your best day."

Merrick inclined his head and said, "We're burning midnight. Let's go."

Lysander slid an arm around Cerise's waist, but his attention was still on Merrick. "You can't afford to be distracted for even an instant. Your best chance of saving Alissa is to stay alive and fight. Don't forget that."

Merrick's grim expression left little doubt that he understood what he had to do, even if he didn't like it.

Without another word, Lysander's wings beat and they rose into the deceptively silent night. When they were about fifteen feet above the roof, she felt the cable become taut as Merrick was lifted into the air. Even with the added weight of two additional bodies, Lysander's flight through the clouds was swift and steady.

"One for luck," she whispered and pressed a kiss onto his cheek.

"One more," he said.

There was no change in their progress across the sky, even when he touched his lips to hers. She kissed him and made it count, knowing it would likely be the last time.

"I'll carry that kiss with me to heaven or hell," he said, and for an instant, the rest of the world seemed to fall away. There was only him and the knowledge that he would hold on to the memory of what they'd had for eternity.

Cerise closed her eyes, not wanting to let go. Mist chilled her cheeks; she inhaled the scent of sandalwood and amber, felt the press of his cool skin and hard muscles, and she didn't regret anything. He saw her exactly as she wanted to be. Powerful and spectacular. He loved her as she wanted to be loved. Without hesitation or limitation. And more than anyone else in the world. Whatever the battle's outcome, she would always have that.

Her lids flicked open, and she studied his face.

I love you.

"Whatever happens," she said, "I'm not sorry we met."

He smiled a brilliant white smile that fractured the light around him so intensely it made her squint. "You love recklessly."

"All your favorite people do," she said.

He nodded. "And they rush headlong into battle with me just as recklessly. I'm fallen. I don't deserve such loyalty, but I'm grateful for it."

Smoke wafted through the air, and she turned her head. They were two hundred yards from the clearing in front of the cave, and white flames rose fifty feet into the air. Cerise's heart lurched as screeching ripped through the night.

A portal was already open.

Chapter 30

When the emergency alert went out to every member of Etherlin Security, the mobilization took a full seventeen minutes less than the required fifty-minute time set for drills.

The briefing took seven minutes. Their mission was simple. Recover the Etherlin muses and bring them home alive. If anything stood in the way of accomplishing the mission, kill it.

Armed and ready, the air units left the center of the Etherlin within thirty minutes. The ground units shortly thereafter.

The first ES officers still arrived on the scene eleven minutes too late.

The smell of muse blood triggered the ventala thirst. Several times, Tamberi had to force her men back with shoves and threats. Fangs descended and snarling with hunger, they pressed forward over and over.

Reziel struck one down with a blade through the heart. His bloodred eyes were as flat and deadly as any she'd ever seen, and the ventala fell back.

Her eyes darted to her watch. The human sacrifices at the other locations had already begun. They only had moments left to complete the ritual.

"I have to return to the other side, so I can emerge as flesh!" Reziel yelled over the roaring wind that whooshed out of the cave. "Finish the rite! Kill Rella, then Xenakis, then North. Do it as fast as you can, then get out of the way."

Reziel's eyes rolled back, and Hayden fell to the ground, his body seizing.

She shouted the words from the tablet, speaking faster and faster. When the last word was out, she slashed Ileana's throat. Blood sprayed onto Tamberi's face and chest, into the fire, and onto the ground. Deep within the cave, the earth cracked. She rushed to Dorie Xenakis, but was knocked back by her own men, who'd charged forward at the spilling of Rella's blood. They ripped Rella's body down and covered it, sucking the blood from her wounds and biting into her veins.

A mass of monstrous demons flew from the cave, screeching and snapping their teeth.

Tamberi grabbed Dorie Xenakis's hair and yanked her head back. Her knife hand was jarred just as she started to drag the blade across the girl's throat. A blow to her head knocked Tamberi forward, and she landed on her knees. She jumped up and spun to find Cerise Xenakis racing toward her.

It can't be!

Kill her!

Tamberi swung her blade around. She would cut Cerise's throat and drain a fourth muse bitch's blood in the center of the triangle. Then nothing would be able to close the gates of hell. The world would definitely fall!

In the final moment before they clashed, Tamberi knew something was wrong. Cerise's brown eyes lightened to hazel green. Only distracted for an instant, Tamberi slashed at her. Cerise's upper body arched back as though she were a gymnast in a backbend. Tamberi's blade sliced the air above Cerise, not connecting, and Tamberi's momentum pulled her to her left side. Cerise's torso sprang forward at the waist, and Tamberi felt the kiss of a blade, then sharp pain as it drove into her, dividing her heart into two pieces.

Tamberi's broken scream was over by the time she hit the ground.

She's killed me. The bitch—

Staring at the sky, Tamberi watched burnt-red demons circle like vultures. There were dozens of them already, and then she saw him—the one with massive black horns.

The prince of darkness himself!
She choked out a wheezing laugh.
They're too late. We still won.

Cerise slammed the hilt of her dagger against the spike that tethered Dorie's arms to the rock. Cerise had to free Alissa and Dorie and get them out of the ritual site.

A deafening screech made her look up. A demon swooped. She crouched so she could use the retractable blade.

Drawing on her muse magic for inspiration, she whispered to herself, *Do it! Fight like him! Tap that power!*

The magic flowed through her and her senses heightened. The smallest sounds became piercingly clear, the smallest movements became obvious. It was as though part of her spirit slipped from her body and watched from above as she spun and dove, slashed and thrust. She wasn't quite quick enough to avoid all the blows. Some sent her sprawling and claws scraped her skin, but she was able to spring back to her feet. She killed one and then another.

A roar caused her gaze to jerk upward. Black wings with gold tips. Reziel in his massive archangel body. Seven feet tall and ripped. He locked eyes with her and dove straight for her.

Fear cramped her stomach. She bent her knees, readying herself, but she couldn't remember what strategy Lysander had told them to use against him.

She jerked up, but couldn't reach to stab him. Reziel's foot-long blade swung down in a blur of speed. She lurched, wasn't fast enough.

The blade would've decapitated her if it hadn't encountered Lysander's.

Reziel cursed and recoiled, flipped backward in the air, touching down and springing up. Lysander leapt into the air in pursuit, but three other demons swarmed her.

Cerise rushed to Dorie and managed to free her, then to free Alissa.

"Cerise?"

"Yeah, Liss, it's me."

"Are we very outnumbered?"

Cerise glanced up. There were dozens of demons in the sky. There was no way—

"Yes, very."

"We have to close the gate."

Dorie's scream made Cerise whirl around. One of the ventala tackled Dorie and sank fangs into her throat. Cerise darted around the fire, but Merrick got there first and hauled the ventala assassin back and took off his head with one swing of a blade.

"Get them to cover," Merrick shouted, shoving a stunned Dorie toward her.

Merrick sprinted back to the thick of the battle where Lysander had been joined by another winged angel with bronze hair. The light around the angel was wicked bright.

It must be Nathaniel! Thank God!

More and more demons poured from the cave. A helicopter landed and ES officers spilled out. They couldn't defeat the demons, but at least they could fight the ventala and get Dorie and Alissa to safety.

"ES!" Dorie cried. "We're here!" she screamed to them.

"No!" Alissa said. "We have to go into the cave. We have to close the gate!"

"But—!"

"It may take all three of us," Alissa said.

"She's right, Dorie. Come with us," Cerise said, waving for her.

Dorie hesitated, then bit her lip and rushed to join them.

It was a battle to get to the cave with demons shrieking and dive-bombing like prehistoric birds. Blood dripped from Cerise's sliced cheek and shoulder. There were an overwhelming number of demons in the sky already. Even if they managed to close the portal, it was probably too late, but they had to try.

Inside, the cave smelled rancid and damp. They all gagged, and Alissa vomited clear fluid.

"She's hurt! Hayden hit her in the back of the head. She bled a lot," Dorie said, taking Alissa's arm to guide her. "She tried to stop this before it started. I should've done more to help her," she yelled with tears in her eyes. "I didn't know! Did you see Merrick save me? I—"

"Never mind. It's all right," Alissa said soothingly, power packed into every word. "Help me now."

"Stay behind me. I may need to stop and fight," Cerise said.

"Together! Come together," Alissa said.

Dorie and Alissa stood shoulder to shoulder, and Cerise backed up until her back touched them.

"Create a small pool of our blood, Dorie. Make sure it's mixed together," Alissa said.

Dorie moved her leg and dragged a nail over her wound. It bled. She did the same to Alissa's head and Cerise's shoulder.

"We'll say the words as one," Alissa said.

"What words?" Dorie asked.

"By muse blood and breath, I command you to close," Alissa whispered.

A moment later they spoke at once and all forced as much magic as they had into the command, but the stench and flow of demons through the gate continued.

"We can't command them. Demons are former angels—a higher power than we are," Cerise said.

A wing slammed into Cerise as a demon flew past. It knocked them all down.

"You're right," Alissa said. "Even together, we're not powerful enough."

Cerise stared into the darkness, feeling the waves of malice pounding from the cracked earth. "They've wedged bodies into the opening. Hundreds of demons are holding the gate open for the others." She couldn't really see through the darkness. The crack was a hundred feet farther into the cave and at least fifty feet down, and yet in her mind, there was a clear image of a blue-eyed demon with a claw mark on his shoulder. He raged at the lesser demons, cutting and shoving them. They wanted to fly to freedom, but he slaughtered any who broke formation.

Four more high-ranking demons pushed their way through the portal.

"We have to force the lower demons to scatter," Cerise said, searching for a solution. She couldn't call for Lysander and Nathaniel to fight at the gate. They'd only get dragged down into hell by the clawed hands of the demons wedged in the crack. But there was no way they could fight thousands of demons and survive, either.

"Push!" Uriah roared.

Dread wailed through Cerise.

"Oh God! He's trying to make the hole bigger," Cerise said, her eyes flying open. "Alissa, you opened a portal to the ancient muses. How?"

"The muses won't cross into our world, and even if they did, what good would it do? They can't fight demons."

"No, but the archangels once had to fight the Greek gods and monsters to force them out of the world. Let's bring forth the ancient monsters that they banished. They're mortal enemies. It will even the odds."

"I don't know how to summon them," Alissa said.

A sharp pain pierced Cerise's back and she cried out. She jerked forward and reached behind her, but there was no blood. She saw Lysander fall. The pain had been his wing breaking.

Oh, no!

"Hurry!" Cerise yelled. She touched the pool of blood, humming a song she'd written with Griffin called "Come One, Come All."

"Sing with me," Cerise said and shouted the lyrics over the rushing air.

They sang together and power coursed through them. Like an ancient siren song, it called the monsters of their ancestors. Cerise felt the barrier between worlds begin to melt; she smelled lemon and licorice and the spices that her grandmother had cooked with. Then she smelled the ocean, and the wind rushing from the cave turned warm.

"Keep singing," Cerise said, and Alissa and Dorie sang at the top of their lungs while Cerise spoke, power flowing through her melodic voice. "Come Minotaur, come Cyclops, come Kraken and Medusa. You can banish those who banished you. Come and slay your enemies. Force them from the world of men."

The first clash shook the cave and the mountain.

Cerise, Dorie, and Alissa fell into a heap of tangled limbs, but none of them tried to rise. They felt the flow of energy. They'd opened the source of their magic and anchored on the floor of the cave between the past and the present, they controlled the war.

Cerise saw the battle. She realized she was watching it through the eyes of one of the lesser demons in the crack—*Griffin*, she realized, going rigid.

"Oh no," she whispered and closed her eyes, horrified by his plight, but also consumed by the desire to close the gateway to hell before any more of them emerged.

The monsters of ancient Greece attacked the demons. They were all forsaken by heaven and therefore all equal now.

The muses continued to sing, thrusting power into the ancient monsters. As the creatures clashed, the demons lost their grip, broke formation, and slid back toward hell. White light blazed through the cave.

"Close your eyes!" Alissa shouted.

They all closed their eyes as hot pulses thrummed through the hollows. They felt the gateway to hell slam shut, and the walls of rock smash together, closing the portal.

Dorie yelled in triumph.

"We have to send the ancients back," Alissa said. "Quickly, before they escape into the world. Concentrate and blow your breath into the cave."

They whispered and exhaled in unison and felt the ancient creatures hesitate and wander toward the outside then back toward the door to their own world. For moments, they moved without clear purpose, then the first of them returned to where they'd made their home, to where all the creatures of their kind resided.

When the Minotaur, the last of the monsters, was gone, the three muses whispered, "By the breath of the muses, we command you to close," and the second supernatural door that had been opened with their blood swung shut and sealed.

Chapter 31

The bloody battle against the demons took hours. More and more men joined the fight, but Lysander, Nathaniel, Merrick, and Cerise did the bulk of the slaying. When she and Merrick stood back-to-back to fight Purim, she was overcome with satisfaction. They were extensions of Lysander, heaven's ultimate warrior.

She let go of herself and lived up to her pure intentions. Whatever happened, she would have done her best. Blood streaming from her cuts, muscles aching and strained, she still felt the buzz of adrenaline, of heaven's grace. When she was close enough to Lysander, she stole a kiss. "For luck," she'd said with a wink before rushing back into the fray. She's seen the ghost of his glorious smile and carried it with her for all the hours that came afterward.

Toward the end, she chased a demon into the woods, where Reziel lay in wait for her. She felt him, but pretended she didn't.

He tucked his blade away and stretched out his massive hands. She recognized his intention. He would rape and strangle her and break her neck. He would stretch her broken body out for Lysander to find.

Her nerves hummed, but it wasn't fear that wove through her soul anymore. It was rage mixed with anticipation. Reziel couldn't defeat Lysander in a fair fight, so he'd tricked and betrayed him. Then Reziel had gone on to exploit those who were weaker than himself. He didn't just want to steal their souls. He wanted to destroy them. To leave them damaged and without hope, just as he'd once left Cerise dazed and confused and aching from a wound she couldn't heal or even comprehend.

But things were different now. The damage he'd done to her while she was with Griffin was done casually. She'd been a means to an end, someone with whom to toy. Not so anymore. Now he hated her. She'd seen it in his eyes. All night he'd watched her fight alongside Lysander and felt their bond. It enraged him.

Still not immune to jealousy, Reziel? she thought as she waited. She was ready now. It wasn't only her own blood coursing through her veins. The blood that fed her muscles was archangel blood. And using muse magic, she'd channeled it like no other human being ever could have.

Reziel hovered, rustling the leaves. She didn't smell demon. He'd rolled in pine needles to disguise his scent. He smelled like winter, like Christmas.

When he was close, he dove in a blur of speed. The rush of air blew back her hair as she dropped to a knee and pivoted. She thrust her blade up and released the spring. The blade sliced his flesh, nicked his ribs, and slid straight into his heart. He plummeted to the ground, which drove the spike through him.

She shoved his body off her and rose to her feet, pulling out her gun. She leaned over him, pressed the muzzle to the base of his neck, and pulled the trigger. The bullet severed his spine, and he went flaccid. She knew it wouldn't kill him, wouldn't damage him forever. She just needed his undivided attention for a few moments.

She knelt with her knee in his lower back and leaned her mouth near his ear, closing her hands around his massive throat and squeezing.

"The next time you choke someone, I want you to remember how it feels to suffocate." She tightened her grip for effect. "And I want you to understand that the pain and terror you reap take you further away from what you long for," she whispered.

"Yes, I know what you want more than anything, Reziel. More than revenge. More than mankind's destruction. More than God's grace and the warmth of heaven. More than all things, you want him." She shoved her knee deeper into his back. "Don't you?"

She let go of his throat and pressed the tip of her dagger to his flesh where his left wing emerged from his back. "I don't blame you. He's beautiful."

She pricked his skin and a drop of blood welled up, staining the blade. "It would drive anyone crazy to have lost him. But you betrayed him . . . and yourself." She exhaled, her breath rustling his hair. "That's why you can't have him back. He belongs to heaven and to me. And we'll never let you take him."

Reziel's body twitched with impotent rage. Cerise thrust the knife into his back and felt his terror as she sliced him open. She winced, but shoved her foot against the base of his wing and stomped. Then she rocked with the entire weight of her body against its root. The wing cracked, and she threw her shoulder against it and allowed gravity to slam her to the ground, wrenching his wing from his back and cracking all his ribs.

His agonized scream seemed to last forever. Lysander came crashing into the woods as Reziel's body turned ashen and died.

"You managed to take one of his wings," Lysander said, astonished.

"I did," she said and added in a whisper, "Retribution. He took something precious from me once and was trying to do it again."

She sat on a fallen tree, resting her weapon next to her. Lysander sat beside her, close enough for their thighs to touch. He was blood-smeared and dirty, but gorgeous and glorious, too. He was born a warrior and he'd just fought hard and come through a great war. The white of his smile was almost blinding, and the urge to kiss him had never been stronger.

"I cracked my wing again, but only a small break this time. I think it'll be healed in a few hours."

"Good. I hate to see you grounded. You're meant to be in the air."

"I don't regret being recently earthbound. Time spent with you feels as great as flying. The way you and Merrick fought Purim, sublime. And the kiss you gave me after, equally so."

"That was hardly a kiss. It lasted two seconds."

"Did it? It felt longer. I definitely carried the effects for longer," he said, glancing down at his lap.

She laughed.

"Did you notice that even full of my blood, you were able to use your muse gift? The divine power of one doesn't extinguish the other. A good sign. The muse daughter you want to give the world could be part mine."

"If there's time before you're called back," she said, glancing at the sky.

"I don't know that I've earned my redemption yet. We could be here for many more years," he said, not sounding sorry. She smiled.

"How is everyone else?" she asked, thinking of Ileana's dead body that ES had removed from the ritual site.

"While I fought Uriah and Nathaniel fought a pair of lesser demons, Lucifer attacked Merrick."

She leaned forward.

"Merrick vanquished him." Lysander smiled, clearly proud. "Of course, I'll never hear the end of this. How he defeated the prince of hell single-handedly." Lysander rolled his eyes. "I suppose I'll have to concede that being married hasn't taken all the bite out of his blade. And his wife's contribution to helping you close the gate was significant. If you hadn't done that, we would've been overrun." He ran a hand through his hair and his smile widened. "It was a great fight. If I hadn't known what would come next, I would've hated to see it end."

"What comes next?"

"You reward me for saving the world." He glanced sideways at her with a sly look. "And I reward you."

"Ah, the spoils of war," she said, running a finger over his chest. "Can't beat those."

"For certain," he said, but then he turned his head and his smile faded.

A glow bathed the sky and lit the horizon. The air shimmered, and she could just make out the impression of a large angel. He looked as though his breastplate was made of silver and his body carved from crystal.

Lysander rose. "Hello, Gabriel."

"You finally had a battle with the forces of hell that was worthy of you," Gabriel said.

"Better late than never I hope," Lysander said.

Gabriel nodded. "You kept your promise. We're pleased to keep ours."

Lysander glanced over his shoulder at Cerise. "Cerise is one of the Etherlin muses. You saw her contribution?"

Gabriel nodded. "We understand she's not ready to leave here yet. Bound to you, she couldn't stay alone. But her gift and her willingness to defend mankind against hell deserves consideration. Heaven bade me to tell you that it will release the binding if you both wish. You'll ascend, and she'll stay and live the remainder of her life."

Lysander stiffened and raised his brows. "If we're no longer bound, will she forget me?"

"It's the best way. Connections to an archangel invite demon attention. You know this to be true. And it will be easier on her if she can't remember what she's lost."

"The others?" Lysander asked. "They'll forget as well?"

"Merrick's nephilim. For him, you won't completely fade. But the others, yes. There will be occasional dreams, momentary glimmers, but otherwise they won't have known you. It's for the best." Gabriel stepped forward. "I'll leave you to say your good-byes. Congratulations, Lysander. Welcome home, brother." Gabriel gripped Lysander's arm, and a burst of white light engulfed them. Lysander sucked in a breath and shuddered.

Cerise felt the difference immediately. The gold of his skin glowed, and warmth radiated from him all the way to her. Gabriel turned and walked to the wood's edge.

Cerise forced herself to smile. "Congratulations."

"I always thought when this moment came . . ." He looked away, and she felt how torn he was.

She stood and walked to him. "You belong there." She swallowed. "And even if I can't remember, I think a part of me will always know I loved you."

He glanced at the sky, then at her. "I don't want you to forget."

"What choice do we have?" she asked gently.

"Are you ready?" Gabriel called.

"No," Lysander said.

"Another few minutes?"

Hidden between their bodies, the fingers of Lysander's right hand closed around hers. Tears shone in his eyes, and he clenched them shut.

She felt his struggle. He belonged to heaven and couldn't refuse to return home, but he couldn't stand to lose her, either. And by his reaction, she knew he was upset by more than a few years' separation. For an immortal, her lifetime would pass in moments.

"What's wrong?" she asked.

He didn't speak, but she felt the answer.

"If we're unbound and I don't remember you, I might fall in love with someone else?" she whispered. "You and I might never be reunited on the other side?"

He nodded, eyes still closed. It was as though all the blood was being squeezed from her heart, slowly suffocating her. Would she really be forced to give up even the memory of him? *Forever?* As a tidal wave of regret threatened to engulf her, she thought, *there's just no way . . .*

A tear spilled over her lashes, and she put her hand on his cheek.

"I—" Her voice cracked, catching on raw emotion. She waited, but he didn't ask her to choose him. He just stood silently, eyes closed, face anguished. She couldn't stand the way it hurt. Suddenly nothing mattered except that she had the power to take away his pain.

"All right," she whispered, touching his lips. "I never want to lose you, either." She kissed him softly. She swallowed and spoke loud enough for Gabriel to hear. "I don't want to be unbound."

"Thank God," Lysander whispered, then rubbed his eyes and opened them. He looked at her, and his eyes were emerald green and breathtaking. All the muddiness that had made them moss-colored was gone.

"Are you sure?" Gabriel said, walking toward them.

"She's sure," Lysander said in a low, steady voice. He looked over his shoulder at Gabriel. "As am I."

"Lysander, you can stay on earth as an angel of the flesh, and heaven will allow you to marry this girl. It's been done. But if you're called back, her soul will have to come. She'll die instantly—whether there are small children left behind or not, no matter the circumstances of your life here or hers. You understand that? The nephilim will be left without your protection or hers. If you both come now, there will be no one left unprotected. It would be simpler."

"But it would be wrong to rob mankind of Cerise's gift prematurely. And of the legacy she wishes to leave it. We'll stay as long as we can," Lysander said with a questioning look at Cerise.

She nodded.

"If there are children, we'll make arrangements for someone to watch over them. We both have family here."

Gabriel smiled. "For a warrior, you have always been surprisingly sentimental."

"For a warrior, love is rarer than war," Lysander said, tightening his hold on her, "which makes it more precious."

Keep reading for a preview of the
first in a brand-new series

Revelation: A Novel of the Seven Signs

by Erica Hayes
*Coming October 2012 from
Berkley Sensation!*

In the dim green-lit laboratory, Dr. Morgan Sterling sighed, defeated, and dropped her long glass eyedropper into its metal dish. Her digital microscope's screen glared smugly at her, and she switched the display off and wristed back her sweaty hair.

Another no-result. The virus-infected cells on her slide just squirmed and evaded the serum until it imploded and died. She'd been trying for two weeks to work up some kind of anti-body reaction, but none of her solutions sustained the smallest effect for more than a second or two.

Damn it.

Morgan slid off her stool and unpeeled her plastic gloves, dropping them in the trash. "Lights," she ordered, and the white fluorescents flickered on, illuminating her laboratory's stainless steel benches, glass-fronted refrigerators, and banks of digital tissue analysis equipment. All this technology, and this damn Manhattan virus still eluded her.

She unbuttoned her white coat, laid it over a chair, and fluffed out her long dark curls. To be fair to herself, this was the Babylon Chief Medical Examiner's office, not a disease control lab, and she was no expert virologist but just a junior pathologist who did autopsies for a living. City Hall had called in the WHO and the infectious diseases crew from the CDC in Atlanta, and from the daily email updates, no one was making any more headway than she.

But Morgan knew enough about virology to be disappointed

she couldn't do more. She'd probably get fired for using CME resources for this, even though she was doing it on her own time. Which was why she was in the office at 9 p.m. on a Thursday night, instead of at home or dating her nonexistent boyfriend. Morgan wasn't big on boyfriends. Sure, she liked men, and they generally found her attractive. She just didn't have time for relationships when lives were at stake.

And lives were always at stake.

Beyond an internal window covered with half-open venetians, the office TV blared in shimmering 3-D, a newscast featuring some religious nutter raving on about God's will and the end of the world.

Morgan snorted. Yeah, right. If there really was a God, It didn't give a shit one way or the other. She'd seen religion ruin enough lives to figure that out. It was the main reason she'd become a doctor—science meant explanations, answers, truth. Religion offered only lies and maybes.

And you sure saw a lot of those on TV these days. Twenty years of a hard-line right-wing White House had spread the war on terror to a third of the globe. The United States had made a lot of enemies, foreign and domestic, and citizens under constant threat of homegrown terror turned to God and extremism to justify their paranoia. The global economy was just one more theater in the conflict. Wall Street soared on the back of clandestine arms deals and aggressive corporate shock tactics, and the rich got richer, while uptown, urban decay ruled and warring gangs killed each other on the streets in the name of God. The fanatical incumbents in City Hall whipped up the tension with discrimination and overzealous police presence. Some called it a new age of prosperity and righteousness—the new Babylon. Others called it asking for trouble.

Morgan pushed through double plastic doors into the deserted office. The religious nutter on the TV wasn't screaming or waving his hands, she saw. He was well-groomed and handsome, with short dark hair, a neat suit, and calm Latino eyes. He spoke intelligently, articulately, without hyperbole.

Didn't mean he wasn't a frickin' nutter.

They shouldn't try to cure the Manhattan virus, he said, because the disease represented God's will. It was His way of exposing sinners. The Bible said only those carrying the Beast's mark would be affected. Everyone else was safe. All we need to do is pray for *deliverance, amen!*

Morgan watched for a few moments, her lip curling. God's will was a city in fear? Twelve hundred fatalities in a week, the National Guard barricading the streets and a temporary morgue in Central Park overflowing with corpses?

Preachers, churchmen, evangelists. No matter what religion, they were all the same. All liars. This guy on the TV was more dangerous, because he seemed normal. People would believe him. And when he turned on them, they'd stare and sob and say *What the hell happened? He seemed so nice and genuine.*

Her throat tightened, angry, and she gripped the asthma inhaler in her pocket and forced herself to breathe. "TV off," she snapped, and the screen flicked silent.

The cultist who'd seduced her mother had seemed nice and genuine, too. Right up until fourteen-year-old Morgan had hopped off the Lexington Avenue subway after Spanish class at Hillary Clinton High to find her mother on the living room floor, her Bible in her hand and a shotgun beside her. Blood everywhere. Bits of her brain dripping down the walls.

The cops had found the emails inciting suicide on her mother's tablet, but the cult leader who sent them had long skipped town. Similar suicides were discovered throughout the city. All part of the bastard's plan.

All her family's money had gone to the cult. All their possessions. Morgan had to pay her way through college and med school on full scholarships and part-time jobs. But she'd made it, without any help. Whenever she faltered, her mother's messy death sustained her. Depending on others was deadly. Blind trust was a killer.

But Morgan Sterling, MD, junior assistant medical examiner for Babylon County, controlled her own destiny now. And she wouldn't pray for deliverance from anyone.

The door banged open, and Suhail, the lab assistant, pushed in a trolley loaded with tissue samples in yellow plastic ice-boxes, the black biohazard symbol printed on the side. "Another load for you, Dr. M," he said cheerfully, a grin on his young face.

Suhail was studying at med school and worked at the morgue part-time, when he wasn't smoking dope and raising hell with his numerous lurid gang boyfriends. He had messy dyed-blond hair and a tongue stud, and wore a T-shirt with a cartoon of a phallic-looking rocket launcher and the words STICK THIS UP YOUR JIHAD.

He also sported a cut lip and the remains of a juicy black eye. Morgan guessed that in gang-happy Babylon, full of militant Latinos and Aryan white supremacists, a mouthy gay Arab anarchist got beaten up by pretty much everyone. But like Morgan, Suhail doggedly made the best of what he had, even if it wasn't much.

"Thanks, So-so," Morgan said. "In the last fridge. I'm almost full up." Manhattan virus was virulent and so far 100 percent lethal, but not particularly infectious. It could be transmitted by blood and fluid contact, like biting or access to an open wound. Only level-two precautions were required for samples in the lab, the same as hepatitis C or HIV. But in the wild, it was another story. When it came to making new friends, Manhattan's victims were cunning—and determined.

"Sure thing. A few more homicide DOAs down in the morgue, too." Suhail leaned his skinny brown elbow on his cart like the first-class time-waster he was, and lowered his voice conspiratorially. "So how's it going? You finding anything on the hush-hush?"

"Nope." Morgan bit her lip. Medicine couldn't solve every problem. But neither did it promise all the answers. She'd helped the CDC track down the virus's likely zero point, which was a start. But it was far from a cure.

"The boss, has he figured you out yet?"

His delight made her smile. Suhail liked breaking the rules, and he'd covered for her enough times, hoarding samples and fiddling paperwork and making excuses to the boss. She snorted. "J.C.? Like he'd stick his head out of his office for me."

"This is not what I hear." Suhail scratched his tight-jeaned ass loftily.

"Well, you heard wrong."

He winced. "Oh. Sorry. Bad date?"

"Something like that." Morgan sighed. "I'd better go prepare those autopsies, just in case. Give me a reason to be here so late."

"Yeah. Clear out a few fridges, why doncha? We're still

swamped, even with the deadhouse tent in the Park." He chuckled. "Babylon County, stiffs 'R' us."

She stifled a laugh. The irony of a crazy gangboy like Suhail working in the county morgue didn't escape her. Half the corpses she examined were gang-related deaths. Still, you had to keep your sense of humor, and at least Suhail didn't spout religious platitudes while he was raising hell. "Sorry, tell me again why you're studying to be a doctor?"

He grinned. "Gotta contribute to society while I'm tearing it down."

"Well, you'd better hurry, or these damn nutters on TV will get in ahead of you. What are they trying to do, scare people?" Frustration crept into her voice. She'd volunteered for duty down at the temporary morgue. Of course she had. But her boss held a lottery, and she'd lost out. Someone still had to deal with the boring old gunshot homicides, gang assassinations, honor killings, and victims of impressionist serial killers. Babylon's moniker as 'crime capital of the country' was well earned, and the happy-sick funmongers didn't all take a vacation just because a nightmare plague had broken out.

Suhail fiddled with his twin-pinned steel earrings. "Hell, I believe in God. Maybe it's the end of the world, just like that preacher guy's saying. God's plan, and all that?"

She smiled. "I don't think so. The world's tougher than we think. We were all going to die of arctic flu, too, remember? Global warming? We're still here."

"I thought you believed in science, Dr. M." Suhail winked slyly.

"I do, smart-ass." Morgan tossed a rolled-up ball of paper at him, and he caught it, grinning. "What I don't believe in is scaremongering, and conjecture masquerading as data. I want proof before I'll batten down the hatches. How about 2012? That turned out to be bullshit."

"My grandma said she prayed all night that night. Just in case."

"Well, good for her," said Morgan shortly. The very idea that one person's blind wishes could alter events offended her. Even the White House chief of staff, who warned nightly on the news in her severe blue Air Force uniform that the Manhattan virus might be a biological attack by terrorists—or the paranoid conspiracy theorists on the Internet who insisted that The Government Did It—made more sense than that.

And that made it all the more important to Morgan that a cure for Manhattan was found. If it could be cured, it was no miracle.

"Yeah," agreed Suhail cheerfully, wheeling his cart toward the fridge. "She said I'll burn in hell, too. Not sure if that was for being nice to all those lousy unbelievers or for taking it up the ass, but still." He shrugged, tolerant. "Pity the mean old tart isn't still alive. She could try her praying mojo out on this one. Can't hurt, right?"

"Guess not," Morgan lied, smiling weakly for politeness' sake. Yes, it could hurt. It could hurt very deeply. "I gotta go. See ya."

"Have a good one, Dr. M," he called, already loading her samples onto the stainless steel shelves.

Morgan grabbed her flash memory voice recorder and hurried out, through the office doors and down a long vinyl corridor. More fluorescents gleamed, the lemony scent of anti-viral spray hanging. At this hour, no one was about—*oh, hell.*

The CME poked his dark head from his office door, tie loose around his unbuttoned collar. "Morgan? You still here?"

"Sure am, Dr. Torres. Just finishing up tomorrow's prep." She kept walking, like she had something better to do and the work was keeping her.

Juan Carlos Torres was a fine doctor and a good boss. But lately, he kinda gave her the creeps. She should've known dating him would be a mistake. Sure, he was a little older than she—midforties to her thirty-something—but he was good-looking and clever, and she'd thought they might have something in common. Something they could talk about.

Turned out they did. All he wanted to talk about was work. He hadn't asked her a single question about herself. They'd discussed cases and autopsy techniques all evening, and the worst part was, she'd had a good time.

A good time. Christ. Emotional avoidance much? He hadn't even tried to kiss her. If that was her idea of a hot date, she really needed to get out more.

Dr. Torres smiled absently, already heading back to his desk. "Don't stay too late. All work and no play."

"Sure thing." She snorted under her breath. *Physician, heal thyself.* Like he didn't sleep here half the time. Although, given the influx of work lately, a bed in the office wouldn't be a bad idea . . .

Ouch. That settled it. When she was done here, she was going out for a drink. A nice modern bar had opened on Third Avenue, just around the corner from her building, where no one did drugs or started gang-related fights, at least not yet. Maybe she'd even talk to a man. One who wasn't wearing a white coat or pushing a sample trolley.

Or lying on a cold metal slab. Dead guys were low-maintenance, but their conversation sucked.

She grinned, and walked down the steps to the mortuary.

Thick plastic sheets sealed in the air-conditioned atmosphere, keeping the pressure constant, and she keyed in her passcode and entered the cool sanctum. Pale vinyl floor punctured with drains, rows of steel autopsy benches, and sinks under bright lights. A digital thermostat on the wall kept the temperature even, and the ventilation system hummed. Steel trolleys carried rows of stainless instruments on white paper lining.

She strode past the benches to the refrigeration area, where one wall was filled entirely with square steel doors, their handles shining. Bodies could be stored here for months awaiting court rulings, though more commonly, autopsies were completed and the bodies released to the families within a few days. Mostly, samples sufficed for long-term storage, though lately a backlog had built up.

She checked the plastic clipboard hanging on the wall. Two new arrivals, signed in with Suhail's scrawled initials. Fridges 21 and 22. Initial autopsy prep involved checking the body for obvious trauma, making sure it correlated with the police's suspected cause of death, reading through the police notes for any factors that might mean the autopsy needed to be done urgently, and noting any irregularities that might call for the CME's personal attendance to be scheduled. It was paperwork, diarizing, prioritizing. Mortuary triage. Menial work, but it required a qualified ME.

Yes. Just what any self-respecting single girl should be doing at 9 p.m. Hanging out with dead guys. At least there was no chance of date rape.

Morgan shrugged into another white coat, snapped on plastic gloves, and opened fridge 21.

The trolley slid out easily on greased wheels, loaded with its black rubber body bag. She slid the handwritten notes from the pocket on the front, flipping past case ID codes and serial numbers.

Caucasian male, twenty-eight to thirty-five, DOA, single stab wound to the chest plus multiple lacerations. Dumped in Battery Park, no witnesses (yeah, right, probably a dozen people standing right there and no one saw a thing), and no weapons found on the scene. Big guy, too, if the bag's shape was any guide. She set her recorder on the trolley and pulled the zipper down.

It jammed. She gripped the plastic edges and pulled harder. The bag popped open, and something white and fluffy puffed into her face.

She jumped back, waving her hands to clear the air. Shit. If that was white powder, she was going to march down to 1st Precinct homicide and shoot whoever wrote those notes. Once she finished dying of anthrax.

But as the fluff settled, she realized it wasn't powder.

Feathers.

The body bag was stuffed with soft white feathers. Downy little ones that drifted and curled on the air, as well as long sleek ones with thick pale cores. They smelled of sugar, or candy. Some were smeared with blood.

Morgan sneezed, and waved her hands again. Nice prank. Any evidence on the body would be contaminated. She yanked the zipper fully open, and scraped the feathered heap, revealing pale flesh, strong limbs, a heavily muscled torso.

Single stab wound to the chest, all right. This guy had been run through. Gingerly, she touched the puncture wound, between two ribs just to the left of his sternum. Something had pierced clean through the intercostal muscles and into his heart. Bone fragments were shoved in deep, the flesh torn, like the weapon had been twisted to make the kill. A sharp piece of metal or alloy, broader than a knife. A sword, or maybe a spear. Babylon gangs had all kinds of weapons these days.

She brushed feathers from his face, and pursed her lips. *Well, hello, gorgeous.* Even in death, this dude was hot. Long golden hair, stained with blood. Beautiful lips, fair lashes on ice-carved cheekbones purpled with bruises. Worked out, too, his chest and abs defined like an athlete's.

She tore her gaze away, flushing. *Perving on a dead guy. Wow, Morgan. That's totally normal. Set the 'mortuary attendants aren't all necrophiliacs' campaign back fifty years, why don't you?*

More feathers wrapped under the body—if smart-ass Suhail did this, she'd stick something up his jihad, that's for sure—and she tugged them free.

They wouldn't come. She tugged harder, and the body's shoulder twisted, revealing . . .

She stumbled backward, hands flying to her mouth.

Holy shit on toast. The guy had wings.

Honest-to-god, feathered wings. Jointed to his shoulders like an . . . well, like a guy with wings.

It can't be.

She edged closer, holding her breath, poking at his shoulder to lift it. Pale dead skin, curving over his scapula. Tiny feathers thickening over a large spheroid joint, and . . . a wingbone, long and thick like a second humerus, lined with muscle and tendon. Damn. If this was body-modification surgery, it was the best she'd seen. No scar tissue at all, and the feathers . . . well, they'd been *growing*. She could see new ones pushing through underneath. She poked harder, and the joint twisted easily, ligaments flexing beneath the skin. Just like the real thing.

It had to be the real thing.

Excitement tingled in her bones. Amazing. She'd never seen anything like it. Hell, no one had seen anything like it, apparently including the idiot CSI who'd stuffed this into a body bag without noticing a thing. *Caucasian male, my ass. It's the fricking bird man!*

Her mind raced. *Calm down. It could be a hoax. Do some tests. Get proof.*

She should call Dr. Torres, get some corroboration . . . *No, don't call Torres yet.* If it was a body-mod, it was expensive and purpose-built. It could be military. She should get pictures first, email them to herself in case someone tried to cover up her discovery before she could find corroborating evidence.

Paranoia? Maybe. But this was the age of spin and secrecy, and both City Hall and the Feds were ruthless, even if she didn't believe they'd planted the Manhattan virus. Seekers for truth—scientists, journalists, hackers, whistle-blowers—had a habit of disappearing.

She sprinted back into the cutting room for the tiny digital camera. Battery full. Excellent. She skidded back, fearful, but the bird man was still there. Unbelievable.

She folded the body bag back neatly, and started snapping shots from every angle. The flash fired, lighting the room in glare. Sweet. She should roll the body over, get some close-ups. Just one more shot . . .

White light erupted, brighter than any flashbulb.

She gasped, dazzled. Breeze ruffled her hair. Her elbow hit the trolley, and the camera jolted from her fingers.

A hand gripped her arm, steadying her. A man's voice, deep and unfamiliar. "Sorry, lady. Are you—oh, shit."

Her vision cleared, and she scrabbled on the floor for her camera. "Jesus, you scared the hell outa . . . oh!" She looked up, and fell right back onto her ass, her nerves in disarray.

Whoa. Not just tall, or big. *More*, in every way compared to . . . well, compared to a normal man.

This guy wasn't normal.

Black hair, blacker than soot and wilder than music. Blue eyes, hotter and deeper than summer sky, luminous pale skin, long dark lashes any woman would kill for. Arms thicker than her thighs in a dark shirt with no sleeves, strong wrists that made her weak, hands that could crush rocks. And his thighs in those jeans . . . long, powerful, rippling as he moved.

His face was familiar, she realized. Those carven cheekbones and, umm, luscious lips. The bird man. Only Birdy was blond, and this guy was dark and . . . tasty.

His gaze lasered onto hers, relentless, and she shivered. He looked dangerous. Driven. Not a patient man.

Morgan scrambled up, struggling to keep her mind on the issues. This was Babylon, the psycho-killer capital. Well-adjusted guys didn't break into morgues after-hours. But how Mr. Huge-dark-and-oh-by-the-way-totally-hot had gotten in here was beside the point. So was how easy it'd be for a guy his size to tear her limb from limb, or worse.

He'd seen Birdy's body. She couldn't call security. Not yet. Not before she'd preserved the evidence.

She licked her lips. "Um. Hi. I was just . . ."

He strode up to the trolley, and his fingers clenched the edge, hard enough to dent the steel. On drugs. That explained the crazy swirl in his eyes. "You found my brother," he said stiffly. "I guess asking how he died is redundant."

"Umm . . . he's . . . well . . ." Morgan stuttered, unable to keep it in any longer. "He's a frickin' bird man! Who the hell are you?"

He turned, and to her surprise, he laughed.

Her guts melted, like warm honey, and she shivered again. So beautiful. So smooth and melodic. She wanted to press her thighs together, feel his tingling warmth . . .

Or not. Her indignation sparked. He hadn't answered her question. Who the hell was he?

The guy with the Rohypnol laugh shook his head. "Bird man. Christ. You people. Never believe what's right in front of you."

"Sorry, but I'm a scientist. I believe what I can see." Morgan folded her arms, defiant, and edged closer to the wall where the alarm button was. Screw collecting more evidence. This guy was seriously creeping her out, and it wasn't just because he had her thinking about sex instead of squirting him with capsicum spray.

"You do, do you?" His gaze flicked to the alarm button, and back to her, and swift as the flashbulb he dived forward and grabbed her arm. "Then believe this."

Light shimmered again, dazzling. And glossy black wings burst from his shoulders in a rain of golden glitter.

Morgan's heart catapulted, and she gulped for breath. The golden light glimmered, and dissolved.

But his lush midnight feathers didn't. And he held her, his body close in the heady scent of altar smoke. His whisper rumbled through her chest. "I'm sorry. I can't let you call your security. My name is Luniel. That's Ithiel, my twin. He's an angel. And so am I."

Morgan struggled, her mind blanking. It couldn't be true. Not possible. She must be dreaming. Yet . . .

She wriggled, beating at his massive forearm. "Let me go!"
He let go.

She stumbled away, rounding on him. More fool him. Whatever this guy was, he wasn't to be trusted. "Sorry. Not possible. I don't believe in angels."

"Not my problem." The man—Luniel—shrugged, feathers ruffling. His accent was elusive, a mixture of exotic and familiar, like he came from no place in particular.

"It'll be your problem when I call the cops, you freak." The dude still wore a shirt with no sleeves, and the wings—*his* wings—fit easily into the cutaway space. Blacker than black, like soot, broader than his massive shoulders, and long, the tips of the feathers reaching to midcalf. It looked so real.

Morgan's mind stuttered. She must be dreaming. But if this was a dream, surely he'd be wearing white robes and a halo? Instead of all dark and smoldering and . . . and sinful, like some insane Mardi Gras biker?

She sidled backward, toward her desk in the cutting room. A girl didn't grow up in Babylon without learning some self-defense. Her pistol was in the drawer. Maybe she could get away, lock him in, call security. Nine-one-one was a waste of time, despite her threat. Resources were stretched, and police response to anything short of a terrorist plot in progress just didn't happen.

Luniel stalked her, midnight wings flaring. "Freak? Wow. I'm so pleased to meet you . . . I'm sorry, what didn't you say your name was?"

"I'm Dr. Morgan Sterling. This is my mortuary. You're trespassing." Behind an autopsy bench, a few steps closer to the desk.

He circled, leaning over the bench on two hands, muscles flexing. "As they say these days, Dr. Sterling: whatever. Tell me where they found my brother."

She fumbled against the desk, feeling behind her. "Screw you."

"Is that an offer? I'm touched." His hot blue gaze drilled her, magnetic. "But not distracted. Come on, doctor, it's important."

She ripped the drawer open and grabbed the pistol, leveling it at him two-handed and thumbing the safety off. "So's this. Back off."

"No." He vaulted the bench with ease, landing silently

before her on wafting wings. Careless of her pistol. Unruffled, like a panther facing a hissing pussy cat, some small, insignificant creature who posed no threat.

His delicious scent paralyzed her, a rich toffee sweetness. Her mouth dried. He was luminous, dazzling, too perfect to be real. Certainly too perfect to be telling the truth. "Get away."

"Wait, let's see. Umm . . . no." He cocked his head, and reached for her hair, stroking it with one finger. "You're very pretty, Morgan Sterling. Pity if that got spoiled. Tell me about my brother."

Now her gun was trapped between them. Her hands quivered, her memory of defensive moves a blank. "Get away! I'll shoot!"

"No, you won't." He wrapped her hair around his fingers, and leaned closer, sniffing her. "You're a doctor. You don't hurt people."

"Don't bet on it." She inhaled, and squeezed the trigger.

The shot thundered. Blood exploded on his chest, spattering her face. She let out a shuddering breath.

But Luniel didn't fall.

He just cursed—most unangelic—and stunned her immobile with a burning blue glare. His palm flashed up, and impossible light welled from it, and her last thought before sinking into velvety black nothingness was that it was just typical that a lying bastard of an angel should be so infernally beautiful.

NALINI SINGH

ARCHANGEL'S BLADE

New York Times *bestselling author Nalini Singh is back in the shadows of a deadly, beautiful world where angels rule, vampires serve, and one female hunter must crawl out of the darkness to survive . . .*

Savaged in a brutal attack that almost killed her, Honor is nowhere near ready to come face-to-face with Dmitri, the seductive vampire who is an archangel's right hand and who wears his cruelty as boldly as his lethal sensuality—the same vampire who has been her secret obsession since the day she was old enough to understand the inexplicable, violent emotions he aroused in her.

As desire turns into a dangerous compulsion that might destroy them both, it becomes clear the past will not stay buried. Something is hunting . . . and it will not stop until it brings a blood-soaked nightmare to life once more . . .